HOW TO BE A PROPER LADY
Amazon Top 10 Best Book of 2012

HOW A LADY WEDS A ROGUE
"The characters are textured, deep and believable.
The writing is strong and lyrical, easily supporting
agile, polished dialogue . . . an intriguing,
engaging plot and healthy doses of both humor
and emotion . . . a delightful Regency jaunt."
Kirkus Reviews

Recommended by
Woman's World Magazine

WHEN A SCOT LOVES A LADY
"Lushly intense romance . . . radiant prose."
Library Journal (*Starred Review*)

"Sensationally intelligent writing, and a true,
weak-in-the-knees love story."
Barnes & Noble "Heart to Heart" *Recommended Read!*

IN THE ARMS OF A MARQUESS
"Every woman who ever dreamed of having
a titled lord at her feet will love this novel."
Eloisa James, *New York Times* bestselling author

"Another gem of a love story. . . .
Immersive and lush. . . . Ashe is that rare author
who chooses to risk unexpected elements within
an es...

KATHARINE ASHE

I MARRIED THE DUKE

∽ The ∽ Prince Catchers

AVON

An Imprint of HarperCollinsPublishers

This is a work of fiction. Names, characters, places, and incidents are products of the author's imagination or are used fictitiously and are not to be construed as real. Any resemblance to actual events, locales, organizations, or persons, living or dead, is entirely coincidental.

AVON BOOKS
An Imprint of HarperCollins*Publishers*
10 East 53rd Street
New York, New York 10022-5299

First Avon Books mass market printing: September 2013

Avon Trademark Reg. U.S. Pat. Off. and in Other Countries, Marca Registrada, Hecho en U.S.A.
HarperCollins® is a registered trademark of HarperCollins Publishers.

Printed in the U.S.A.

10 9 8 7 6 5 4 3 2 1

To
Marcia Abercrombie
Anne Brophy
Meg Huliston
Mary Brophy Marcus
&
Barbara Tetzlaff

Sisters of my heart.

And to Noah Redstone Brophy

A true hero.

Blessed are they who hunger,
for they will be satisfied.

I
MARRIED
THE
DUKE

The Orphans

A Fair Somewhere in Cornwall
April 1804

*T*hree young sisters of no rank and even less fortune sat in the glow of lamplight before a table draped in black velvet.

Upon that table was a ring fit for Prince Charming.

Veiled in ebony, the soothsayer studied not her clients' palms or brows or even their eyes, but the ring, a glimmering spot of gold and ruby amidst the shadows of everything else in the tent.

"You are motherless." The Gypsy's voice was rich but as English as the girls'.

"We are orphans." Arabella, the middle sister, leaned forward, tucking a lock of spun copper behind an ear formed as delicate as a seashell. Only twelve years old and already she was a beauty—lips pink as berries, cheeks blooming, eyes sparkling. In appearance she was a maiden of fairy tales, and just as winsome of temper, though any storyteller would be obliged to admit that she was not in the least bit meek.

"Everybody in the village knows we are mother-less." Her elder sister Eleanor's brow creased beneath a golden braid tucked snugly into a knot. Bookish as she was, Eleanor's brow often creased.

"Our ship wrecked and Papa adopted us from the foundling home so that we would not be sent to the workhouse." With the simple candor of the young, Ravenna explained the history she did not remember yet had often been told. She was but eight, after all. Restlessly, she shifted her behind on the soft rug, and the fabric of her skirts tangled beneath her slippers. A tiny black canine face peeked out from the muslin folds.

Arabella leaned forward. "Why do you stare at the ring, Grandmother? What does it tell you?"

"She is not our grandmother," Ravenna whispered quite loudly to Eleanor, her dark ringlets bouncing. "We don't know who our grandmother is. We don't even know who our real mama and papa are."

"It is a title of respect," Eleanor whispered back, but her eyes were troubled as she looked between Arabella and the fortune-teller.

"This ring is the key to your destinies," the woman said, passing her hand over the table, her lashes closing.

Eleanor's brow scrunched tighter.

Arabella sat forward eagerly. "The key to our true identity? Does it belong to our real father?"

The Gypsy woman swayed from side to side, gently, like barley stalks in a light breeze. Arabella waited with some impatience. She had in fact waited for this answer for nine years. Each additional moment seemed a punishment.

From without, the sounds of the fair came through

the tent walls—music, song, laughter, the calls of food sellers, whinnies of horses at the trading corral, bleats of goats for sale. The fair had passed through this remote corner of Cornwall every year since forever, when the Gypsies came to spend the warm seasons on the flank of the local squire's land not far from the village. Until now, the sisters had never sought a fortune. The Reverend always warned against it. A scholar and a churchman, he told them such things were superstition and must not be encouraged. But he gave freely of his charity to the travelers. He was poor, he said, but what little a man had, God demanded that he share with those in even greater need—like the three girls he had saved from destitution five years earlier.

"Will the ring tell us who we truly are?" Arabella asked.

The soothsayer's face was harsh and stunning at once, pockmarked across her cheeks but regal in the height of her brow and handsome in its strong nose and dark eyes.

"This ring . . ." the Gypsy intoned, "belongs to a prince."

"A prince!" Ravenna gaped.

"A prince?" Eleanor frowned.

"Our . . . father?" Arabella held her breath.

The bracelets on the woman's wrist jingled as she ticked a finger from side to side. "The rightful master of this ring," she said soberly, "is not of your blood."

Arabella's shoulders drooped, but her dainty chin ticked up. "Mama gave it to Eleanor to keep before she put us aboard ship to England. If it belongs to a prince, why did Mama have it? She was not a princess." Far from it, if the Reverend's suspicions were correct.

The fortune-teller's lashes dipped again. "I do not speak of the past, child, but of the future."

Eleanor cast Arabella an exasperated glance.

Arabella ignored it and chewed the inside of her lip. "Then what does this prince have to do with us?"

"One of you . . ." The woman's voice faded away, her hand spreading wide above the ring again, fingers splayed. Her black eyes snapped open. "One of you will wed this prince. Upon this wedding, the secret of your past will be revealed."

"One of *us* will wed a *prince*?" Eleanor said in patent disbelief.

Arabella gripped her sister's hand to still her. The fortune-teller was a master at timing and drama; Arabella could see that. But her words were too wonderful.

"Who is he? Who is this prince, Grandmother?"

The woman's hand slipped away from the ring, leaving it gleaming in the pale light. "That is for you to discover."

Warmth crept into Arabella's throat, prickling it. It was not tears, which never came easily to her, but certainty. She knew the fortune-teller spoke truth.

Eleanor stood up. "Come, Ravenna." She cast a sideways glance at the Gypsy woman. "Papa is waiting for us at home."

Ravenna grabbed up her puppy and went with Eleanor through the tent flap.

Arabella reached into her pocket and placed three pennies on the table beside the ring, everything she had saved.

The woman lifted suddenly wary eyes. "Keep your coins, child. I want none of it."

"But—"

The Gypsy grabbed her wrist. "Who knows of this ring?"

"No one. Our mama and our nanny knew, but we

never saw Mama again, and Nanny drowned when the ship sank. We hid the ring."

"It must remain so." Her fingers pinched Arabella's. "No man must know of this ring, save the prince."

"Our prince?" Arabella trembled a bit.

The Gypsy nodded. She released Arabella's hand and watched as she picked up the ring and coins and tucked them into a pocket.

"Thank you," Arabella said.

The soothsayer nodded and gestured her from the tent.

Arabella drew aside the flap, but the discomfort would not leave her and she looked over her shoulder. The Gypsy's face was gray now, her skin slack. A wild gleam lit her eyes.

"Madam—"

"Go, child," she said harshly, and drew down her veil. "Go find your prince."

Arabella met her sisters by the great oak aside the horse corrals around which the fair had gathered for more than a century. Eleanor stood slim and golden-pale in the bright glorious light of spring. Sitting in the grass, Ravenna cuddled the puppy in her lap like other girls cuddled dolls. Behind Arabella the music of fiddle and horns curled through the warm air, and before her the calls of the horse traders making deals mingled with the scents of animals and dust.

"I believe her."

"I knew you would." Eleanor expelled a hard breath. "You want to believe her, Bella."

"I do."

Eleanor would never understand. The Reverend admired her quick mind and her love of books. But the Gypsy woman had not lied. "My wish to believe her does not make our fortune untrue."

"It is superstition."

"You are only saying that because the Reverend does."

"I for one think it is splendid that we shall all be princesses." Ravenna twirled the pup's tail with a finger.

"Not all of us," Arabella said. "Only the one of us that marries a prince."

"Papa will not believe it."

Arabella grasped her sister's hand again. "We must not tell him, Ellie. He would not understand."

"I should say not." But Eleanor's eyes were gentle and her hand was cozy in Arabella's. Even in skepticism she could not be harsh. At the foundling home when every misstep had won Arabella a caning—or worse—she had prayed nightly for a wise, contemplative temperament like her elder sister's. Her prayers were never answered.

"We will not tell the Reverend," Arabella said. "Ravenna, do you understand?"

"Of course. I'm not a nincompoop. Papa would not approve of one of us becoming a princess. He *likes* being poor. He thinks it brings us closer to God." The puppy leaped out of her lap and scampered toward the horse corral. She jumped up and ran after it.

"I do wish we could speak to Papa about it," Eleanor said. "He is the wisest man in Cornwall."

"The fortune-teller said we must not."

"The fortune-teller is a Gypsy."

"You say that as though the Reverend is not himself a great friend to Gypsies."

"He is a good man, or he would not have taken in three girls despite his poverty."

But Eleanor knew as well as Arabella why he had. Only three months before he discovered them starving in the foundling home, and Eleanor about to be sent off to the workhouse, fever had taken his wife and twin daughters from him. He had needed them to heal his heart as much as they needed him.

"We shan't have to fret about poverty for long, Ellie." Arabella plucked the ring out of her pocket and it caught the midday sunshine like fire. "I know what must be done. In five years, when I am seventeen—"

"Tali!" Ravenna's face lit into a smile. A boy stood at the edge of the horse corral, shadowy in plain, well-worn clothes.

Eleanor stiffened.

Arabella whispered, "No one must ever see it but the prince," and dropped the ring into her pocket.

Ravenna scooped up the puppy and bounded to the boy as he loped forward. His tawny skin shone warm in the sunlight filtering through the branches of the huge oak. No more than fourteen, he was all limbs and lanky height and underfed cheeks, but his eyes were like pitch and they held a wariness far greater than youth should allow.

"Hullo, little mite." He tweaked Ravenna's braid, but beneath a thatch of unruly black hair falling across his brow he shot a sideways glance at her eldest sister.

Eleanor crossed her arms and became noticeably interested in the treetops.

The boy scowled.

"Look, Tali." Ravenna shoved the puppy beneath his chin. "Papa gave him to me for my birthday."

The boy scratched the little creature behind a floppy ear. "What'll you call him?"

"Beast, perhaps?" Eleanor mumbled. "Oh, but that name is already claimed here."

The boy's hand dropped and his square shoulders went rigid. "Reverend sent me to fetch you home for supper." Without another word he turned about and walked toward the horse corral.

Eleanor's gaze followed him reluctantly, her brow pinched. "He looks like he does not eat."

"Perhaps he hasn't enough food. He has no mama or papa," Ravenna said.

"Whoever Taliesin's mama and papa were, they must have been very handsome," Arabella said, fingering her hair. She remembered little of their mother except her hair, the same golden-red as Arabella's, her soft, tight embrace, and her scent of cane sugar and rum. Eleanor remembered little more, and only a hazy image of their father—tall, golden-haired, and wearing a uniform.

The fortune-teller had not told her everything, Arabella was certain. Out there was a man who had no idea his three daughters were still alive. A man who could tell them why the mother of his children had sent them away.

The answer was hidden with a prince.

Arabella's teeth worried the inside of her lip but her eyes flashed with purpose. "One of us will wed a prince someday. It must be so."

"Eleanor should marry him because she is the eldest." Ravenna upended the puppy and rubbed its belly. "Then you can marry Tali, Bella. He brings me frogs from the pond and I wish he were our brother."

"No," Arabella said. "Taliesin loves Eleanor—"

"He does not. He hates me and I think he is odious."

"—and I aim to marry high." Her jaw set firmly like any man's twice her age.

"A gentleman?" Ravenna said.

"Higher."

"A *duke*?"

"A duke is insufficient." She drew the ring from her pocket anew, its weight making a dent in her palm. "I will marry a prince. I will take us home."

Chapter 1

The Pirate

*L*ucien Westfall, former commander of the HMS *Victory*, Comte de Rallis, and heir to the Duchy of Lycombe, sat in the corner of the tavern because long ago he had learned that with a corner at his back he could detect danger approaching from any direction. Now the corner provided the additional benefit of a limited landscape to study.

On this occasion the landscape especially intrigued.

"Ye've got the air o' a hawk about ye, lad." Gavin Stewart, ship's physician and chaplain, hefted his tankard of ale. "Is she still looking at ye?"

"No. She is looking at you. Glaring, rather." Luc took up from the table the letter from his uncle's land steward, folded the pages and tucked them into his waistcoat pocket. "I think she wants you gone."

"Wants to get at ye. They all do. 'Tis the scar." Gavin lounged back in his chair and scratched his whiskers, salty black and scant. "Wimmen like dangerous men."

"Then you are doomed to a lonely life, old friend. But you were already, I suppose."

"Hazard o' the vows," the priest chortled. "Bonnie lass?"

"Possibly." Pretty eyes, bright even across the lamp-lit tavern, and keenly assessing him. Pretty nose and pretty mouth too. "Though possibly a schoolteacher." A cloth cinched around her head covered her hair entirely, and her cloak was fastened up to her neck. Beneath it her collar was white and high. "Trussed up as tight as a virgin."

"The mither o' our Lord was a virgin, lad," Gavin admonished. Then: "An' what's the fun if a man's no' got to work for the treasure?"

Luc lifted a brow. "Those were the days, hm, Father?"

Gavin laughed aloud. "Those were the days." He was broad in the chest like his Scottish forbearers, and his laughter had always been a balm to Luc. "But since when do ye be knowing a thing about schoolteachers?"

Since at the age of eleven when Luc had escaped the estate where their guardian kept him and his younger brother and blundered onto the grounds of a finishing school for gentlewomen. With a soft reprimand, the headmistress had returned him home to a punishment he could not have invented in his worst nightmares.

Luc had not believed his guardian's rants about the evils of temptation found in female flesh. Of course, he hadn't believed anything the Reverend Absalom Fletcher said after the first few months. Bad men often lied. So he escaped the following day and ran to the school, hoping to find the headmistress out walking again, and again the following day, and again, seeking an ally. Or merely a haven. Each time the footmen dragged him back to his guardian's house, his punishment for the disobedience was more severe.

He had borne it all with silent tears of defiance upon his cheeks. Until Absalom discovered his true weakness. Then Luc stopped disobeying. Then he became the model ward.

"I know about women," Luc grumbled. "And that one is trouble." He took a swallow of whiskey. It burned, and he liked that it burned. Every time she looked at him he got an awfully bad feeling.

Her movements were both confident and compact as she surveyed the crowded dockside tavern with an upward tilt of her chin as though she were the queen and this a royal inspection. Clearly she did not belong here.

Gavin set his empty tankard on the table. "I'll be leaving ye to the leddy's pleasure." He dragged his weathered body from the chair. Not a day over fifty, the Scot was weary of the sea that he had taken to for Luc's sake eleven years earlier. "Don't suppose ye'll be wanting to have a wee bit o' holiday at that castle o' yours after we leave the crew off at Saint-Nazaire? Visit yer rascally brother?"

"No time. The grain won't ship itself to Portugal." Luc tried to shrug it off, but Gavin understood. The famine of the previous year was lingering. People were starving. They could not halt their work for a holiday.

And, quite simply, he needed to be at sea.

"Grain. Aye," Gavin only said, and made his way out of the tavern.

Luc swallowed the remainder of his whiskey and waited. He did know women, of all varieties, and this one wasn't even trying to feign disinterest.

She wove her way through the rowdy crowd, taking care nevertheless to touch no one in her approach. Only when she stood before him on the other side of the table could he make out her eyes—blue, bright, and wary. The hand clutching the cloak close over her bosom was slender but the veins beneath the pale skin were strong.

"You are the man they call the Pirate." It was not a question. *Of course it wasn't.*

"Am I?"

A single winged brow tilted upward. "They said that I was to look for the dark-haired man with a scar cutting across his eye on the right, a black-banded kerchief, and a green left eye. As you are sitting in shadow, the color of your eye is not clear to me. But you bear a scar and you cover your right eye."

"Perhaps I am not the only man in Plymouth that answers to such a description."

Now both brows rose. The slope of her nose was pristine, her skin without blemish and glowing in the fading sunlight slanting through the window at Luc's back. "There aren't any pirates now," she said, "only poor sailors with peg legs and patched up faces from the war. It is very silly and probably disrespectful of you to call yourself that."

"I don't call myself much of anything at all." Not Captain Westfall, and not the Duke of Lycombe's heir. The latter was an unstable business in any case. Luc's aunt, the young duchess, had never carried an infant past birth, despite five attempts. But that did not mean her sixth could not now survive. So in the year since he had left the navy to pursue another noble goal, he'd gone only by Captain Andrew of the merchant brigantine *Retribution*. Simple and without any familial complications, it served his purposes.

The Pirate was a foolish nickname his crew had given him.

"Then what is your real name, sir?" she asked.

"Andrew."

"How do you do, Captain Andrew?" He nearly expected her to curtsy. She did not. Instead she extended her hand to shake. She wore no ring. Not a war widow, then—the war that for years had kept his brother, Christos, safely hidden in France beyond their family's reach.

He did not take her hand.

"What do you want of me, miss, other than to lecture me on the evils of war, it seems?"

"Your manners are deplorable. Perhaps you are a pirate after all." She seemed to consider this seriously, chewing on the inside of her lower lip. The plump lip was precisely the color of raspberries.

Tastable.

Luc had not tasted a pair of sweet lips like that in far too long.

"I suppose you are an expert on manners, then?" he said with credible disinterest.

"I am, actually. But that is neither here nor there. I need passage to the port of Saint-Nazaire in France and I have been told that you depart for that port tomorrow. And that . . ." She studied him slowly, from his face to his shoulders and chest, and soft color crept into her cheeks. "I have been told that you are the most suitable shipmaster to transport a gentlewoman."

"Have you? By whom?"

"Everyone. The harbormaster, the man in the shop across the street, the barman at this establishment." Her eyes narrowed. "You are not a smuggler, are you? I understand they are still popular in some ports even since the war ended."

"Not this port." Not lately. "Do you believe the harbormaster, shopkeep, and yonder barman?"

Her brows dipped. "I did." A pause, then she seemed to set her narrow shoulders. "Will you take me to Saint-Nazaire?"

"No."

Her jaw took on that determined little tilt that made Luc's chest feel a bit odd.

"Is it because I am a woman and you will not allow women aboard your vessel? I have heard that of pirates."

"Madam, I am not—"

"If you are not a pirate, why do you cover your eye in that piratical manner? Is it an affectation to frighten off helpless women, or could you only find black cloth of that width and length?"

Clever-tongued witch. She could not possibly be teasing him. Or flirting. Not this prim little schoolteacher.

"As I believe the scar makes clear, it is not an affectation, Miss . . . ?"

"Caulfield. Of London. I was recently in the personal service of a lady and gentleman of considerable status." Her gaze flittered down his chest again. "Whom I don't suppose you would know, actually. In any case, they employed me as a finishing governess for their daughter who is—"

"A 'finishing' governess?"

"It is the height of ill breeding to interrupt a lady, Captain Andrew."

"I believe you."

"What?"

"That you are a governess."

Her eyes flashed—magnificent, wide, expressive eyes the color of wild cornflowers flooded with sunlight.

"A finishing governess," she said, "teaches a young lady of quality the proper manners and social mores for entering society and leads her through that process during her first season in town until she is established. But I don't suppose you would know anything about manners or mores. Would you, captain?"

Oh. *No.* Magnificent eyes notwithstanding, he needed a sharp-tongued virginal school mistress aboard his ship as much he needed a sword point in his left eye.

He climbed to his feet. "Listen, Miss Whoever-You-Are, I don't run a public transport ship."

"What sort of ship is it, then?"

"A merchant vessel."

"What cargo do you carry?"

"Grain." To people who could not afford such cargoes themselves. "Now, I haven't the time for an interrogation. I've a vessel to fit out for departure tomorrow."

With that jaunty tick of her chin, she darted around a chair and moved directly into his path. "You cannot frighten me with your scowl, Captain."

"I was not attempting to either frighten or scowl. It is this inconvenient affectation, you see." He tapped his finger to his cheek and stepped toward her.

She remained still but seemed to vibrate upon the balls of her feet now. She was a little slip of a thing, barely reaching his chin yet erect and determined.

He couldn't resist grinning. "You don't look any taller to me standing on your toes, you know. I am uncowed."

Her heels hit the floor. "Perhaps you take pleasure in playing at notoriety with this pirate costume."

"Again with the pirate accusation." He shook his head. "You see no hook on my wrist or parrot on my shoulder, do you? And I have all the notoriety I wish without pretending a part." Heirs to dukedoms typically did, even Luc, despite his estrangement from his uncle. But now the latest letter from the duke's steward sounded desperate; the fortunes of Combe were in jeopardy. However much he wished to help, Luc hadn't the authority to alter matters there. He was not the duke yet. Given his young aunt's interesting condition, he might never be.

He closed the space between them. "As to the other matter, I take pleasure in a man's usual amusements." He allowed himself to give her a slow perusal. She was bound up snugger than a nun, in truth. But her lips were full, and her eyes . . .

Truly magnificent. Breathtaking. Full of emotion and intelligence he had absolutely no need of in a woman.

"I daresay," she said. The magnificent cornflowers grew direct. "Name the price I must pay for you to give me passage to Saint-Nazaire and I will double it."

He scanned the cloak and collar. Pretty, yes. Gently bred, indeed. Governess to society debutantes, possibly. But now she was alone and begging his help to leave Plymouth.

Suspicious.

"You cannot pay double my price."

"Name it and I will."

He named a sum sufficient to sail her to every port along the Breton coast and back three times.

Her cheeks went slightly gray. Then the chin came up again. In the low-beamed tavern packed with scabrous seamen she looked like a slim young sapling in a swamp, and just as defiant. "I will pay it."

"Will you now?" He was enjoying this probably more than he ought. "With what, little schoolteacher?"

The cornflowers narrowed. "I told you, I am a governess, a very good one sought after by the most influential families in London. I have sufficient funds."

With a swift movement he slipped his hand into the fold of cloak about her neck and tugged it open.

She grabbed for the fabric. "What—?"

His other hand clamped about her wrist. Her gown was gray and plain along the bodice and shoulder that he exposed, but fashioned of fine quality fabric and carefully stitched. And hidden beneath the fabric stretched over her throat was a small, round lump.

"Not a little school mistress, it seems," he said.

"As I have said." For the first time her voice quavered.

"You do look like a governess." Except for the spectacular eyes. "More's the pity."

Her breasts rose upon a quick breath, a soft pressure against his forearm that stirred a very male reaction in him that felt dispiritingly alien and remarkably good.

"My employers prefer me to dress modestly to depress the attentions of rapacious men," she said. "Are you one of those, Captain?" Her raspberry lips were beautifully mobile. He wanted a glimpse of the sharp tongue. If it were half as tempting as her lips, he might just take her on board after all.

"Not lately," he said. "But I'm open to inspiration."

The raspberry lips flattened. "Captain, I care nothing for what you believe of me. I only want you to allow me to hire passage on your ship."

"I don't want your gold, little governess."

"Then what payment will you accept?" She sent a frustrated breath through her nose, but her throat did a pretty little dance of nerves. *By God*, she truly was lovely. Not even her indignation could disguise the pure blue of summer blooms, dusky lashes, delicate flare of nostrils, soft swell of lips satiny as Scottish river pearls, and the porcelain curve of her throat. And her scent . . . It made him dizzy. She smelled of sweet East Indian roses and wild Provençal lavender, of Parisian four-poster beds and the comfort of a woman's bosom clad in satins and lace, all thoroughly at odds with her modest appearance and everything else in this port town.

"I can cook and clean," she said. "If you prefer labor to coin, I will work for my passage to Saint-Nazaire." Her voice grew firmer. "But my body is not for sale, Captain."

Governess and mind reader at once, it seemed.

"I don't want that," he lied. His hand slipped along the edge of the linen wrapped about her head. Her eyes were wide but she remained immobile as his fingertips brushed the satiny nape of her neck. Her hair was like silk against his skin, the bundle inside the linen heavy over his knuckles. Long. He liked long hair. It got tangled in all sorts of interesting ways when a woman was least aware of it.

"Then . . ." Her lips parted. Kissable lips. He could imagine those lips, hot and pliant, beneath his. *Upon him.* She would be hot and pliant all over. He could see it in her flashing eyes and in the quick breaths that now pulled her gown tight over her breasts. Cool and controlled she wished to appear, but that was not her true nature.

Her true nature wanted his hands on her. Otherwise she would be halfway across the tavern by now.

"What do you want?" Her words came unsteadily again.

"Aha. Not as starchy as she appears, gentlemen," he murmured beneath a burst of rough laughter from a table of sailors nearby.

"What do you know of gentlemen?"

Too little. Only those moments during the war when Christos was safely stowed at the chateau and Luc had been able to enjoy the company of his fellow naval officers, as the lord he had been born to be.

"An expert on the subject, are you?" His fingertips played.

"No. What do you want?" she repeated flatly.

"Perhaps this?" His thumb hooked in the ribbon about her neck. She gasped and tried to break free. He twisted the ribbon up and the pendant popped from the gown's neck.

Not a pendant. A man's ring, thick and gold with a ruby the size of a six pence that shimmered like blood.

"No." She slapped her hand over the ring.

Luc released her and stepped back. Lovely, yes indeed. But she did not look like a man's mistress. She was too plainly dressed and far too slender to please any man with money to spend in bed.

But appearances could deceive. Absalom Fletcher had looked like an angel.

"What is it?" he said. "A gift from an appreciative patron?"

She seemed to recoil. "No."

"He has poor taste to give you his ring instead of purchasing a piece for a lady. You should have thrown him off much earlier. Or haven't you? Are you going to him now?"

The cornflowers shuttered. "This ring is none of your business."

"It is if you intend to carry it aboard my ship. That's no mean trinket you have there. Where are you going with it?"

She stuffed it back into her dress. "I am traveling to a house near Saint-Nazaire to take up a new position at which I must report before the first of September. And what do you think you're doing, reaching down a helpless woman's gown? You should be ashamed of yourself, Captain."

"If you are helpless, madam, then I've something yet to learn about women."

"Perhaps you should learn generosity and compassion first. Will you take me aboard?"

Beautiful face. Gently bred. Desperate for help. A rich man's cast-off mistress. Eager to leave Plymouth. Had she stolen the ring?

He didn't need this sort of trouble.

"No," he said. "Again." He headed toward the door.

A GREAT STONE seemed to press on Arabella's lungs. It could not end like this, rejected in a seedy tavern by a man that looked like a pirate, and all because she had been foolish enough to miss her ship.

But she could not have left those children alone, the little one no more than three and his brothers trying so valiantly to be brave while frightened. The eldest, dark and serious, reminded her of Taliesin years ago, the Reverend's student and the closest to a brother she had ever known. She could not have abandoned the children like their mother did, even if she had known it would cause her to miss her ship.

The ship that would take her to a prince.

He would not remain at the chateau long. The letter of hire said the royal family would depart for their winter palace on the first of September. If she arrived after that, she must find her own way.

She always sent all her spare funds to Eleanor; she had no money to spend on more travel. And she simply must make an excellent impression. She would prepare the princess for her London season. Then perhaps—if she were very lucky and dreams came true—the prince would come to admire her. It would not be the first time one of her employers had turned his attention toward her, liking the pretty governess a bit too much. Not the first by far.

This time, however, she would welcome it.

She twisted her way through the crowded tavern in the captain's wake. His back was broad, his stride confident, and men made way for him.

"I beg you to reconsider, Captain," she called to him as he passed through the door to the street. Her fists balled, squeezing away panic. "I must reach the chateau before the first of September or I will lose my new position."

He halted. "Why didn't you book passage on a passenger ferry?"

"I did. I missed my ship." She chewed the inside of her lip, the only bad habit from childhood that she had not been able to quell. The public coach from London had rattled her bones into a jumbled heap. But anticipating the sea voyage proved so much worse. For two decades her nightmares had been filled with swirling waters, jagged lightning, and walls of flame. She'd been tucked in a corner of the posting inn's taproom, struggling to control her trembling, when the call for her ship's departure sounded. She had forced herself to her feet and out the door by sheer desperation to know once and for all who she really was.

Then, in the inn yard, she encountered the children.

"I had a matter of some importance to see to," she evaded.

Lamplight cast unsteady shadows across the captain's face. Probably it had been a very handsome face before the scar disfigured it, with a strong jaw shadowed now with whiskers and a single deep green eye lined with thick lashes. His dark hair caressed his collar and tumbled over the strip of cloth tied about his head.

"A matter of more importance than your new position at a *chateau*?"

He did not believe her.

"If you must know," she said carefully, "I have three

children I must take to their father this evening before I travel to France."

He looked blankly at her. "Children."

"Yes." She turned and gestured to the curb beneath the eave of the tavern. Three little bodies huddled against the wall, their eyes fixed anxiously upon him. "Their father awaits them across the city. While I was attempting to contact him, my ship departed without me," taking with it her traveling trunk, another trouble she could not think about until she solved her first problem. But the daily cruelties of the foundling home had taught her resourcefulness, and working for spoiled debutantes had taught her endurance. She would succeed.

"I am relieved—" Captain Andrew's fingers crushed his hat brim, the sinews of his large hand pronounced. "I am relieved to learn that you take pride in your progeny even as you abandon them."

"You have mistaken it, Captain," she said above the clatter of a passing cart, making herself speak as calmly as though she were sitting in an elegant home in Grosvenor Square recommending white muslin over blush silk. "They are not my children. I encountered them only in the posting inn yard. Their mother had abandoned them, so I determined to find their father for them."

The captain turned toward her fully then, his wide shoulders limned in amber from the setting sun that lightened his hair with strands of bronze. In his tousled, intense manner, he was not commonly handsome, but harshly beautiful and strangely mythic. His dark gaze made her feel peculiar inside. *Unsolid.*

His lips parted but he said nothing, and for a moment he seemed not godly but boylike. Vulnerable.

She tilted her head and made herself smile slightly. "I can see that I have surprised you, Captain. You must reevaluate matters now, naturally. But while you are doing so I do hope you will reconsider the plausibility of me being mother to a twelve-year-old boy." She paused. "For the sake of my vanity."

He grinned, an easy tilt of one side of his mouth that rendered a pair of masculine lips devastatingly at the command of a grown man indeed.

"How callous of me." He crossed his arms and leaned his shoulder against the doorpost. "I beg your pardon, madam."

"Without any sincerity whatsoever, it seems. I pray you, sir, will you take me to Saint-Nazaire?"

The grin slid away, leaving the vibrant scar dipping over his right cheek yet more pronounced. He must have suffered the injury recently. The war had been over for a year and a half, but he bore the erect carriage and authoritative stance of a naval commander.

It wouldn't matter if he were the head of the Admiralty and his vessel a hundred-gun ship of the line, as long as he carried her swiftly to her destination.

"How did you determine the location of their father's home?" he said.

"I asked about. I can be persistent when necessary."

"I am coming to see that." He pushed away from the doorway and started off along the street. "Come."

"Come?" She gestured to the children and hurried after him.

He looked down at her as she awkwardly tried to match his long strides, and he halted mid-street. He did not seem to heed the traffic of horses and carts and other pedestrians, but stood perfectly solid before her like he owned the avenue. His eye glimmered unsteadily, a trick of the setting sunlight, she supposed. It was a very odd sight. He seemed at once both in thorough command and yet confused.

He pointed at a building across the street. "Give my name to the man that you find on the other side of that door and tell him that I said he is to escort you to the children's home and return you to your inn tonight."

"But— No." Arabella's cold hands were pressed into her skirts. "You needn't. That is to say—"

"He is a good man, in my employ, and you and the children will be considerably safer crossing this town with him than without." He scowled again. "You will do this, Miss Caulfield, or I will not take you to Saint-Nazaire on my ship."

Her heart turned about. "You will take me there?" Upon his ship. Upon the sea.

She must.

He scanned her face and shoulders. "To whose home are you traveling, little governess?"

He was no longer teasing. She must be honest. "I am going to Saint-Reveé-des-Beaux. It belongs to an English lord, but the Prince of Sensaire is in residence there and he has hired me to teach his sister before her debut in London society at Christmastime."

"Saint-Reveé-des-Beaux," he only said.

"Do you know it, Captain?"

"A bit." His brow cut downward. "Miss Caulfield . . ."

"Captain?"

"My ship is not a passenger vessel. There will be no other women, no fine dining or other amusements. Aboard it, you will be at my mercy. Mine alone. You do understand that, do you not?"

"I . . ." She hadn't given it thought after so many people in port recommended him. Naïvely, she had assumed it meant he was a gentleman. But gentlemen had lied to her before.

She had no choice. "I understand."

"We depart at dawn, with or without you."

He moved away, and Arabella released a shaking breath. Forcing a bright smile, she pivoted about and beckoned the children to her.

Chapter 2

The Sea

Mr. Miles, the captain's cabin steward, was a neat little person with a starched cravat, velvet lapels, and high-heeled shoes. When he greeted Arabella as she boarded the *Retribution*, he peered at her gown as though it were made of sackcloth. "You haven't any luggage, madam?"

"My traveling trunk departed for Saint-Malo without me. I must purchase new clothing at Saint-Nazaire." With funds she did not have. After she paid Captain Andrew his fee, she would have one pound three shillings in her pocket, enough to hire a coach to drive her to the chateau. She would arrive wrinkled and filthy, but she would arrive on time.

"The leddy's a sight for weary eyes, Mr. Miles." The day was gray and cool, but the smile of the Scotsman who approached was broad, his sea-weathered skin crinkled about his eyes. He bowed. "Gavin Stewart at yer service, Miss Caulfield. Ship's doctor and sometime chaplain, though o' the Roman persuasion."

"Sir?" she said, uncertain of his meaning.

"Father," Mr. Miles corrected with a pinched nose, turned about on his heel and clip-clopped across the deck, weaving through the dozens of sailors who were preparing the ship for departure.

"Aye, lass. Ma French father had a quarrel with the Presbyterians, ye see, so he raised us Catholic. But I niver mind it, 'cept when there be a bonnie lass aboot." He winked.

She smiled. "I don't suppose you typically have women aboard, do you?"

"Niver."

Her amusement faded. "Never?"

"No' a one, lass. Ye must have a way with persuasion." He offered his arm. "Nou, allou me to see ye to yer quarters. 'Tis a sennight's trip ahead o' us at least, an' it's smelling like rain. Ye'll want to be comfortably settled afore that."

"Rain?"

He patted her hand upon his arm. "No' to worry ye, lass. 'Tis a fine strong vessel."

Her mother had probably thought the same of the ship upon which she put her three daughters to sail to England.

Arabella walked along the deck, averting her face from the open water beyond the busy port and restraining herself from clamping on Dr. Stewart's arm like a frightened child. The farther she moved from the gangplank, the more her stomach clenched.

Everyone else aboard seemed at ease and active. A boy leaned against the deck house, whittling a stick. The others all worked at ropes, planking, and sails, most of them laboring at a massive pulleylike device, hauling barrels from the dock to the deck. They chanted a song that matched the rhythm of their footfalls. Weathered like Dr. Stewart and dressed simply, to a one they looked like ruffians, with missing teeth and scruffy whiskers. But they worked diligently as the breeze sheering off the channel snapped at ropes and sails. Each cast her a quick glance and some tugged at cap brims in greeting then returned to their tasks. Only one young man did not; his attention never wavered from the pile of canvas he was stitching with bony hands.

Dr. Stewart guided her down a steep stairway onto a deck lined with enormous cannons: silent waiting warriors. At one end a narrow corridor gave off onto small curtained chambers to either side and one door directly ahead.

Mr. Miles threw open the door. "Captain, your guest," he said primly.

Captain Andrew sat at a writing desk, his left shoulder to a window, his brow bent to his palm and fingers sunk in his hair. In his other hand was a pen, and upon the desk an ink pot and ledger opened past the first folios. The scents of cheroot smoke and salt mingled with the decidedly masculine furnishings of a dining table, chairs, and a single sitting chair. Beside a mounted sword and a brass mechanism of some sort, only two pictures adorned the walls, one of a ship flying the British flag, the other a charcoal drawing of a boy standing in the corner of a dark chamber.

He turned to look over his shoulder at her. His jaw was darker with whiskers than the night before.

He frowned.

She lifted her chin.

"Ma'am." He stood, the top of his head brushing the ceiling beam. "Good day," he said in a perfectly flat tone. He wore a loose-fitting coat with a waistcoat and plain neck cloth, a pistol strapped to a sash across his chest and a sword at his side. His hair was tousled and a scowl lurked at the corner of his very fine mouth.

She walked toward the lion in his den.

"Good day, Captain." She extended her hand. "Here is the fee I agreed to pay you."

He looked briefly at the purse dangling from her fingers then at Mr. Miles. The steward came forward and took it.

The captain's attention fixed on her again. "Welcome aboard, Miss . . ."

"Caulfield." Her cheeks warmed. *Cretin*.

"Caulfield," he murmured. "I see you've met Dr. Stewart, whom some of my crewmen believe is also a man of religion."

"An' those gadgies in Rome," the Scot mumbled with a grin.

"I have," she said, feeling befuddled and like a complete fool for it. She had dined with heiresses, dressed baron's daughters, and schooled future countesses in comportment. It was idiotic to be tongue-tied in the presence of a rough, crude merchant ship captain, even if the daylight enhanced the wolfish glint in his eye and he looked at her as though he knew her thoughts. "He has offered to make me acquainted with my quarters."

He gestured toward a door to his right. "Be my guest."

Mr. Miles darted forward with a clippity-clop and opened the door. The cabin within was narrow and curved on one side along the curve of the ship. A long cot with wooden sides built into the wall, a small ledge, and four clothing pegs were its only furnishings.

"Will it suit you, Miss Caulfield?" the captain said at her shoulder.

"But— Is it your bedchamber?"

"It was." His smile was slow and his emerald eye danced with deviltry. "Now that you have paid for it, it is yours." His gaze dipped to her lips.

"But—"

"I told you this is not a passenger ship, Miss Caulfield. Bunks are few aboard, and the mattress in my cabin is the most comfortable of those few. Do you concur, Mr. Miles?" he said without removing his attention from her.

"Entirely, Captain," the English Napoleon said.

Dr. Stewart chuckled.

They were enjoying this.

"I cannot—" She had been forced to face plenty of indignities as a servant, but this was outrageous. "That is to say, it would not be proper for—"

Captain Andrew lifted his brow.

"I cannot deprive you of sleep, Captain," she said firmly.

"Dinna fret, lass. He'll sleep fine and dandy with ye in his bed."

Dr. Stewart could not mean what she imagined. He was a priest, for heaven's sake.

The captain slanted him an odd glance.

"Gentlemen," she said, "if gentlemen you can be called," she added under her breath, "this is insupportable, and you know it as well as I."

Captain Andrew laughed softly. It was a wonderful sound—deep and warm and confident and appreciative.

She forced herself to look him in the face. "Captain?"

"I am afraid I've nothing else to offer you, little governess, but a hammock on the gun deck with the crew or a straw pallet with the goats and sheep below. Would you prefer one of those?"

"Not precisely."

"Ye'll have ma cabin, lass," Dr. Stewart said, and went toward the door. "The bed's no' so soft, an there be no door to lock. But ye'll have the privacy a leddy needs."

She released a breath and slipped by the captain to follow.

Dr. Stewart shook his head. "I warned ye she woudna take to it, lad. Some wimmen dinna care to be teased."

"Seems so," the captain said quietly.

She glanced back. He was no longer smiling, but watching her with that same intensity he had revealed for a moment on the street the night before, like he knew not only her thoughts, but also her fears.

Like he was a wolf, and she the lamb.

WITHOUT ANY FANFARE of trumpets, the ship drew away from the dock with a sudden sway that left Arabella's joints loose and her limbs trembling. Dr. Stewart invited her to the main deck to watch their departure. She declined and instead sat on her borrowed cot, clinging to its sides, eyes clamped shut, and thought of her sisters, Ravenna's bright smile and Eleanor's arm wrapped about her shoulder. Her heartbeats were frantic. Her palms grew slippery on the wood.

She opened her eyes and reached for the shutter over the window. She folded it open. The sea stretched before her in undulating swells of white and gray.

She slammed the shutter closed.

A miniature bookcase beside the cot and bolted into the wall held several dozen well-worn volumes. She snatched up the closest, opened it, and read.

When Mr. Miles scratched on the curtain with her dinner, her stomach was too tight to accept food.

Eventually, she slept, restlessly, and dreamed of

storms. She awoke to the steady drum of rain on the ceiling above her head. Mr. Miles brought her breakfast. She left it untouched.

Her second day at sea proved equally eventless and equally exhausting. Her nerves were raw, her skin clammy, her belly cramped. She needed distraction. Not, however, in the form of a wolfish ship captain, whose deep voice and confident tread she occasionally heard through the wall shared between the cabins.

But she was unaccustomed to inactivity. On her third morning aboard she ventured out of the doctor's cabin to stretch her legs and seek out a hiding place aboard that would not put her in sight line of either the captain or the water that surrounded them completely now.

A sixty-five-gun merchant ship, however, while considerably larger in volume than the London town houses in which she had worked, posed a challenge when it came to places a woman could stroll or sit unnoticed. After ducking around barrels and lurking behind cannons to avoid the captain, she found an ally. The cabin boy had been following her about on her tour of the ship's nooks and crannies.

"If you're wantin' someplace to set, miss," he said, "you'll like Doc's place. It's warm and dry, though it rocks somethin' fierce in a storm, seein' as it's in the bow."

He guided her to the infirmary, dropped to his behind on the floor outside the door and pushed his cap over his brow.

"Won't you follow me inside like you have followed me everywhere else this morning?"

He shook his head. "No, miss. I'll catch a wink while you're in with the doc, if you don't mind."

"I do not." She laughed. "But do tell me your name so that I might wish you pleasant dreams."

"Joshua, miss."

"Pleasant dreams, Joshua."

Dr. Stewart welcomed her and she settled on the extra chair in his infirmary, a book on her lap. She was no scholar like Eleanor, and when they hadn't turned her stomach, the doctor's tomes on the treatment of shipboard ailments had nearly put her to sleep. Today, however, she had unearthed quite another sort of book from the captain's day cabin while Mr. Miles served her breakfast—a peculiar book for such a man to own.

Dr. Stewart had set a vast wooden chest atop the examination table and was drawing forth bottles of powders and liquids, making marks in a ledger, then returning the bottles to the chest.

"Ye canna be comfortable there, lass," he said. " 'Tis no place for a leddy to set. Allou me to have the boys set up a canopy for ye atop where the light's better and ye can take the fresh air."

The wooden chair was a torture only less noxious than sight of the sea. "It is quite comfortable, in fact." She turned a page in Debrett's *New Peerage*. "I am quite well."

"Aye, I can see that." He smiled as he placed a bottle in its rightful nook in the case.

She bent to her book. All of her former employers had a copy, so she had long since memorized every page. She folded it closed in her lap. "What do you have in your medicine chest there?"

"Cures that a man might need at sea."

"Two bottles have skulls and crossbones on the labels, I noticed." *Suitable for a pirate captain.* But now she was being ridiculous. "What need do you have of poisons?"

"Arsenic, taken in wee doses, aids the nerves. Otherwise 'tis for the rats. 'Tis a powerful poison."

"Best then that you keep a lock on that chest." She opened her book again. "With a captain such as yours, passengers mustn't be given any opportunity for mutiny, must they?"

The doctor chuckled. Bottles clinked.

"He intrigues ye, daena he?"

Her head snapped up. "What?"

A sympathetic twinkle lit the Scot's eyes. "Ye'd no' be the first, lass."

"Doc?" A sailor stood at the door, a young man of no more than seventeen, clutching his cap in his hand. He was the sailor who had not looked at her on deck when she arrived, nor since, as he avoided her gaze now. His hair was filthy, his sun-darkened skin draped over knobby cheeks and hands.

"What do ye need, lad?" The doctor went to him.

The youth's hollow eyes were fixed on the medicine chest.

"Got me a nasty toothache, Doc." His accent was English—Cornish—the accent that the Reverend Caulfield had drummed out of Arabella after their four years at the orphanage. Young ladies did not speak like peasants, he had scolded. But he was not naturally a harsh man; only her misbehaviors had roused his irritation. Only her. To him, gentle, studious Eleanor could do no wrong. Always off in the stables or woods, Ravenna had rarely ever come under his notice. Only Arabella with her fiery hair and too-pretty face made him fret.

"Can ye gimme somewhat for it?" the young sailor asked the doctor.

"It may have to come out, lad."

The sailor clutched his cap over his jaw. "Naw, sir. Me mum said as I'd best come home with all me teeth or I'd best not come home at all."

"Begging yer mither's pardon, lad, but if it's paining ye, it may need to come out or it'll take the whole bone."

The youth shook his head. With a last quick glance at the medicine chest, he disappeared.

Dr. Stewart shrugged. "Some dinna know what's best for them." He cast her a knowing grin. "Both sailor lads an leddy governesses."

But Arabella had no attention for his teasing. The young sailor did not have a toothache. With the same keen sense of people that made her so good at her work, she knew it of this youth. He wanted something else in Dr. Stewart's medicine chest. Something he could not simply ask for. He had lied.

THE SHIP GROANED against a swell of the sea, drowning out the rasp of Arabella's breathing. The mattress was like a board. Lying rigid on it, she felt every sway of the ship, every wave, every tilt. She should have accepted the offer of a hammock. The crewmen slept perfectly well despite the poor weather, while for four nights now she had barely dozed.

She had not returned to the top deck since she boarded the ship, and she had seen the captain only from afar. That was enough. The ocean terrified her and the captain was large, unpredictable, and a little bit dashing, and she needed only the service of his ship, not teasing or intense scrutiny that made her think about him whenever she wasn't preoccupied by the constant roll and pitch that seemed to bother no one but her.

Instead she should be thinking of the royal family to whom she was traveling. She should be making plans for Princess Jacqueline's debut in London society. Her mind should be bent on how to win the prince's attention despite her servile status.

The ship leaned and she clutched the edge of the bunk. Wind howled. The wall creaked like it would snap.

She squeezed her eyes shut. She was exhausted. But this simply must be borne. She was a world away from comfort now. But soon, *hopefully,* all the canings and scoldings and groping hands and even this heaving ship would be pale memories of a distant past.

Then, she would bring her sisters with her into her fairy-tale life. Eleanor could quit translating texts for the Reverend by the putrid light of tallow candles, and Ravenna could set up her own stable or kennel or even a physician's practice if she wished. They would be together again.

She missed them. She missed the affection they shared, the secrets and confidences and embraces. She had lived too long among strangers, coming to know women barely younger than her only in order to set them out into the world as brides, then being sent off for another assignment, another debutante, another success.

She feared her turn would never come and that she was chasing moonbeams. A prince would be mad to look twice at a governess. Her journey to Saint-Reveé-des-Beaux would win her nothing but further distance from her family. She would be alone in a foreign world living among people who paid for her skills for the remainder of her life.

And she would never know the truth about who she was.

She turned onto her side, but her skirts tangled in the blanket. With no lock on the cabin door, she was afraid to undress for sleep. Her gown was a shambles. With an upturned nose Mr. Miles had offered to press it for her, but she had nothing else to wear in the meantime. And nothing else to wear to meet a prince. It was hopeless.

No. This was fear and weariness speaking. She would not accept defeat.

Wide-awake, she sat up, banged her head on the top of the bed and groaned.

This was insupportable. She had not survived years of canings then scoldings then gropings only to cower in fear and doubt, not now when she had never been closer to her goal.

She crawled over the wooden side of the bed and for a moment stood still in the cramped space, bracing herself against another sway of the ship. Then she pulled her cloak tight about her and drew aside the curtain door.

All was quiet. The door to the captain's quarters was closed. In the other direction sailors slumbered in hammocks strung up between the massive cannons in the dark. A single lantern at the closest stairway cast a wavering glow. All smelled of brine, unwashed men, and farm animals from the hold below. But the faintest whiff of rain touched the air.

It had fallen steadily for three days already. Few sailors would be atop now, she suspected. Dr. Stewart had said that no storm threatened. And she needed the activity.

More than that, she needed to be brave.

Holding tight to posts and cannons against the ship's gentle roll, she stumbled to the stairs and gripped the rail. Raindrops fell onto her hands, but she put one foot on the glistening step, then the next.

She climbed the narrow stair with her heart trapped firmly between her molars, wind grabbing at her hood and skirts.

Water puddled across the top deck and the sky was a thick darkness from which fell a steady, light shower. Rigging clattered in the wind. Far toward the bow lit by two bright lanterns, a pair of sailors huddled. Arabella held onto the stairway railing with both hands and made herself look up at the sails. Only a half dozen of them were unfurled, and they were stretched with wind.

A strange eddy of calm crawled through her.

She released one hand from the rail.

She took a slow, deep breath and felt her feet solid beneath her. The ship rocked. She bent her knees into it.

She could do this.

Her other hand loosened on the rail, then released it.

She did not fly up into the sky and nothing propelled her abruptly from the center of the deck and into the sea. She felt light, giddy, almost weightless. She looked up again and rain pattered on her cheeks.

Pulling in another breath, she moved one foot. Then the other. Then the other. She did not look at the darkness of the water beyond the main rail, only at her feet, at a trio of barrels nearby, at a line stretching from the railing to a sail above, at anything but the sea.

Finally she came to the main railing that ran all the way around the deck. Her fingers curved around it. It was solid and reassuring. She looked into the darkness.

The Atlantic roiled, tossing up whitecaps beneath the starless sky. Only lantern light from either end of the ship lit its surface.

She stared, dizzy and clutching the railing. Twenty-two years ago this ocean had swallowed everyone aboard a ship traveling from the West Indies to England— everyone except three tiny girls. It was a miracle, the Cornish villagers had said. God had saved them.

But God had not seen fit to save their nanny. And their names meant nothing to the villagers, nor to the distant solicitor in London that the village aldermen reluctantly hired to find their father. So, plucked from the horrors of the sea, the three little beneficiaries of a miracle had been deposited in a foundling home where they then learned other sorts of horrors altogether.

The black water churned. Arabella's hands were ice on the railing.

She must conquer this. *She would.*

She sucked in air, fresh and tinny. After the closeness of below, it was a little scent of heaven.

Drops pattered on her hood and shoulders. The sleeves of her gown clung damply to her arms. She shivered. But she was standing erect and stable on the deck of a ship. She could not go below yet. Not until the nightmares were truly and thoroughly bested.

She released the rail with one hand and then pulled the other away from safety.

Her breaths came short. Panic washed over her. The deck seemed to spin.

She grabbed the railing.

"It is unwise to drench oneself while at sea, Miss Caulfield," rumbled the captain's deep voice at her shoulder. "One might remain drenched for weeks if the sun fails to appear."

She turned, clutching the railing hard with both hands behind her.

His stance was square, his face dark in the shroud of rain. His height and the breadth of his shoulders garbed in a coat that reached to his calves shaped an austere silhouette in the light from the front of the ship. In the dark he seemed even larger than before, and powerful and dangerous and . . . *mythic.*

She was ridiculous to think it. He was just a man. But her thoughts were muddled, and he looked so solid and strong.

"I had not considered it," she said.

"Apparently." He seemed to watch her. "Did you return the children to their father?"

She stared. "Children?"

"In Plymouth. You do recall that you missed your

ship's departure on account of three urchin children. Do you not?"

"Of course I do." She only found it remarkable that he did. "Don't be foolish."

A crease appeared in his scarred cheek, deepening the shadow across his face. "You have a remarkably agile tongue for one in dire need of assistance, Miss Caulfield."

"Alas, servitude has not taught me meekness." The open sea yawned at her back like a hole that would swallow her up if she were to lean outward only the slightest bit. "But when one is teased in the dark by a large man who has previously threatened one, one is foolish to behave as a servant."

"Did I threaten you?"

"If I remind you of it, will you make good on the threat?"

He smiled slightly.

"Captain Andrew, are all your crewmen men of good character?" The youth's lie to the doctor in the infirmary bothered her.

In the silvery darkness, his eye glittered. "Would you have cause to expect otherwise, madam?"

"I don't know. I know nothing about the crew of this ship. Or of its master."

He took a step nearer. "The members of my crew are all men of fine character, Miss Caulfield. The very best, given their lot." His attention settled upon her mouth. "Considerably better character than mine, I suspect."

She should not have come out. Her fear aside, she should not have allowed this encounter with him. From the moment at the tavern when he touched her, she had known.

She made herself look directly at his scar. She peered at the puckered slash, angry red against the tan of his skin, and the strip of cloth that covered his eye, and she waited for a shiver of revulsion. None came. His body, so close to hers, seemed to radiate strength and vitality at odds with the disoriented desire in his gaze upon her lips.

Arabella was no stranger to men's lust. She knew far more about it than she wished. And she knew this man was no longer teasing.

Chapter 3

Brandy

Will you have your way with me here on deck, Captain? Or can you wait long enough to first drag me by the hair to your cabin? Don't tell me you are the sort of man to throw a woman over your shoulder." Her bright eyes challenged, then shifted to run along Luc's shoulders. "Though I suppose it would barely require an effort."

It had rarely ever required any effort whatsoever on his part to win a lady's favors. He was Lucien Andrew Rallis Westfall, decorated commander in His Majesty's Royal Navy, master of an enviable ship, not to mention a pretty little property in France, and heartbeats away from an English dukedom. Women had begged him to bed them, and wed them.

"From governess to jade in a mere five days." He forced his feet to remain where they were planted, his hands to remain at his sides. She held the hood of her cloak close about her cheeks. He wanted to see her entire face, to draw away the wool and linen and touch her perfect skin. For five days he had been dreaming of it.

He had avoided her for precisely that reason.

"I had not expected this of you, Miss Caulfield," he said.

"Then you are indeed foolish, Captain."

"I have challenged men for offering me less insult."

"Will it be swords or pistols, then? I haven't any skill with either, so you may as well choose your favorite."

A thread of amusement wound through him, and sanity. But with the rain sparkling in her eyes and bathing her skin in ethereal shadows, she was too lovely for him to be content with sanity.

"A man might look without intending to touch," he said.

"A man might lie through his teeth convincingly if he practices the art of it often enough." She spoke without bravado, but with warmth and the clearest, sharpest tongue he had ever heard from a woman so young.

"Do you know . . ." He bent his head, hoping to catch her scent of roses and lavender on the breeze. "I have been combing my memory to recall who it is that you remind me of, and I have just come upon it."

"You have?" The cornflowers widened in a moment of candid surprise.

"In my youth I saw the Duchess of Hammershire. She was an old termagant, sharp-tongued, with an air of sublime confidence and utter indifference to her effect upon others."

Her lashes flicked up and down once. Her knuckles were white about the railing. His words disconcerted her. Good. The more unsteady he made her, the better. Then they would be on the same footing.

"I am not indifferent to my effect upon others," she said.

He laughed, and her eyes went wide. "You admit to sharp-tongued and sublimely confident, do you, my little duchess?"

A shiver shook her. "I—I am not your little anything."

He allowed his gaze to drop to her lips, not raspberry now, but blue. Her quivers were not from fear.

"You are chilled."

Her chin jutted up. "It is my only recourse to putting you off. I am in your power, recall." She shivered again.

"I didn't say chilly. I said chilled. Has the rain soaked you through?"

"I—" Her body trembled beneath the sodden cloak. "That is none of your business."

"Woman, I have no patience with fools. How long have you been atop?"

"I . . ." Her delicate brow creased, her teeth clicking together.

"Half an hour, Cap'n," the cabin boy's voice piped from close by. "Been standin' there still as a statue gettin' soaked through."

"Thank you, Joshua. What are you doing atop at this time of night?"

"Watchin' the lady, just like you told me to, Cap'n."

The cornflowers shot Luc a confused glance. *Blast the innocent ignorance of children.*

"My grandpa took a chill afore he up and croaked in my grandma's one good bed," the boy said, and his little jaw dropped open. "Is Miss goin' to croak too, Cap'n?"

"I don't believe she would allow that, Josh."

"You mustn't—" Her words ended on a hard shudder.

"Joshua, find Dr. Stewart. Bid him attend me in my day cabin."

"Aye aye, Cap'n." The boy scampered off.

"Truly, Captain, I shan't—"

"You shan't say another word until I say you may." His hand came around her elbow through the fabric of her cloak. His grip was strong and very tight. "Now do allow me to escort you below, madam."

She resisted, then released the rail and allowed him to lead her toward the stairway.

Joshua met them at the bottom. "Took me a few to suss him out, Cap'n, this bein' such a prodigiously grand ship, a'course. But the doc's on his way now."

"Excellent." They passed through the sleeping sailors and came to the cabins. "The lady is in good hands now, Joshua," he said in a gentle hush. "Off to bed with you."

"But, Cap'n—"

"If you wish to stand with the helmsman again on the quarterdeck tomorrow and assist him in steering the ship, you will climb into your hammock and go immediately to sleep. No. Not another word from you. Go now."

The boy hurried into the darkness of the deck.

"Now, little duchess, do follow me." He opened the door to his cabin.

Another shudder grabbed her and Arabella's teeth clacked. "Y-You call me d-duchess yet you speak with greater respect to Joshua," she mumbled.

"He complimented my ship."

"If I w-waxed eloquent on the prodigious size of y-your . . . *ship* would you s-speak to me with deference too?"

"Jade. How is it that you can taunt me so indelicately while soaked and frozen? It is truly remarkable." He pressed her into a chair.

She clutched her arms about her middle and clamped her eyes against a shudder. "I—I did not in-intend in-delicacy."

"Perhaps. I will for the present reserve judgment." A blanket came over her back. She opened her eyes but, doubled over, she could only see his feet, quite well shod with silver buckles and trouser hems of a remarkably fine fabric.

"Are y-you certain you are not a s-smuggler?"

"Quite certain. Is there something written upon the floor that suggests I am?"

"The quality of your tr-trousers and sh-shoes. Men earned fortunes sm-smuggling during the war ag—" An agonizing shudder wracked her. "—against Napoleon," she finished in a whisper.

"Did they? I suppose I chose the wrong profession, then. Ah, Dr. Stewart. You are in time to hear all about the fine quality of my footwear. Duchess, here is the sawbones to see to what ails you."

"Step aside, Captain, an allow a man o' science to come to the rescue."

"You n-needn't rescue m-me, Doctor." Arabella raised her head and opened her eyes, but everything was a bit spotty. "I am w-well."

"I can see yer perfectly hale, lass. But Captain, weel, he's a hard man. He'll make me walk the plank if I dinna take a look at ye." He set a chair facing her and sat. "Nou, be a guid lass an' give me yer hand."

She unwound her arm from within the wet cloak and he grasped her wrist between his fingers. The captain had moved across the cabin and turned his back on them, but his shoulders were stiff and she thought he listened. Dr. Stewart grasped her chin and studied her eyes. His touch was impersonal, not like the shipmaster's.

"Shall I bring another lamp, Gavin?" The captain's voice was gruff, his back still to them.

"No. I've seen enough." The doctor released her

and placed his palms on his knees. "Lass, yer chilled through. Ye've got to get out o' those wet clothes and a dash o' liquid fire in ye or ye'll take a fever."

Arabella pressed her arms to her belly. "I have no other c-clothes."

"Mr. Miles will find something to suit ye."

The captain looked over his shoulder. "What on earth inspired you to wander atop in the rain and dark, duchess?"

"D-Don't call me that."

"'Tis no use, lass. He'll no' listen once he's got an idea in his head. Niver has."

The captain was looking at her, a frown marring his dramatically destroyed face. "He has the right of it. Now, Miss Caulfield, will you allow my steward to dress you in dry clothing and save you from a far worse fate, or will you foolishly destroy the respect I have developed for your courage and fortitude over the short course of our acquaintance?"

He respected her? Hardly.

She nodded and cradled her arms to her.

Dr. Stewart patted her shoulder. "Good, lass." He stood. "I'll fetch Mr. Miles. With a dram o' whiskey in ye, ye'll be singing in chapel again come Saubeth." He went out.

The captain sat back on the edge of his writing table, bracing his feet easily against the sway of the ship. He crossed his arms. He had removed his coat and wore now only a shirt and waistcoat. The clean white fabric pulled at his shoulders and arms. There was muscle beneath, quite a lot of it, the contours of which could not be hidden by mere linen. Looking at it, Arabella got an uncomfortably hot feeling inside her. It seemed to split up her insides, jolting against the cold.

She looked away from the muscles.

"I'll wager you sing in church on Sundays, don't you, duchess?"

"I d-don't believe in G-God any longer."

"That miserable, are you?"

She did not reply. She mustn't care what he thought of her. The less he thought of her, the less likely he would be to worry about her and stand around her with his indecently oversized muscles.

The cabin door opened and the captain's steward entered with an armful of clothing.

"Would the lady prefer to dress herself or to be dressed?" he said primly.

Grabbing the blanket about her, Arabella stood and took the clothing from him and went into the captain's bedchamber on shaking legs.

Impotent frustration rattled in her while she peeled off all but her shift and wrapped her hair in the dry neck cloth in the pile of clothes. But she could not bring herself to don the sailor's garb. She left it folded, bundled the blanket about her tightly and returned to the day cabin.

Mr. Miles greeted her on the other side of the door with an eager step. "I will be most happy to see to your garments, miss."

She clutched her clothing to her. "Th-That will not—"

"Accept gracefully, Miss Caulfield," the captain said in a low voice. "Or I shan't be responsible for the pall his foul humor will subsequently cast over this entire ship."

She offered the steward her wet gown and petticoat, with the stays and stockings tucked inside. "I will return with tea for your guest, Captain." The steward marched to the day cabin door and closed it behind him, leaving her alone at night wearing only a chemise and blanket with the man she had been avoiding for five days so that she would not feel precisely this: weak and out of control.

She stepped back and bumped into a chair. He tilted his head, then gestured for her to sit.

She sat. Better than falling over.

"I continually disappoint Miles in offering him little of variety in my clothing," he said. "The opportunity to manage yours has put him in alt."

"He doesn't c-care for that g-gown," she mumbled.

"Did he tell you so? The knave."

"N-Not in so many words."

"Nevertheless, for offending you I shall have him strapped to the yardarm for a thorough lashing."

"Y-You won't."

"I won't, it's true. How do you know that?"

She did not know how she knew, except that despite his arrogance and teasing, he could be solicitous and generous.

"Where is D-Doctor Stewart?"

"He'll return." He seemed to watch her steadily. She had often felt invaded by men's predatory stares, but never caressed.

Now she felt caressed.

Which was impossible and foolish and proved that she was delirious. A shiver caught her hard and she jammed the blanket closer around her.

He went to a cupboard attached to the rear wall of the cabin, drew a key from his pocket, and unlocked the door. Out of it he pulled a bottle shaped like a large onion, with a broad base and a narrow neck, and two small glass tumblers, then moved before her and sat in the chair that Dr. Stewart had vacated. His legs were longer than the Scotsman's and his knees brushed her thigh, but she could not care. She told herself she *did not* care.

He set the glasses on the table and uncorked the bottle.

"What are you d-doing?" she said.

With what seemed extraordinary care he filled one glass then the other, took up a tumbler and lifted it high.

"To your imminent comfort, duchess." He emptied the glass in a swallow. He nodded. "Now it is your turn."

When she did nothing, he reached forward, his fingertips sliding over her thigh. She flinched.

He grasped her hand and the blanket gaped open. She snatched it back. His brow lifted. But he said nothing about her dishabille, only reached again for her hand and pried her fingers loose from the blanket.

"I am not trying to take advantage of you, if that is what worries you," he said in a conversational tone, and wrapped her palm around the tumbler. "Dr. Stewart will return shortly with possets and pills and what have you, and Mr. Miles with tea. But while Gavin might not quail, if Miles found me in the process of ravishing a drunken woman he would serve notice, and then where would I be? It is remarkably difficult to find an excellent cabin steward, you know." He pressed the glass toward her mouth, his hand large and warm about her shaking fingers. "Barring a fire, which I am loath to light aboard my ship, this is the only route to warming your blood swiftly. One of two routes, that is, but we have just established that the other is not an option."

"*Cap—*"

"Now, drink."

Her outrage could not compete with her misery or the heat of his hand around hers. Liquor fumes curled up her nostrils. She coughed. "Wh-What is it?"

"Brandy. I regret that we are all out of champagne. But this will do the trick much quicker in any case."

She peered into the glass. "I've n-never—"

"Yes, I know, you've never drunk spirits before." He tilted her hand up, pressing the edge of the glass against her frozen lips. "Tell me another bedtime story, little governess wearing a king's ransom around your neck."

She did not bother correcting him. She drank. The brandy scalded her throat, and the base of her tongue crimped. But when the warmth spread through her chest she understood.

He released her hand and watched her take another sip. She coughed again and her eyes watered.

"You needn't drink it all in one swill," he murmured.

"I told you I haven't drunk b-brandy before."

"So you say."

"C-Captain, if you—"

"How do you feel? Any warmer?"

"Why m-must you always interrupt m-me?"

"We haven't spoken enough for an 'always' to exist yet. You have done all in your power not to come within twenty feet of me since you boarded my ship and refused my bed."

Her gaze shot from the glass to his face.

He lifted a brow. "True?"

"N-No."

She didn't think he believed her.

"Now another," he said, sliding the bottle across the table toward her.

"I will b-become intoxicated if I h-have another." Her head was muddled already. But she was warm. Warmer than she'd been in days. She feared it had less to do with the brandy than with the man's quietly wolfish gaze upon her.

He leaned back in the chair, his long legs stretching out to one side of her, trapping her against the table. He folded his arms over his chest. "What are you afraid of, duchess? That under the influence of alcohol you will abandon your haughty airs and do something we will both regret in the morning?"

Men had attempted to cajole her, to seduce her, to make love to her with words so that she would succumb to them. They had treated her to endless flatteries, and when that had not sufficed they had forced her. No man had ever spoken to her like this, so frankly. And no man had ever made her want to do something she would regret in the morning.

But his words now were not meant to seduce.

"You are ch-challenging me, aren't you?" she said. "T-Testing my m-mettle, like you would test any sailor aboard your ship."

"Do you wish to be a sailor now, Miss Caulfield? Trade in the dreary life of a governess for adventure on the high seas? I suppose I could arrange that."

She set her glass on the table beside the bottle. "F-Fill it."

He chuckled. She liked the sound of it. When he looked at her with amusement, she imagined he actually found her amusing.

She was not amusing. She was serious, professional, determined, and responsible. Except for boarding a ruffian's ship and sitting before him wearing a blanket, she'd done nothing especially adventuresome since she could remember.

She lifted the glass to her lips. "I am n-not afraid of anything. Especially not of m-men."

"I begin to believe it." A smile lurked at the corner of his beautiful mouth. The cabin was a haze of mellow woods and salt-smelling air and heat growing inside her. She could not seem to look away from his mouth. It was not in fact wise to sit before him wearing only a blanket.

"This is u-unwise," she heard herself say.

"Medicine is rarely easy to swallow." His voice seemed a bit rough.

She dragged her attention to her glass.

"Why do you cover your hair?" he said abruptly.

"Because I do n-not wish it to be seen by rapacious s-sea captains." She took another sip of brandy. "Next question."

He laughed. She did not like it. She *loved* it—warm, rich, and confident. His laughter burrowed into her, into someplace deeply buried.

"What thoughts had you so lost in bemusement atop that you did not notice even the rain, duchess?"

"I have t-two sisters." She could not tell him of her fear. "I have not seen them in an age. I m-miss them."

"Tell me about them." The golden lamplight cast his features in light and shadows so that he did look mythical. It was not her imagination or the brandy. It was him.

"Why?"

"I have a brother." He gestured to the framed drawing on the wall. "Common interest. And, given your earlier refusal of my bed, we've nothing better to do tonight."

"D-Do you speak to all women in this manner?"

"Only governesses wearing little more than a blanket."

"Do you come across th-those often?"

"Never before."

Over the rim of the glass she met his gaze. The brandy rushed down her throat. She sputtered.

He reached into his pocket and withdrew a neatly pressed white kerchief. He set it on the table between them. She took it up and dabbed at her watering eyes, studying the charcoal drawing. The boy's eyes were shadowed sockets of fear, his shoulders hunched, the lines of his face severe. Yet the skill of the artist had brought forth his natural beauty, despite the darkness.

"That p-picture is of your brother?"

"A self-portrait."

"At s-such a young age he is an artist?"

"He is now six-and-twenty. He drew that from memory. Now tell me of your sisters."

She set down the handkerchief. "Eleanor is g-good and fair, with golden hair and golden-green eyes, and t-tall and slender like a Greek m-maiden of old."

"Athena, warrior goddess."

"Wise, but not a warrior. She would rather read than ride or walk or do j-just about anything else. She spends her days tr-translating texts for the Rev— for our father from Latin into English. No one knows. Others th-think it is his work. When I asked her once if she m-minded, she said she preferred it."

"She is modest."

"Perhaps."

He leaned forward to refill her glass, and she smelled clean sea and warmth upon him. What would it be like to be held in his muscular arms?

She must be drunk already.

She had been grabbed, groped, clutched. She had never been held by a man.

He poured brandy into his glass and set the bottle on the table. "And your other sister?"

"Ravenna is a Gypsy."

The glass halted halfway to his mouth.

Arabella chewed the inside of her lip. "Dark eyes. D-Dark hair. Cannot be indoors. Cannot b-be still. Cannot be quelled."

"That last is like her sister, it seems." He drank the contents of his glass in one swallow.

"I am responsible for them." The words tumbled from her tongue in a rush.

He refilled the glasses. "You?"

"It is why this p-position I go to now is so important. I must . . ." His glass was empty again. She swung her gaze up to him. "Why are you dr-drinking too? You are not chilled."

"A gentleman never allows a lady to drink alone." He held the glass in the palm of his hand with ease. Except he was not at ease. Tension seemed to set his shoulders, and his jaw was hard with restraint.

Restraint?

"You are not a g-gentleman. Are you?" she said. "You did not seem so when you denied my request for passage in Plymouth."

"Which I then recanted."

"And teased me about your b-bed."

"A show of gracious generosity on my part."

"Not just now."

"That was to put you at ease."

"What sort of women d-do you usually speak with so that you could imagine *that* would have put me at ease?"

His eye hooded. "I am a sailor, Miss Caulfield."

Oh.

But . . . *champagne*? And his clothing . . . it was very fine. Handsome. He looked like a gentleman, except for the scar and black kerchief and shadow of whiskers on his jaw and wolfish glimmer in his eye and havoc he was wreaking with her insides.

She wasn't thinking straight.

"Gentlemen tr-treat ladies better," she said.

"So I hear."

"Some gentlemen."

He leaned forward, his knees coming around hers. "Not all?"

"Not . . . most." She lifted her attention from their knees locked together.

Hungry.

His gaze upon her was hungry. Like the wolf looking upon the lamb.

He stood abruptly, the chair scraping back, and swiped his hand around the back of his neck. "Not this one, apparently."

She got to her feet and the blanket drooped open. But she was warm finally. Her teeth clacked but deep inside her swirled heady heat. The lamplight threw his good eye into shadow, but she saw the confused desire there. He was both unsteady and authoritarian and he looked at her like no man ever had before, like he wanted her but did not understand that he did.

"I think you should go to bed, Miss Caulfield." His voice was low. "Now."

She could not think. The brandy stole her reason. Her head spun. Dr. Stewart was right: she was intrigued. More than that. She was *infatuated*. Upon so brief an acquaintance. Like a schoolgirl. Like the schoolgirl she had never really been because even then she had been serious, learning to be a lady despite all. When the other girls at school nursed *tendres* for the dancing master, she did not. She had remained directed and determined, waiting for a prince to come along and tell her the destiny that was just out of her grasp.

Now, with only two glasses of spirits, a piratical shipmaster threw her into foolish infatuation.

It was ridiculous.

She must halt it before it got out of hand.

"Why d-did you order Joshua to follow me about ship?" She said it like an accusation.

"So that I would know where you are."

"D-Doctor Stewart s-said—"

"What did he say?" He stood so close she could feel the heat from his body.

She was having difficulty breathing. "He said I would not be the first."

The door swung open. "Captain, I have hung the lady's garments in the warmest location aboard. Shall I make up the bed?"

The captain stepped back from her and nodded, turning his head away. "Do."

His steward went to the little cabin off the captain's day cabin. A dart of panic shot through Arabella. On wobbly knees she moved toward the door.

"No escaping, duchess." The captain stepped forward and swept her up into his arms. "Not this time." He carried her into his bedchamber. To his bed. She could not catch breath. His arms gave her no quarter. Thrillingly muscular arms. And hard chest. *She was touching his chest.* A man was carrying her to his bed, a man with desire in his eyes who smelled of salt and sea and heat and power, and she was frightened because the drunken part of her wanted him to carry her.

"No." She struggled. "You must n—"

He dropped her onto the mattress and backed out the door. "Rest well, duchess." He disappeared.

She pressed her burning face into the pillow while Mr. Miles tucked the blankets around her and made clucking sounds like a nurse settling an infant into a cradle.

"Dr. Stewart will be in within an hour to see that you haven't taken a fever," he said. He left. No key sounded in the door, nothing trapping her except the softest mattress she'd slept on in years and a cocoon of warmth bearing her into sleep.

HE SHOULD NOT have drunk a drop. He should have remained sober so that when the magnificent cornflowers
grew hazy then wild then caressed him like a touch, he
would not have started imagining peeling the blanket
off her to reveal the woman beneath.

With nothing to conceal it, the ruby ring had dangled
from its modest ribbon where the blanket gaped at her
breast as though it weren't worth five hundred guineas
and she had no cause to hide it. Only the sight of that
ring, and some remnant of gentlemanly honor his father
and the Royal Navy had drummed into him, had restrained him from doing as he imagined.

She claimed she did not belong to any man. Except
for her saucy tongue, she responded to his decidedly
ungentlemanly teasing as predictably as any virginal
governess.

But that ring told another story. Unlike his rakish
cousin the Earl of Bedwyr, however, Luc preferred his
women unentangled. Also, not shivering. Or tinged
blue.

He climbed the companionway to the main deck. The
rain had let up while he'd been below fantasizing about
undressing a woman while she sat before him. Wind
sheared off the ocean to port cold and fresh. Within
two days they would make harbor at Saint-Nazaire and
his passenger would set off toward the castle, *his* castle
to which he himself had not been in many months but
where his brother, Christos, and his friend, Reiner of
Sensaire, were now in residence.

She was going to *his* house—his chateau that had
come to him from his mother's family, the mother who
abandoned her young sons upon the sudden death of
her husband, to then cast herself into the hands of revolutionaries in her home country. Now, a beautiful little

English governess had sought him out to take her there so she could work for his friend.

What were the odds? Luc wasn't much of a wagering man, but he suspected they were pretty damn slim.

The sea spread out around him, and the solid boards of his ship and the bleached sails above were peace. With a turn of his head he could see in every direction. He passed the remainder of the night as he usually did, watching the stars. Though he would have liked his hands around the ship's wheel, he had drunk too much brandy, and while seven months ago that wouldn't have much affected his ability to steer his vessel, he wasn't so much of a fool that he believed he could steer both foxed and one-eyed.

A *pirate*. He laughed. The One-Eyed Captain they would have called him if he had remained in the navy. Now when he returned to London he would be the One-Eyed Heir. And someday, perhaps, the One-Eyed Duke.

That one-eyed duke would require an heir.

He tried to imagine the society debutantes he had been introduced to in his youth before he escaped to war. The only face he could conjure was hers. Even pale and shivering, she was stunning. And she was not as disinterested in the company of a man as she said. Brandy had revealed a longing in her eyes that had gone straight to his groin.

He didn't need that sort of trouble. There would be women to spare in Saint-Nazaire who could satisfy his needs quite satisfactorily.

If he could endure two more days of not touching her.

Her hair bound up beneath that linen was driving him mad. Each time he'd glimpsed her across deck he nearly ordered her locked in the bilge so he wouldn't be tempted to accost her and strip that damn turban off.

She had to know that binding any part of her tightly away from sight made her all the more tempting. Especially that hair.

It was glorious. Golden-red. The linen had slipped while she drank his brandy, and a crest of luxurious color showed above her brow. Like spun copper. He'd drunk with her to avoid snatching that turban away and seeing all of it. Then he had thrown her into his bed, despite her protests. That he had removed himself from the bedchamber was a miracle he was still too foxed to fathom.

He reached up and pressed his fingertips into his right eye. A spark flashed, a tiny thread of lightning across the black, like his memories, fleeting yet devastating.

As the first stirrings of gray crept onto the horizon, Luc got to his feet and—carefully, as he did everything now—made his way to the companionway and below. The dawn crew had stowed their hammocks, and sailors cupped tins of tea and biscuits in their palms. They nodded. A few nostalgic fools even saluted as he walked by and entered his cabin. He drew open the door to his bedchamber.

In a chair propped against the wall, Gavin came awake with a start. He shook his head free of slumber. "How much brandy did ye give her, lad? She's been out cold the nicht."

Luc cupped his palm around the back of his stiff neck, remembering her distress at the tavern in Plymouth, knowing her sleeplessness on board. "I think it is entirely possible that she hadn't slept in days before this."

"Aye." Gavin nodded. "So ye put her to sleep."

"It seemed the swiftest solution."

Gavin took up his satchel and patted Luc on the shoulder. It was a familiar gesture, banal, and yet Luc felt the affection as though it were the wool blanket that cocooned the woman in his bed.

"She's no taken fever. Ye've done guid, lad. As ye always do."

He stepped back to allow Gavin through the door. Then he entered his bed cabin and sought out her form in the dimness. Miles—the old mother hen—had wrapped her in his own favorite blue wool blanket and tucked it around her neck. Her breaths were deep, her mouth open slightly.

"When you examined her," he said over his shoulder, "you touched her face."

"Aye."

"What did her skin feel like?"

The Scot's grin rolled through his words. "Fancy the lass after all?"

"No, damn you." The inevitable pause. "Yes." He shrugged. "She took those children upon herself at no thought to her own disadvantage." And she was a servant to society debutantes. So he, heir to a dukedom, might as well lose his head over her.

"Ye've got a weakness for a soft cheek, lad."

"And you have a weakness for dancing girls. Hang me for my vice and choke on the rope, old friend."

Gavin chortled and went across the day cabin. "Ye'll have to dose her wi' drink again to settle her belly. Take a dram yerself while yer at it, lad. Ye look like ye coud use it."

Luc turned to the sleeping woman.

Wrapped in the fine wool, she barely made a dent in his cot. He knew she'd taken little to eat aboard; Miles and Joshua had both reported to him. But she looked like she hadn't eaten well in weeks. In the dimness of dawn stealing in through the shutter, her lips were dry and pale, her cheeks slightly sunken, and her skin less silken than he had been fantasizing, rather more like sailcloth. When she awoke, those brilliant cornflowers would open wide with surprise, or flash with indignation or warm with feeling she could not entirely conceal. But for now only the triangle of orange hair at her brow relieved the severity of her face.

He acted next purely from desire and without hesitation: he reached over and tugged the linen head covering back.

A halo of satin fire hugged her skull like a knit cap. Not orange or red. Flame, burning hot toward white. Like polished copper.

He pulled the covering entirely off, freeing a length of fiery beauty that caught his breath in his throat with awe that sank straight to his groin. There was *so much of it*. It would reach to her waist when she stood. It was impossible not to imagine her above him, the shining tresses cascading over her bared shoulders and breasts and draped across his chest. Or spread upon white sheets, his hands tangled in her glory as he worked his way into her.

He stifled the groan rising in his chest. He should move away.

He went to his knees beside the cot and touched his fingertips to her brow. He had felt the satin before at the nape of her neck. Now he turned his knuckles against her skin, teasing himself only, and drew them through the straight, heavy strands, closing his eye and feeling the caress deep in his body, then deeper.

It felt good. "Dear God." *Too good*.

Her breath stirred against his skin. "Praying, Captain?"

Chapter 4

The Servant

*L*uc withdrew his hand and sat back on his heels. "Always, duchess. A man like me needs all the help he can muster."

The summer blooms trained upon him were wary and rimmed with red. He stood, went into his day cabin and returned with a cup.

"You wish me to be drunk today too? Perhaps so that you can fondle my hair a bit more?"

He did not withhold his smile. A servant she might be, but she certainly didn't seem to know it. "Water with a splash of brandy. Doctor's orders."

She frowned, but drew her arms free of the blanket and pushed herself up to sit. She accepted the cup. The gold and ruby ring winked against her skin where the blanket gaped. Her arm was like cream, untouched by sun and supple from shoulder to wrist.

"My physician says you have avoided taking fever." He spoke to prevent himself from staring. The short, unadorned sleeve of her chemise showed at her shoulder. The gown she'd worn aboard was simple too. Her beauty and character demanded silk and lace. But on her, even the plainest linen seduced. "Congratulations, duchess, on possessing a hardy constitution."

"Not hardy enough to retain my clothing, it seems. Where is it?"

"Oh, somewhere about." He waved vaguely.

"Do not let my calm suggest to you, Captain, that I am comfortable sitting before you in this state," she said with perfect composure. "I assure you, I am not."

He withheld a grin. How this woman had been born into the servile class he could not fathom. "You mustn't allow it to bother you," he said. "Sailors routinely lose their garments to the elements. Or thieves. Brigands. Pirates. You know how it goes."

She returned the empty cup to him. Her hair spilled down her back like a waterfall. "You have had your clothing taken too, I am to guess?"

"Only the eye."

"You should not have done it."

"I didn't. The other fellow did."

"You should not have gotten me drunk. A dram would have sufficed."

He leaned back against the wall and crossed his arms loosely. "Is it magical? Do you keep it bound up to preserve its mystical properties?"

"Foolishness again." She turned her face away. "Don't you mind being foolish?"

"Good God. The ladies used to call it charming. But I suppose Napoleon soured everyone on charm. Charm is so French, after all."

"You said you would not take advantage of me," she said quietly but firmly.

"Our terminologies are clearly not in accord. For I am most certain I would remember having taken advantage of you last night if I had."

She did not respond but remained with her head bent and face averted.

"Samson," he murmured.

"Samson what?" she replied.

"Wasn't he the one with the hair that gave him strength? Or was that David? Forgive me, I forget my catechism at moments like this."

"Moments like what?"

"Moments in which a beautiful woman reclines upon my bed and I find myself not reclining with her."

She finally faced him again. Luc's breath slid away. A single drop of moisture rested on her pale cheek, its trail like silver.

She lifted a hand and passed her fingertips beneath her eyes, but not to rub away the tear. It was as though she did not know it was there.

"Are there dark smudges?" she asked.

"Barely," he managed to utter. "Beautiful, recall? I speak only truths, you know."

"I told you, I don't know anything about you."

Which was nearly true, after all.

She took up the linen neck cloth and, as he sat entirely bemused and wholly aroused, she twisted the mass of spun copper into a knot and secured it beneath the covering.

"Have you regained your strength now, Lady Samson?"

"Have you tamed your piratical manners, Captain Andrew?"

"Is it vanity?"

"Your arrogance?" Her brow went up, a spark lighting her eyes again that he felt in his chest. "Most certainly, I imagine."

He smiled. "If you don't like it to be seen, why don't you have it cut?"

"So that I can torment men like you with it, which I have also already told you. Really, you don't pay attention to a word I say, do you?" She tucked final strands beneath the linen.

How much money would he be obliged to part with to convince her to loose all that hair again? Just once. Once so that he could run his fingers through it and feel the surge of pure, uncomplicated lust. He could make her an offer that would render her compensation from Reiner laughable.

The notion intrigued.

He would add a bonus if she agreed to wash it.

"Every word," he murmured. "As though they were pearls."

She cut him an inscrutable glance, then swung her legs over the side of the cot. The hem of her chemise poked out from the blanket, the dullest white linen without ornament. It was an astoundingly prim garment from which a glimpse of her calves and feet emerged. Luc's mouth went dry.

"If I allow my ankles to dangle in your sight for a bit," she said, "will you forget about my hair?"

"Probably not, despite how comely those ankles are." Like the rest of her, a wrinkled and rumpled governess and none too clean yet still breathtaking. A beautiful servant on her way to his castle. "How will you travel to Saint-Reveé-des-Beaux, duchess?"

"I will hire a coach, though I hardly see how that is your concern."

Rather, entirely his concern. "If I choose to follow you, will you call the *gendarmes* down upon me?"

Her delicate brow dipped, the cornflowers wary once more. "Why would you follow me?"

"My brother lives nearby." In the chateau. He could tell her. He should tell her. "It is on my route."

"If you remain at a distance, I don't care if you follow me the length of the continent and back again."

"That is a comfort to hear." He stood and offered his hand.

Her shoulders stiffened. She climbed off the side of the cot without his assistance and pulled the blanket tight about her again. "I must find Mr. Miles and retrieve my clothes. When will we arrive at Saint-Nazaire?"

"Tomorrow if the wind holds. And Mr. Miles will bring your clothing when it is dry. Today you must remain here."

"In your cabin?" Her cheeks flushed. "Your bed?"

He allowed himself a slight smile. "Yes, but alas, without me in it. I have work to do elsewhere today."

Her quick breath of relief caught him. She had not expected to have a choice in the matter. A servant with her beauty . . .

He felt like a fool for teasing her. Worse, a scoundrel. He should have known. Other men did not always accept no as an answer.

Other men had not lived through the hell he had.

Luc reached for his hat hanging on a peg. "Last night you asked after the character of my men? Why? Has someone bothered you?"

"No. But there is one young man . . ." She chewed on the inside of her lip, a habit she had to which he was developing something of an addiction.

"Tell me," he said. "Now."

The cornflowers flashed anew. "You are remarkably autocratic."

"It comes with the ship." He allowed himself a moment's satisfaction. *The duchess was back.* "Tell me."

"The other day he visited Dr. Stewart's infirmary and claimed a toothache, but he was lying."

"How do you know he lied? Did Dr. Stewart suspect him?"

"No. But . . . I felt it. Whatever it is that sailor wishes from Dr. Stewart's medicine chest, I believe he has ill intentions." She spoke with confidence again, uncowed by his anger and unafraid of his authority. He had never known a woman of such beauty that was both modest and vulnerable, yet assured and resilient. She astounded him. He could not look away from her, but he could not speak.

"I felt it," she repeated earnestly.

"How did you feel it, little duchess?" he said, and lifted a hand to her chin. "As you feel—"

She jerked away from his fingertips. "Don't touch me again."

Luc stepped back.

On his eleventh birthday, pointing a pistol with a shaking hand, he had said those words to Absalom Fletcher. So Fletcher had found another victim. A younger victim.

He turned to the door. "I will take your warning under advisement."

He left her then to his bedchamber alone. Having stolen his peace and sanity, yet offering him nothing with which to remedy those losses, she did not protest his departure.

HOWEVER MUCH SHE needed the sleep, Arabella could not remain in his bed. Only one wicked temptation might have enticed her to linger: the opportunity to fill her senses with his scent that made her a little dizzy. But the bed linens bore only the mild scent of soap.

She had shared beds with her sisters enough to know that the scent of a person clung. She loved curling up in the sage-smelling warmth Eleanor left on the pillows when she rose at dawn to study and write. Ravenna's spot in the bed was always tangled and crumpled, strands of wild, Gypsy-dark hair mingled with Beast's silky black hairs and occasionally a mangled rope toy lost in the coverlets. Many times alone upon her plain cot in the servants' quarters of whatever house she had served, Arabella had imagined being cuddled beneath the old four-poster with her sisters, keeping warm from the winter and laughing. Always laughing, even in the depths of poverty and want, for that was love.

She had slept in Captain Andrew's bed, yet his scent was absent.

Mr. Miles served her breakfast in the day cabin but informed her that due to the rain her clothing was not yet dry. When he left, she bound herself up in the coat he had offered her the night before and carried her aching head to the infirmary. Sailors cast her curious glances as she went. She hurried by. They'd all no doubt seen considerably more than the hem of a woman's chemise. *I am a sailor, Miss Caulfield.*

None of the sailors would bother her. The captain would not allow it.

Only he posed a threat. Everything he did and said made her feel confused and out of control. For the first time in years of determination and work, she was behaving recklessly, standing in the rain, drinking brandy, and sleeping in a man's bed—and wanting to do it all.

She did not want him to touch her again. He was autocratic and arrogant and he made her uncomfortably hot all over when he looked at her. Always before, men's attentions had repulsed her. But when she had awoken to his caress, she wanted to turn into his touch.

The cabin boy Joshua had left off his vigil, and she went alone down the companionway and along the orlop deck to the infirmary. The door was open a crack. She pushed it wide and halted.

The skinny youth from three days earlier stood above the medicine cabinet. The drawers were open. His hand was clutched around a brown bottle prominently marked with skull and crossbones.

She moved toward him. "What do you have there?"

He tucked the bottle into his pocket. "Begging your pardon, miss. Doc said I was to take this medicine—"

"He could not have meant for you to dispense it yourself, or for you to take that bottle in particular."

The youth looked hard at her, his attention dropping to her chest.

The ring. She had not thought to tuck it away. She had only been thinking of her ridiculous infatuation.

"Set down the bottle," she said.

"Give me that ring, then, miss, and I'll give you this bottle." His attention darted to the door. No one had been on the orlop deck when she came, and the winds blew especially hard today. The ship creaked furiously and the animals in the hold were restless and noisy. If she screamed it was entirely possible no one would hear her.

"I'll leave the bottle, I promise," he said. "I don't mean any harm, miss. Just gimme the ring." His eyes looked wild above his sunken cheeks. Perhaps he was ill. Perhaps he was merely starving. Perhaps desperation drove him to this.

She understood desperation.

"Return the bottle to the case and leave now," she said, "and I will pretend you have not tried to bribe me."

His eyes again skipped between the door and her ring.

She extended her hand. "Give me the bottle," she said in her most authoritative governess voice.

The sailor slipped his hand into his pocket and withdrew a slender blade.

Her throat caught.

He grabbed her wrist and pushed her to the wall. His body was wiry but he was tall and surprisingly strong.

"If you won't trade, I'll have both." The blade gleamed close to her face.

"What foolishness is this?" she managed to utter, nerves spinning through her. His grip bruised her arm and his hand holding the dirk grappled at her shirtfront. He could cut her even without intending to. "We are at sea. Your crime will be discovered immediately."

He yanked. The ribbon sliced into her neck. She threw her weight into her leg and thrust up her knee between his thighs.

He staggered back, gasping for breaths. He opened his fist and the ring winked like blood in his palm. She dodged for the door. Face twisted, he staggered toward her.

"THEY'RE DOING WHAT?" Luc squinted across the whitecaps. Sunlight glinted off dozens of white sails three hundred yards portside, casting the nearby naval vessel in a glorious glow.

"Standin' about with the sheep, Cap'n." Joshua chewed on a straw, his little thumbs hooked into his suspenders like a farmer.

Across the water Luc could not clearly see faces yet, but he knew well the cocky stance of the man posed proudly atop the quarterdeck of the ship opposite. Tony Masinter had been the best of first lieutenants and of friends. Luc could not have wished for a finer man to take his place as the master of the *Victory*. But why in Hades his old ship was bearing down on his new one now was anyone's guess.

"Cap'n?" Joshua said.

Luc glanced at the deck of his brig. It was peculiarly spare of sailors, given the company that had appeared on the horizon an hour earlier. It wasn't every day a hundred-twelve-gun naval frigate escorted a humble merchant ship into port. But it seemed as though Tony intended to do just that.

"Twenty of the men, you say?"

"P'raps more. But I've only got twenty fingers." Joshua shrugged.

Luc turned his back on the other ship, leaned against the rail and folded his arms. "Why do you suppose the men are doing such an odd thing, Josh?"

"P'raps on account of the women's flimsies hanging from the beams, sir."

Luc stood up straight. "Women's flimsies?"

"There's one bit, Cap'n, ain't nothin' more than a scrap of nothin', but it's got them all castin' wagers as to who gets it. That is, if she forgets to take it with her when we make port, you see." The boy winked.

"I see. Thank you, Joshua." He strode toward the companionway. He should send Miles to see to the matter. But he'd be damned if his crewmen and blasted steward would ogle her undergarments while he had to content himself with heated fantasies.

What in the devil had Miles been thinking to hang her clothing to dry in the livestock pen? Warmest location aboard, *hell's thunder*.

Halfway to the hold he heard her scream.

Sailors' heads came up around him.

"Orlop deck, sir," one of them said.

He leaped down the stairs and bolted toward Stewart's office, men in his wake. No time to load a pistol. He reached for his sword and slammed the infirmary door open.

With her back pressed to the wall and color flushed across her cheeks, she wielded a bone saw in one hand and a pewter jug in the other like a Valkyrie, with regal fearlessness. A yard away, the sailor pointed a dirk at her neck. His other fist was clutched tight, but between the awkward bones shone gold and red.

"I told you they would come." Her voice was strong but compassionate, as though her pale throat were not inches from the lad's blade. "You should have listened to me."

He was one of the new men that Luc's quartermaster had hired on at Plymouth. Barely old enough to raise a beard, now he stared at Luc with fear, the dirk shaking in his grip.

"He told me he'd pay me three guineas to do it," came his raspy reply. "Three *guineas*."

"Whoever he was that made you such a promise, boy," Luc said, lifting his sword and stepping between them, "he's left you to swing for it alone."

The youth made no move to resist. The dirk fell to the floor with a clatter and he seemed to crumple in upon himself.

Luc gestured for one of his men at the door to take up the dirk, then he reached for the thief's hand and pried the ring from the slack fingers. He nodded to his crewmen crowding the door. With a growling cheer, they burst into a volley of shouts, grabbed the thief and shoved him before them from the cabin.

Her eyes were wide, her face pale now. She lowered her arms. Luc took the saw and jug from her and set them on the examination table.

"He carries a bottle of arsenic in his coat," she said.

"The men will find it. Are you—"

"I am well," she interrupted him. Her throat constricted but her chin ticked up. "I am well."

"You showed great bravery. Greater than many a man I've seen when threatened."

"He was frightened. He did not want to do what he had agreed to do." Her attention went to the ring in his hand.

He placed it upon her palm and she wrapped her fingers around it.

"I regret to have misled you, Miss Caulfield. He's a new man aboard. I should have taken better care."

"What will you do now? Will he be tried by a court when we reach port?"

"He has already been convicted. He will serve his sentence within minutes."

Her eyes snapped to the door where the sounds of the cheering sailors had faded. "What sentence?"

"Theft aboard ship is a flogging offense."

"Flogging?"

"Twenty-five lashes."

"Twenty-five?" It would kill him. "Here? Immediately?"

He nodded.

"No. No, he mustn't be beaten."

Captain Andrew slid the sword into his belt. "The law is clear, Miss Caulfield."

"You are the captain. Does that not make you the law on this ship, as you warned me? Spare him." She stepped forward. "I beg of you."

He looked down at her, his scrutiny intent now. "He has stolen from you. And you say he stole from Stewart as well. Why do you wish him spared?"

"I cannot be the cause of a man's death." The ring was meant for life, not death.

"Perhaps you won't. Perhaps he will live." The captain turned and left the cabin. She rushed after him. Ahead, the cheering of the crew on the main deck came down the stairway.

"He is starving," she said behind him, gripping the stair rail. The sea spread out to all sides of the ship, brilliant in the sunlight. "Can you not see that?"

"Then he should have availed himself of the plentiful rations aboard this ship," he said without turning to her.

She made herself release the rail and step out onto the open deck. "If he's new aboard, how would he have known the rations would be plentiful?"

He halted and turned to her. The deck was crowded, her view of the frothy sea and the activity around the forward mast limited. *What she could not see could not hurt her.* Her limbs loosened uncontrollably. She felt dizzy.

"You are defending a thief, Miss Caulfield. A man who intended harm to you."

"But the objects of theft are restored and he did not commit murder." She clasped her hands together before her in supplication. "Captain, you must see reason."

"Madam—"

"I cannot bear the burden of this man's punishment upon my soul."

"Then you should not have come aboard my ship with a possession worth stealing."

He was not speaking only of the ring. He was speaking of her. She had put him off, told him not to touch her, and now he was making her pay for it.

It could not be. She could not be infatuated with a man who could be so cruel. But she had trusted in a man's character and suffered for it before.

Dr. Stewart approached. "Captain, the men be ready for ye to pronounce sentence."

Arabella swung to him. "Doctor, you mustn't allow this."

He shook his head. "'Tis the way o' it, lass."

She pushed through the crowd toward the mast. The crewmen made way for her. The youth stood lashed about both wrists to the yardarms to either side of the mast. His ribs poked out.

Three guineas. A fortune for a common sailor. Enough to feed his family for a lifetime.

"Look at him, Doctor," she said. "He is skin and bones."

The Scot frowned. "Lass—"

"He stole nothing," she said. "I gave them to him. I gave them to him!" she shouted.

The sailors went silent amidst the clatter of rigging in the wind and the creak of planks and the ever present whoosh of the ocean.

"If you will flog anyone today, Captain," she said, "I am afraid it must be me. I discovered a rat in my cabin and I borrowed the bottle of arsenic from Dr. Stewart's cabinet to dose it so that it will not visit me again tonight. This sailor was helping me with the task. And—" She faltered.

Captain Andrew's knuckles were white around the hilt of his sword.

"And I gave him my ring in thanks," she said firmly. "I—I gave it to him as a gift. I am . . . *terrified* of rats, you see."

Not a man aboard made a sound.

"Lass—"

"It is true, Dr. Stewart." She pivoted to him. "I gave it to him. So he did not in fact steal anything. Captain, you must let him free now."

Slowly, with deliberate movements, Captain Andrew

sheathed his sword and walked toward her. "You gave him both the bottle and ring?"

"I did. I— Yes." She trembled. The wind whipped through the flimsy skirt of her chemise below the concealing coat. She felt undressed and out of control, as always with him.

"What do you say to this, Doctor?" he said without removing his attention from her. "Shall I flog the little governess for stealing poison from your infirmary to treat a miscreant rodent?"

She gulped over her alarm. *He would not.*

"Cap'n, I admit, I maself gave the lass the poison for the rat," the doctor said.

She sucked in breath.

The captain nodded. "Gentlemen," he said, still watching her. "Release the prisoner. Our guest has an item of value that she must return to him."

Reluctantly the sailors untied their captive and shoved him toward her. Head hanging, he shook like the rattling rigging. In his sunken eyes fear and uncomprehending gratitude warred.

Her throat closing, Arabella reached into her pocket for the ring.

"Naw, miss," the youth rasped. "I can't take it, now I think on it." His words came quickly. "My ma, she wouldn't like me taking gifts from a lady. She'd think she owed her life to you and she'd never let me hear the end of it." He backed away a step.

"Mr. Church," the captain called to his lieutenant. "Escort Mr. Mundy to the brig, if you will. And give him his dinner ration now. No one—not even those saved from a whipping by heavenly intervention—goes hungry aboard this ship."

The lieutenant grasped the youth's arm and led him

away. Arabella's fingers clamped around the ring in her pocket.

The doctor came to her side. "Ye've done a fine charity, lass. Bless ye."

"Thank you, Doctor," she whispered. "Thank you."

"Miss Caulfield." The captain strode toward the stairway. "Do attend me in my day cabin, if you will. I have a matter I should like to discuss with you in private."

Dr. Stewart shook his head then turned to the gaping crewmen. "Back to work," he ordered. "All o' ye nou."

The day was warming, the sun poking through wispy clouds. But Arabella shivered as she went to the captain's cabin.

He stood with his back to the door, facing the open window. On the sea beyond, a huge ship flew the flag of England. His stance was rigid, his hand on the hilt of his sword.

"You would not have flogged me," she said.

He turned about. "Wouldn't I have? How do you know? I thought you said you knew nothing of me."

"I could not allow him to be punished for my foolishness."

"Foolishness?" He moved toward her. "Was it upon a whimsical order from you, duchess, that he removed the poison from Dr. Stewart's medicine cabinet?"

"Do not call me that."

"Why not? You behave as one, mismanaging justice according to your wishes."

"I could not—"

"Are you his confederate?"

Her eyes flew wide. "*No*. No, of course not."

"How did you know?" He was angry, emerald flashing in his eye, but controlled, restrained. The night before she'd sensed his restraint with her too. "How did you know he intended theft? Harm to another? Even my quartermaster who is an excellent judge of men had no idea. How did you know he was lying when he asked the doctor for medicine?"

"I . . ." He would not understand. The Reverend never had.

"You?"

"I can read people."

"You can *read* people?"

"I can read people I encounter." Except him.

His eye narrowed. "You can read a man's thoughts?"

"No. It's not like that. I can sense feelings—desires and fears—and I guess at the reasons for them. Usually . . ."

"Usually?"

"Usually I am correct. It is what makes my services so sought after in society. It is very useful when seeking status or connections to know the unspoken wishes of others."

He took another step toward her. "You do this with everyone?"

"Only if I wish to."

"Do you wish to read me?" It was not an idle curiosity. But there was no desire in his gaze now, no teasing, only that intensity that had frightened her in the tavern in Plymouth.

She willed her feet not to retreat. "Yes."

There was a moment's silence.

"And what have you discovered of my desires, little duchess?"

"Nothing."

"What prevents you from making the attempt?" He moved close. "Fear?"

"I have tried." *She should not tell him.* "I failed. I don't understand you."

"Convenient," he said.

"Not at all."

He did not speak. She could no longer meet his gaze.

"What will you do now?" she finally said.

"Make you walk the plank, of course."

Her eyes shot up. His face was hard but the anger had gone.

Her lungs filled. "Of course."

"Miss Caulfield, do not interfere again with the justice that I mete out, do you understand?"

She swallowed over her relief and nodded. "I understand."

He studied her face. "What did he intend to do with the arsenic?"

He believed her. He believed that she could read people. Or he believed her to be the thief's accomplice.

"I don't know."

"No?"

"I told you, I am not a mind reader. I only . . ."

"Only?"

"Feel. I feel the emotions of others, Captain, because I have none inside myself to stand in the way."

He stared at her. "A remarkably candid admission, especially from a woman who claimed minutes ago that a man's punishment would be a burden upon her soul."

Her heart beat too swiftly. "What will you do with him?"

"Remand him to the navy."

"That ship—"

"A naval vessel. Its captain will make good use of him. The lad will not realize how fortunate he has been for many years, I suspect. But eventually he will."

"You will let him go free?"

"Have you ever rowed in the galley of a hundred and twenty-two gun frigate, Miss Caulfield? It's hardly freedom."

"But, he is a thief."

He lifted a brow. "Now you wish to see him flogged? Little governess, do make up your mind."

"Why did you spare him? Everyone knew I invented my story."

"And dragged the good doctor into it," he said ruefully. "Clever witch."

"Witch?"

"Another word came to mind, actually. I edited it before speaking."

One moment in anger, the next teasing. "You are a strange man, Captain Andrew."

"And you are a most unusual governess, Miss Caulfield."

"I thank you for the compliment."

The crease appeared in his cheek. "Was that what it was?"

Arabella's heart thumped again, but not from fear. "You must at least question him. Someone hired him to steal poison, it seems. Perhaps his employer wished one of your crewmen harmed. Or dead. Perhaps . . ."

"Me? Perhaps he wished to kill me? Mutiny, perhaps?"

She nodded.

"Not to fret, Miss Caulfield. The lad will be suitably questioned."

"Are you typically the target of murderers, Captain?"

"Not usually."

"Yet it seems not to surprise you that another man could wish you harm."

He lifted a brow and smiled slightly. "I find that somewhat disingenuous coming from a woman who has made no secret of her opinion of my imperfect character."

"Can you not be sincere about anything? Do you laugh at everything? Even real danger?"

"I was perfectly sincere in my fear for you when I entered that infirmary."

Arabella's throat got thick. "Fear?"

A knock came at the door.

"Come," the captain called, still watching her.

"Sir," Mr. Miles said, "Captain Masinter wishes an audience with you."

He frowned. "Now? Before we make port?"

"His passenger insists upon it."

"Who is his passenger, Miles?"

Mr. Miles's voice seemed to pucker. "His lordship the Earl of Bedwyr."

Earl?

But Arabella's surprise was nothing to the captain's, apparently. All amusement slid from his face. "I will pay a call on the *Victory*. Tell Mr. Church to ready the boat."

"Aye aye, Captain."

"Miss Caulfield, I will instruct Mr. Miles to return your clothing to you immediately." He moved toward the door. Then he paused and returned to her to stand very close again. "Do not leave this cabin while I am absent. Unless Dr. Stewart is here with you, lock the door and only allow Mr. Miles to enter." His gaze scanned her face slowly, carefully. "Do I make myself clear?"

Little hot nervous jitters slipped through her. His gaze lingered upon her lips then rose again to her eyes.

"Do I?" he repeated roughly.

She nodded. "Yes."

"Then good day, ma'am." He reached for his hat on the table and went from the cabin.

Arabella's knees gave out. She sank to a chair.

An *earl* wished an audience with a ruffian merchant ship captain? She had never seen him, but she knew of the Earl of Bedwyr by reputation. They said he was astoundingly handsome, a seasoned gambler, and the sort of man from whom a mother should steer her innocent daughters far away. What on earth did a rakish lord want with her ship captain?

Her cheeks flushed with heat.

He was not her ship captain. His ship was merely the means to an end. In two days she would never see him again. In two days he would be nothing to her but a memory.

Chapter 5

The Duke

The Devil take you, Luc! My men welcomed you aboard like a Messiah returning from the dead. It's damned lowering, I say." Captain Anthony Masinter of the Royal Navy pushed away his dinner plate and poured another full glass of wine, then refilled Luc's as well. His moustached scowl was jocund.

Luc settled back in his chair at the fine mahogany table he had chosen for the captain's day cabin when he outfitted the *Victory* for its maiden voyage six years earlier. Considerably more spacious than his quarters aboard the *Retribution*, it was the place from which he had commanded hundreds of sailors and half a dozen officers for over five years.

"The men remember the war and the glory enjoyed after battles, Tony. I am merely a reminder of that."

A cabin steward worked silently about them, removing the remnants of their meal. He caught Luc's eye.

"Blast it." Tony's palm came down on the table. "Even Cob here knows you're blowing smoke. I tell you it's damned provoking, captaining a ship full of sailors who want their old master back."

"I would never say so, sir," the steward said, and carried the dishes from the cabin.

"He would never say so," Tony grumbled, wiping wine from his neat moustaches with an embroidered handkerchief. "Balderdash!"

"Speaking of smoke, shall we, Anthony?" From across the table, the Earl of Bedwyr's voice held a studied air of indolence. Though cavalry once upon a time, after acceding to the earldom, Charles Camlann Westfall had cast off every vestige of the military. He wore now not the dashing gold-corded blue of the Tenth Hussars, but a plum cutaway coat with large silver buttons, a silk waistcoat embroidered with roses, and a mask of supreme ennui upon his face.

"Capital idea, Charles." Tony stood and brought a box to the table, lit a cigar, and pushed the box toward Cam. "Then you don't want the *Victory*?" he said loosely to Luc.

Not since he'd found another mission worth pursuing. "You know I don't want her."

"He couldn't have her even if he wished," Cam drawled.

"Right." Tony shook his head. "The old duke doesn't like him in the line of battle. Poor sot." He clapped Luc on the shoulder.

"Rather," the earl said, lifting eyes shadowed by a thatch of artfully arranged golden hair, "the old duke's widow." He slipped a hand draped with lacy cuff into his waistcoat and drew forth a letter bearing a wax seal. He tossed it onto the tabletop. "What say you to those tidings?"

"Luc, by golly, you're a duke! My compliments. This calls for a toast, and a second to follow. Cob, bring the brandy!"

"He is not a duke yet, Anthony. Merely duke-in-waiting."

Luc stared at the unopened letter in his palm. "When did it happen?"

"When did old Uncle Theodore go to his maker?" His cousin's voice did not rise above its habitual drawl, as though coming one step closer to the dukedom himself meant nothing to him. Which it probably didn't; Cam preferred indolence to work. "Three weeks ago, after a nasty turn for the worse. Really, Lucien, if you stayed in touch you might have known this was coming."

The steward returned with a crystal carafe and three glasses.

Cam played absently with his gleaming watch fob, smoke curling about his shoulders. "I suppose you are still pursuing the activities you commenced when the navy ejected you?"

"Didn't eject him. He wanted to go," Tony said, puffing a cloud. "Noble fellow."

The cabin was cool, the late summer wind coming off the Atlantic sifting in through the broad windows. But sweat gathered along Luc's scar. "Why did Adina send you to tell me, Cam?" Theodore's wife, young, beautiful, and equally as vain and vapid as her late husband, was devoted to her much older brother, Absalom Fletcher. This news would not be welcome to Fletcher. It would mean, of course, that Luc would finally return home. And so would his brother.

But Fletcher was no longer a mere cleric. Recently elevated to the episcopate, he was a powerful and influential man. The Bishop of Barris could hardly fear anything from his former wards. Nevertheless, Luc had remained at sea and Christos in France. Now, however, that would change.

"She did not send me. I volunteered." Cam lifted a brow. "I came to commiserate, cousin."

Tony frowned. "Now see here, Combe is a pretty place. Wouldn't mind having a castle like that myself."

"Luc already has a castle, Tony."

"Not in England!"

"The title would be welcome to him, Anthony, as would the estate," the earl murmured. "Rather, if the duchess were to lose this child like she has lost all the others, or if she were to bear a girl-child, the necessary padding of heirs to the duchy would swiftly diminish to . . . none."

Tony choked on his brandy. "I don't like you speaking of a man's brother like that, Charles. Wouldn't be surprised if Luc called you out for it. And if he don't, I might."

"He knows I won't, damn his two eyes." Luc slipped the letter into his pocket. "And you won't either."

"I'll challenge the blackguard if I like, even if I do owe him a hundred guineas from that faro disaster."

"There is a note enclosed from Adina, Lucien," Cam said. "Are you not interested in reading our auntie's heartfelt pleas for you to return and make it all better for her?"

"Bed her already, did you, Cam?"

Tony sprang to his feet, knocking his chair over behind him. "Damn all three of your eyes. The poor girl's only just been widowed."

"Sit down, you chivalrous fool." Cam laughed with languor. "Luc is merely taunting. And the duchess is not to my tastes anyway."

"She's not female and married, then?" Luc finally took up his glass.

The duke had died. Long live the duke.

In the nineteen years during which Adina had been Theodore's wife, she had lost five infants before birth. The life of the poor child she carried now was not by any means a certainty. After the fifth still birth, Theodore's demand that Luc relinquish his command in the navy had made his concerns upon that score eminently clear.

But Luc had always assumed his uncle would recover from his illness and continue trying to make heirs. Others had grimly suggested that delicate Adina would not survive the next difficult birth, and that Theodore would swiftly take a second wife whose ability to produce heirs might meet with more success.

Now that was not possible, and because of it everything had changed.

The face of the sailor Mundy haunted Luc, like the little governess's pleas to save the starving youth. A year after the famine now, hunger still ravaged the poor. Failed harvests the year before had decimated seed reserves, and this year's crops were scant. He'd seen it in Portugal in the spring, France in the summer, and again in Cornwall and Devon before he departed Plymouth: peasants' hollow cheeks, the bone-thin limbs of villagers, and children dying everywhere. Even his own family's patrimony, a sprawling Shropshire estate, still suffered.

But he had no choice now. His current cargo must sail to Portugal without him.

Now he had one goal: he must have an heir. With the duke dead, while Adina awaited the birth of her child, the duchy was in abeyance. But if the child did not survive, or if it was a girl, Luc would inherit. He must leave his ship and return to London to find a suitable bride.

The French property was modest, the Rallis title honorary; his brother Christos, who had lived at the chateau for years, could manage those. But the dukedom must never come to him. The weight of responsibility and authority would kill Christos as surely as if it were a guillotine.

Finally, Luc could no longer remain abroad. For the first time in eleven years, he must go home.

In doing so, he could see to the troubles at Combe while he still might. Theodore could not name him principal trustee to the estate. He feared that Fletcher, his uncle's longtime friend, had been given that honor instead. Luc had only until the birth to wield authority at Combe. After the birth he would have none . . . or all.

"In point of fact, coz," Cam said, "the duchess isn't in any condition to be rolling about in the hay with anybody. Lovely Adina is nearly in her confinement."

Luc's gaze snapped up. "Already?"

"Oh, how the months fly."

"Poor girl." Tony shook his head. "With her record at the track, likely as not it's all for nothing. Still, Luc's got to hang about twiddling his thumbs waiting. Damn the aristocracy, yanking a fellow about this way and that all his life. Much better to be a commoner, I always say."

"Your father is a baronet, Anthony," Cam said with a slight smile.

Tony waved his cheroot about. "Nobody cares a sow's ear about a wretched little baronet. Least of all his fifth son, don't you know."

"When is the child due?" Luc said.

"November."

Less than three months. Three months, after which Absalom Fletcher could very well be the de facto master of Lycombe for years to come. Or three months until he himself became duke. It all depended on a fragile widowed duchess and her unborn infant.

Luc rubbed his scar. Casually, Cam turned his head away. But for the first time in six months, Luc did not have the urge to plow his fist into his cousin's perfect face.

"Still and all, Luc, the poor girl could probably use a man about the place." Tony patted the hilt of his saber. "Best you hurry home."

"What is that monstrosity?" Cam passed an arch look over the sword. "Good God, Tony, it looks like the crown jewels."

"Family piece." Tony's chest puffed out. "My great-grandfather had it as a gift from King Willie himself after his smashing success at Cherbourg, don't you know."

Luc stared distractedly at the glittering gems on the sword handle. A ruby caught his eye, but not nearly as large as the jewel on the little governess's ring. He could not follow her to his chateau after all. It was for the best. He had no business courting trouble with a governess, no matter how brave and vulnerable and foolhardy she was, and no matter how her magnificent eyes looked at him with barely veiled desire and her tongue surprised him at every turn.

He swallowed the brandy in his glass, all of it, as he had the night before when he shared the darkness with a beautiful little sodden servant.

"I'll leave the *Retribution* in Church's command," he said. "Will you head back to England immediately?"

Tony snorted. "The Admiralty has commanded that I put my ship at your disposal. The *Victory* sails at your leisure. Again." He grinned upon a scowl.

Luc met his cousin's dark gaze. Cam stared back at him, his eyes hooded.

"Why did you really volunteer to bring me the news, Cam?"

The corner of Cam's mouth crept up. "Serendipitously, at the moment of our uncle's demise I found myself with the pressing need to be absent from London."

"A woman, I presume." Luc's scar ached. Six months ago it had also been a scandal with a woman that drove his cousin from England to France. A girl, rather. But that time Cam had surprised him. His cousin's vice had not been what Luc imagined. By the time he understood the truth of it, of course, it was too late. His eye had been the casualty of his misjudgment.

Cam absently twirled the stem of his brandy glass. "It is always a woman that drives a rational man to behave contrary to his interests, Lucien. That you are too blind to see that"—he finally looked directly at the kerchief about Luc's brow—"is no one's fault but your own."

Luc scraped back his chair and rose. The door opened and the *Victory*'s first lieutenant entered.

"Captain," the sailor said to Masinter, "we've interrogated Mundy. He'll admit only that he was hired in Plymouth by a man he had never seen before to find the *Retribution*, join the crew, and steal poison from the infirmary. He was to await further orders when they arrived in Saint-Nazaire." He turned to Luc. "I believe he is telling the truth, sir."

"Put the thumbscrews on the lad, did you?" Cam drawled.

"He gave you no name for the man that hired him?" Luc asked the lieutenant.

"He said he didn't know it, sir. As to thumbs . . ." He glanced at the earl. "Mundy said that the man lacked a thumb on his left hand."

"Thank you, Park," Tony said. "That will be all."

"Aye, Captain." The officer left.

Tony scowled, this time with no pleasure. "Blast it, Luc, I don't like a thief going freely about my ship."

"Hold him in the bilge if you wish. I will speak with him during our return." And learn what could be learned of the lad's attempt at thievery. If her instincts were to be believed—her ability to read men, as she said—Mundy was not a thief by inclination but by desperation. But the poison was worrisome.

Luc went to the door. "I will see you in port, gentlemen."

"All plans to make a sojourn to that lovely little chateau of yours are off, I suppose," Cam said with a sigh of regret.

"Deuced shame. But old Luc's got to take up his responsibilities after all."

That, and avoid further private audiences with a beautiful little copper-haired servant. He would send her on to Saint-Reveé-des-Beaux and be rid of the temptation.

"DR. STEWART, WHY is the Royal Navy escorting us into port?" Arabella stood at the day cabin window, watching the ship keeping easy pace with them across the water.

"'Tis a great honor, lass."

They would be at Saint-Nazaire shortly and she would be leaving the sea behind. But her nerves were stretched. She told herself it was because she was now within reach of her new position—within a day's ride from the port, Dr. Stewart had told her. It was most adamantly not because she would be obliged to speak to Captain Andrew before disembarking. They had not spoken since he went aboard the naval ship the night before, and she was glad of it. Her dreams had not been of churning seas and thunder, but of him touching her.

She had never wanted a man to touch her before. That

she dreamed of *him* doing so—and woke breathless, with her skirts in a tangle and skin hot—was preposterous.

"I am grateful for the care you took of me while I was chilled, Doctor. I wish I could offer you suitable compensation."

"Ye needn't be thanking me." He chuckled. "And there's no need for compensation."

She dug into her pocket and withdrew her largest coin. "Will you accept this?"

Gently he pressed her hand away. "There be no shame in accepting charity, lass. Nor sin."

"The sin lies in the pride that leads one to reject charity." Captain Andrew filled the doorway to the cabin.

She was not prepared to see him again. She probably would never be. It had not been the brandy or sleep or the young sailor's attack that muddled her when he was near before. It was rather him—simply—his strangeness and destroyed beauty and intense gaze that gentled so abruptly and grew hard again as swiftly.

"Are you a theologian now, Captain?" she said.

"I dabble in many endeavors, Miss Caulfield."

His glimmering gaze made her want to tease too. *She mustn't.* But after today she would never see him again. She would return to work and determination and her goal. "Like what?" she let herself say. "Other than sin, that is."

He leaned a shoulder against the door frame and crossed his arms over his chest. "A bit of this, a bit of that. You know . . . apprehend jewel thieves, rescue damsels . . ." He waved a negligent hand. "The usual sorts of things."

Dr. Stewart cast him a slanted look and went out.

Arabella drew a steadying breath. "I did not steal the ring."

His brow went up. "I did not say that you had."

"Why do you mistrust me about this? Have I given you any special reason to?"

He assessed her with that odd intensity that made her knees feel watery. "You are not what you appear, Miss Caulfield. The ring you bear suits your character better than the governess's gown. Will you deny it?"

She wanted to. It was on the tip of her tongue. He spoke foolishness. She was a poor girl from a poor family. An orphan. A servant.

But when he looked at her, he made her feel like . . . *a duchess*.

She grappled at reality. "Why is the British Navy escorting your ship? In French waters, no less? Have you done something wrong?"

"Ah, the little duchess believes she may ask any question she wishes while refusing to answer those put to her. Interesting, though to be expected, I suppose." He nodded toward the gun deck. "We will shortly come into port. Perhaps you would like to take in our arrival from atop."

He gestured her through the doorway, and she went before him. But he stayed close, too close, and as she climbed the steep stair to the main deck, his hand brushed hers upon the rail.

He grasped her fingers, halting her ascent. The breeze twining down the hatchway whipped around her cloak and their joined hands.

"Sir," she whispered, but her throat was constricted and the wind snatched away the sound.

He released her and she hurried the remainder of the way up.

The wind was strong on the main deck, and the *Retribution*'s sails were full like those of the naval ship close by. Sailors were active on deck.

"Have you lost your gloves, Miss Caulfield?" The captain spoke at her shoulder, low and intimate, as though they were not standing in broad daylight surrounded by dozens of men.

She turned. Color shone high upon his cheekbones and his lips were parted.

"In Plymouth," she said, "I sold my gloves for food."

"Food for those children you found."

She nodded.

He stared at her mouth and his chest rose sharply, and she feared he would kiss her here before his crew in the light of day, like a man might kiss a woman of ill repute—where he wished, when he wished. For all his talk of governesses, he must believe her to be what he had first suggested in Plymouth. She was traveling alone and in possession of a ring that only a wealthy man would own. Captain Andrew had no reason to think her other than a fallen woman, or any other justification for staring at her with undisguised desire.

"I am not what you think I am." She bit her lip. She had not meant to speak. She needn't justify herself to him.

"I don't believe you have the faintest notion of what I think of you. Now look behind you."

She turned.

Arrayed like a bride on her wedding day, the estuary shone bright and sparkling in the sunshine, broad across and festooned with vessels. The near bank stretched gold and white with long, lazy beaches giving way to rows of docks cluttered with ships, banners proclaiming them from every nation on earth, it seemed.

Tucked beyond, inside the mouth of the river, the town of Saint-Nazaire was little more than a collection of quays and shipyards, with a church spire poking above the cluster of buildings that rose from the shore.

"Here amidships you are unlikely to fall overboard, duchess," he said quietly at her shoulder. "You can release the railing now."

She started. Her knuckles were white around the stair rail. "I . . ."

"I noticed," he only said. "Welcome back to land, Miss Caulfield." With a bow he strode across deck and to the helm.

Chapter 6

Two Louis

Je suis désolé, mademoiselle," the innkeeper said without a shadow of desolation on his narrow Gallic face. "*Mais*, there is no carriage in the carriage house. And one cannot fabricate a carriage from the air like the magician, can one?" His lips pursed.

Arabella's fingers gripped the coins she had shown him, every penny she had. "This is because I am not offering to pay you more, isn't it?"

He shook his head. "*Je vous ai dit*, the horses and coach, they are not available until *jeudi*."

Thursday. Two days away. She could not afford to stay even a single night at the inn and also hire the carriage to Saint-Reveé-des-Beaux.

"Is there another place I may hire a carriage in town?"

"*Non non, mademoiselle.*" He shook his head again as though he were filled with sorrow over her plight.

"But I passed a stable walking here, and I saw a perfectly good carriage and two horses doing nothing at all," she said firmly. "How do you explain that, monsieur?"

"There is no arguing with innkeepers in this country, my dear," a languid voice came from behind her. "Now that they have tasted revolution, the French have little respect for anything but avaricious acquisition. Pity, really. They used to be so delightfully ingratiating."

Golden like a god, with wavy hair and warm brown eyes, dressed in dark velvet, with draping lace at throat and cuffs, and boots that shone with champagne polish, the man standing in the doorway looked like a prince out of a storybook.

But no prince would peruse a lady from brow to toe. In comparison, Captain Andrew's lustful stares seemed positively safe. *No.* That was not true. There had been nothing safe about Captain Andrew's stares, because despite herself she had wanted them.

"Monseigneur, bienvenue!" The innkeeper bowed deeply. "How may I be of service to you?"

"You may cease distressing this lady." He came to her. "Clearly she is in great need of assistance."

"Which she is unlikely to accept from you." Captain Andrew strode through the door. "I think you will find she is adamantly self-sufficient." He bowed to her. "Madam."

Arabella battened down on her tripping pulse. "Captain."

The gentleman's languid eyes went wide. "How is it, Lucien, that you have the pleasure of this diamond's acquaintance yet I do not? It is positively criminal."

"Miss Caulfield, allow me to—with all reluctance—introduce you to the Earl of Bedwyr," the captain said with a sideways glance at the earl. "Cam, Miss Caulfield took passage aboard the *Retribution* from Plymouth."

The earl's mouth curved into a slow grin and he

scanned her anew. "Ah, now is fully explained the presence of a passenger aboard your ship otherwise *rempli des bêtes*. Well done, Lucien."

The captain accepted a key from the innkeeper.

"Festival in town, tomorrow," came through the door before the man who spoke it. "Great guns, gents, we're to have uncommon entertainment." Black-haired, with moustaches that curled dramatically upon either cheek, he wore a naval uniform, the splendid plume of his tricorn draping over blue eyes. He saw her and halted abruptly.

"Well, *bonjour*, mademoiselle." He swept off his hat and scraped the plume to the floor. "Sight for sore eyes, ain't she, gentlemen?"

"It seems that Luc's eyes are not quite as sore as ours, Anthony," the earl drawled. "Rather, eye."

"Miss Caulfield, this is Captain Masinter of the Royal Navy." Captain Andrew said, coming to her side. "Tony, she is not French."

"I don't think Anthony is particular when the beauty is so marked," Lord Bedwyr said with a smile.

"And she is not married," the captain said flatly, cutting the earl a sharp glance. Then he looked at her. "Are you?"

She swallowed over the catch in her throat. The earl was frankly gorgeous, and the naval captain dashing. But standing beside the scarred, autocratic merchant shipmaster when she had expected never to see him again made her knees watery. He carried himself with absolute authority, and she had not needed to tell him she feared the sea for him to know it. She could not read him, but it seemed he could read her perfectly well.

"I am not married."

"My sympathies, Cam," the captain said without any show of humor, then looked down at her and his gaze glimmered. "Monsieur Gripon, have you assisted Miss Caulfield to her satisfaction?"

He had done this before, speaking to another while looking at her. It was as though he knew everyone's attention would always be on him, waiting for his words, no matter where his attention was directed.

"Hélas, monsieur!" The innkeeper clasped his hands together as though he were in great distress. "The preparation for *le jour de la fête* tomorrow, you see, it has commanded *toutes les ressources de la ville.*"

The captain frowned.

"I wish to hire a carriage to travel to the chateau," she said, "but he said there are none to be had, although I saw one in the stable, and horses."

He turned to the innkeeper. "Is this true?"

"Le chariot is to bear the holy image of *le roi* Louis IX in the procession tomorrow night, Captain. I cannot send it away now." The innkeeper shook his head sorrowfully. "But the mademoiselle, she does not understand."

The captain nodded. "I see. Miss Caulfield, I am afraid in this he is probably telling the truth. How many days yet before you must arrive at your destination?"

"Five, but I should like to arrive before then." She had no choice. She hadn't the funds to linger even a day in Saint-Nazaire. She could not have come this far only to be thwarted now. "Will the festival last many days?"

"Only one." Captain Masinter removed his gloves. "It is the Feast of Saint Louis, Miss Caulfield, one of those medieval crusading blokes, and ancestor to the newest Louis, don't you know. Ought to be great good fun tomorrow." He gave her a broad smile. "Continental Catholics, you know, throw a splendid party."

"Why don't you remain in town a night and enjoy the celebration, Miss Caulfield?" Lord Bedwyr said with an elegant bow. "I should be honored to escort you about the festivities."

"I've no doubt you would." Captain Andrew looked back down at her. "Miss Caulfield, if your claims of having spent time among London society are true, you will know better than to trust in Lord Bedwyr's intentions."

"I am barely acquainted with him, Captain Andrew. I should not presume to make a judgment."

"Perhaps then you can trust in my word."

"Yes, Miss Caulfield," Cam said with a sly look at Luc, "by all means trust our friend Captain *Andrew* here rather than me. For all that he looks like a villain and addresses a lady like a cad, he is a *noble* fellow in truth, while I am but a poor man alone in an alien country, innocently seeking a lovely lady's company for an evening stroll." Cam's grin slipped into the smile he had practiced upon hundreds of pretty females with enormous success.

A pale flush stole over the little governess's cheeks.

Luc ground his molars. The rakehell always had such an effect on women. Luc had never cared. Not once.

Now he cared.

"Camlann, don't tease the lady," he said, unsurprised at the gravel in his voice.

"You are to be the only man allowed that privilege, I suppose?" A gleam lit Cam's eyes.

"Captain. My lord," she said firmly, her chin inching upward. "I would very much like it if you would not speak about me as though I were not standing here." She turned to the innkeeper. "I will hire a chamber for tonight and tomorrow night, monsieur, in the hope that you will make the carriage available to me the following day. How much will it be?"

The innkeeper looked questioningly at Luc.

Her cheeks flamed. But her slender shoulders remained square. "I am barely acquainted with these gentlemen, monsieur, and not a member of their party. I will pay for my own room and for the carriage to Saint-Reveé-des-Beaux."

"Saint-Reveé-des-Beaux?" Cam said with a quick glance at Luc. He stepped toward her. "Why, my dear, that is precisely my destination as well. I have an itch to see my old friend, Prince Reiner, who is in residence there as the guest of . . . Now who is that crusty old fellow that owns the castle, Tony?"

Tony lifted a brow and casually twirled a moustache between forefinger and thumb. "Don't know if I quite recall."

"Ah, yes, the Comte de Rallis." Cam gestured with a lacy wrist. "Monsieur Gripon, the carriage the day after tomorrow will be on my bill. I insist. I will, of course, allow you privacy during the journey, madam. I shall ride ahead and clear the road of ruffians and knaves." He gave her a winning smile and went to the door. "Now, Tony, why don't we find that smart little brasserie we passed and command a roasted capon. Lucien, I trust we shall see you anon."

"Capital idea, Charles." Tony swept a deep bow to Miss Caulfield and departed.

She said, "You count earls and naval commanders among your close friends, Captain?"

" 'Friend' loosely employed in the case of Bedwyr."

"That, at least, is obvious. I have no intention of accepting his assistance in traveling to Saint-Reveé-des-Beaux."

"That is probably wise." If there were a horse or mule to be spared in town, he would send a message to the chateau and have a carriage sent for her. As soon as Miles had finished packing, he must see to it.

She studied him for a moment longer, the flush still high in her cheeks. "Good night, Captain."

He watched her follow the innkeeper up the stairs, her back as straight as any duchess's. He had no doubt that the young ladies she trained for society were among the fortunate few.

THE INN SAT at the far end of town at the edge of a stretch of beach bordered by a grove of shrubs and mottled plantane trees. Monsieur Gripon gave her a bedchamber the size of a closet at the head of the stairs from which Arabella heard every footstep and uttered word of every guest in the crowded hotel as they passed by her door. It seemed that having the acquaintance of both an English nobleman and a captain in the Royal Navy did not ensure a poor woman an enviable bedchamber in a French inn. The bed linens were thin and worn, the mattress a straw pallet, and the posts and headboard eaten through with tiny holes by some hungry resident.

It required little to soothe herself with the reminder that in two nights' time she would be sleeping in a castle.

For now she stared out the window at the black waves breaking on the beach where two hours earlier the sun had disappeared in a blaze of fire into the inlet. From this distance and the safety of land, the water seemed dramatic and powerful, but no longer frightening. Even its scent, mingled with comforting aromas of the meal served earlier in the inn's dining room below, seemed less wild and ferocious.

Her stomach growled. If the passage of other guests traveling up and down the stairs did not keep her awake all night, her empty belly would. But she hadn't enough to pay for the room and dinner.

Captain Andrew would purchase dinner for her if she asked. Then she would owe him a debt and he would expect payment from her in return. They usually did. She had rarely met a man who did not look at her as though she were a thing to be cajoled, commanded, or purchased. Or despised. Like the man her sisters called Papa.

She believed the Reverend Martin Caulfield to be a good man, sincere in his intentions and affectionate in his subdued, scholarly way. He admired Eleanor's modesty and was proud of her fine mind. And Ravenna's interests in every beast and bird in the village amused him; he imagined her an amateur naturalist of sorts. But he had never cared for his middle adoptive daughter. Once, when she was very young and disturbed him at his work, he scolded her, telling her that her vanity drove her to disrespect him.

But as she grew older she had seen something else in his eyes when he looked at her. Disappointment. Disgust.

Then, on her fourteenth birthday, he discovered her talking with the blacksmith's son. A strapping lad, he had brought her a bouquet of flowers plucked from a garden, and she laughed at how he escaped the gardener's notice. The Reverend found her there, grabbed her wrist and dragged her home. He called her immodest and read to her the story of Jezebel from scripture. He told her he had long suspected their mother was a woman of ill repute. Who else but a red-haired harlot would send her children away from her as she had? Arabella must fight against that tendency in her blood, for the good of her sisters' reputations and for the good of her soul.

After that she ceased seeking his approval or affection. She sought instead to educate herself so that she could find her mother and prove him wrong. Eleanor's prolonged illness made it possible. Instead of her elder sister, Arabella went off to school with the funds he had saved, and learned there what she must to enable her to forge her destiny—and to someday, hopefully, find the man who had sent for his daughters across the ocean to claim them as his own.

Now her fingertips stole to the linen wrapped about her head. She remembered her mother's hair well, all silken and bright in the tropical sun.

Her own was wretchedly dirty. And her scalp itched. She could not meet Princess Jacqueline looking like a nun. But if she put down her hair without washing it, she would look worse.

Taking up the stub of tallow candle Monsieur Gripon had given her, she left her chamber and climbed down the four narrow flights of stairs to the parlor. The hour was late already. She peered into the corridor leading to the back of the inn. A woman marched toward her, her cheeks ruddy, hair trussed, and black silk skirts starched.

"I'm Madame Gripon." She spoke like the downstairs maid in the town house of Arabella's last employer. "Cat got your tongue, miss?"

"I desire a bath." Arabella adopted her best upper servant hauteur. "I should like hot water sent to my bedchamber immediately."

"Well, we're all high and mighty now that we've got the eye of his lordship, aren't we, then?"

"I beg your pardon?"

The woman set her fists on her hips and looked her over again. She shook her head. "Seeing as he's not paying the bills, though, I don't suppose I'll be able to serve you that bath after all."

"You will indeed."

The woman laid her palm out flat before Arabella. "That'll be two louis."

"Two . . . ? But that is robbery."

The fist went back to the hip with a rustle of expensive fabric. "Two louis is the price of a bath in my hotel, miss. If you haven't got it, then I haven't got the hot water."

"Then bring me cold water and I will make do with that."

The palm jutted out again. "That'll be three pennies, miss."

Arabella pressed down on her irritation. "Good night, madam." She walked as calmly up the steps as she could, the candle quivering in her hand.

When she entered her room, she set down the candle, tore the dirty linen wrap off of her matted hair and threw it onto the bed. Her hair fell in a thick, lusterless clump to her waist, her stomach accompanying with a mighty howl. Frustration and helplessness and exhaustion and sheer yawning hunger overcame her. She dropped her face into her hands.

Nothing came. No sobs. No tears. Not even a drop of moisture.

It never did. She was as dry in her heart as she'd been since the day after she received her first caning at the foundling home. Switch in hand, the Mistress of the House laughed at her, and Arabella had vowed aloud to the woman and to God that she would never again weep.

She went to the window, threw open the shutter and stared out at the black sea. Below in the stable, the horses that she was not permitted to hire because a saint had previous claim to them nickered softly.

Her stomach clenched with nerves—the tingling sort

she used to get when she was about to do something she knew the Reverend would dislike—the sort she hadn't felt in years, since she had become a respectable, responsible, professional, and highly sought-after caretaker of young ladies of breeding.

She stared down at the stable. No lamp or torch lit the outbuilding, and no other house was within sight of it. Earlier she had watched the stable hand close the door behind him and walk off toward the center of town. There was no one within.

She had spent her childhood in the countryside with a sister enamored of farm animals. Where mules and horses bedded down for the night, there would be water.

She could not. If she were discovered . . .

She doused the candle and lay upon the bed in the dark. But she remained awake, submerged in the violent music of the surf, the sea air damp and salty on her skin. She felt grimy all over, sticky from her journey and not a woman that a prince would ever consider.

But he *must* consider her.

So she simply must be beautiful when she met him.

She would not be discovered.

She climbed out of bed. The wooden floor was cold on her bare feet as she moved to the door, taking up a threadbare blanket as she went, and slipped out of her bedchamber. The stairwell was inky and she felt her way, only one or two risers complaining as she descended. From one chamber by the landing came the furious creaking of bedsprings. Arabella's cheeks warmed, but it was nothing that she hadn't heard in servants' quarters before, and perfectly foolish to be missish about when her own mind had strayed to the very thing far too many times when Captain Andrew had turned his gaze upon her.

She stole on silent feet to the ground floor.

She needed soap. Where in a French inn she would find soap appropriate to wash hair, she hadn't an idea.

She began in the kitchen. An old dog slept on the warmth of the stones by the hearth. It opened an eye as she crept toward the pantry, flicked one ear, then closed the eye, snorted, and breathed deeply again.

She found a pot of soap behind a jar of dried plums. *Curious location.* Then she opened it and stuck her nose inside.

It was not mere soap but the most luxuriant paste of lavender she had ever smelled. She dipped a fingertip in, rubbed it, and nearly crowed with glee. Bath oil. Exceedingly fine bath oil, worth a great deal more than two louis. If she possessed such a thing in a public house, she would hide it behind the prunes too.

She stole out of the inn. The night was lit with the slenderest crescent moon, the shadows deep across the few yards to the stable. The ocean crashing upon the beach fifty feet beyond the plantane trees drowned all other sounds, like prowling night creatures. Far better than bright moonlight and silence, she told herself. What she could not see or hear would not frighten her.

The stable was dark, but shards of thin moonlight darted across the straw as she opened the door. The horses snuffled in quiet sleep, and the air tasted dry, less salty, more like the earth. It smelled like home, like England. She filled her nose with it, and her lungs.

She found a full bucket of water beside the first stall. She stood for a moment, longing to pour the entire contents over her, and felt confounded.

Her gown would be soaked. Her petticoat too. Even if she washed bent over, she was bound to end up sodden like that night aboard ship.

Her heart did an uncomfortable turnabout.

She could not afford that sort of problem now. For a whole host of reasons.

The horse within the stall stared at her with eyes the color of tea as she shed the blanket, then her gown, petticoat, stays, and stockings, set them neatly aside, went to her knees, and bent her head into the pail.

Cold, blessedly clean water tickled through the matted strands of hair, freeing her scalp. Tiny fingers of pleasure scampered all over. She shivered in perfect delight. After weeks of the tight linen wrap, this was freedom. It felt *magnificent*. She moaned in pure satisfaction.

Nearby, a man cleared his throat.

She whipped her head out of the bucket, pushed streaming strands from her eyes and clasped her hands to her breasts. She blinked into the dark. "Who is it?"

"You might consider all the wonders of the world, duchess, before you bury your head in the sand."

Water dribbled along her nose, over her shoulders and between her breasts, trickling down her belly beneath her shift. A little tremor shook her. "You might have announced your presence sooner, Captain."

"I could claim you acted too swiftly for me to do so. But that would probably be a lie."

She saw him now, a shadow standing with his back to a stall as though it were perfectly normal for him to stand in the dark in a stable in the middle of the night. As normal as it was for a respectable governess to wash her hair in a horse bucket, she supposed.

"Don't let me interrupt." He gestured, and a spot of moonlight caught the gold of a ring on his hand. "I pray you, continue with whatever it is you were doing. Drowning yourself, perhaps? I hope not on my account."

"You are absurd."

"You have chosen a poor method for ending it all."

"I am not—"

"I know this from experience, you see."

Her heart stumbled.

She forced disdain to her tongue. "Do go away now."

He crossed his arms, stationary and large in the shadow. "I was here first."

She rolled her eyes, suppressing the memory of the muscles in those arms and the way that looking at them made her feel peculiarly tight inside. "Are we nine then, Captain?"

"If we were nine, duchess, I would not wish to remain here."

Heat rushed up through her in little spikes. "I want to . . ."

He remained silent.

"I want to wash my hair," she whispered as though she were about something scandalous. Which of course she was. "But I cannot do it with you watching."

"I won't watch. I cannot see you anyway. Not well at least. Pity."

"Go away. *Please.*"

There was a lengthy silence during which the swoosh of the waves sounded muffled without and the soft rustlings of horses within.

"I will pay you for it." The rumble of his voice was deep and serious.

The tremor shook her again, this time of regret. Of all men, she did not want this man to wish to purchase her. She did not want him to believe she was a woman to be used and discarded. Foolishly, she wanted him to be different. "I told you—"

"To wash your hair here, now, before me. Only that."

Only that? "I don't—"

"You haven't the funds to pay for a night in this inn or a carriage to the chateau. You haven't even a change of clothing. Aside from a ring of which I will not speak, you have a cloak, a sorely abused gown, and a cravat my cabin steward has lent you. You cannot intend to enter the castle of a nobleman clad in worn garments, even through the servants' door. They will expel you as a beggar."

It was true, of course. But she could not admit it.

"I will pay you sufficient money to hire your room tonight and to purchase new clothing," he said, "if you continue with your bathing now."

"I will not—"

"Only your hair, Miss Caulfield. And I will remain standing here."

"Will you also cease interrupting me?"

"Will you do it?"

Her gown was within arm's reach. She should cover herself. But in order to do so she must first expose herself for a moment. The idea of it sent a wicked thrill through her. This was not how her journey to France to meet a prince was supposed to progress. But for the first time in ages she wanted to feel *something*. She wanted to allow herself a moment of purely irresponsible and thoroughly unwise pleasure.

She mustn't.

"I do not believe you will remain there," she said hesitantly.

"Then I wish you luck with your bills."

"Your charity is not so unselfish now, is it, Captain?"

Another pause. "If I offered you gold for doing nothing, would you accept it?"

"No."

"You do not trust in charity."

Arabella had encountered too many men of the world to trust that anyone would ever give her something for nothing.

"Charity always comes at a price," she said.

"I am offering to pay for your charity now." He shifted his stance and his voice eased. "Come now, duchess, amuse a sailor who has been at sea far too long with only the beauty of the blue horizon to please him. Allow him to enjoy a beautiful woman. Innocently."

There was nothing innocent about him. His words teased again now, but he was not a man of light temper, and if he wished to hurt her he could quite easily.

But she did not believe he would. He might have already at any time aboard his ship—when she was drunk and in his arms, in his bed, in his power. But he had not. He had mercy on desperate thieves and he looked at her like a man starved.

"It is a simple transaction, Miss Caulfield," he said. "You wash your hair, I give you gold. Nothing more. Nothing less."

"Yes."

In response, he was silent, not even a nod to indicate that she agreed to his salacious proposition.

Arabella turned her face from him, willing her sixth sense that felt him close to obey. *What she could not see or hear would not frighten her.*

She bent and scooped a handful of water from the bucket, and as she spread it on her hair and scrubbed, she hoped that he did not see her trembling now, or that if he did, he would think her merely cold.

Chapter 7

The Bath

Shreds of moonlight peeking through the stable door doused her in silver. Luc was as good as his word, but through no particular nobility of character. In truth, he could not have moved if he wished it. The image of the little governess on her knees, her pale, lovely arms stretched up and tightening the damp linen across her breasts, paralyzed him.

Her hair fell in dark rivers down her back and over her shoulders, rivulets of soap sliding down as she worked her hands in it. Eyes closed and lips tight, she moved with purpose, not intending to seduce, yet seduction was inevitable. He had imagined those slender arms, those small breasts, and the curve of her buttock to her thigh, and now they were before him like a banquet.

He was famished.

His body responded. Of course it did. He hadn't seen an unclothed woman in months. The heir to the duchy of Lycombe did not spread his seed carelessly. No low-born by-blows must mar the Westfall family tree; that much his uncle Theodore had taught him. As Luc had been content to share his bed with women of experience and discretion, he'd never had need of common tarts. But willing widows were in short supply at sea. It was no wonder that watching the beautiful little governess now made him hard. He was only a man.

She lifted her behind from her heels and spread her thighs to hug the bucket, then bent and submerged her hair once more, and Luc lost his senses. He wanted the bucket gone and her legs wrapped around him. She splashed water onto her head, and her breasts, perfect peaches ripe to be tasted, strained against the chemise. A woman of experience would know what this did to a man—what it was now doing to him. Either this woman was intentionally taunting him or she was a virgin and knew no better.

A virgin. *Dear God.* He could not bear it.

She twined the stream of hair into a thick cord, dropped it over her shoulder to fall heavily down her back, and stood. Then she turned fully to him.

"I have done it," she said. "I need only enough to purchase a new gown and shoes and to hire the carriage. Give me only that."

The pain of complete denial was too great to withstand. He went forward to be closer to her, because he knew now that he could not have more of her.

She stood her ground, her chin tilting up almost as an afterthought. Her arcing throat was entirely bare and beautiful, glistening with moisture, and he thought he might go mad. She put on a brave facade but she was thoroughly innocent, a child playing with a lit taper yet defending her play even as fire burned down the house around her.

He halted close—close enough to touch her if he dared, and close enough for the distance to be torture. His hands wanted her. The soaked linen undergarment clung to her, the soft swell and contours of her breasts and waist on display for him in the moonlight. The thatch of hair at the apex of her thighs showed dark through the wet cloth, and her nipples stood out in taut glory. *Cold.* Her body was cold, he told himself. But color shone in spots high on her cheeks and along the column of her satin neck down to the clinging chemise. Her lips like raspberries parted, and a soft sound escaped them.

But she was uncertain. Her eyes were luminous, not seducing, instead questioning. Brave, warm, and wary.

"It gleams even in the dark." His voice was husky. "Your hair. Even wet." He must make himself speak or he would touch her. "By what conjurer's trick does it do so? Are you a witch after all, merely disguised as a governess?"

"Yes. But what of you? Are you a prince disguised as a pirate?"

He could not mistake the glimmer of hope now in the cornflower eyes that at other times flashed so sharply.

He stepped back. "Not a prince." Rather, a man whose mission to produce as many of the most uncontestably ducal heirs as possible should be at the forefront of his desires now, not a bedraggled little underfed governess of uncertain virtue crossing France alone in search of a castle.

As he swung around toward the door, he must have imagined the sinking of her proud shoulders and the light sigh that followed him from the stable.

He went to his bedchamber but could not sleep. Instead he paced like an animal in a cage. As always. But for the first time in years he had cause.

Heirs to dukedoms did not tarry with governesses unless they wished to murder a tradesman or tradesman's son on a field at dawn. Women like this one inevitably had stalwartly rash fathers or brothers prepared to defend them against the ravages of the libertine aristocracy. At least, such stories were common enough in the gossip mills.

He could not offer her a more permanent arrangement either, not this little thing with a quick tongue and spine stiff with pride. She had proved tonight that in desperation she could be bought. But he did not want a desperate woman in his bed. Even upon the remote chance that she would agree to it, he suspected she would make an exceptionally uncomfortable mistress.

Snatching a handful of shining new coins from his travel bag and a candle from the mantel, he climbed the stairs to her bedchamber. He stood before the door and imagined breaking it down, imagined what he would find on the other side. Would she welcome him? Would she scream for help? *Would she even be there?*

He really was going mad.

He knocked.

No reply.

He turned the latch and the door gave way. He studied the latch. No lock. Not even a bolt to protect her. Gripon was a worm.

The room was frigid. There was no glow at the hearth, no coals lit for warmth. Nothing more than the stub of a greasy candle already burnt through.

She was curled up at the corner of the bed beneath a blanket thinner even than her chemise. Her undergarments were carefully arranged on a chair by the hearth, too flimsy and thin for travel and now at least one of them wet.

She was so desperate to reach the princess of Sensaire

that she had allowed her luggage with all her clothing to sail to another port without her.

At dinner his cousin had interrogated him about his lack of forthrightness with the lady, and asked a question that now pressed at him: Why did he believe that she was who she claimed?

Because he had no other reason to believe otherwise. Honesty lit her eyes when she looked at him. She had put herself in jeopardy to save a starving sailor. And those children in Plymouth . . . He knew she had in fact helped them. He had spoken with his clerk, who assisted her.

The greatest confirmation, though, was her integrity. With her beauty, she might be much grander than a governess. A sennight in the right rich man's bed could have easily won her a shop, a modiste's or some other respectable profession allowed to poor gentlewomen. Longer might have merited a house of her own. Gowned and perfumed, she would be a courtesan to drive men wild. But she did not trust men. She had been propositioned before, certainly. She had clearly refused.

None of this explained why a woman of her beauty and spirit was yet unwed. Unless she was unfit to wed a respectable man. Unless she was not in fact a virgin.

Her glorious hair, draped across the bolster, was still damp and tangled. She wore no cap. She would catch a chill and perish because he was too much of a coward to see that she dried her hair by a proper fire. He should bring wood for the grate, wake her, find her a comb and make her dry that hair.

But he could not wake her. In sleep, her cinnamon lashes hid the sparks in her eyes. She was less beautiful asleep. *Not* beautiful, in fact, merely a too-thin maiden past the bloom of youth, or perhaps only scored by the trials of servile life.

But he could not cease staring. She did not feign sleep, this much was clear, and he knew himself to be the only real fool between them, wakeful and wanting still.

On the bedside table, he deposited the coins he owed her from his self-inflicted torture episode and went out. In the stairwell, he pressed his back against the wall and felt the heaviness of his limbs, the dizzy imbalance of his legs on land, made worse by the narrowed field of his vision.

In the darkness, he strode from the building toward the beach. Scaling the woody ridge, he tore off his coat and waistcoat. His neck cloth caught on the wind, which blew harder now, and it fluttered for several yards before it came to unsteady rest on the sand. His boots went next. The crashing of the waves drowned out his curses at the crescent of the moon, which even so shone too brightly for him now, and more curses at the white froth of waves that seemed to illuminate the beach in a holy glow.

Stripped to his drawers, he threw away the black kerchief that he never went without now and walked into the ocean. The water was icy. He strode to his waist then dove into a breaker.

It hit him in his face and across his shoulders. The scar hollered, and he dove again, then deeper, farther from the shore and docks and ships and civilization. He turned away from the moon to the south, his arms commanding the current. He closed his eye. His chest grew tight, his breathing hard, the taste of cold sea in his mouth and the scent and sound of it everywhere, and always the current urging him away from the beach. He let it carry him.

After a time he turned onto his back, filled his lungs and stared at the stars.

"Blast and damn," he cursed at the moon again, for

the sheer pleasure of cursing aloud. The water lapped about him, rough at the estuary, submerging him in swells then laying him level. He could no longer see the shore; it was too distant and the shimmer of the water overtook all else. But he knew where it was. The stars and moon would not abandon him.

With slow, measured strokes he began the journey back. The current caught at his arms and legs, pulling him out, but he fought it now.

When his feet finally touched land and the waves knocked him about, he dragged himself from the surf and onto the rough sand, and he went to his knees. Exhausted, he bent forward and his hand brushed cloth.

He opened his eye and laughed. Hooking his thumb around the kerchief, he lifted it and returned it to its rightful place over his ruined face. Then he turned onto his back on the sand that still embraced the warmth of the day's sun.

For the first time in months he slept until daylight.

WHEN SHE AWOKE, Arabella discovered beside her bed five gold coins emblazoned with the French king's profile.

She rose, and with skin covered in gooseflesh, dressed in her chemise, stockings, stays, petticoat, and wrinkled gown. She tied on her boots, donned her cloak, and went downstairs and out of the inn. The morning was so new that the mists clung to the street, and she pulled her cloak tighter, willing the sun to rise from pinkish uncertainty to gold. In the sunshine, she might be able to forget the night and moonlight in the stable and how he had made her feel.

The shutters were opening over the front of a bakery. The baker greeted her with a smile and a curt, *"Bonjour, mademoiselle.*" She chose two hot rolls and a twist of pastry laced with preserves, paid the man, and walked swiftly back to the inn. A man pulling a cart laden with trinkets passed her and tipped his cap. A boy sitting in a crevice of a wall stared at her food. She gave him a roll, tucked her cloak tighter about her, and went toward the beach. She would not give the innkeepers the pleasure of seeing her breakfast like a peasant.

The pastry beckoned to her. She stared at it with eyes like the captain's staring at her last night. As perhaps she had stared back at him.

She mustn't think of it. She mustn't admit it to herself. After breakfast she must simply hide in her bedchamber until the festival was over. Then she would hire the only witnesses to her shame and their carriage for the drive to Saint-Reveé-des-Beaux.

Through the trees, the barest hint of sunlight cast the sand in layers of pale gold and shadow. Tiny blue crabs skittered about, rushing forth from their burrows then darting back, and gulls circled overhead, searching for breakfast. In the center of the beach a naked man lay on his back on the sand.

Arabella halted, consumed in confusion.

The captain's arm moved at his side, and he covered his face with his hand.

She should leave. She should run away. *Now.*

She could not make her feet move.

He sat up. His back was broad and golden brown in the dawn rays, sand clinging to it and his arms. He brushed it off absently, watching the ocean.

She *must* leave. He would stand up and she would see . . .

He drew up his knees and propped his elbows on them, and her nerves collapsed in a quivering heap. He wore drawers. She was safe.

She drew in a shaking breath.

He could not have heard her; the crashing of the waves drowned out all else. But he turned, and she understood that she was not safe. Not in the least. She had never known a live man could be so beautiful. The shift of his muscles as he twisted around to see her, his evident strength in even this slightest movement, rooted her feet to the sand now.

Words from the Reverend's sermons—words like *girded loins*—came to her, and she drew in an unsteady breath. He had seen her. She must be courageous. She could not run away.

He climbed to his feet and she nearly lost courage. But she must return some of the coins, for he had certainly given her too many. And, quite simply, she could not walk away, or run, or even crawl on wobbling legs. She could go to the inn, wait until he dressed, and speak with him then. But she might never see a man like this again. She would never see *this* man again.

He walked toward her.

She made herself go forward to meet him as though it were nothing unusual for her to meet a half-naked man on the beach at dawn, regretting her earlier wish for sunlight. Newborn gold illuminated his skin, casting the muscles into breathtaking contours. She had the most frightful urge to touch him. She had never before wanted to touch a man except him, and certainly not a man's unclothed body. She tried not to stare. She failed.

But when she thought he would halt several feet away, he did not.

She stumbled back and thrust out her hand. "Stop! Keep your distance."

He grasped her hand and pulled her to within inches of his bare chest. "If you wished distance you might have gone already." He gripped her fingers with little effort, and his skin was warm. How he could be so warm when he was nearly naked, she could not fathom. He had shaved off his piratical whiskers the night before, but now his jaw was again shadowed.

Arabella tugged at her hand and he released it.

"I . . ." With her feet sunk deep in the sand and the sunlight dancing across his cheek, she felt wretchedly out of control. She knew she mustn't look away from his face, but his attention dipped to her mouth, and yearning curled through her.

"Why don't you just kiss me?" she blurted. He was so beautiful—from his wide shoulders and muscular chest to the drawers slung low on his hip bones. A man's body. A beautiful man's body, and he stood before her threatening her without even touching her. The truth was awful—that she wanted him to demand a kiss so she would not be at fault for being kissed by him. "I know you want to," she said.

"I have not kissed you because, despite what you believe of me, I am a gentleman and you have not invited me to." His voice was low. "Invite me now."

Yes. "No."

His breaths seemed to come hard, his attention entirely upon her mouth. He bent his head and unkempt locks bronzed by the sun fell over his brow. He whispered across her lips, "Just a kiss."

She mustn't.

So close yet not touching her, he inhaled deeply.

"Mm. Roses and lavender. Come now, duchess," he murmured. "Don't make me beg."

"No." She ached for his mouth on hers. "No."

Slowly his hands curled into fists at his sides. He stepped back from her, his emerald gaze hot and not entirely focused.

He walked away. Around and past her and toward the inn.

He walked away.

She stared at the footprints he left in the sand. Nearby a man's coat lay on the beach, and beyond that a waistcoat and trousers, and farther off, a shirt. He was walking away, and the wound-up coil of anticipation inside her screamed in frustration.

She swung around and her throat made a little sound of misery. Men never walked away from her. She walked away from them. More often she ran. She did not know this was an option. She had never met a man who respected her wish to not be touched.

"You have forgotten your clothing," she called across the wind.

"Keep it," he threw over his shoulder without breaking stride.

"That is ridiculous. What need have I of a man's shirt and coat?"

"Give it away. Sell it. Do with it what you will. I have more. Plenty more."

"You have already given me more money than you should have." She dug into her pocket for the coins. "You must—"

He halted and pivoted toward her. His brow was remarkably dark with the slash of black kerchief across it. Arabella backed up a step.

"I am not ridiculous." He came toward her again. "Or absurd. Or even unreasonably arrogant, given all." His strides were long and certain. "I am merely a man who wants to kiss a woman who wants to be kissed—*by me*, mind you—yet claims she does not." He halted before her, tall and nearly naked.

"I—" Everything inside her was tangled. The wind

whipped at her cloak, and her lips were cold, and after this day she would never see him again. "I—I do want to be kissed by y—"

He covered her mouth with his.

She had been kissed before. She had been pawed and groped and grabbed and forced. She'd had wine-soaked tongues thrust into her mouth and cold hands shoved beneath her gown.

This was entirely different.

He held her with only the pressure of his mouth upon hers, firmly, intentionally, as though he wished to feel her in this manner only. His kiss was warm, like he was the sunlight himself. She stood perfectly still, his sunlight spreading inside her, twining around her stillness and catching at her belly and her breaths.

Gently, he cupped his hand around her shoulder and captured her lips more securely beneath his. She did not move. In moments he would demand more. He kissed her again, closer it seemed, holding her bound so that she was waiting for more, waiting for the demand so she could throw him off. He slipped his hand to her neck. Fingertips gently upon her throat, he tilted her face up and made her meet his mouth fully for one endless moment of sweet, hot connection.

He released her lips.

She gasped and blinked, and a little sigh of astonishment escaped her.

He scanned her face. His chest rose roughly.

"Again?" he said.

"Again," she whispered.

His hand cupped the back of her neck and he brought their mouths together. Confidently, completely, he guided her, making her meet his lips for one caress, and a next, then another and another. Now she did not wait for the opportunity to throw him off. Now she let herself be kissed and hoped he would not cease before she had enough of him, enough of his touch, heat, and the aching he was making inside her. She wanted him to kiss her until she forgot what it was to not feel pleasure in a kiss. He was tender and thorough and she imagined he would know every feeling and desire of hers now. He would know that she was frightened and wanting and that for the first time in years she did not feel alone.

Foolishness. Men cared nothing about feelings and loneliness, only lust and satisfaction.

He coaxed her lips apart and she allowed that too, knowing he wanted from her only what any man did: her body, her acquiescence. But she did not wish to resist him. He asked no more of her than she was willing to give, eager to give. He had often looked at her with hunger, and now she was hungry for him.

She pressed onto her toes in the sand, seeking him deeper. Scooping his hand around her head, he bent to her and she opened, letting him use her as he wished, letting him command her. She wanted more—more of the growing ache inside her that sought him with a sort of desperation.

He caressed her tongue with his.

She dropped the pastries.

He did it again and she was wild inside. Her hands jerked beneath her cloak. He sucked on her lower lip and a soft whimper escaped her. He caught the sound with his mouth and stroked her tongue again and she heard sounds from her own throat she did not recognize, sounds of astonishment and need and misery. She mustn't want this but she ached for more. She wanted to be closer to him. Her arms were pressed to her sides, trying to hold in the need.

His hands came around her face and he took her mouth completely, and she gave it to him, allowing him entrance, allowing him to know her. Their breaths came fast. Her breasts brushed his chest. Heat burst inside her. He groaned.

"Duchess." It was a sound of frustration and restraint. His hands swept down her back. Upon her moan, he pulled her against him.

He tasted like salt and wind and heat, and he was hard everywhere, his thighs and chest powerful and his arms holding her to him strong. She wanted to touch him. He was hot skin and strength and beauty, and she was penniless and bedraggled yet felt like the most beautiful woman on earth—beautiful and innocent for the first time in years.

The back of her throat tightened and heat prickled behind her eyes. It was a fantasy. She was inventing fantasies.

She wanted to push him away. But he was *real* and she could not seem to detach herself from him.

His fingers slipped into her hair, dislodging the linen wrap, and for the second time he stripped her of it. But he found only a tightly wound braid beneath, the kind she had learned to make from Eleanor long ago. She had bound it purposefully today.

The braid stopped him. His hands fell and he released her abruptly. But he was breathing roughly and frowning. Wind whipped a lock of her hair over her eyes. She dragged it aside with a shaking hand, and the sunlight danced in the strands as they stared at each other.

"I will escort you to Saint-Reveé-des-Beaux tomorrow." He did not sound pleased to have kissed her, or even frustrated. He sounded angry.

She shook her head. "I don't need your help."

He scowled but his gaze was upon her lips. "Yet you will have it."

"I don't want your help. I— Please don't offer it."

His chest rose on a harsh inhale. For a moment he looked as though he might speak.

He turned and strode toward the inn.

Arabella ran her fingertips over her damp lips and felt him there. "That was not just a kiss," she said. Panic sped through her. "That was not just a kiss," she shouted.

He did not pause, but flipped his hand in the air impatiently. "Terminology, Miss Caulfield. Terminology."

Chapter 8

The Dinner

$\mathcal{A}$rabella did not hide. The festival filled the streets of Saint-Nazaire with music, and delicious aromas wafted to her open window where she stared down at the stable in which she had been scandalously immodest the night before and at the beach upon which she had been even more immodest.

Tucking the coins he would not accept back into her pocket, she donned her cloak and left the inn. Vendors were everywhere, calling their wares—melons, cherries, pâtés, cheeses, nuts, olives. The warm air smelled of flowers and roasted meat and garlic as she had only ever smelled in London houses that boasted French chefs, more intriguing and considerably better than anything she had come across in weeks, except one confusing ship captain who smelled of the sea and yet of whom she could not seem to get enough.

The festival was far more than a regular market, rather like the Gypsy fairs she and her sisters used to wander about during the summers when they were girls. A man dressed in purple and yellow did tricks with cards and a hat, a trio of acrobats tumbled about the street, and another man swallowed an entire sword as delighted bystanders watched. People of all sorts looked on: peasants by their dress, prosperous looking shopkeepers, and a handful of gentry. There were fiddle players and pipers and a drum played by a lanky boy in blue trousers and coat with buttons polished for the occasion.

"That one no doubt drummed Napoleon's troops on to battle." The Earl of Bedwyr's smooth voice turned her around.

"Good day, my lord." She curtsied.

He smiled slightly. At a booth nearby, Captain Masinter flirted with a shop mistress whose cheeks were turning brilliantly red.

Arabella scanned the crowd.

"He isn't here," the earl said, twirling his gold watch fob. It glittered in the sunshine like the gold stripes on his waistcoat and the waves of his hair. "He is on his ship doing God knows what to prepare for putting it in the hands of his lieutenant. But he does not care for these sorts of gatherings anyway." He gestured to the festive crowd around them. "Not anymore, at least." He lifted a gloved hand and laid his forefinger upon his handsomely formed cheek so that it pointed to his right eye. "A man of action does not like to be surprised."

She should turn the subject. She should not encourage her curiosity.

"You and he are well acquainted, it seems," she said instead. "The scar is not old. Did he suffer the injury during the war?"

The earl's brow lifted. "Why don't you ask him yourself, my dear?"

Because she was afraid to know more of him. She

was afraid that the more she knew of him the more she would want him to kiss her.

She remained silent.

"Ah," the earl murmured. "She is as unforthcoming with him as he is with her, it seems. Interesting." He took her hand and placed it upon his forearm. "He lost the eye in a quarrel six months ago, Miss Caulfield." He began to move along with the crowd, drawing her with him. "Dreadful spat. Sword point. Nasty business, duels, of course."

"A duel? But dueling is illegal."

He patted her hand. "Only if one is caught, my dear."

"Over what was the duel fought?"

"A gentleman cannot say."

Her stomach soured. "A woman."

"A girl, rather. Not precisely as you imagine it," he said quietly, "though naturally I do not presume to suggest you know anything about such sordid matters. Or not sordid, actually, as the case was in the end."

"Lord Bedwyr, you are speaking in riddles. To confuse me, I guess."

"It is a sticky business, Miss Caulfield," he said, "admitting to having cut out one's friend's eye, you know. You cannot expect me to be entirely rational about it."

She withdrew her hand. "You blinded him? Over a girl?"

"He accused me of a rather nasty vice," he said without evasion now. "While I freely admit to being an aficionado of any number of sins, that is decidedly not one of them." He drew her arm through his again. "He had some reason to leap to that particular conclusion, though, so I forgave him in the end."

"After wounding him."

"That does tend to happen when one fights with swords. But it is well behind us now." He smiled. "I

suggest you put it behind you as well, forgive the poor
fellow for his wrong-mindedness and me for my pride
that allowed him to goad me. Let us instead enjoy this
charming festival."

"The procession from the church to the dock begins
at noon." Captain Masinter approached behind them, a
paper cone of spiced nuts in one hand, a glass of ale in
the other. "Apparently they carry Saint Louis through
the streets on a palette for a bit before they send him
out to sea on a boat. Off to the crusades anew, poor old
chap. Splendid stuff, I say." He offered her a nut.

"Never too highbrow for amusements intended for
the masses, are you, Anthony?" The earl grinned at her.

Between a pasty seller's booth and a cluster of people
watching a marionette show peeked the window of a
dress shop.

"My lord. Captain. I must visit a shop just here." She
nodded good-bye and moved away.

"I should be glad to accompany you," the earl said,
and gestured for her to precede him. "I count myself
something of an expert in fashion."

Captain Masinter grinned. "I'll wait out here." He
jerked his chin toward the marionette stage. "Take in
a show and all that." A buxom woman brushed by his
sleeve and he turned and followed her without another
glance at the marionettes.

The shop was filled with silks, cottons, velvets, and
wools, all in beautiful colors. The shopkeeper rustled in, a
petite woman in a sublimely fashionable ensemble of pale
violet muslin. A flicker of her lashes at the earl's elegant
clothes and another at Arabella's plain gown and travel-
worn cloak, and her swift eyes went perfectly neutral.

"Monsieur, how may I assist you?" she said in English colored with a soft French accent.

"It is rather the lady who is in need of assistance, of

course. I am only here on her sufferance." He wandered past a case of laces to a chair and ensconced himself in it elegantly.

Arabella's eyes went first to a bolt of luxurious velvet the color of winter, then to a mannequin garbed in a glorious gown of blue silk. It was layered with over-skirts of gossamer tulle embroidered with sequins of silver, black, and gold that almost seemed like butterfly wings, light and sparkling, as though the lady who wore it might take flight if she wished.

The modiste's red lips curved upward. She looked to Lord Bedwyr.

Arabella's cheeks heated. But of course this woman assumed the worst of her. She was not the first. *Only a harlot would bequeath such hair to her daughter and then abandon her children as your mother did.* Only a harlot. A woman who took money from a man for giving him pleasure.

The coins burned in Arabella's pocket.

"I shan't be purchasing a gown today, after all," she said to the modiste, and left the shop.

SHE ALLOWED CAPTAIN Masinter and Lord Bedwyr to escort her to the procession. The crowd sang a solemn hymn along the route, and the ritual reminded her of a coronation. She supposed that was intended.

After the gilded and painted life-sized statue of Saint Louis had ceremonially embarked for the Holy Land on a boat nearly too small for its own sail and the single sailor manning it, she excused herself from her companions and returned to the inn.

As dusk fell she brushed out her hair, bound it in a knot, and smoothed out the creases in her old gown while her stomach complained at its emptiness. A modest dinner awaited her at a little tavern she had discovered near the church. Most of the celebrations had moved down toward the water, and she made her way in the direction of the church through the increasingly empty streets of the town. She would have dinner, sleep, then take a short journey to the chateau. Then she would meet her destiny.

She drew her hood up and tugged her cloak more firmly about her and turned the corner into the alley before the tavern.

Four men blocked the narrow passageway in the gathering shadows. Three stood together in a cluster, another against the wall nearby.

She paused.

But already it was too late.

"La voilà," one of the men exclaimed.

There she is? She had never seen them before.

"Où est votre homme, ma petite dame?" he said as he came toward her, looking behind her. "Where is your man?" he repeated with a thick tongue.

One of the others followed him. *"Eh, signorina?"* *Italian?*

She backed away. They laughed roughly and spoke to each other so she did not understand. The man in front gestured, beckoning her to him.

"Va be. Noi vi abbiamo ora. Allora, ucciderlo." He put his hand over his crotch and tugged.

She pivoted and ran. The street before her was deserted, the sounds of the festival distant. Footsteps smacked the street behind her. A hand jerked on her cloak. She yanked free. Her skirts twisted about her legs and her foot caught on a boot scraper. She pitched forward. Their laughter came close.

She stumbled toward a spot of light—a doorway—people, she prayed.

They grabbed her cloak, then her arm, and swung her around.

"No! Release me!"

The man laughed. His teeth were black, his cheeks sunken. The eyes of the next man tilted left and right. *Drunk.*

She fought, twisting to free herself, but the drunken man grabbed her other arm. A third man appeared behind.

They pushed her back against the wall, slamming her shoulders into the stone. One of them reached for her skirt.

She screamed.

LUC STRAIGHTENED HIS neck cloth.

Miles held forth his coat. "Your grace, I have not yet—"

"Your grace?" Luc peered at his valet's reflection in the mirror.

"As you did not see fit to inform me of your uncle's demise, Lord Bedwyr did," Miles said with a sniff.

"I see." Luc straightened his cuffs. "I am not yet a duke, as you well know."

"You will be."

"You're a grim fellow, Miles."

"The child could be a girl. As I was saying, I have packed a traveling case with clothing suitable for the chateau, and have arranged for a mount to be delivered here for you this evening so that it will be available for your departure with Miss Caulfield. The carriage is ordered for seven o'clock."

"Fine." He would drive her there and see her safely settled with his staff and Reiner. If she allowed it.

He should not have touched her. The little governess

had been kissed before, but he wasn't so certain that had gone well for her. She'd stood like a marble statue in his arms. Yet her kiss was like living fire. He was quite certain she would not welcome his escort to Saint-Reveé-des-Beaux, but he did not intend to give her any say in the matter.

After that he would depart for London, find a bride, and become so busy getting heirs upon whatever young lady of the ton he chose that he would forget entirely about the beautiful little governess who—if character had any say in the matter—should have by all rights been born a duchess.

And pigs would fly come Eastertide.

She was not forgettable.

"After you have settled my bill, Miles, you may enjoy a day's holiday here in town," he said. "I won't be more than a day at the chateau."

Miles's back stiffened. "I would not dream of abandoning you to a footman, your grace. There will be ladies present."

"I'm sure Reiner won't mind me borrowing the services of his personal man for such a short visit."

"Absolutely not. I shall accompany you to the chateau and return with you to the *Victory* when you so desire."

"Of all the people I know, Miles, you are the only one who treats me with such impertinence."

"I am sure I don't know what you mean, your grace. Miss Caulfield does too, after all."

Luc went down to the parlor, then to the inn's dining room, where he found no trace of Cam, Tony, or Gavin, or of the governess.

Gripon minced toward him. "*Bonsoir*, Captain. Will you take dinner now?"

"Where have my traveling companions gone, Gripon?"

"The doctor, Captain Masinter, and my lord dined

early, then went to take in the show by the docks. Mademoiselle departed not a quarter hour ago."

"She departed alone? To the festival?"

"Oui, monsieur."

"And you did not counsel her to await an escort?"

Gripon folded his hands before him. "She was in great haste, Captain. And the festival, it brings all of the families and farmers into the streets. She will be well—"

But Luc was already out the door. A horse was tied before the inn. He snatched the lead, swung into the saddle and pulled it around.

He cantered toward the bottom of town where the festival crowds had moved for the evening's entertainments, the horse's hooves clattering on the cobbled streets and then the docks as he searched.

He did not find her in the streets or the brasserie. He followed the procession route backward. She would not have strayed from the populated parts of town. She was far too wary of men to do anything so—

A scream echoed against the stone walls of the alley ahead.

He charged forward.

They had her against the wall, hidden behind a stack of crates, two at her arms, holding her still, covering her mouth, another grabbing her legs, pulling them apart. Another one waited in the shadows of the alley beyond.

Luc drew his sword and sliced the blade through her attacker's shoulder before any of them even looked up at the horse bearing down upon them. The man screamed and staggered back. One of the men at her sides bolted, running into the dark of the alley where the other had already disappeared. A fourth man came at Luc from behind.

"Captain!" she cried.

The wooden crate hit him broadside against head and shoulder. Everything turned black. He barely had the sense to release his feet from the stirrups and leap free of his horse. He rolled to the ground, dodging hooves, and shoved himself to his knees. The street tilted beneath him and he choked in breaths, his hand searching blindly for the sword he'd thrown in the fall.

"Here!"

He swung his head up. A yard away she was grabbing the sword from the ground, but her cloaked shape wavered, doubled, blurred. Luc shook his head. The ruffian hit him with the crate again. It caught him on the shoulder. He went down and his stomach heaved.

The horse's tread sounded farther away. Bolted.

The man grunted as he lifted the empty crate again.

"No!" She ran at his attacker with the sword.

Luc rolled onto his side, over his shoulder, his useless right eye to the ground. Someone howled. He shook his head, grappling with sight, looking for the man with the crate.

She'd gotten there already. He was bleeding from beneath his arm and shouting, and he'd dropped the crate. Another of the attackers grabbed her from behind and twisted her arms behind her. The sword clattered to the street. The wounded one stumbled toward her, cursing.

Luc struggled to stand, to make his body function. Nothing would act. They were pulling her back, dragging her heels, bearing her to the ground. The bleeding man was upon her, grabbing at her skirts. She kicked viciously.

Luc shoved to his knees, made his limbs perform. The sword lay inches from his hand. *Blessed woman.* She had kicked it to him.

He lunged for the weapon. Lurched to his feet.

He struck her attacker with the flat. The other released her, shouting, and ran. Her attacker staggered away, groaning and hurling curses back as he fled.

Abruptly, except for the woman, the alley was empty.

Luc's head swam. He stumbled. She grasped his arm. Then her arms were around him, pressing her body to his. Everything was astoundingly hazy.

"Don't *fall*." Her voice was strained, her arms tight.

She was holding him up? *Preposterous.* But the alley was a tunnel of blackness, his limbs heavy and ears ringing.

"We must go to a more populated place quickly," she said. "But if you fall I am not strong enough to pull you to your feet again." She shoved her shoulder beneath his arm, banded her arm about his waist and pushed him forward.

Luc blinked, and a fuzzy spot of light became a torch ahead, then a lantern before a door. Then another. His head throbbed and whirred to the music now filtering up the street. He blinked again, then harder, and more came into focus. His shoulder ached like the devil. He focused on the woman beneath his arm. Her hair, bound into a knot and uncovered, glimmered like fire.

He pulled away from her.

Arabella stood shaking. "But are you—"

"Yes." The street rocked. He grasped her arm and drew her along. They turned a corner to a street with lanterns before each door. People clustered around a pair of jugglers, flaming torches flying between them. Captain Andrew pulled her around the crowd into shadows and swung her to face him. His eye was ablaze.

"Goddammit, what were you thinking to walk about town alone? Where were you going?"

Arabella could not control the shaking that had taken over her body. "To dinner."

"Dinner?"

"I was hungry."

"You were—"

"Hungry! I haven't eaten an entire meal in weeks, and with the wretched coins you insisted on giving me for doing what I should not have done, I intended to eat." The explanation tumbled from her tongue. "After this morning I could not risk dining at the inn and encountering you because I do not wish to do things I mustn't again. But . . . I was hungry."

His gaze seemed to swim. He stretched his hand out to her and she flinched.

He dropped back a step. "I— Forgive me."

"How can I presume to forgive you for anything when you have just now saved me from those men and my own poor judgment? You are absurd." She did not want to be beholden to him. Her insides twisted with panic.

"You were not afraid," he said in a strange voice.

"On the contrary." Her knees were water. She had been unutterably foolish, thinking only to escape him and of nothing else.

He came toward her, but he only took her hand and wrapped his around it.

"You are safe now," he said simply.

"I do not wish to be in your debt," she said, because they might as well have the truth between them.

"That is perfectly clear to me," he murmured beneath the music of a fiddle nearby. "You were brave. If you'd had Stewart's bone saw and pewter jug at hand, you would not have even needed my help." A smile lurked at his beautiful lips. His fingertips came beneath her chin and he tilted her face up. "As I am now in your debt as well, shall we call it even?"

She nodded. He studied her for a silent moment, then with a tight breath released her and turned away. A trickle of crimson stained his neck cloth.

"You are hurt."

"No more than I have been many times before." He gestured her from the shadows. "Now I believe it is time you had that dinner you sought."

"I've lost my appetite. I didn't see everything that happened when . . . What did they do to—"

"Nothing," he said shortly. "Come."

She went at his side along the narrow streets. People strolled arm in arm or lingered by doorways of over-flowing establishments. All were celebrating.

They came to the brasserie near the inn. He opened the door for her and she saw his grimace of pain.

She halted. "I will not dine until you have seen to your wounds."

"Blackmail? Miss Caulfield, you were wasted to have been born anything less than a duchess, in truth." There was something very strange in his gaze as it dropped to her mouth.

"Perhaps I shall someday marry a duke and fulfill my potential," she said with a forced smile. "Until then, however, I make an exceptional governess."

"I have no doubt." His voice was low.

"Your wounds?" she said briskly.

His mouth tilted up at one end. "Or a nanny, if not a governess."

His half smile made her feel peculiar inside and out of control. Everything about him made her feel out of control. She made rash decisions because of him.

She moved away from the door into the street. "My nanny was a wonderful woman." She must remain light, speak of nothings, then there would be nothing between them. "I remember little of her; she died when I was three. But I remember her black hair and—"

He grabbed her wrist and turned her around to him.

"I don't wish to know about your nanny." He spoke low beneath the sounds of merriment all about. "I don't wish to know anything more about you at all. I am nearly mad with wanting you in my hands, and the madness worsens with every word you speak."

"About my *nanny*?"

"About anything. Everything." His gaze covered her, and like in Plymouth it was both bemused and commanding. "You have only to move your lips and I want you."

"Then I shall be silent!"

"I don't imagine you can be silent, and it wouldn't matter anyway. I would still want you, though perhaps less acutely, admittedly."

"You speak to me as no man ever has. So frankly. As though—" As though in making his intentions clear he was putting the decision to act upon them in her hands, as he had that morning on the beach. "I wish I had never met you," she said.

He spoke with quiet intensity. "Destiny, it seems, Miss Caulfield, is a contrary master."

Destiny?

She whirled away from him and into a stream of people moving along the street. The music of trumpets and drums and pipes were suddenly upon her, firelight dancing off walls and glittering brass and sparkling fabrics. Revelers were laughing, talking, and singing as they jostled along. But the music was familiar now, rich and free. She caught a glimpse of the players, a Gypsy band, unmistakably different from the townsfolk and farmers with their dark skin, thick black locks, and the shimmering gold loops in the men's ears and on the women's wrists. She had danced with her sisters every summer of her girlhood to music at the Gypsy fair.

They danced the very day the old soothsayer told them their fortune and Arabella declared she would someday wed a prince. That it was her destiny.

Dreams. Fantasies. Like the fantasy she chased now, rushing to a castle to find a prince and instead falling into the hands of men who would hurt her because she was alone.

She wove her way against the crowd, knowing he was following. He would not allow her to go alone now. She squeezed between people, holding her cloak close and peering into faces, not seeing the men who had attacked her, her heartbeats wild. The band drew closer on the street and the crowd pressed her back. Hands grabbed at her in passing. She dragged her cloak free. Her head felt dizzy, disoriented. She could not stop trembling.

He grasped her arms and blocked the crowd from her. Revelers complained with good-natured laughter and went around him.

"Are you all right?"

She nodded. He touched her only where he held her arms, protecting her with the shield of his body. She looked up. His face was shadow and light.

"I don't know what cruel twist of fate brought you to me, duchess," he said roughly. "But I would rather a moment of madness with you now than the promise of sanity for a lifetime."

"I . . . Please." Her breaths were short. "Do not ask of me what I cannot give."

"For what exactly do you believe I have asked?"

"I will dress your wound and then you will leave me alone and that will be an end to it."

For an instant his grip tightened. The crowd had thinned, the music fading into the darkness. Nearby, the brasserie patrons laughed and drank wine in the warm night.

He took her hand and without speech led her. The inn was close, the rhythmic whoosh of the river meeting the sea mingling with the Gypsies' music. He led her there, releasing her hand only when they came to the door of the inn and gesturing for her to go before him. She climbed the stairs, breathless and fashioning the words she must say to put him off.

When they came to her bedchamber and he opened the door, she turned to face him.

"I must retrieve a lost horse now," he said. "We will depart for Saint-Reveé-des-Beaux early. Until then, I wish you a good night's sleep, Miss Caulfield." He bowed and went swiftly down the steps.

THE NIGHT WAS still warm and the festival celebrations continued undeterred by the approach of midnight. But the careful, thorough search through Saint-Nazaire's quieter alleys cooled Luc's blood and distracted him from the pain in his shoulder and his aching head. He carried with him pistol and dagger, and his sword, which he had cleaned in those first moments after leaving her at her door when he still doubted that he could in fact walk away.

The trail of blood from the place where they had attacked her was not difficult to follow. A handful of coins passed to a prostitute in a slatternly house by the docks revealed the wounded man lying on a pallet in an upper room. His shirt and coat were crimson with blood. He did not open his eyes when Luc spoke to him.

Luc gave the woman a few extra coins for burial expenses and sought from her the names of his companions. She did not know them. They were sailors and foreigners, she claimed. She had not seen them before tonight.

He continued on until the dark town had finally gone to bed. His search awarded him nothing. The other three men had vanished.

There was nothing left but to find his horse. It had returned to its master's stable and stood nervously outside the paddock, reins dangling to the ground. He soothed it, climbed into the saddle with extraordinary discomfort, and turned back toward the inn.

In the inn's stable, the little governess stood in the golden circle of a candle's light.

He removed his mount's bridle, saddle, and blanket and drew the animal into a stall. Then he shut the half door and allowed himself to look at her. She stood straight and proud, the pale oval of her face framed by the hood of her cloak.

"Clearly you have learned nothing from your adventure this evening of the dangers of wandering about alone at night in this town," he said.

"I was not ignorant of the dangers of such 'adventures' before tonight, Captain," she countered. "Though never four men at once, it's true." Her voice wavered but her chin inched up, as though to deny that such encounters had ever distressed her.

Luc's chest felt inordinately tight.

"I see you found your horse," she said. "I presume it did not require the entire four hours you were absent to do so."

"I lingered for a spell at a watering hole," he said. "Drink, you see, can be useful to dull undesirable— ah—desires. When one drinks alone, that is. When one drinks with a beautiful governess it can have quite the opposite effect, as we already know."

She came toward him until she stood nearly touching him. Luc's heart beat hard. She reached up, slipped her slender hand about his neck and went onto her toes. She tugged on his neck.

He dipped his lips to hers. Her kiss was firm and deliberate.

She released him swiftly and took a step back. "You have not been drinking. There is no scent of spirits about you."

"Witch."

Her hood had fallen back and the cornflowers were wide. "You went to find those men."

"Would you rather they went free?"

"I would rather you did not again endanger yourself on my account."

"There was little danger. I am not unknown for my skill with sword and pistol. Wooden crates notwithstanding."

"Do they not teach wooden crate fighting in pirate school?"

"Not the one I attended."

"You hadn't sufficient skill with a sword to protect your eye in the duel you fought with Lord Bedwyr."

"A curiosity, that mistake. As he would have admitted if he weren't trying to impress you."

She paused. "Was the moment of madness you spoke of a curiosity too?"

"No." He struggled against that madness pressing at him now. She was like no other woman. Without flirtation, she was direct and forthright and vulnerable all at once. And beautiful. So beautiful that despite the wretched night he'd had, he still ached for her. "Rather, the regular state of things lately."

Her eyes were wary. "I am doubly in debt to you now."

"I don't expect payment." He backed away from her. "I don't want payment. Your debt is hereby cancelled."

"I don't want to pay you. I don't intend to pay you," she said swiftly. "I only want . . ." Her lashes flickered with uncertainty, then entreaty.

Luc counted to ten. To twenty.

She said nothing.

He turned and strode out of the building. He went through the trees toward the water, seeking refuge and sanity where he had always found them.

She came after him and touched his arm, and he succumbed to madness.

HE PULLED HER into his arms, bent to her mouth and kissed her. He kissed her quite thoroughly, with no pretense of hesitation, and Arabella did nothing to halt him. It was what she most wanted and why she had run after him. He made her want things she should not want and do things she should not do, and this was no doubt the worst of all because she did not only want to be kissed. She wanted to feel weak-kneed from something other than fear. But the only thing other than fear that had ever made her feel weak-kneed was him. He made her forget that she had been kissed by men who did not want to please as they took pleasure.

He clearly wished to please. Flat across her back, his palms slipped to her waist and he tugged her against his body. She allowed this too. He was hard and strong and she wanted for a moment to lose control.

He sank his fingers into her bound hair, tilted her head back and put his mouth on her throat. She sighed, pleasure fanning through her until it was everywhere inside her, in the tips of her breasts and between her legs. It made her want to touch him, to feel him with her hands. She trailed her fingers along his arm, then grasped gently. The muscle beneath his coat shifted beneath her touch. A sound of pleasure rumbled in his chest.

"You have hands after all, do you?" he murmured behind her ear, his mouth hot upon her skin making her feel wild inside. "Use them on me, duchess."

"I mustn't."

"I invite you to."

"You frighten me."

He released her. His chest rose upon a hard breath. "This is worse than war. At least in battle a man knows where he stands from one moment to the next. Usually."

"I am only being honest with you! I—"

"*Yes* or *no*?"

"Yes." She closed the space between them and laid a light palm upon his chest. His hands covered her behind and pulled her flush to him and his knee came between her thighs.

Arabella lost her breath. She lost all thought. She felt only the hard shock of his muscle against her most intimate place.

He kissed her neck and tugged at the fastening of her cloak.

"What are you doing?" she whispered, her words lost in the rhythm of the surf and need inside her.

"Undressing you. Touching you. Let me touch you." His palm smoothed along her collar and over her breast. But she did not move away or chastise him or tell him no. She knew it was wrong to let him touch her, but she wanted to feel pleasure. She wanted, even for a moment, to be as mad as a pirate.

SHE DID NOT push him away. She met his kisses, and Luc filled his hands with her as he had fantasized.

The reality of her was sweeter. It made him insane

for more. Her breasts were small in his hands and he wanted to suck on them until she moaned and came for him. But she was motionless, barely touching him, her eyes closed and shoulders stiff. He pressed his hand along her spine and cinched his arm low around her waist, trapping her to him, making her straddle his thigh. She arched her back, tightening the fabric of her gown across her breasts.

"Unbind your hair." The words were too abrupt, like a command he might give his men aboard ship.

Miraculously, she obeyed. Reaching up to remove the pins, she separated the thick cords of copper from the binding. But she watched him through lowered cinnamon lashes. When all of her hair fell down her back, he slipped his hand beneath the magnificent mass and speared his fingers into it. It was heavy, like water and silk and molten copper, and warm. Strands of it stirred in the night breeze, fluttering across her raspberry lips. He wanted to see it clothe her, sliding over her naked body—nothing but her hair and his hands.

"You did not purchase a new gown?"

"I did not."

"You are obligated to. It was our agreement." He turned her around so her back was to him and still she did not protest. Swiping the hair aside, swiftly he unfastened the gown's hooks at her nape then the tapes that crossed beneath her breasts.

"Will you undress me here," she said, "in the open where anyone might see?"

"All are abed, including the moon." He bent to her neck to taste the satin of her skin, and she sighed. "Only I will see."

"I am not beautiful," she whispered. "Not round and voluptuous. You will be disappointed."

"You are not beautiful," he lied, because at thirty he knew the folly of trying to convince a woman of what she refused to believe about herself. He peeled off the bodice and drew the sleeves down her arms. "You are too lean. A woman should have more flesh." Flattening his palms over her abdomen, he hooked his thumbs around her hips and drew her tight against him. Soft and round, she cushioned his erection. "Much more."

"You have no regard for my vanity." She arched her neck and his fingertips dipped. She caught her breath. "You haven't since the first."

"Vanity is not the worst of your faults, duchess." He kissed her neck, breathing in her scent of lavender and roses. "It is pride."

"As though I held a monopoly on pride here. I should not have concerned myself over owing a debt to you. You are no gentleman, after all."

"And you have a sharp tongue, which no man can like." He turned her to face him and lost his words. The petticoat barely covered the stays and her chemise was thin, the mere scrap of fabric he'd seen through in the stable. The heavy ring hung in the shallow gully between her breasts, strands of bright copper silk tangling with the plain ribbon. Her skin was like cream, the curve of her hips exquisite.

"My sharp tongue is irrelevant at present," she said. "We were not speaking of my character faults, but my lack of beauty."

"I want you. Now." He could think of nothing else.

Her quick breaths pressed her breasts against the stays. "Yes," she whispered.

He flung his sword, pistol, and coat to the ground and went to his knees before her and put his hands under her skirts. Her legs were glorious, and she wore stockings of a noisomely practical kind he wanted to tear off. He slid his hands up her calves to her thighs and she said nothing, did nothing, moved not at all. But he could feel her trembling.

He needed her beneath him. Seeking with his palms, he cupped her buttocks. Her hand clenched on his shoulder.

He drew her to the ground.

She let him kiss her lips, the arch of her throat, the swell of her breasts, and she let him drag the petticoat and shift down so that the stays no longer contained her breasts. Her nipples were taut, and dusky like her lips against the pale of her skin in the dark. *Beauty.* Pure beauty. He stroked a fingertip across one peak. Her trembling was fierce but she did not speak and her eyes closed. Bending to her breast, he circled his tongue around her arousal—soft as rose petals, her skin, her breaths. He passed his tongue across the peak, tasting her, and her lips flew apart on a silent gasp of pleasure.

He was undone.

He sucked on her, his cock pushing at his breeches. Her breaths quickened, and he bit. She arched beneath him, her palms pressing into the ground.

A groan of frustration broke from him. She was his fantasy, naked and unbound for him, lying on her back, finally acquiescing. But she was stiff and silent beneath the whoosh of the pounding surf.

He didn't want her acquiescence. He wanted her fire.

"Open your eyes, duchess." His voice was too harsh. It had been too long since he'd had a woman, and too long wanting this woman. He could not wait. "Speak."

"I feel," she whispered upon a jagged breath. "Is that not enough for you?"

He pushed up her skirts, tore at the fall of his breeches, and thrust deep into her.

Heat. Tightness. Wet.

"Oh, God." He was dying. His cock surged forward. He would come now. Blessed quick release. Too long without. So hot and tight. She was beauty and angel and seductress, and she was saving him.

But she was gasping, clutching the cloak beneath her, her throat working.

Ice slithered down Luc's spine, lodging in his balls. He grabbed her chin, surrounded her face with his hand, willing her eyes to open.

"You are a virgin," he said like gravel.

"I—" She tried to pull her face away but he held her firm. "I told you I was not what you believed."

"Open your eyes." His body shook with restraint. He was in agony. *"Open your eyes."*

She obeyed. "Don't . . ."

He heaved in air and braced his arms to remove himself.

"Don't go." She grabbed his sleeve. "Do it."

"Forgive me," he whispered, and thrust into her. He could not do otherwise. He pulled out and thrust in again, deeper, groaning from the sheer relief of it, the power and pleasure of taking her. He worked his way into her, slowly at first, pushing against her resistance, and then because he was not able to continue slowly, he went faster.

She was immobile beneath him, her wrist slung over her eyes, her lips closed.

"Now," he groaned. "Duchess, I beg of you." He grabbed her hips and pulled her to him and she cried aloud. He forced himself into her again and her lips opened upon a moan. Her hand clutched his arm, and her hips jerked against his. She sought him now, moving in rhythm with each thrust, her beautiful lips parted.

Words came from his mouth, prayers, curses. The ecstasy on her face now drove him and his urgent need to fill her. Her fingers gripped him hard and her eyes snapped open, astonishment in the cornflowers. Then she was gasping again, throwing back her head and calling her pleasure.

Chapter 9

The Vows

$\mathcal{A}$rabella laid her wrist over her eyes and shut out the stars, witnesses to her ruination.

Men had been groping and pawing at her for years. She had fought off amorous upper servants and employers, twice at the cost of her positions. But she'd had no idea what those men really wanted, no idea of the pleasure that could be had in the act, and no idea that she could feel such sensations or that with his touch a man could wind himself around her heart and make her want to sing and laugh and scream and beg for more all at once. And give him everything.

Now she knew.

Lying on her back, her body warm with satisfaction, she pressed down on the panic. She had ruined herself. The virtue she had guarded closely for years was now gone forever. She could not retrieve it.

She had tried to remain unmoved when he touched her. She hadn't wanted to fight him off, only to live for a moment of madness not in the distant, hazy past or the uncertain future, but in the present. She thought she could let herself feel pleasure for that moment.

Instead, she lost control. She had let him into her.

Was this how her mother had begun, with one man? One act? One moment of madness?

What had she done?

"No payment, hm?" he said.

He sat away from her with his back to a tree. In the bluish hue of starlight she could see that he had unbuttoned his waistcoat and untied his neck cloth, and his elbows rested upon his knees. His broad shoulders were rigid.

"That was not intended as payment," she said. Only the need to experience a moment of danger that had nothing to do with violence or force, but with her need and her desire. "I told you the truth."

"You might have told me the entire truth." He was silent a moment. "Why didn't you stop me?"

She pushed up to sit, combed her hair with her fingers to free it of sand, and began the long process of braiding it again. She could not quite look at him. "I did not want you to stop," she said to the length of hair in her hands. "I wanted to feel what it would be like." *With him.* Something inside her had panicked that she would never see him again and must have something of him to carry with her into the uncertain future. "After tonight and those men . . ." Not only those men. Plenty before. "What happened frightened me."

"You said I frightened you." His quiet words were almost lost in the sound of the surf.

"I wanted it to be on my terms." Her fingers worked the hair swiftly, twisting, binding. "By my choice."

"I ought to feel used, but in such a noble cause I suppose I cannot."

"Don't mock me."

"Forgive me."

"You are foolish."

He came to her and wrapped his palm around the side of her face. His touch was warmer than the night and he brought with him the scents of sea and danger and intoxication. She didn't need brandy. He made her drunk simply by coming near.

"I am not in the habit of deflowering governesses."

"I am not in the habit of being deflowered by pirates. Shall we consider it a draw?"

But he did not laugh as she intended. His grip tightened. Where his collar gaped, she saw a man's body, bone and muscle and skin so unlike hers. Even after everything, the mere sight of him made her feel shaky.

"I must braid my hair now," she made herself say. "Release me."

His hand slipped from her and he sat back on his heels. Arabella's fingers shook but she hid them in her activity.

"Tonight I have done this," she said, "but tomorrow—"

"Tomorrow is another world," he said gravely.

She knew his gaze remained on her while she bound her hair securely. The evening air touched her damp neck. The cool and control felt safe and familiar.

"I have not been honest with you," he said.

She stood, grabbed up her cloak and pulled it about her. "I may have quite recently been a virgin, Captain, but I am not entirely naïve. Men are never honest with women they wish to bed."

"There is something I must tell—"

"No." She backed away, her heels sinking in the sand. "You claimed to have no wish to know more about me and I share that sentiment in reverse. Good night, Captain."

The moon had disappeared, the only light now from the stars and the lamp at the inn's door. He did not follow her; she knew he would not. He commanded dozens of men and the respect and friendship of naval captains and lords of the realm, but he had never forced her to do what she did not wish to do.

Except sleep in his bed without him.

She strode toward the inn swiftly, pressing down on the rising panic inside her. When she heard the captain's oath behind her, she imagined he uttered it because of her flight. Then she heard the other men's voices and knew he had not.

HE HAD NO time to defend himself. His sword and pistol lay in the sand yards away.

But the dagger was in his boot.

It didn't matter. Just as the crash of the waves had obscured their approach, the darkness obscured sight of them. His thorough bemusement, and simple exhaustion from the beating he'd taken earlier and more recent exertions, ensured his fate. They were upon him before he could react. Two of them seized his arms from behind while the third sprang from the trees to his right. His bruised shoulder lodged an agonizing protest.

A glittering flash of steel cut through the starlight.

The pain was not immediate, only the shock and ice in his gut. He wrenched an arm free and swung out. His fist snapped against a jaw.

Then the pain came, complete and crippling. He doubled over, grappling for his dagger. His fingers grasped it and yanked it free.

Blindly he swiveled, thrust with the dagger, and met flesh. Someone howled. He prayed it wasn't him.

A woman screamed. His attacker fell back.

Luc struck again.

A boot slammed into his leg. His injured shoulder hit the ground. He could only groan.

The ice slid free of his gut, and his attackers spoke to each other in furtive whispers. *Italian.*

Then they were gone.

Were they? The darkness enveloped him. The surf lulled. He panted for breath. He tried to move.

Ohh, God.

Right. Stillness was better. Stillness was in fact superb.

He curled around the hole in his belly, pressing inward hard with his knuckles, cursing. He mustn't bleed to death now, not after all the other injuries and horrors he had sustained and yet survived. To die now would be idiotic.

But after a moment, as the strength went out of his arms and he could no longer even stanch the wound sufficiently, so he found himself bleeding through his fingers, a quick death seemed a perfectly reasonable option.

ARABELLA WAS CLOSE enough to see the men run and to see one of them stumble not far beyond the tent and fall. He did not rise.

She ran forward and threw herself to her knees beside Luc. His face was contorted.

"No." She grabbed for his arm and drew it back from his waist. He did not resist. His waistcoat and shirt were soaked in blood. *No.* "No no no."

She had nothing to halt the bleeding. She pulled his coat aside and searched for a kerchief.

"Now you use your hands on me?" he whispered. "Poor timing."

"I didn't know I might not have another opportunity."

Her words caught in her throat. She found his kerchief and pressed it to the darkest patch of blood.

"Not—" His jaw was like a rock. "Not what I had in mind."

"Be still." *What could she do?* The man on the ground beyond the treeline had not moved. But the others might still be close. "You mustn't speak."

"Bedwyr," he said on a tight breath.

"No. Those men will return. I cannot leave you. Where is your sword?"

"Go."

Biting back on her fear, she ran.

The earl opened the door to his bedchamber bleary-eyed, his shirttail hanging over his breeches and feet bare.

"He is hurt. Badly. You must hurry."

He went into his chamber and came forth with his boots and a pistol. Pulling on his boots, he gestured down the corridor. "Wake Masinter and Stewart."

Captain Masinter swung the door open, sword in hand. "Wh-What?" His eyes went wide. "Good God."

Dr. Stewart's eyes were shot with red but instantly alert. He grabbed his medical bag off the floor.

They went swiftly and quietly out of the inn along the path to the beach.

Luc lay as she had left him, motionless. But now his face was slack.

"No!" She leaped forward.

Captain Masinter grabbed her arm. "There there, Miss Caulfield. No place for a lady."

She pulled away from him. "But—"

"Father Stewart knows best what must be done." The earl set a lamp beside Luc and the priest kneeling before him.

"Too much bluid's been lost," Dr. Stewart muttered. He set aside the saturated kerchief.

The earl looked down at him. "Will he die, Gavin?"

"You . . ." The barest whisper. " . . . wish."

Arabella's heart lurched. Luc had not moved.

"Occasionally." Lord Bedwyr knelt on the ground in his elegant breeches. "But not so ignominiously, you know. I am not as insensible to our amicable past as you are."

She dropped to her knees on Luc's other side. His breaths were so shallow she could barely see them.

"What would you have me do now, Lucien?" the earl said. "I am yours to command."

"God's breath, lad. Not nou." The priest thrust aside another reddened cloth. He opened the satchel beside him and drew forth two small bottles and a leather envelope. A needle and spool of thread were within. "Chairles, yer cravat."

The earl unwound his neck cloth and put it in the priest's hands. "If we are not to speak of it now, Father, then when shall we?" he said, and returned his attention to the wounded man. "What say you, cousin?"

"Cousin?" Arabella dragged her gaze from Luc to the earl.

"Yes, Miss Caulfield. I share in the blood that is now discoloring this beach." The earl tilted his head. "Ah, a detail not confided to the lady, Luc?" He smiled slightly. "You rogue. But I suppose you simply cannot abide it that we own the same blood. Not since our little quarrel, that is."

"Damn . . . you." Luc did not open his eye.

"Damning me with your final breaths is shockingly poor form, old boy." The earl settled back, stretching his long legs before him and leaning on one hand. If not for the dark, he might have been at a picnic. But there was no real pleasure in his face. It was an act, Arabella thought. Lord Bedwyr was pretending nonchalance.

"Consider this, Lucien," the earl drawled. "When you die, which you may very well do shortly—and no, I do not intend to speed it along—"

"Good . . . of you."

"The two of you are horrible. Captain Masinter, make them stop this." Arabella pressed her palms to her cheeks. "This cannot be real."

"It is, my dear," the earl said. "Terribly real. And Luc is pondering that very thought at this moment. More precisely, he is thinking that if he dies today, indeed momentarily, he will die childless."

"Childless?"

"Childless, Miss Caulfield. Without issue," the earl said very carefully it seemed.

Luc's face had become more drawn, his breaths quick and shallow. Father Stewart was sewing the wound closed and she knew the pain of it must be agonizing, but even so, Luc remained conscious. His life was flee-ing, his strength and vitality and passion, and inside her she was screaming that it simply could not be. He had kissed her, made love to her, and never forced her. He had seen her drunk and said she was not beautiful and she thought perhaps she loved him a little bit for that.

"What does it matter if he is childless?" she de-manded. He was *dying*.

"What does it matter, Luc?" the earl repeated. "Is your heir fit to fill your shoes, old friend?"

"His heir? Heir to what?"

The earl remained silent.

"Captain Masinter, tell me!"

"His property. Whatnot. Usual sorts of things." He was frowning, eyes intent upon the earl.

"This cannot be real." She turned to Lord Bedwyr. "You cannot possibly be speaking to him in this manner now simply because you have quarreled and should he— should—" Helpless anger washed through her. "He has a brother."

"That he does."

"Is that what this foolishness you speak of is about? His bad blood with you or his brother?" She looked between the three men. Luc was very still. She knew he had not slipped into unconsciousness only by the tight lines on either side of his mouth. Father Stewart still worked at his side, and a bitter scent twined through the air. She could do nothing for him. *She could do nothing.*

All her life she'd fought against helplessness. At the foundling home when they neglected her infant sister she had complained and was beaten for it, but Ravenna had not gone hungry. When the Reverend had said she must be the daughter of a harlot because no modest woman would have such hair, she made him promise upon the cross never to say such a thing in her sisters' hearing if she cut it short. When her employer's son had accused her of seducing him after she fought him off with teeth and nails and then was dismissed, she warned his mother that if she did not write a glowing letter of reference for her next position she would tell the world how her youngest daughters were not her husband's. And when a fortune-teller had promised that a prince would reveal the truth of her past, she had worked until she found her way to a prince's doorstep.

She had never accepted helplessness. But now she could do nothing, and they spoke of a man's life ending as though only possessions mattered.

"I cannot believe this is what you speak of now," she uttered.

"It is what he wishes to speak of, my dear," Lord Bedwyr replied.

"No. No. I—" She struggled to her feet. "There must be something I can do." She could not remain idly by and watch him die. "I must—"

"Duchess." It was barely a whisper. Luc's hooded gaze was black in the pale glimmer of predawn.

"Aha." The earl leaned forward. "So you are thinking what I am thinking, cousin." He nodded. "I had imagined so. But will the lady be amenable?"

Luc's eye seemed to glaze then slid shut again.

Father Stewart placed the final cloths beside him, saturated with blood. "No, Chairles." He shook his head. "'Tis no' possible."

"Of course it is possible. You are a priest and he needs a wedding. *Allez-y, mon père.*"

"I'm no' a priest o' yer kirk, lad."

"A wedding?" Arabella's stomach churned. "But to who—"

"To the only person present here who could potentially be carrying his heir." The earl lifted a single brow to her.

Heat filled Arabella's cheeks, then all of her.

Wiping the blood from his hands, Dr. Stewart shook his head, but his sober eyes suggested that she should not deny it.

"I—"

"You needn't explain, my dear." The earl smiled confidentially. "We are men of the world, aren't we, Gavin? Tony? And in any case, we haven't time for it." He waved an imperious hand at the doctor. "Go ahead, Father. Pull out your little book and stole and do your magic."

"'Tis no magic, lad," the priest said, and set the reddened cloth down. "An ma kirk woudna condone it."

"His French mother was Catholic and we are in France, a Catholic country. Are we not? You, a priest of Rome, can marry him to whomever you choose. And whatever the hasty deed itself does not satisfy, I'm certain a pretty little parchment with a gold seal will take care of."

"Sufficient for those fellows in Rome, perhaps, but not for the codgers in Parliament," Captain Masinter muttered.

"Parliament?"

"Being the carousing naval hero that he is, dear Miss Caulfield, our delightful captain knows nothing of the laws of marriage. Don't listen to him." Lord Bedwyr met Dr. Stewart's regard firmly. "Now, Father, your services are required."

"I won't." Arabella clutched her cloak about her, but her hands were stained with his blood and she fought sobs. "You are all mad. Let his property pass to his brother. *Oh, God.* Let it."

"But you see, madam, you have leaped to a spurious conclusion. It is not a quarrel that motivates my cousin's last wish. Is it, Luc?"

"Not fit," he bit off on a shallow breath.

"You see, Miss Caulfield. His brother is unfit to inherit."

She gripped her fists. "Captain Masinter?"

"S'truth, ma'am. Sorry to say it. Worse than you imagine, I daresay."

She swung to the priest. Dr. Stewart's brow was tight. He nodded confirmation.

She couldn't draw breaths. "But no one in England would accept such a marriage to be legitimate, done in such haste and by a Catholic priest. It is outrageous."

"Do study the situation," the earl said calmly. "If you do not shortly find yourself in—shall we say?—an interesting condition, then you might consider the entire thing a Roman farce and go about your merry way none the worse for it. But if you do, with the assistance of yours truly"—he bowed—"you could petition the Church of England for validation. Thereafter you and your child would want for nothing. My cousin's property is . . . extensive."

"But, even if there were a child—" Her mind grappled. "It would not be legitimate. This wedding—"

"Comes after the fact?" the earl supplied. "True. But Captain Masinter and I would never tell, would we, Tony? And the good father can adjust the date on the official record, as it were."

Father Stewart frowned but said nothing. He was watching Luc's face. Then he reached into his bag and drew out a book threaded with colored ribbons and a long, thin strip of cloth. He laid the stole around his neck and opened the book.

"What? No!" Arabella shook her head. "You cannot force me—"

"Dinna fash, lass. 'Tis anither sacrament."

She shook her head. "Another?"

"Extreme Unction, Miss Caulfield," the earl murmured. His attention on his cousin was sober now. "Last rites."

"Good God," Captain Masinter said in a strangled voice. He turned his face away and his shoulders heaved.

Arabella had never seen a man weep. They loved him—this sailor and nobleman and priest—because he was worthy of love. But her heart was cold, as she had known for years.

Then what was this desperate aching in her chest?

"Are ye sorry now for all yer sins, lad?" Dr. Stewart said. He pried the stopper out of a tiny glass bottle and pressed his thumb to the opening.

Luc's gaze came to her. "All . . . but one."

She fell to her knees beside him and reached for his hand. But she jerked back and did not take it. She dared not touch him.

"They are mad," she whispered.

"I . . . pray . . . you." Strain hardened his mouth.

"You will not even be able to say the vows." Each word hurt to utter. *She could not bear this.*

"Beautiful . . . wife." The lines about his mouth loosened. "I'll . . . try."

"You are a liar. Earlier or now, but I don't care to know which." Tears scalded her eyes, then her cheeks. "This is wrong."

His cloudy gaze slipped to the earl. "Tell . . . truth."

She could not see through the tears. "The truth that you are a madman, and not only for a moment?"

"Want you . . ." A labored breath, his throat working. ". . . to—"

"I will do it."

"There we have it!" The earl clapped. "The lady is in fact amenable. Father, make it so."

The Scot shook his head but he turned the pages in his book. Then he raised his hand and drew a cross sign in the air between them.

"In nomine Patris et Filii et Spiritus Sancti . . ."

In the warmth of the late summer dawn Arabella shivered. This was not a legal wedding. It was a farce for the earl's benefit, and Luc's. But now he watched her with hooded gaze and she could not regret it. When he might have abandoned her, he had helped. And when he might have hurt her, he had given her pleasure. She must give him this gift, however false it was.

She had not paid attention to the Reverend's church lessons and had not studied like Eleanor; she understood nothing of the Latin incantations that preceded the vows.

"Lucien Andrew Ral—"

"Yes, yes, he knows his name," the earl interrupted. "Time is short, Father. Move along."

"Luc, will ye take this woman to be yer wife?"

"I will." It was barely a breath across his lips.

"Lass, yer name?"

"Arabella Anne Caulfield."

Luc's hand unclenched, his broad palm opening. The priest spoke the words that asked her to commit herself in marriage to him, and she responded as they wished.

Abruptly, the earl got to his feet and walked swiftly toward the inn. As she watched, stunned and shaken, the priest returned to the earlier place in his book and began speaking softly and rapidly beneath his breath. He laid his hand on Luc's brow. Captain Masinter stood with his back to them, his arms crossed tightly over his chest and stance wide as he stared at the sea.

Gray crept into the sky and the calls of gulls came across the morning wind. Arabella sat numb, only panic twining through her blood.

Dr. Stewart's hand slipped away from Luc's brow and the priest bowed his head.

No. *No.*

She sprang to her feet and whirled about, staggering on bandy legs.

Lord Bedwyr caught her arm. "Mustn't neglect the formalities, my dear."

She stared at the foolscap and ink bottle in his hand. "Why have you done this?"

"You must trust me." He drew forth a pen from his coat. "Like your husband." He returned to Luc's side and knelt again, unfastened the cap on the ink bottle and flattened the blank sheet of paper on the doctor's satchel. "Here will do." He pointed to the bottom of the page.

With numb fingers she signed it.

"Arabella," the earl murmured. "Beautiful name your wife has, Lucien. Shame you won't have the opportunity to employ it." He laid the pen in his cousin's upturned palm. "Now it is your turn, old boy. Try not to stain it with blood."

Arabella turned away.

"Excellent," the earl muttered. "Now Tony, then Father. Must have witnesses and officiator."

Captain Masinter's face was white.

"New . . . gown," Luc whispered. "Shoes."

"You would like to be buried in a new gown and shoes?" the earl said. "Odd request, but a man's last wishes are sacrosanct. I won't tell a soul and neither will Tony," he added, but Arabella saw the misery in his eyes now.

Impulsively, she gripped the earl's hand. "He wishes me to have a new gown and shoes before arriving at the chateau. We made an agreement. Tell him you will help me purchase new garments and take me there." Her voice rose. "Promise him."

The earl's mouth cut a line across his face and he cast a hard look down at his cousin. "Of course I will help her, you bastard." He pulled his hand from Arabella's. "Anthony, help me carry him inside."

Captain Masinter came forward.

She could not look at Luc's ravaged face, only at his outstretched hand. She longed to take it, to place hers in it and give him her life.

Chapter 10

The Widow

They would not allow her in his bedchamber. She did not protest; they had known him a lifetime. She went to her chamber, washed her hands clean of his blood, and her tears fell into the stained water.

She sat at the window, watching the sea. Footsteps and voices came and went on the stairs. After a time she wrapped herself in her cloak and curled up on her bed. Her body was bruised in the places the men had grabbed her and tender where he had made love to her.

Near dusk Captain Masinter came to her. His face was haggard, his knuckles white around the hilt of his sword.

"Miss— That is, ma'am, I— That is to say—" He passed the back of his hand across his eyes. "I'm dreadfully sorry, m'dear."

"It cannot be." She felt blind and breathless. "May I go in now?"

The captain shook his head. "Don't think he'd care for that."

She could not fight it. Whatever the paper she'd signed might say, in truth she had as much business with him now as a stranger. Since she had wished for precisely that, she supposed it was a fitting punishment.

THEY TOOK HER to the constable and showed her the still, white face of the man that Luc had killed on the beach. She recognized him. He had been one of the men in the alley that Luc fought.

"They attacked him in retribution for defending me," she whispered numbly.

The burial would take place at sea the following day. Then, Lord Bedwyr said, he would settle his cousin's affairs and join her at the chateau. Until then it would be best if she continued on to her destination. He handed her into the private carriage where Mr. Miles awaited her, and with a burly sailor from the *Retribution* riding on the box with the coachman, they set off for Saint-Reveé-des-Beaux.

THE CASTLE APPEARED before them abruptly through a parting in the woods. In Gothic magnificence it arose from the river itself, gleaming gold in the pale evening light with thrusting, pointed turrets and graceful arches, all trumpeting its aristocratic splendor and all reflected in the water's mirror.

The weakness gripped her that she'd felt aboard ship when they had come to Saint-Nazaire. But now Luc did not stand behind her to assure her, nor did she feel the touch of his hand holding hers as she had then. Her only companion this time was an odd little man with stiff collars and high heels who had not spoken to her on the day-long journey except to offer her food and pillows.

She supposed Mr. Miles was mourning too, in his way.

Now he leaned to the window and said, "As you see, the chateau is French Renaissance at its whimsically elegant best, madam. Brilliant architecture. Exquisite artistry."

It was a fairy-tale castle out of a storybook and it gave her no pleasure.

"The dowager *comtesse*'s charitable work in the area saved it from the Revolutionaries and maintained it in the family," he continued. "She perished some years ago, but her younger son continues to reside here in his brother's absence. Are you acquainted with his lordship or his royal highness?"

"No. The prince hired me by letter, and I know nothing of the *comte* except that he is a minor English lord who has been absent from home for some time. I heard nothing of him in society." She stared at the castle. "The people for whom I typically work have no interest in absentee lords, only those in London who might take notice of their daughters."

Mr. Miles's lips were tight. "The *comte* is heir to a title and property of extraordinary prestige in England, madam."

In two month's time Prince Reiner intended to introduce his sister into London society for the purpose of finding her a suitable husband. Perhaps he now visited the *comte*'s chateau in the hope of allying their families.

"Is he married?" she asked.

Mr. Miles turned his attention to the window. "Quite recently, in fact."

They approached the castle with its walls that swept into the azure sky from the silver river like a fantasy. Two men came from within, liveried in blue and gold and bearing swords at their hips. Another man appeared, his black coat corded in silver, perhaps a butler. He opened the carriage door. Mr. Miles climbed out, stepped back and said, "Miss Caulfield, cousin to Lord Bedwyr. She has come to take up her post with her royal highness. His lordship the earl will be along in several days, I believe."

Arabella was now cousin to an earl. She had not given a thought to it.

She took a footman's hand and stepped out.

The butler bowed. "This way if you will, miss."

Within, the chateau was yet more splendid than without. The foyer glittered with a crystal chandelier and mirrors to either side that turned her reflection into infinite images. She snapped her gaze away and allowed the butler to take her cloak. He guided her up a magnificent spiral staircase carved of stone to a corridor lined with lush red and gold carpets and portraits of ladies whose coifs rivaled the castle towers and men draped in purple robes trimmed in white ermine. He opened a door figured with gilt onto a drawing room of perfect splendor.

Silhouetted by light from the window, tall and slender, a lady turned. Amidst Egyptian brocaded chairs and sparkling pianoforte and gilded harp, and gowned in plain white muslin and a drab lace shawl, she looked nothing like a princess.

"Miss Caulfield?" she said.

Arabella curtsied deeply.

The princess came to her with eager steps. "Why, you are so young! And beautiful!" She spoke perfect English with the softest turn of her tongue that marked her as foreign. She took Arabella's hands and bent to offer her two kisses, one upon each cheek. "When Reiner told me he had hired the redoubtable Miss Caulfield of London, I commenced quaking in my slippers. For who other than a perfect termagant of a governess could place so many young ladies in advantageous marriages? But you are not severe and horrid at all. What great fortune this is for me."

"The fortune is mine, your highness."

"I am Jacqueline to my friends." She appraised Arabella's face with open, intelligent eyes. The princess was a plain girl, with black, straight hair, a long nose, and a wide mouth that smiled easily. Her only adornment was a pearl pendant upon a filigree chain about her neck. "We shall be fast friends, I think."

"I hope so, your—"

The princess squeezed her fingers. "Jacqueline," she corrected. Her dark brows bent. "Unless you are a horrid, wicked, villainous witch of some sort and hide it well behind your lovely face and pensive smile. Are you?"

Witch.

Arabella pressed down on the ache in her chest. "You will discover that in due time."

The princess laughed again and drew her to a sofa. "You must be fatigued after your journey. But Reiner understood from his secretary that you were to have arrived days ago."

"I intended to. Then, unexpectedly, I suffered the loss of . . . a close relation."

"Oh, I am terribly sorry, dear Miss Caulfield. I saw the black drape upon your carriage and imagined it was for the old duke. I had no idea you were in mourning. Yet you came to help me. You are better than I even imagined."

That the princess understood little of the obligations of the serving class did not bother Arabella. Jacqueline was bright and kind and her hazel eyes shone with sincere sympathy now. Arabella nodded and wished for her sisters, to whom she could have confided the truth. Tonight she would write to Eleanor and Ravenna.

"The old duke?" she said.

"The Duke of Lycombe, uncle to the *comte*. He died little over a month ago, leaving our host as heir to his unborn child, it seems. I have never known an English duke. I always thought they were all pale and gray and severe. But my brother says the *comte* is a fine man, so if he should inherit his uncle's title, my notion of English dukes will be quite dashed away." She smiled. "Of course, Reiner likes horses and hunting dogs better than most people, so I don't know that his recommendation can be taken without sober reflection. In fact, my brother is off hunting at a neighboring estate at present and shan't return for at least a sennight."

"I understood you were to depart for the winter palace within days."

"Reiner is having too splendid a time here hunting and riding. So am I. It is ever so nice a place to read and write. We have decided to go directly from here to London."

She might not have hurried. She might not have taken passage with Luc, and he might now be alive.

She struggled to make words come. "Is the *comte* here now?"

"No. His brother was in residence until a few weeks ago when he went off with my mother and Reiner's courtiers to Paris. Since then it is only me and Reiner and a few of my waiting ladies who are all quite nice and deadly dull. But what a lovely holiday Reiner and I have been having. I do wish it could go on forever." She sighed. "It cannot, of course. Reiner intends to wed me away to some old stodgy English lord, and I suppose since I have expected this since I can remember, I mustn't think anything of it."

"It is the reason he hired me."

"But he cannot demand that you work when you are in mourning. Miss Caulfield, I propose that we continue on holiday through the month of September. Then you might mourn in peace and I might delay the inevitable a bit longer. If you agree, I vow that come October I will learn everything you wish to teach me in half the time. Do you think I can do it?"

"That all depends on whether you are a very foolish pupil"—*like her teacher*—"or a very wise one." Was this typical grief—regret and pain and longing at once? It was difficult to breathe. Difficult to speak. She had made a life of pretense and yet she had never suffered through it before.

Jacqueline cracked a grin. "Does it?"

"Oh, yes." She forced her tongue. "I like the wise pupils best, of course, but I can make something of the silly ones as well. What they lack in character they typically make up for in a strident devotion to conformity. Since most of the gentlemen of the ton are likewise un-original and predictable, matches are rarely difficult to facilitate."

"Oh, Miss Caulfield—"

"Arabella."

"I do believe, Arabella, that we are going to get along fabulously."

As fabulously as two friends could when one was hiding grief and the other was running from her future.

AFTER TEA THE butler, Monsieur Brissot, led Arabella to her bedchamber. She took one look at the sumptuous four-poster bed arrayed in ivory silks with golden tassels, the Italian marble fireplace and thick carpet of pale pinks and gold, and backed away from the threshold.

"I beg your pardon," she said. "I thought you meant to show me my chamber."

"*Ça y est, madame.*" He gestured within.

"No, monsieur. It must be a mistake."

"It is no mistake. Lord Bedwyr's instruction was quite clear." He said this as though it meant nothing to him that a servant of lesser status than he was being assigned a bedchamber fit for a noble guest.

For four days Arabella kept largely to that bedchamber, joining the princess for walks in the park that spread to one side of the river and for tea and dinner. On the fifth day Prince Reiner sent the carriage to collect his sister for a party that was to be given in her honor by his host at the neighboring estate.

"I would beg your company, Arabella," Jacqueline said with a kiss on either of her cheeks. "But I suspect you would rather remain here. Indeed, like I would." She smiled ruefully and went off to the party.

Arabella went to the terrace overlooking the river and stared into the water, which terrified her even in its mirrorlike tranquility. She drew the ruby ring from her gown and ran her thumb over the symbols embossed in the thick gold.

When Jacqueline returned she would bring her brother with her: the prince. Arabella knew she should feel the same tug of anticipation that every step toward discovering her true identity had given her. But she felt only emptiness. She would have thought it was heartbreak, but she must have a heart for that, and she'd long known she no longer possessed one of those. Neither weddable maiden nor truly wife or widow, the notion that she might someday be a princess now seemed like an ambition from another woman's life and foolish beyond measure.

FOR SOME TIME there were nightmares of dark and desert and thirst and more nightmares and more thirst. Then came moments of light and brief, godsent satisfaction on his tongue and in his throat. Following these came more thirst and more nightmares, punctuated by the screams of a boy then a woman. In the darkness, he could never find them. The thirst consumed him.

Then the light spread. It became pearly gray, then white.

"Ah, Lucien. Welcome back to the world of the living."

"Wine," he said.

His brow was heavy.

The heaviness vanished, and coolness replaced it. It was heaven.

"Wine."

"Why, I believe he's said something, Charles!"

"Of course he said something, Anthony. He is conscious. Thus the lucid open eye. Speak up, cousin, or I shan't be responsible for what I pretend to hear you say."

"God's breath, Luc! You gave us a wretched scare for a bit there."

His mouth was parchment, his tongue five sizes too big. *"Wine."*

"All right, all right. No need to shout, old fellow."

"Fetch him a glass of wine, Anthony."

He tried to rise. Pain seized his belly, then spasms. He gasped.

"It will be best if you refrain from movement." Cam's

voice came beside him. "You've a nasty hole in your side and none of us wish it to open up again, least of all Gavin who has had to sew it back together twice because you are too strong to be held down in a raving fever by no fewer than all three of us at once, even as ill as you were, damn you."

Luc closed his eye and concentrated on not fainting. *Agony everywhere.* He breathed shallowly, testing his limbs one after another.

A hand hovered above his chin. A hand with a cup. But his head was too heavy to lift.

"Damned wretched business," Tony muttered. He reached around the back of Luc's neck, tilting his head forward. "Drink up, old man. Must recover your strength speedily. Don't want to leave that pretty wife of yours a widow for too long, now do you? A girl like that'll find the fortune hunters beating down her door in no time."

Luc sputtered out the wine. *"Widow?"*

"Now look what you've done, Anthony. You have confused him and he hasn't even been conscious for ten minutes yet."

"I'm *alive.*"

"Objecting to the widow part," Tony said, and stood again. "See here, Luc, old man, it had to be done. Poor girl. Devastated, don't you know. But it was better that way. Safer for her."

"Throt—" Pain twisted his bowels. He gasped for air. "Throttle the both of you."

"I dare you to try." Cam's voice was smooth.

Luc relinquished the struggle. From the bone-familiar lull of his body as he lay still and the smooth oak ceiling above he knew he was in the captain's quarters on the *Victory*. He was weak and his bedclothes were cold and damp. He'd been in fevers before. Even muddled, he recognized the aftermath.

He closed his eye and let himself sink into the cool bed linens. "Tell me."

"Wise man." Cam's voice came closer. "You have perished, Captain Andrew of the *Retribution*. Your remains were deposited at sea from the deck of your old naval vessel upon which we are now sailing up and down the Breton coast."

He waited.

"Why, you might ask, have we staged your premature demise yet labored in secret for lo this sennight to make ourselves liars? Because, you see, we believe you are a marked man. Or, rather, that you were. The assassins, having done the deed, are now presumably off the job. Until you are once again revealed to be alive, you've nothing to fear in your weakened state. In short, we wish you to recover fully before placing yourself in the line of danger again."

Luc's hands curled into fists. The pain in his gut spiked with each breath of anger.

"Let's wait to explain the rest, Charles. Old boy's looking terribly white about the mouth. Father Stewart, do bring—"

"Where. Is. She?"

"At the chateau," Cam said. "Miles accompanied her there the day after the attack and placed her in Reiner's care. She is safe there, and until we discover who it is that sought your death no one need know anything of her elevation to the aristocracy, which we believe to be optimal and with which you will no doubt concur. For her part, she seems disinclined to accept the validity of your hasty nuptials, which is for the best until we have gotten to the bottom of this."

His scar ached. His shoulder ached. Breathing hurt. It all made him atrociously tired.

"Cutpurses," he mumbled, sleep tugging at him.

"Assassins." A crinkle of paper unfolding. "Look."

He cracked his eyelid open and tried to focus on the page Cam held before him.

His face stared back at him. It was a perfect portrait, including the scar and kerchief. And it was quite clearly his brother's work. Even signed at the bottom: *Christos W.*

"Anthony found this on the fellow that you killed on the beach. The other two men have not been found, but we believe from tracing their lodging in Saint-Nazaire that at least that one was Sicilian. Mercenary left over from the war, perhaps?"

"Scum," Tony spat.

"So you see, cousin, we have cause to believe that somebody wishes the duke-to-be dead."

"Not Christos," Luc whispered.

"He is not at the chateau, Luc," Cam said. "I have had a message from Mr. Miles. Your brother departed Saint-Reveé-des-Beaux a month ago claiming that he was off to Paris. He has not been heard from since."

Luc's mind was fuzzy. "A month . . ."

"A month ago, after our uncle died, bringing you perilously close to the dukedom, and young, mad Christos next."

"No." *Impossible.* "Impossible," he whispered, then sleep dragged him under.

HE AWOKE IN the dark and struggled to place himself, then to recall.

"Cam?" His throat was on fire.

"Abed, lad," Gavin said by his side, then helped him to drink. "Ye gave us all a guid fret. He's no' slept in a sennight."

"Guilt." He would laugh if it wouldn't plunge him into agony.

"Devotion. Luves ye like a brither. Always has."

Which was probably true. And given the deed of which he had unjustly accused his cousin seven months ago, Cam had been forgiving to only cut out his eye.

"Christos?"

"Anthony's sent a man to Paris to find him."

"Wasn't him."

"Aye, lad. But we've got to be certaint, nou dinna we?"

"Cam must go—" Pain shot through his gut, gripping his lungs.

"To the chateau. Aye. He's already packed to leave in the morn."

Luc managed a grimace. "Seems I'm not needed for anything," he whispered.

"Anly to heal up fast. There be a lass who'll be happy to see ye hale."

That, or discovering him snatched from the brink of death, she would finish the deed herself.

THE PRINCESS AND prince returned from the hunting party a mere hour after the housekeeper told Arabella that the Earl of Bedwyr had arrived at the chateau.

Arabella awaited her royal charge in the parlor. Jacqueline spared no time in seeking her out there. With the train of her riding habit slung over her elbow, she drew off her gloves as she hurried into the chamber.

"Dear Arabella, how I missed you! I feel quite like you are my sister already. That is how urgently I wished to tell you every little thing that happened while I was away."

"You honor me, your highness."

The princess slanted her a suspicious eye. "Don't tell me you are to become all stuffy and governesslike now that my brother has returned."

"I—"

"No! I told you not to tell me, and I fear you are about to do just that. Instead come with me to my dressing chamber while I do away with this awful habit. I simply loathe riding to hounds, but that was all anybody would talk of—this hunter and that bitch and of course the countless foxes bagged and strung up for decoration."

Arabella smiled. "Was it dreadfully dull?"

"I swear to you, Bella, I had nothing whatsoever to say to anybody the whole time. But that really isn't anything out of the ordinary. I am horridly shy in company."

Her disbelief showed.

The princess shrugged her straight shoulders. "I am wonderfully comfortable with a book or pen, and not at all at my ease with gentlemen and ladies of society. My tongue ties." She linked her arm in Arabella's and drew her into the corridor. "That is one of the reasons I like you. You never say a thing that makes me want to retreat behind the tapestries."

"I cannot believe you."

"But it is all too true. Sadly. Reiner knows my trouble, you see, and I'm afraid he hired you under false pretenses. I suspect you imagined you were to have a pupil who could open her mouth in regular company, but instead you are saddled with a filly that balks at the merest glimpse of a dog and positively runs in the other direction when a fox is near."

Arabella laughed. It felt awful and a great relief at once.

"Ah, the sweet laughter of a lady," came the earl's voice from behind them. "What balm to the weary masculine soul."

Arabella turned. Beside her, the princess gasped.

Lord Bedwyr stood at the other end of the corridor before the drawing room door, typically resplendent, his linens snowy and a hint of lace dripping from his cuffs. His hair was artfully disarranged and his smile was gorgeous.

Beside him the Prince of Sensaire seemed downright ordinary.

Arabella had once seen the Prince Regent of England from a distance. He was a florid-faced man of enormous girth and flamboyant dress, and certainly above fifty. At that moment she had cast off any childish imaginings she'd had that the prince she would wed would be young, handsome, or dashing.

Prince Reiner was not handsome or dashing, but in appearance he was as far from the Prince Regent as he was from the Earl of Bedwyr. Quite tall, he was lean from jaw to leg, lending him a lancelike air. He wore a neat white coat with military epaulettes, his color was robust, and his face, though not truly handsome, featured a fine, laughing pair of eyes.

"Reiner," the earl said, "may I make you acquainted with my cousin, Miss Caulfield?"

The prince bowed. *"Enchanté, mademoiselle."*

Arabella curtsied.

"And, Bedwyr, I must introduce you to my sister," the prince said. "Jackie, I am pleased to have you know the Earl of Bedwyr, Westfall's close companion since childhood."

"Your highness." Lord Bedwyr offered the princess an elegant bow.

Jacqueline dropped her eyes to the floor.

The earl turned away from her. "Reiner, old friend, news has come from England. Westfall is nearly Lycombe."

"I heard. The ducal uncle is dead."

"God bless his damned soul."

"Have you heard from our friend lately, then?" the prince said. "Has he hurried back to London to await his fate, leaving you to enjoy his chateau in his stead?"

"In fact he is in France and intends to pay a call upon our merry party here." He smiled at her and the princess. "Now, until our host arrives, whatever shall we do with our time?"

"YOU MUST ATTEND me at dinner every night, Bella," Jacqueline insisted. "Those foolish waiting ladies my mother chose for me cannot be counted on to make interesting conversation, and I . . ."

She was infatuated with the earl. Arabella needed no special powers of observation to see that.

"You are shy in company," she only said.

"I am shy in company." The princess's cheeks were not pink, but sallow. Apparently she found more distress than pleasure in her infatuation. Arabella understood well.

"Please, Bella. I would very much like it."

It was what she had dreamed for years: to be thrown into the intimate company of a marriageable prince. Now she hadn't any interest in it, but she did as Jacqueline requested.

A SENNIGHT LATER the princess announced to Arabella her readiness for schooling. "I wish to be less . . . reticent."

"You are not naturally reticent." Only befuddled by a man. "You need only the smallest instruction to be able to make your way comfortably in London society." Not all gentlemen in society were as handsome as the earl, she wanted to say. Nor as provoking. He had not spoken to her of his cousin, but occasionally he glanced at her assessingly. When she caught him out he would grin then say something outrageously flirtatious to one of the waiting ladies or invite the prince on a ride or make some other transparent excuse in order to avoid her. But she had no more wish to speak to him of Luc than he had to speak with her.

It was not until a fortnight had passed that he sought her out.

"Good heavens, my dear," he said, coming toward her across the rose garden green, hat in hand and hair glimmering in the sunshine. "Are you still wearing your governess uniform? I thought you promised to purchase a new gown. And shoes, if I recall correctly."

"I see that three weeks of mourning has not cured you of inappropriate raillery, my lord." She turned away from him to the basket into which she was placing roses that she cut.

"As it has not cured your propensity for doing the work of servants. Hasn't Reiner gardeners for this sort of thing?" He gestured to her basket.

"I enjoy it. And I am a servant."

For a moment the silence was punctuated only by the merriment of birds in the hedgerow nearby and the snap of her clippers.

"I am here to make good on my promise to my cousin." His voice did not tease now.

"To purchase for me a new gown and shoes? That is as ridiculous as any other part of it all."

"Not to purchase a gown." His face was quite sober.

"You bear no responsibility toward me, my lord."

"Indeed I do." His gaze slipped down to where she held her hands tightly together at her waist, and then she understood. He would remain with her until she knew whether she carried Luc's child.

"I could lie to you," she said, a strange, sorrowful desperation building in her. "I could bear another man's child and claim it was your cousin's in order to take advantage of my connection to you, a lord. How do you know I would not do that in the hopes of securing my future so that I will never again have to be a servant?"

"Because I know my cousin. A great deal better than you, it seems."

Her lungs stung. "I came here to marry a prince," she said nonsensically.

"My dear, in all things but title you already have."

It could not be. She was not meant to have wed him. He had not been a prince and he had not recognized the ring. And he was gone.

He was gone. The finality of it swept down upon her.

The earl stepped forward and drew her into his arms. She pressed her face against the exquisite lapel of his coat and wept.

ARABELLA RETURNED TO the gardens the next day and the next, and for the sennight following. Grand yet tranquil, the labyrinthine pathways allowed her hours of solitude in which she was not obliged to suffer the earl's scrutiny. She strolled between manicured flower beds then wandered a wooded path to a fountain fashioned of stone caryatids elevating a shell. As she walked she composed letters to her sisters which she never wrote.

When a carriage drawn by four matching gray horses rumbled up the drive, she paused and from a distance watched its passengers disembark. Four servants in the black and silver livery of the house came forth and flanked a gentleman, walking protectively around him up the stairs.

Arabella returned to the house and sought out Jacqueline.

"Has your mother's retinue returned?"

"Oh, no, not yet, thank heaven." Jacqueline dipped her pen into an ink pot. "The *comte* has come home at last."

"Is he an elderly man?"

"He is Lord Bedwyr's age, only a few years younger than Reiner, I believe. Why do you ask?"

"He walked slowly into the house, attended by hovering servants." Arabella drew the curtain aside and looked at the opulent coach disappearing into the carriage house.

"He has been ill, apparently," the princess said, "and is only now convalescing. We are unlikely to enjoy his company for several days. But how lovely when he is fully recovered it will be to augment our little party by a gentleman. It almost makes one wish my mother will never return with the rest of the court. Oh, but I wished that already, didn't I?" Her hazel eyes twinkled.

AS THE FOLLOWING afternoon was fine and warm, Arabella suggested that Jacqueline practice the English art of taking high tea. The servants set out the repast on the terrace that jutted out from the castle on the bank of the river overlooking the formal gardens.

Jacqueline accepted a cup from Arabella and turned her head to Prince Reiner sitting over a chessboard with Lord Bedwyr.

"Tell us about the *comte,* brother. Is he handsome?"

"How should I be able to say one way or the other, Jackie?" He leaned over the game. "I am not a lady."

Two of Jacqueline's waiting ladies giggled. They had taken the lesson in tea as cause for dressing in their smartest frocks, no doubt for the earl's benefit.

Arabella poured a cup for herself and walked to the balustrade. The queen's chosen companions for her daughter had not accepted her in their circle, and after three weeks still looked at her with mildly veiled suspicion. She did not begrudge them. After years on the edge of society, she was accustomed to it.

"Is the *comte* handsome, Lord Bedwyr?" Jacqueline had finally managed to leave off stammering and blushing in the earl's presence. It seemed to have no effect whatsoever on him. He treated her and her waiting ladies with the same easy amusement.

Lord Bedwyr leaned back in his chair, awaiting his opponent's next move. "I regret to report, your highness, that he is a great beast of a man. Not a'tall to ladies' tastes."

Jacqueline's lips twisted. "He owns this chateau and the vineyards, and a house in England, I understand. He must at least be very rich."

"What sort of a thing is that to say, Jackie?" her brother said. "Miss Caulfield, you are remiss. You must take your charge in hand and teach her manners." He smiled.

"I beg your highness's pardon." Arabella's fingers tapped on her teacup, paper thin porcelain with gold ribs. It was a cup fit for a princess, like her sumptuous bedchamber and the gardens she stared out at now without a scrap of feeling. "I shall endeavor to improve my methods of instruction."

"I expect you to." Prince Reiner grinned and returned his attention to the chessboard. He was a kind man, pleasant to all, and generous and affectionate with his sister. He stirred in Arabella no interest whatsoever.

"Well, is he rich, my lord?" Jacqueline said.

"If I had half of the *comte*'s funds, Princess," Lord Bedwyr replied, "I should be swimming in horses, carriages, houses, and jewels."

"You know, brother," Jacqueline said, "you should not fault me for wondering about a gentleman's worldly characteristics. It is what Maman has taught me to consider most important in all men since I was six."

"How tragic that in ladies' estimation a man's courage, heart, and nobility of character should fall behind his fortune and appearance." The earl sighed theatrically and moved his white knight.

"You needn't worry over that, my lord," the princess said, looking directly at him, her gaze perfectly clear.

He lifted a brow. "Ah, but my fortune is far from enviable, Princess."

A smile tweaked the corner of her mouth. "Lord Bedwyr, you are outrageously conceited."

"Jackie!"

"Princess!"

The earl cast the princess an oddly knowing sideways glance then returned his attention to the board. "Your sister is frightfully honest, Reiner. You ought not to have sent her to a convent for schooling. Girls learn all the worst sorts of morals from nuns, you know."

Jacqueline's cheeks were pink but her eyes were serene. Perhaps she had taken the earl's measure after all.

The door onto the terrace opened and a footman announced, "His lordship, *le comte de* Rallis."

A gentleman stepped into the sun—a tall, broad-shouldered man with impeccably tailored clothes, gleaming top boots, and a black slash of a kerchief about his brow that covered his right eye and part of a horrible scar.

The teacup slipped from Arabella's fingers and shattered on the stones at her feet.

Chapter 11

La Comtesse

Luc watched the color flood back into her cheeks, which had gone pale as parchment, and he nearly marched over to his cousin and strangled him. When Cam last sent word to the *Victory*, he said that she now knew his true identity. Unwisely, Luc had believed him.

A girl with the tall, dark appearance of Reiner rushed to her. "Arabella!"

Arabella.

"Bella, are you ill?"

"No," he barely heard her say. "No, I am well." Her chin ticked up as she met his gaze, but the cornflowers swam with confusion.

"Ah, Luc!" Reiner clasped his hand. "Bedwyr promised you were to come, but I never believe a thing he says."

"I would be well advised to follow your example." He looked over Reiner's shoulder to her.

"My friend," Reiner said, turning to the others.

"Allow me to make you acquainted with your guests, my sister and her ladies-in-waiting."

The women came forward. He was trapped, acting the gallant host to the party while the single person who most deserved his attention stole away down the terrace steps to the garden. No one seemed to notice. She still wore the plain governess's gown. It seemed that neither Cam nor she had told Reiner or anybody else of the events at Saint-Nazaire.

He would remedy that swiftly. But not before he spoke with her alone.

"Your lordship," one of the ladies said, "will you take tea?"

"I should think he might wish something a bit stronger. Don't you, Rallis?" Cam said with a lifted brow.

"Wine it is, then," Reiner said.

Luc bowed to the ladies, sent his cousin a silent command, and followed the prince inside. With a wave he dismissed the footman and turned to his cousin.

"Damn you, Cam."

Bedwyr leaned against the sideboard negligently. "I don't suppose you recall damning me when you were shedding your life's force in the sand. Really, Lucien, you are repeating yourself tiresomely."

"You deserve every moment of damnation you are wished."

"Probably, but that is hardly to the point. When did it become my responsibility to negotiate your tortured love affairs for you?"

"Goddammit, Cam. Have you no conscience?"

Reiner poured a glass of burgundy. "The two of you still argue like you did when you were eighteen."

"Then, he was merely a careless hedonist. Now he is a liar and a manipulator. Why did you lead me to believe you had told her?"

"Tell me, Lucien," Cam said as though Luc had not spoken, "during your convalescence did you by chance flirt with trading in the old blindness for the new? Or are you simply doubly blind now?" Cam gestured with his glass to the terrace doors. "But I think I have my answer already."

Reiner pushed a glass of wine into Luc's hand. "Drink this, my friend. It seems you need it."

Luc set down the glass. "Did he tell you?"

"That I was to ensure the safety of the stunning governess but not step within ten yards of her? Yes. He failed to mention it had anything to do with you, though."

"It was not my news to share, of course." Cam flicked an imaginary speck of lint off his coat sleeve. Finally he met Luc's gaze squarely. "From the beginning. As you wished."

Cam was right. Luc knew he should have told her the truth the moment she first asked his name. He could have told her at any moment since then. He hadn't because in hiding his identity he imagined he would be able to remain aloof from her.

But Cam had known. Somehow the rakehell swiftly understood what he had indeed been too blind to see.

He started toward the door.

"Now, wait here a moment, Luc," Reiner said to his back. "Have you installed your mistress in this house as my sister's governess?"

"She is not my mistress." He yanked open the door. "She is my *comtesse*."

ARABELLA WENT BLINDLY through the garden, no tears in her eyes but a cyclone of relief and joy and pure, titanic anger crowding her senses as she hurried along the hedgerow toward the wooded paths.

He was *alive*.

She needed a moment alone to think, to collect her thoughts, to understand.

To *revel*.

He was alive. Alive and well and able to smile and bow handsomely to the princess's silly waiting ladies.

Alive.

Alive enough to have told her that he had not in fact died before she discovered it in this manner.

For weeks she had shed tears for him. *Weeks.* While he had lied to her. For what reason, she could not fathom. Had he thought that if she knew the truth she would try to entrap him into marriage? But she had held him off more than once. She had objected until the very last moment. He had entrapped *her*.

The hedgerow ended in a long stone wall that stretched alongside a field of rows of pruned grape vines. She halted. Her steps had not taken her to the woods. She was lost. But certainly she had not walked so far to stray from the estate. *His* estate. The *comte*'s estate.

He was alive. And he was a titled nobleman. The heir to a dukedom.

She should have known. Men had lied to her before.

Never like this. *Of course.*

Her breaths came shallow. She reached out a hand, grabbed the wall and held tight to a rock while incomprehensible reality settled upon her. Then she continued walking until she came to a building. Low-roofed, long, and dark, she recognized it at once as a wine press. No one was about. The harvest was over, the sun low, and the building and naked vines cast long shadows across the grass.

She leaned up against the stone wall and closed her eyes. She would return and confront him and try not to hurl herself into his arms and breathe him in while she told him exactly what she thought of how he had treated her.

Perhaps it had all been a game to him. And his cousin, Lord Bedwyr, must have been part of it. But the men who attacked him, and his wound, had not been make-believe.

Why had he done it?

She pushed away from the wall and turned in the direction she had come.

She heard the dogs barking first, then hoofbeats. Rounding a corner of the high stone wall that bordered the nearest field, four of them scampered around her, tongues lolling, bearing friendly welcome.

A whistle cut the air and the beasts leaped away from her and back across the field.

He cantered toward her upon a great black horse like a man out of her dreams. He wore a dark green coat of superb cut and a black duster, buckskins that stretched over his thighs to extraordinary advantage, and a tall-crowned hat. Even with the kerchief and scar, he looked like a lord.

She did not wish to hide. That her hands shook and her throat closed should not matter. But as he came down from the horse, with the dogs cavorting about his boots, she drank in the sight of him.

"Good day, madam." He came toward her.

She backed up. "Should you be riding?"

"Probably not. But according to the footman, who had it from the gardener, you set off in this direction at quite a pace and I could not imagine how I was to find you before dusk if I made the attempt on foot. The grounds are extensive." He smiled ever so slightly. "So if my wound should open from the ride and I die from it, rest assured it will be your fault."

"How could you—" Her voice failed. He stood there so tall and handsome, yet lighter of flesh than before and somewhat taut about the mouth. She wished he was in vile pain and prayed that he was not. "You are cruel."

"Ah. We come directly to the point. No fond reunion kisses first." He sighed. "I should have expected it after the shattered teacup, yet I held out hope."

"How could you not tell me?"

"I thought Bedwyr did. He said that he had."

"He had not." Her voice wavered. She forced it to steadiness. "I was obliged to learn it abruptly when you walked through that door."

Luc reveled in the luxury of seeing her face. Her cheeks were touched with pink, her cornflower eyes were wide, and her lips were perfect, as always, soft and pink as raspberries and ample. He wanted his on them. He wanted a reunion kiss that would end up with them in the grass and half dressed, as they'd been on that beach too many miserable weeks earlier for him to contemplate.

But she looked sick to her stomach.

He halted at a distance from her. "I am sorry I failed to tell you the entire truth about myself." He bowed deeply. The cutting pain in his side had not been so acute in a sennight, but this was worth it. "I beg your forgiveness."

The cornflowers opened wide. "You are sorry you did not tell me the *entire truth*? What sort of partial truth could you have told, I wonder?"

"Partial truth?" Luc's impatience got the best of him. "Are my title and position so abhorrent to you?"

"Your *title* and *position*?"

He shook his head, befuddled. Then the reason for her astonishment struck him in his sore gut like another cold knife.

"Bedwyr did not tell you that I was alive." *Not possible.* "Did he?"

"He did not." Her throat worked against emotion.

"Dear God." He stepped forward. "I never imagined he would not. He did it to punish me rather than you, undoubtedly. But I should kill him for it. I was unable to travel until yesterday, but if I had known, I would have written to you."

With a squaring of her shoulders, she seemed to make a decision. "Why didn't you tell me before who you really were?"

"I would have." He rubbed his jaw. "I intended to."

She looked away. "Men deceive as a rule."

"I intended less to deceive than to—"

"It matters nothing to me. You are nothing to me."

"Yet your eyes were bright with relief when you saw me at the house. You deceive yourself, duchess."

"Do *not* call me that."

"That you care at all what I call you is instructive." He moved closer. Her shoulders seemed to flatten against the wall behind her. He traced her lovely profile, and his fingers itched to play in the coppery strands that dangled from the heavy knot of hair at her neck. "You care for me," he said.

"I cared for you when I believed you dead." Her voice quivered. "You were more interesting then."

A constriction in his chest loosened. "If it will hold your attention, I shall gladly die again. Name the date and time."

"You are outrageously amusing, my lord. You ought to gather a theater troupe and put on a traveling show." Still she would not look at him. "Perhaps invite Lord Bedwyr to join you. The two of you would make money hand over fist."

"I have enough money already. And I simply cannot

hear you call me 'my lord' in that disgusted tone. It makes me want to write the king and tell him I won't have the title after all."

Finally her lips twitched. Then she seemed to lose the battle within her entirely; her brow softened and she turned her face to him. Luc thought he could die now indeed. To have her gaze upon him with such grace and charity was the blessing of heaven.

"I am . . ." She seemed to struggle for words. "I am glad you are well."

"Glad? Is that all I am to have from you?" He reached for her and curved his hand around her cheek. Arabella jerked away.

Anger flashed in his eye. "You will not let me touch you? You let Bedwyr touch you."

"I did not."

"He said you embraced him. Did he lie about that too?"

"I—" She sought in her memory. In the garden the earl had held her. "I did—"

"You allowed that raking libertine cad of a—"

"It was an embrace of comfort only, the briefest—" She cut off her justification. "I needn't defend myself to you."

"You jolly well do."

"I wept! Don't you see? I wept for you, for your death that I caused, and he comforted me. That is all. Mere momentary comfort. Now here you are, having lied to me and made me grieve, and you expect me to fall into your arms?"

"Yes."

She gaped. "Your arrogance seems to have survived along with your body."

He flattened his palm to the wall behind her head and leaned in. "My body survived, indeed, and it remembers the touch of yours. Quite well."

Now her body betrayed her. His teasing she could withstand. His closeness she could not.

"My cousin says that you intend to marry Reiner," he said.

"He told you *that*, but he neglected to tell me you were alive?"

"He is a contrary fellow," he said a bit grimly. "Too much untrammeled adulation, I think." He leaned in to the side of her face and seemed to breathe in deeply. "But by God, what seeing you does to me. All else fades away." His lips brushed her earlobe, stirring soft pleasure deep in her. "What are your intentions toward Reiner?"

He was alive, well, and he was touching her. She had dreamed of this. She had wept through entire nights dreaming of this.

She must make herself form sensible words. "I haven't any intentions toward him. I hadn't any since the moment I allowed you to touch me on that beach." *Days before that.*

"Good," he murmured. The tip of his tongue traveled the tender dip beneath her ear, then his mouth found her neck. "Because I would have to call him out for marrying my wife. As I am the better shot, he would perish, then his country would be left leaderless and there would be a whole international incident. It wouldn't be pretty. It is far better this way."

She dragged herself from pleasure and sidestepped out from under him. "I am not truly your wife."

His arm fell to his side. "The priest said, 'You have declared your consent to be man and wife.' I believe you are."

"I did not hear him say that."

"The moment must have overcome you. I understand that is common with brides."

"It was not a legal wedding."

"You signed a marriage contract."

"I signed a blank page."

"It is no longer blank. Friendly elves that I encountered whilst convalescing in the woods revealed the invisible ink on that page that now makes it quite clear you are wed to me. Isn't magic remarkable?"

"How can you jest about this?" she cried.

He came forward, took her face gently between his hands and brought his mouth an inch from hers.

"I jest not. We are wed. Truly and validly." His breath feathered over her lips, and all the life in her seemed to heat up.

She had trusted him, believed in his honor, given him her body, and all along he had been lying to her.

"If I tell you to release me," she said, his scent and warmth all around her, tangling her thoughts as he always did, "you will do so."

"Are you certain?" His voice was deeply husky. His lips brushed hers like a whisper. She closed her eyes against the sensations of her weakness.

"Yes. I am certain. Release me now."

For a taut moment he did not move. Then with a snarl he released her and backed away.

"What do you want of me?" he demanded. "Another apology? A dozen apologies? Then you have them." He threw forth his hand. "I was wrong. I made a mistake. I was accustomed to playing that part and saw no reason to inform you otherwise."

"I don't care why you lied to me, only that you did. Don't you see?"

"I see that given the outcome, you are making a mountain of a mole hill."

"You forced me to marry you under false pretenses!"

"I have never forced you to do anything." He advanced on her again, coming as close as he could without touching her. "But I will now, little governess. I will force you to care. I will make you care more than you can bear."

"Now you threaten me?"

"How you can consider that a threat, I have no notion."

He was a lord. She finally understood his arrogance and authoritarianism and persistence. He could have any woman he wanted. He could not truly want her, poor, a servant with a sharp tongue. He was like other men after all. When she would not allow them to have her, they had sought to ruin her. Like those men, he simply wanted to win.

Now she was entirely in his power, his wife, his to command not for the duration of a brief journey but for a lifetime. The panic that she had felt so many times with him threaded through her afresh.

"You don't understand," she said. "I *cannot* be married to a lord."

"You cannot be married to a lord," he repeated without inflection. "You are the most difficult woman I have ever known."

"Given that, I wonder that you could want me."

"You wonder," he said, his gaze shadowed again with that bewildered need she did not understand. "You wonder, do you?" He kissed her, at first the softest caress, taking her lips and making her feel him. Then it became possession. She welcomed it, leaned into him, pressed her palm to his chest, felt his life beneath her hand, and parted her lips for him.

It was too brief. He released her.

She covered her lips with her fingertips and turned her face away, seeking control. He reached up as though to pull her hand away, then halted and instead backed up.

"God *damn it*." With a swirl of his coattails, he pivoted about and strode to his horse.

She watched him mount from the ground despite the wound that must still pain him. He circled the horse about and, with the dogs barking and leaping, spurred away. She watched him go.

He always left her. Only once had she walked away from him, but each time he made her need him, she watched him go. He expected to win and it was entirely possible that he would.

SHE RETURNED TO the chateau in the gathering dusk to find a parade of carriages lining the drive and servants laden with traveling trunks and bandboxes hurrying about. The butler stood in the center of the commotion, directing the flurry of activity.

"Monsieur Brissot, who has arrived?"

"The queen has returned, mademoiselle. I advise you to attend the princess *tout de suite*."

Arabella passed through the busy servants and swiftly to the princess's chambers.

"Oh dear, Bella. I thought we might be spared Maman a bit longer. Alas, it is not to be." Jacqueline shrugged her square shoulders, then she grinned. "So I have asked the *comte* to throw a party."

It seemed he had told no one of his marriage. She understood nothing of him, only that he was unpredictable and authoritarian and he made her positively weak with longing.

"I thought you disliked society," she managed to say.

"I do mostly. Only, Maman must always have something upon which to direct her thoughts. Since lately that direction has been my marital prospects, I thought to give her something else upon which to turn her attention. At least for a few days."

"Is the party to be soon?"

"The day after tomorrow. The *comte* was excessively keen on the idea. Everybody around is to be invited." She grinned. "Before the ball gowns and waltzing commence, however, you must teach me something utterly practical so that Maman will be immensely impressed with your instruction and double your wages."

THE QUEEN WAS not impressed. When she entered her daughter's chambers before dinner, she gave Arabella one sweeping glance and said that now that the court had returned her services would no longer be needed in the evenings, distant cousin to an earl or not. Jacqueline protested but the queen went to the chamber door and opened it herself. Arabella left happily.

The prince's objections overruled his mother's directive. A minute before the dinner bell rang, Jacqueline flew through the door of Arabella's bedchamber.

"Hurry. You must dress for dinner." She went to the clothes press. "Reiner has insisted that you join us. The *comte* seconded. He is quite the gentleman." She gaped at the empty drawers. "Arabella, have you no other gown but the gray one you wear everyday?"

"I am—was—am in mourning," she stammered.

"Then you might at least have two gray gowns," the princess said with the practical sense of a girl that had not gone a day in her life with fewer than three dozen gowns. "I'm afraid I have nothing so drab, but all white and pastel, as Maman insists. So you must wear color tonight." She went to the door. "Now make haste. The longer we make everybody wait for dinner, the more they will stare at us when we appear, and I should dislike that excessively. It is one thing to be stared at when one is the most beautiful woman in the county like you, but another altogether when one is me."

THEY MADE HASTE, but everybody stared anyway. Arabella only felt the gaze of one person.

Then he ignored her entirely—not only throughout dinner, but for the next three days. Gracious and welcoming to the queen and her courtiers, including her ladies-in-waiting, whom he treated with utter charm and deference and without any particular show of arrogance or authoritarianism, to her he said nothing at all. As the household whirled into a frenzy of preparations for the party, he did not seek her out or even come within speaking distance of her. No one else spoke to her as anything but the princess's governess, Miss Caulfield. Even the earl had ceased to send her studying glances; he had largely disappeared from company.

No one knew the *comte*'s wife resided beneath the roof of Saint-Reveé-des-Beaux, and Arabella began to believe that she had imagined their interview in the vineyard.

WHEN A MAIDSERVANT came to her chamber bearing the gown Jacqueline promised to lend her for the party, she shook her head.

"This cannot be intended for me."

Draped on her bed, it was a confection of pink gauze and the finest, thinnest silk, with tiny cap sleeves and stars picked out in silver beads across the bodice and overskirt. It was a gown fit for a princess, certainly, but not for the hired governess, no matter how much her charge liked her.

"Mais oui, mademoiselle," the maid said earnestly. "The princess, she chose it from her gowns and had it tailored especially for you for *ce soir*."

"But I cannot accept another gift—"

"You can." Jacqueline poked her head in the door, a box in her gloved hands. "This one." She came forward, removed the lid, and drew forth a glittering crescent of diamonds.

"Princess," Arabella whispered. "You should not have done this."

"I didn't." Jacqueline placed the sparkling tiara above the gown on the bed, as though dressing the coverlet for the party. "It is from the *comte*."

The maid's hand flew to her mouth. *"Jésus, Marie, et Joseph."*

"Clearly, he admires you," the princess said. "As well he should. And he isn't the only one. I've seen at least four of Reiner's courtiers casting you interested glances down the dinner table—and two of them married, the philanderers."

Arabella stared at the delicate tiara, a sprinkle of diamonds fanning out from a gathering of gems in the center set in the shape of a rose. "I cannot wear it."

The maid made a moue of displeasure.

Jacqueline peered at her. "Do you dislike the *comte*? Really, Bella, if a man gave me a tiara this lovely I would wear it whether I liked him or not. All of my tiaras are royal heirlooms, thoroughly ugly and old-fashioned. This one is perfect."

He intended to follow through on his threat, after all. He did not know that extravagant gifts meant nothing to her.

She dressed and left the tiara on the bed. But the princess barred the door and forbade her to leave the chamber unless she wore it.

Arabella allowed the maid to set it on her head and stared at herself in the mirror. She looked like a princess. She touched the diamond ridges with a tentative fingertip. "Why did he not give it to me himself?"

"I suspect he feared that if he tried, you might throw it at his head." Jacqueline's brow went up. "You have a way of putting out barbs when he is in the room, Bella, and truly I cannot understand why. If any man should inspire a lady's suspicions it is Lord Bedwyr, not the *comte*. Why, for all that he is a naval hero and bears that dashing scar, he is the veriest puppy."

Arabella did not believe it. He had enlisted Jacqueline's aid so that she could not refuse his gift, and yet he had not yet told anyone the truth. He was playing a deep game, like he had played with her from the beginning, and the panic he stirred in her washed against her relentlessly.

He was not a puppy. He was a wolf.

A CENTURY EARLIER, a grand room for balls had been built onto the castle's farthest end to reach across the river, completing the bridge from one bank to another. A corridor from within the arched colonnade led into the magnificently high-ceilinged room, a door at the opposite side letting out onto a trellised walkway into the woods.

Tonight the ballroom sparkled with hundreds of candles and the reflection of torches set in buoys upon the river glittering through the windows that stretched from sparkling parquet floor to stucco-sculpted ceiling. The prince's musicians were adorned in blue and gold livery, playing brightly to fill the vast chamber. Footmen in the silver and black colors of the duke's household moved through clusters of guests, offering wine.

The guests were likewise magnificent. This was his world, the men and women of his society of whom she had only ever caught glimpses while readying her students, gowned and garbed at the height of fashion and all with an air of sublime superiority. The ladies, their lips stylishly rouged and necks draped with jewels, turned long-lashed eyes upon her and lifted their fans to whisper.

Arabella held her chin high, unfurled the lacy fan Jacqueline had given her and went into the crowd.

The queen entered on Prince Reiner's arm, with Jacqueline behind. Guests dipped into bows and deep curtsies as the royal party made its way to the dais, where the prince deposited his mother in a gilded chair. Then he took his sister's hand, led her down the dais step, and came directly to Arabella.

Astonished gasps were audible throughout the chamber.

He released his sister and bowed deeply over Arabella's hand. *"Comtesse,"* he said quietly, "I should very much like the honor of a dance with the beautiful wife of my fondest friend."

Jacqueline gaped.

Arabella could do nothing but allow him to lead her into the set. He smiled pleasantly, and it was all as if there were nothing unusual about a prince dancing with a governess.

"You should not have done this, your highness," she whispered when the pattern brought them close.

"I could not do otherwise. It would evidence the greatest lack of gratitude on my part to fail in soliciting your hand for the first dance. This is, after all, your house." He smiled.

"The guests think you are dancing with a servant."

"The guests will know differently soon enough."

Across the glittering room Luc stood in a cluster of

ladies and gentlemen. As though he felt her regard, he turned and looked at her.

The dance came to an end and the prince bowed and went off. Jacqueline glided to her side.

"*Comtesse?* Good heavens, Bella, what have you hidden from me and why does my brother know when I do not?"

"He must have told him." She grasped Jacqueline's hand. "I am sorry I did not tell you. I didn't know—"

"Oh, none of that. We all have our secrets, after all, though admittedly yours is an enormous one. I don't know why you and the *comte* are hiding this from everyone, or why you are acting as a servant when you are the mistress of this house. But—" She looked through the crowd again, this time at Luc. "I must compliment you. Your husband is very handsome."

"I don't know what he wants of me," she said honestly.

The princess's wise regard settled on her. "Perhaps you should ask him."

He was walking toward them. Jacqueline squeezed her fingers and moved away.

Then he was before her, taking her hand and bowing over it.

"How beautiful you are this evening, duchess. As always." He brought her hand to his lips, turned it over and kissed the center of her gloved palm. Tingles shivered over her.

She dragged her hand away. "What are you doing?"

He smiled comfortably, confidently. "Making myself immeasurably frustrated. Come with me to the terrace."

"No. Everybody will think you are trying to seduce the governess."

"Hang everybody. And anyway I already accomplished that weeks ago. Come with me."

He already accomplished that. "No."

"Your greetings still leave much to be desired."

"I suppose I haven't sufficient practice being fondled in public."

"Since I prefer fondling you in private, I will allow you this point."

"That beach was hardly private."

"True. But my imagination has run ahead with all sorts of plans for us."

Her hands fisted. "Why do you tease me as though there is nothing else to be said?"

"What else should be said, then? How's this: this ball is for you."

"For *me*? But you—"

"Call it an betrothal party of sorts." He glanced about them. "Now everybody is actually staring. Apparently a man is not allowed to speak at length with a beautiful lady in a ballroom. You must dance with me to soothe their outraged sensibilities."

"I thought you said hang everybody."

"Dance with me, duchess."

"You *confuse me*."

"And you bedazzle me." His gaze slipped down her neck and caressed her breasts, then continued to her hips. He was handsome beyond her dreams in a dark blue coat that made his broad shoulders seem as though he could lift his ship from the water himself, and a single large sapphire the color of the night lodged in his neck cloth. A pristine black silk band covered his eye and even the scar seemed dashingly elegant. If she were a woman to have her heart stolen by a man's consequence and beauty alone, she would be lost. But she had no heart to be stolen; she was safe.

"You must dance with me," he said. "I will not accept refusal."

"You enjoy having the upper hand."

"Rather, I enjoy having my hands on you. It puts me in mind of that brief but memorable sojourn on the beach. Before the unfortunate incident with the knife, of course." He smiled.

Her cheeks were hot. "I have heard you talking with the ladies-in-waiting. You do not speak to all women in this frank manner."

"No. Only my wives, and among them only those who refuse my request for a dance." He moved a half step closer and looked down at her. "Will you dance with me, Arabella?"

He had not spoken her name before. He seemed to caress it.

"I—I—" He tangled her thoughts and intentions. She knew he did it intentionally. "For three days you have not tried to speak with me alone, yet now you tease me as you did aboard your ship, as though nothing has happened in the meantime."

"For three days of agony I have held myself aloof from you to allow you to become accustomed to the truth in your own time. Clearly that was the wrong tactic." He glanced at the tiara tucked in her hair.

"Only a man of poor character would seek to cajole a woman with extravagant gifts."

"You are no doubt correct," he said. "Dance with me anyway."

She could not resist him. She nodded.

Lord of the manor, he merely lifted a hand, and far across the chamber the orchestra commenced the new set. Then he took her fingers in his. His hand slipped around her waist and then up to the back of her ribs, unnecessarily caressing, but she accepted it. She lifted her hand to lay it upon his arm and he drew her into the waltz.

"Haven't tried this since that reprobate put out my

eye," he said quietly, a smile in his voice. "I beg your pardon in advance for stepping on your toes."

She looked up into a countenance of such simple pleasure that something tender and painful caught in her chest. Perhaps Jacqueline was right. Perhaps he was not always a wolf.

That assessment lasted less than a minute.

"Dear God. How I want to kiss you." His voice was husky, his attention entirely upon her lips. "I need to kiss you."

"If you kiss me here you will shame me."

"If I kiss you here I will—" He broke off. "Was that a tacit acceptance?"

"I—"

"Not acceptance of the location of the kiss, of course. But of the kiss itself."

She could not bear it. He made her want to laugh and cry and dance all at once. She directed her gaze pointedly over his shoulder. "You are—"

"Absurd. Yes, you have noted that before."

"You cannot help but interrupt me. I was going to say that you are as much of a reprobate as your cousin."

"In desire, perhaps. But my deeds are confined to one woman." His fingers spread upon her back, teasing the edge of the gown then steeling over her skin. "His are distributed rather thinly amongst many. *Regardez*."

Seeking distraction, sanity, anything to stanch the agitated heat gathering inside her, she followed his gaze. Lord Bedwyr stood at the center of a group of ladies, laughing as they waved their fans before their cheeks.

Arabella frowned. "I do not understand why he insisted on that farcical wedding."

Luc drew her closer, beyond propriety's separation, so that if she fought the strength of his arms she would trip.

"It was not farcical," he said above her brow. "And he did it because he knew I wished it."

"You did not wish to marry me anymore than I wished to marry you. You wished only to have me that once, as I did. We thought you would die. It should never have come to this."

Finally it was said aloud.

She held her breath, biting down on the inside of her lip.

He did not deny it.

His hand tightened on her back. He drew her close and bent his head beside hers. "It has been more than a month, Arabella. Long enough to know." His voice was rough. "Tell me. Do you carry my child?"

Crumbling a bit inside she whispered, "I do not."

He said nothing.

"If the duchess's child is a boy," she said, "you needn't worry about your brother inheriting."

"Bedwyr told you."

"No one needed to tell me. The whole household knows of your family's situation. The ladies-in-waiting were gossiping about it all morning." She could not meet his gaze. "I will accept an annulment without protest. I will expect nothing from you in return for it. No one else need ever know."

There was a long silence.

"I do not wish an annulment," he said.

"You do. You must."

"No, I mustn't, little governess who levels commands like she was born a duchess. What will you command next, I wonder. That I must find a fresh knife and continue the project those fellows began on the beach? Or perhaps you would command me to cut a bit higher, to carve out my heart and put it in a box on the shelf so it will not inconvenience you again."

He could not mean it. He did not mean it. He flirted and teased as though it meant nothing, when it meant everything to her.

It meant everything to her.

The heart that she had thought did not exist now beat in a full galloping panic beneath her ribs. She had always run—from the foundling home, from the Reverend, and from the men who had tried to use her. But she could never run from him. The worst of it was that she did not wish to. She wished to be lost again, this time to him. Willingly she would lose herself and then she would be gone forever.

She broke free of his hold. They stood like Greek statues amidst the swirling skirts and coattails and sparkling jewels of dancers all about them. In his face she saw the truth. He had not told her everything about their hasty wedding. He was still lying to her.

"You speak as though your words have no consequences," she said. "But this game is over. You must cease playing it."

"I will not release you, Arabella."

She reached up and dragged the tiara from her hair. "You cannot cajole my sentiments or purchase my obedience, my lord."

Couples around them slowed and halted, watching.

He did not move to accept the tiara. "Now who seeks to shame whom?" His voice was a dark rumble.

"I am the only one shamed here. In trusting you I shamed myself."

He snatched the tiara from her fingers, and in his face was furious vulnerability.

With her chin high as she passed between the guests, she fled. Every ounce of her self-possession fought not to run.

Chapter 12

The Bride

hey talked of it for hours." Jacqueline stood behind her at the dressing table, passing the bristles of a silver-backed brush through Arabella's hair. "French aristocrats are routinely scandalous, but they never expect it of the English. Your waltz and quarrel with the *comte* came as a refreshing surprise." Her laughing gaze met Arabella's in the mirror.

Arabella's own eyes were clear. After she left the ball, she had removed the gown meant for a princess and gave it to the maid to take away. Then she sat by the hearth until the sounds of revelry faded and Jacqueline came to her bedchamber.

"Everybody would have known of the origin of the tiara soon enough anyway," the princess said, brushing slowly. "The servants were probably gossiping from the moment I gave it to you. No information remains secret for long in a house such as this."

"None?"

Jacqueline's lips twisted. "Except perhaps the news that you are not in fact a governess."

"I am a governess."

"Only until the *comte* announces your secret wedding. Reiner thought he intended to do so tonight. Your quarrel must have thwarted him. Oh, Bella, you must make it up to him immediately so I can embrace you publicly as my friend and no longer my servant."

Arabella stood and went to the clothing press and opened it. Jacqueline had lent her new undergarments; her old linens were folded neatly within. She moved aside the petticoat and revealed the ring nestled upon the chemise. She withdrew it and tied the ribbon around her neck. Wearing the ball gown, she had missed the weight of it. It was familiar. Comforting.

"Why is your marriage a secret?"

"Jacqueline, I cannot remain here."

The princess set the brush down on the table. "You will not tell me the trouble between you and the *comte*, will you?"

"I am leaving tomorrow."

"Does he know?"

He would discover it swiftly enough. But hopefully, with distance his lust and pride would cool and he would see that it was for the best. In the meantime she would begin searching for her father, this time without relying on a prince to reveal him to her.

"You must do what you need," Jacqueline said. "I know nothing of the complications of married life, of course. But I wish you would remain."

"I cannot." The moment of panicked terror she felt during the dance had passed, but not the agitation to be gone and away from him.

"Bella," the princess said, "I must admit to being sorry that you will not be with me in London."

"You know all you must to acquit yourself splendidly."

"I am uncomfortable with gentlemen," she said with a serious twist of her brow. "I had hoped you would school me to become better accustomed to them."

"I fear I would be no more knowledgeable than my student in that matter." Not if Luc Westfall was her examination.

"That cannot be true. I am confined to whatever castle or party my brother and mother choose, and have known so little of men. But you have lived amongst London society. You must have had many adventures."

"If by adventure you mean did I trust a man who promised to introduce me to"—*a prince*—"a possible employer and then discovered that he meant to introduce me instead to his own lust, why then, yes, I had an adventure."

"Arabella! Was he a guest in the house at which you worked?"

"He was the elder brother of the children I cared for, and I had considered him a friend until then." Her fingers curved around the ring dangling against her collar. "I told the housekeeper about what he did. She informed my employers, but they were unmoved by my story. They said I had seduced him. I was released from service."

"They were unjust."

"It was my fault." It had always been her fault, from the first days at the foundling home to the terrible mess she was in now. "I was naïve. And I foolishly assumed that good character must always accompany a man's fine appearance and wealth."

The princess did not speak at once. "I see," she finally said.

Arabella went to sit at the dressing table again and reached up to begin braiding her hair.

Jacqueline grasped her hand. "Will you leave tomorrow?"

"In the morning."

"I will instruct the coachman to make the traveling carriage available for you." She went to the door and paused there. "I will miss you, Arabella, as I would miss a sister, had I one. I do hope we will meet again soon."

Arabella went to her and embraced her.

After Jacqueline left a maid entered to build the fire against the cool night. Arabella sat before the blaze plaiting her hair. But an hour later, wrapped in a blanket and staring out the window onto the black river, all the party lights doused and the magic gone, she was still cold. The castle was three hundred years old, and autumn had brought a damp chill to its chambers; it was no surprise she could not make herself warm enough to sleep. And she would never see him again.

She climbed onto her down-filled mattress and drew the draperies around her. The linens were all soft and scented of roses, and she was surrounded with ivory and gold. It was a princess's bed, and for one more night she could pretend.

SHE AWOKE TO amber firelight spread across the coverlet from the foot of the bed. The *comte*'s silhouette showed dark as he parted the drapery. She saw only the contours of his shoulders and his arm holding aside the curtain and the outline of his waist; the full masculine beauty of his form was now concealed by the dark, where on the beach it had been revealed by the sun.

She sat up.

He said nothing but his chest expanded and, in the silence softened by the crackle and hiss of the fire, she heard his hard breath.

She went forward on her knees to the end of the mattress. He reached down and his hand curved around the side of her face, large and warm and strong. She turned her lips against his palm. He bent and lifted her to him and their mouths met.

He kissed her hungrily, holding her to him with his hands about her face. His thumb stroked along her jaw and down her chin, opening her mouth to him. He tasted of wine and heat and his desire for her. His tongue stroked hers gently, then sought her deeper. She took him in. With each meeting of his flesh and hers he made her want more of him.

"Sweet Arabella," he whispered against her cheek. "What consequence could you fear so greatly, my little governess, that you run away from me?"

Loss. Betrayal. Heartbreak. The patina of too much pain lingered beneath her skin and circled her heart like a guard. She must not love him. But to remain with him and not love him was impossible.

"What are you doing here?"

"Enjoying what is mine by right." He nuzzled her throat and she lifted her chin to allow him.

"You do not own me like you own this house and your ship."

"Give me a wedding night. Finally."

"We should not be wed. You should not be my husband."

"Duchess." He cupped her face in his hands and made her look at him. "You are my wife in God's reckoning."

"I don't believe in God any longer."

"Then believe in me."

"Blasphemer."

He grinned. "Hypocrite."

"Kiss me." *Kiss me again and again, until I believe in God once more, because then I would know that this is a miracle and not merely a dream.*

He stroked his fingertips over her face reverently, then he did as she bid him. She knew the flavor of him, the sublime shape and pressure of his mouth upon hers, the deep, pulling thrill inside her when his tongue touched hers. She knew the scent of sea and wind that even now clung to him.

Finally she allowed herself to touch him. Putting her hands on him, she followed the contours of his neck and shoulders with her palms and fingertips, learning his skin and sinew like she knew his character—strong, powerful, confident. His body was hard and large, and she knew he would never be hers, no matter what he said now, or did. He did not intend to hurt her; he would do so without even knowing it.

"You make me feel when I do not wish to," she said, and to save her pride added, "And you are overbearingly arrogant."

His thumbs caressed the undersides of her breasts. "Can we not call a truce?"

"As we did on the beach when you had me?"

"Perhaps for a bit longer than that." He cupped her breast and she leaned into him. Then he stroked across the nipple. Her breaths stuttered. He caressed and she thought she might shatter into little pieces of desire if he ceased.

She clung to his shoulders. "You may have me now."

"Yes, I was just coming to that."

"Don't laugh at me." Inside her, everywhere, she needed him. "You don't know what this does to me."

"I know." His hand swept down her back to her behind

and pulled her against him. "Because it does it to me."
He kissed her deeply. She wanted to climb up him, to
wrap herself around him. Her hands sought his chest,
then his waist, needing to touch him everywhere and
needing him closer. Her fingers collided with uneven
flesh and his breaths caught. In the dim light the fresh
scarring showed as a dark slash along his side.

"Ah," he said low. "Minor inconvenience."

"Inconvenience?" She had spoken wedding vows because of this wound.

"Rather, opportunity." He tugged her from the bed,
pulled her to him and kissed her. His hands ran over
her back and down to her buttocks, then her thighs. Her
nightrail slipped over her knees, his palms hot on her
skin as he made her part her legs. She gasped, her body
exposed to his, and he dragged her against him and her
tender flesh met the fabric of his breeches.

"I—" She pressed into him. "I will fall."

"I am here to catch you." He drew her onto the bed,
onto his lap, and made her straddle him. She did not
understand what he wanted but she did it because he
wished her to and because she longed to have him close.
He kissed her, one hand tight around her hip, the other
around her head. His fingertips dug at her bound hair.

"Dear God, why this infernal braid?" he cried as
though in suffering.

She laughed.

He fumbled with the hair ribbon. "I will give you
anything." His voice was very rough. "Half—three-
quarters—*all* of my worldly possessions if you will but
help me here."

She stilled his hands and easily unfastened the tie.
"I don't want those things." She set to unbuttoning his
breeches.

"Oh, duchess, duchess," he groaned, spreading her hair over her shoulders, his gaze heavy with desire. "You may be the death of me yet."

"I shan't allow you to die because of me again."

"I am dying now because of you." His chest rose hard. "Touch me. Touch me now or watch me perish."

"Another threat?" Her fingertips strafed his abdomen and the hard muscle there flinched.

"It is a threat only if you would regret my death." He breathed unevenly. "Arabella, I beg of you."

She touched him. Desperate though she had been to hold him off again and again, now she wished only to please him.

It was not what she expected. He moaned his pleasure, which she had thought he must feel, but she felt pleasure deep in her too as she touched him, exploring. He covered her hand with his and showed her what he wanted, moving her hand on him until he released her and aided her with the thrust of his hips instead.

"Is this all you want of me?" she said with a shaky voice.

"Yes— *No*." His voice was strained. "God no."

"Then what?"

"I want you to get on me." His hands came around her hips. "But first . . ." He tugged the chemise from beneath her behind and dragged it up. Her arms and hair caught in it. He held her still, arms raised, hair spilling everywhere. "Oh, God, duchess."

"I cannot see your face," she laughed behind the curtain of her hair, "but you sound pained."

"Pain, yes." His hand encompassed her breast, warm and teasing the nipple. "Yes." Then his mouth was on her, around the nipple, hot and wet. He bit lightly. Pleasure rippled through her.

"Free me."

He dragged the nightrail off. Her hair fell in cascades. He twined a lock around his hand and by it he drew her to him.

She smiled and it felt glorious to allow herself for this moment to enjoy happiness. "Then you are, after all, the sort of man who will drag a woman to your quarters by her hair?"

"Not when she has already invited me into hers."

"I did not invite you. You picked the lock."

"The door was unlocked. You expected me." His fingers stroked a tress from her brow. "You fight me. But you wanted me to come."

She took his hand and placed it on her waist, and then with her other hand she found his arousal. She went up onto her knees and he said nothing as she fit herself to him, but he watched her face and his breaths were uneven. It was not the same as she remembered it from the beach after those first moments of pain. He was enormous and she was awkward.

His hand tightened on her waist. "Arabella, let me—"

She pressed her lips to his and he sank his fingers into her hair and held her to him as he kissed her.

"Come, beauty," he said against her lips. "Open for me. Let me give you what you seek." The tip of his tongue traced her lower lip, his hand curving around her breast. He stroked a thumb over the nipple and she shimmered like raindrops within. She bore down on him and was stretched, then full, then overcome. There was so much of him. Too much in her body and too much of him in her raw heart.

"You will not break." He tilted her head back and kissed her throat as she sought breaths. "You were made for this," he murmured, his mouth hot on her neck, his fingertips trailing down her belly. "For me."

His thumb slid through the hair on her pubis and

stroked her intimate flesh. She heard herself make a sound, a whimpering moan, and could not stop. He caressed her and spoke to her softly, and she pressed to him, desperation surging in her.

"More," she whispered. "Please."

He thrust her onto him. She moaned and went onto her knees then took him inside her again. Deep, in the back of her throat and everywhere, he pleasured her. He was solid, his hands strong, and she wanted all of him at once. She held his face in her palms and kissed him and greedily took him farther into her. She wanted more. She wanted him inside every part of her.

When the moment came, he held her, and she did not shatter into pieces or break or fight him. Instead she clung to him and when she would have cried his name, she bit her lips.

His skin glimmered with sweat, his chest rising and falling in heavy breaths. She ran her palms down the contoured muscle to his belly and allowed her fingers to cover the wound so near to where they were joined.

"You lived," she whispered.

"I was well motivated." He stroked the hair back from her face and pulled her to him. He kissed her tenderly, gratefully, she thought. Her heart was too full.

She drew away and separated them, and he lay back on the mattress and released a great breath. Cold in her damp skin without his body to warm her, Arabella wrapped the coverlet around her and curled up on her side facing him.

"Have you had what you wanted, Captain?"

His eye was closed but a smile lurked at the corner of his mouth. "I have had what I wanted, little governess." His voice was a quiet rumble, as though he were already half asleep.

"I am leaving here in the morning."

"The hell you are."

"I am."

"How?" He turned his head then rose onto his elbow to face her. "Will a caravan of wandering Gypsies arrive and steal you away?"

"There will be no stealing away. I will simply leave as I arrived, through the front door, in a carriage."

He stroked a fingertip along her shoulder, pushing the coverlet down her arm, his gaze following. "I don't believe you. But if I did, I would not allow it."

"Will you instruct the servants not to let me go? Will you lock the doors against my departure?"

His nostrils flared like an angry horse. "No."

"Then I will leave."

He got off the bed, and pulling his breeches over his tight buttocks and fastening them, moved to the bell-pull and snapped it down. "Then you will need sustenance for your journey," he said in an unremarkable voice, with the same lordly charm he used with the rest of his houseguests. He took up the dressing gown he had draped over a gilded chair and shrugged it over his shoulders. It was black and satin.

She sat up, drawing the bedclothes with her. "Even dressed as a lord you look like a pirate."

He smiled and went to the door. "If you believe I look like a pirate, then you've never seen a real one."

"Have you known real pirates?"

He went into the corridor, drawing the panel nearly closed behind him. But his speech with the servant he had summoned was sufficient to announce to the household that they were lovers, if the gift of the tiara had not already.

He returned, closed the door, and crossed to the hearth.

"I was eleven years in the navy during wartime," he said, placing a fresh log on the grate then taking up the fireplace poker. "I have known everyone."

"You were heir to a dukedom. Why did you go to war?"

He settled in a chair before the restored fire. The scarred side of his face was lit with gold light. "My uncle wed a young bride. I was never expected to be the final heir. In any case, after the Treaty of Paris, I withdrew from the navy."

"But you did not return to England. And you did not answer my question."

"I was at Cambridge when my brother escaped his guardian and disappeared into France."

"France?" In the middle of war against England.

"Though I tried for a year, I could not find him, protect him. I . . ." His brow drew down. "Gavin Stewart was our family's physician for many years, and a friend. He suggested that I put myself to good use instead of fretting to distraction." He rubbed a hand over his face, pressing his fingertips momentarily against the scar. "And I am fond of boats."

"Did you . . ." She had never imagined he had lost someone too. "Did you ever find your brother?"

"He found me. By then I had control of an allowance through the property my father gave me, although not yet my fortune. But my brother was still too young to claim independence from the man who had been our guardian after our father's death, and our uncle, who was our legal guardian, refused to intervene. So I sent Christos money."

"You sent money into France? Was that not illegal?"

"And so we return to the subject of pirates." He grinned but there was little real pleasure in it, and although he sat relaxed, his hands draped over the chair arms were tight.

"Where is your brother now?"

His eye shuttered. "Paris, I believe."

A knock sounded on the door.

"Ah," he said. "Sustenance arrives."

He brought the tray inside himself, not allowing the servant to enter, and he set it on the bed. She removed the silver lids.

"This is enough food for half-a-dozen people," she exclaimed.

"Or one underfed governess." His voice was quiet.

She looked up from the delicacies before her to his face and saw a mixture of satisfaction and vulnerability. The back of her throat tightened.

She ate, and she drank the wine he poured for her. He leaned back on the bolster with a silver plate of ripe purple figs balanced on his flat belly, the dressing gown falling in satin folds to either side, and Arabella lost her appetite for anything but watching him. She wanted to caress him with her mouth as he had done to her. He made her blood run hot and fast and he frightened her. With him, she could forget everything. She could forget even her need to know who she truly was. She had denied it for weeks, fought it and him, yet still she fell.

She pushed the tray to the bottom of the bed and crawled toward him. Afraid to touch him and renew the feelings from before, she only lay down on her side and watched him.

"Luc . . ." *I love you.*

He set the dish of fruit aside, bent over her and kissed her. "Call me by my name again, beauty, and I shall give you a dozen tiaras. A hundred."

"You cannot purchase me."

"I do not wish to purchase you," he murmured against her neck. "I wish to make you happy."

"Diamonds will not make me happy." She held onto his shoulders as his kisses descended.

"What, then?"

"I want to know my family," she whispered the truth finally that she had never spoken aloud to anyone.

"Your adoptive father, Reverend Caulfield, pastor of a poor parish in a tiny border hamlet," he said. "Your elder sister, Eleanor, spinster scholar. Your younger sister, Ravenna, in service to—"

She pushed him off. "How do you know this? I never told it to you."

His brow creased. "It was not difficult to discover, duch—"

She pressed her fingertips to his lips. "You mustn't call me that."

He kissed her fingers, then drew one into his mouth. The caress of his tongue on the sensitive pad echoed between her thighs and in her toes. She closed her eyes and let herself feel what he did to her. *Just this.* She must want only this now, not anything else of him. Now that she knew her weakness, she could guard against wishing for more. She could still save herself from being completely lost.

He set his lips to her palm, then to the tender inside of her wrist. "How then shall I bring you happiness, little governess?"

"Let me go." She stretched her neck and he kissed her shoulder, pushing the coverlet aside then entirely off her.

"I cannot." He traced a trail with his tongue between her breasts, then he circled the swell, and finally the hungry peaked nipple. "Everyone would think I was a terrible scoundrel for seducing the governess then discarding her. Would ruin the reputation of the family, you know."

She arched to his kisses on her belly, breathless. "You tease but you do not understand."

"I understand that when I am with you, inside you, there is nothing else." His hands circled her hips.

"There is always something else."

"What else is there but your speaking eyes, your glorious hair, your sharp tongue—"

"My mistrust of you."

He urged her knees apart and placed his mouth upon the inner curve of her thigh. "Your scent of roses."

My heart that can now be broken.

He bent to her and his tongue skimmed her most tender flesh and she gasped. "Your intoxicating flavor." He licked again, slowly. Her back bowed.

"What—" She struggled for breath. "What are you doing?"

"Tasting you." He dragged his tongue across her. "Intoxicating myself upon you."

It was perfect pleasure, soft and wet, and she was drowning. "I am not brandy."

"You are heaven. My heaven." He sucked gently and she almost jumped off the bed. She clutched the bedclothes and held herself still and he sucked on her until she was blind with the pleasure and weak with yearning for more than this alone.

"This must be wrong." She struggled for control beneath the caresses of his mouth, fighting her need.

"Trust me, Arabella," he said and his hands held her securely.

She wanted it. She wanted to be his whole world as she feared he was now hers.

She let him do to her with his tongue what he wished, and she cried out when the pleasure came through her, rocking her body with such force that she could not withhold her cries. He came into her then, his thick shaft driving into her without tenderness or murmured encouragement this time, but urgently. He thrust hard, then harder. After the soft seduction of his mouth she welcomed it, and she imagined he needed her. She pulled him to her.

"My God, Arabella," he growled. "You drive me mad." His shoulders caped, and with a powerful moan he finished inside her.

He did not release her at once. Instead he wrapped his arms about her and held her beneath him, and dipped his brow to her shoulder. She ran her hands along his damp sides, memorizing the texture of his skin and the shape of him. When her fingers came to the wound, he sucked in a sharp breath. He pulled away but his gaze remained upon her.

"You should not have done that," she said.

"I could not stop myself from doing that."

"In that manner," she clarified, touching a single fingertip to his side.

Moving carefully, he drew the coverlet over her. "I am undisciplined."

Another lie. He was so thoroughly confident of the discipline he imposed on his crewmen and friends and servants that he could not even fathom deviation from his will.

She closed her eyes and turned her face into the bolster. He touched her brow, stroking back a lock of hair, his fingertips lingering on her cheek for a moment before he drew away.

"Why do you mistrust me, duchess," he said quietly, "when I would give you everything?"

"Why do I mistrust you," she whispered, "when you lied to me and continue to withhold the truth from me?"

She needed him to deny it, to assure her that there was nothing he was hiding about the reason for their wedding that had been done in such haste, and why his injury was kept such a secret.

He said nothing and she pressed her face into the linen that held the scent of him.

"Will you accept the diamonds as my wedding gift to you?" he said quite seriously.

"I cannot."

He left her then. She had expected him to leave, but the bedchamber grew cold swiftly. She pulled the blanket around her, burrowed into the mattress, and waited for sleep.

Chapter 13

Lord of the Manor

$\mathcal{A}$re you in there, your grace?"

Luc cracked his eye open. His valet stood in the open doorway of the boathouse. The sunlight framing his compact silhouette suggested midday.

Luc leaned forward on the cushioned bench and rubbed his face in his hands, then through his hair, shaking himself awake.

"What is it?" After a night of making love to a beautiful, passionate woman, he ought to feel spectacular. But his side hurt like the devil and despite all she had remained intractable.

"A letter arrived this morning from Canterbury, your grace, and another from Mr. Parsons." With military precision Miles proffered the correspondence. Luc scowled. His valet's gesture reminded him too much of how Arabella had thrust that blasted tiara into his hands the night before.

He had made a mistake. Yet another mistake with her. She was too proud to be cajoled. But what the woman wanted from him he could not fathom. He had never met a female who didn't turn sweet over jewels. Or seduction. Apologies hadn't even worked.

He took the letters. "Coffee. Pack. Traveling coach. In that order."

"I have taken the liberty of instructing the butler to instruct the cook to prepare another breakfast for you and several of your guests who have arisen late due to the festivities last night. Before she departed, her grace—"

"The *comtesse*."

"—and her royal highness breakfasted—"

"Departed?" Luc's head snapped up.

His neat little man milliner of a valet—dressed to the nines, starched and pressed as impeccably as he'd always been when playing cabin steward on Luc's ships—turned his nose into the air.

"Her grace wished to pay a call on the mantua maker in the village. I assured her that the woman would come to her, but she expressed a keen desire to be away from the house, where it seems she is the object of considerable scrutiny today among your guests—my lord Bedwyr and his and her royal highnesses excepted, of course."

Luc rubbed his sore neck. Sleeping upright never bothered him unless he slept particularly hard. But his troubles were not truly physical. She had exhausted his body while leaving the rest of him a confounded mess. She was passion and courage all bound up in fiery audacity that he now knew masked tender uncertainty. With each touch and each word she made him need her more.

She might fight it, but she had no choice in the matter. She was his.

He flipped over the letter in his hand and snapped apart the wax seal. "The mantua maker?"

"Her grace wishes to purchase a traveling gown."

"Mm hm." The letter was short and to the point. The archbishop would not accept the validity of the wedding ceremony performed by a priest of the Roman confession under uncertain circumstances and without benefit of the proper banns being read. Lord Westfall was urged to make haste in returning home and securing a license to wed Miss Caulfield with the full sanction of the Church of England or risk the danger of placing his mortal soul in peril through the sin of fornication.

Luc stuffed the letters into his pocket.

Damn prelates. It was a mere inconvenience. If she conceived a child now, however, it could prove a problem if it were born short of nine months from the valid wedding date. He would take her home to England swiftly and the issue would be moot.

He stood up and Miles stepped back for him to exit the boathouse. He had not returned to his bedchamber after visiting hers. After she rejected his gift again, he had come here without thought. Only close to water did he sleep well. His ancestor who purchased Saint-Reveé-des-Beaux might have had him in mind.

Miles trailed after him, his Louis XIV heels clicking along the dock beneath the arched tunnel.

"Will we be departing soon for England, your grace?"

"Today. And stop calling me your grace. It's disrespectful and not a little ghastly."

"Very well, your grace. And shall I instruct Monsieur Brissot to place the household under her grace's authority when she returns?"

"From the dress shop?"

Miles's pencil thin brows rose. "Do forgive me, your grace, but I assumed her grace would return here from

Paris. But perhaps she will continue on to join you in England afterward."

"After what? What in the devil are you talking about, Miles?"

"Monsieur Brissot informed me that her grace intended to depart for Paris today directly from the modiste's."

Luc halted and closed his eye. He should have known. She had told him. He was a complete fool. Worse, he was blind. And he was coming to see his little governess's character in a whole new light.

"When did she leave for the village, Miles?"

"Not a quarter of an hour ago."

"Make the arrangements for our departure today. We will spend the night at Guer and wherever else necessary en route to Saint-Malo. And inform Lord Bedwyr that I will be leaving within the hour. If he wishes to join me and my wife, he should be prepared to depart then."

He strode across the dock and into the bottom level of the house where the clean, alive scent of the river mingled with aromas from the kitchen of baking bread. He would find her at the dress shop and then . . . He didn't know what. She was irrationally resistant. What woman did not wish to be a *comtesse* and next in line to be a duchess, for God's sake?

She wanted him; that was obvious enough. He need only maintain a steady course until he came within range of her guns. Then, as the more experienced of them, he would outmaneuver her. As he had already tried to do several times without any success.

Perhaps if he got himself stabbed in the belly again she would come to him willingly. He must keep that in mind.

Striding to the stable, he pulled the letter from

Combe's land steward from his pocket. Parsons had nothing good to report. The estate was producing well enough; its income had not decreased. But the tenants were suffering. The famine was over, yet the farmers seemed to be less prosperous than ever, laboring hard yet with nothing to show for their struggles. And now Parsons was begging him to see to it. The estate could not wait until the matter of the title was settled. The steward was calling on him to return as swiftly as he could.

He must, and not only because the estate was in dire straits. Parsons's letter confirmed it: Theodore had named his old friend and Adina's brother, Absalom Fletcher, principal trustee should Adina's child be a boy. Luc had been named second. In two months time the Bishop of Barris could be de facto master of Combe for the next two decades.

Luc needed no further urging. He was eager to return to England. As eager as he was to know who it was that wished him dead.

The men who attacked him on the beach had not done so in retaliation for their companion killed in the alleyway. That she had come upon them first was sheer unlucky coincidence. Or perhaps they knew she had come off his ship and meant to use her to draw him out. But the sailor Mundy continued to insist that he had been hired in Paris without any notion of what he was to do with the poison once he acquired it. Tony and his lieutenant both believed him.

In England he would find answers.

Cam found Luc in the stable as he led his horse into the yard.

"I understand that your lovely *comtesse* has gone shopping for gowns." He leaned a shoulder into the door and crossed his gleaming Hessians. "How you could convince her to do so when I could not, I confess I am in astonishment."

"Perhaps my powers of persuasion are greater than yours."

"I doubt that."

Luc adjusted the stirrup and ran his hand along the animal's sleek withers. "You are not dressed for the road."

"I regret that you must make this journey without me, cousin." He glanced across the drive to where Princess Jacqueline rode with a groom. "I have interests I must see to here before returning home."

Luc frowned. "She is an innocent, Cam. And, I needn't add, she is also our friend Reiner's sister."

"Then why did you add it?" He grinned lazily. "But that is not the sort of interest I have in her, so be at ease, oh ye stalwart defender of ladies' virtue. Excepting one lady's virtue, of course."

"Take care how you speak of my wife," Luc grumbled.

His cousin accepted the reins of a great white horse from a groom.

"Perhaps it is you who should take care, Lucien, or despite the effort I have gone to on your behalf, you will lose her."

"I will take that under advisement." He put his foot in the stirrup and hauled himself up, biting back on the pain.

"I see we are not yet entirely ourselves again, are we?" Cam said. "Are you certain you wish to set out quite yet?"

"I'll not hide in a hole like a frightened rabbit." He shook his head. "Tony's men have returned from Paris. Christos is not to be found there."

"And the portrait found on the Sicilian who tried to kill you?"

"I haven't an explanation. But Christos did not hire them."

"You are concerned for him. For his safety," Cam said, because he knew.

"Always." He ran a hand around the back of his neck and released a hard breath. "When I saw him last, in December, we quarreled."

"I assumed as much."

"Did you?"

"I could not imagine another reason for you to accuse me of misusing a girl of twelve," Cam said smoothly. "After our little conversation with swords, I wrote to your brother. He told me that before you found me in Paris you and he had spoken about Fletcher."

"I asked Christos to return home with me."

"He refused, presumably."

"He said he had no wish to return to England or Combe." He took a breath. "My reaction to finding you with the girl was a regrettable consequence of my . . . frustration."

"Ah." Cam tapped the crop against his boot.

"How is she?"

"My ward is well, thank you. She would send you her affections, I'm sure, but she is deathly afraid of you. Understandably so."

"If you had shared with me that you had a ward for whom you were searching before I found you alone with her in a Parisian brothel, I might not have reacted quite so violently."

"I daresay. What were you doing in that brothel anyway, cousin? Never seemed quite your style."

"I was looking for you, of course. I hoped that since you were in France you might talk sense into my brother." His scar ached. Both of them. "He hides here from the past, and yet I don't think he remembers any of it, Cam."

"Would that you did not as well."

Luc met his cousin's sober gaze. "I was a fool to have imagined even for a moment that you resembled Fletcher in any manner."

"Ah, he finally apologizes." He sighed theatrically. "What a tangle. And now you are blind because of it. But it cannot have been helped. The timing was unfortunate, and you are predisposed to protect the weak. You poor chivalrous fool."

"Enjoying the speechifying, cousin?"

"Merely reveling in the freedom that my lack of concern for the good of others provides me."

Luc pressed his mount forward. "Enjoy the chateau, Cam, if not the princess." He spurred toward the village.

THE DAY WAS warm and the door of the dressmaker's shop stood open. Luc halted upon the threshold, heart in his throat.

In the center of the shop she stood with her face turned away from him. She wore a gown of blue the color of the sea that caressed her subtle curves and exposed her neck and arms and the dip of her bosom. Her hair, cinched with a simple ribbon, tumbled down her back in waves of fire.

"Wear that on our wedding day, duchess, and make me the happiest man alive."

She whirled toward him, her eyes wide. "Wedding day?"

He stepped into the shop. "A formality for the Church of England's satisfaction only, of course. But it must be done soon. We depart today."

"To—" She looked to the modiste. The woman's brows were perked high, her attention eager.

Luc gestured for her to depart. She curtsied and scurried into the back room of the shop.

Arabella stood poised upon her toes as though she would flee momentarily. "You wish to depart for England today?"

He seemed to study her. "Unless it interferes with your travel plans."

She pressed her hands against her waist. "You said that you would not stop me from going."

"I said I would not allow my servants to lock you into the house. I said nothing of myself."

"You will *lock me in*?"

"Of course not." He walked toward her. The ruby and gold ring on its plain ribbon glimmered in the crevice of her bosom. "Did you intend to leave alone?"

"Yes. The princess offered me the use of her brother's traveling carriage and the escort of a guard."

"Ah. You concluded that you could not effectively escape me in my carriage. That is, your carriage."

She said nothing.

He reached up and she did not flinch as he took the ring in his palm and studied it.

"Is it the man who gave you this costly trinket that you go to meet in Paris?" The words came from him without his will. "Is it he that draws you away in such haste?"

She did not respond at once. "If you imagine me capable of giving myself to you as I did last night while intending what you suggest," she said, "then you have much to learn about me, my lord."

She might have slapped him. He dropped the ring but could not move away from her. She bound him as surely as if she used lock and key. He could not outmaneuver her. He was moored securely.

"Why do you wish to run away to Paris, Arabella?" His heart beat hard. "What do you hope to find there that I am not able to give you?"

"A man." Her hand wrapped around the ring and she held it tight to her breast. "But not as you imagine."

"What do I imagine?"

"I have told you before what sort of woman I am, yet you do not believe me." She backed away. "Tell me, my lord, is it my hair alone, the harlot shade of red, that convinces you I know nothing of chastity or constancy? Or is it my beauty? Or perhaps it is the immodesty I have exhibited with you. It would not make you unique among men to believe the worst of me. Rather, quite common."

"I do not believe the worst of you."

She met his gaze squarely and her chin tilted up in that manner that caught at his chest.

"I will be a good and dutiful wife. I will go with you to England and give you what you wish when you wish it. Upon my word your heir will be yours in truth."

"I never imagined it would not be," he managed to utter.

"Then why did you come here to stop me from going to Paris?"

Because he needed her. Because he could not allow her to come to harm. Because he felt insane—not with her but without her. Because for the first time in his life he felt truly unbalanced and that, perhaps, his brother's madness was not unique, that he would succumb to it as well.

The delicate sinews in her neck constricted. She came forward, moved around him and out the door, leaving him with only the scent of roses and the hated, familiar biting pinch of helplessness.

IN THE MOST unremarkable manner, as though informing her of the weather, at the inn en route to the port Luc told her he would not share her bed. His wound, he said, troubled him greatly. It required more time to heal.

On the road to Saint-Malo he rode alongside the carriage she occupied with Mr. Miles and a maid. They dined alone at the inn, and he spoke to her with civility about the villages they had passed through and the port city to which they were traveling and at which they would await Captain Masinter's ship to convey them to Portsmouth. After dinner he saw her to her bedchamber, bowed, and with a simple "Good night," left her.

In much the same manner, they traveled the remainder of the journey to Saint-Malo. In the walled port city they awaited the *Victory*'s arrival before Luc's impatience seemed to get the best of him. Mr. Miles informed Arabella that they would not wait for Captain Masinter's ship, but that the *comte* had hired passage on a ferry. They would continue on their way to England in the morning.

They embarked early. By noon the sky had grown gray and by mid-afternoon the rain began. By dusk the ocean swells were lapping at the windows of the cabins belowdeck.

The captain of the little ship assured her it was a mild storm and that since the winds were holding steady they were making excellent time. Mr. Miles offered her tea that sloshed in the cup and ran over the table. He mopped up the spill, all the while telling her tales of gales of a much worse caliber that the *comte* had mastered easily.

"Of course, his lordship is not captaining this ship, if a sloop can rightfully be called such," the little man said with a persnickety shake of his head. "So who is to say, my lady, how well we will fare in this squall?"

The night came and she lay on her side in bed, curled around her clasped arms, her hands cold and damp and her breaths fast. The ship creaked madly and the wind howled, buffeting the sides of the vessel until she could not hear even her thoughts. Exhausted, she sank into nightmares of violence and suffocation.

She awoke to the dark and the warmth of Luc's hand curving around her cheek. She reached for him and held onto his fingers like a buoy.

He sat on the edge of the bed and drew her into his arms.

"Do not be afraid, little governess," he said beneath the groaning of the ship and the lash of rain. "I am here. You are safe." He held her securely. She burrowed her face against his shirt and clung to him. He kissed the top of her head and smoothed his hand over her hair and down her back. "You have survived much worse."

The beat of his heart, strong and steady, played against her cheek.

"You know about the shipwreck?" she whispered.

"I know," he said against her hair. "A man in my position must know something of the woman he weds."

She lifted her head and in the darkness saw only the shadow of his features. "It matters nothing to you? That I know nothing of my real family? That my mother sent three tiny daughters off to an uncertain fate? That she might have been a—"

He captured her lips.

He kissed her softly, tenderly, then deeply until she

wrapped her arms around his neck. With great gentleness he bore her down to the mattress. Her fingers tangled in his hair and he drew her close with his hands around her waist and she pressed against him. Strong and solid and warm, he held her to him and kissed her so that she knew only his mouth and her need for him and the safety to be had in his embrace.

"Thank you," she whispered, because she had never said it to him.

He kissed the corner of her lips, then beneath her ear, then her neck. Then he shifted his arm to pillow her head.

"Sleep now." He stroked a single fingertip across her cheek. "I promise, when you wake the sky will be clear and you can again practice standing atop with all the advantages of gravity on your side."

She curled into the shelter of his body, the rolling of the ship only a distant threat.

"Will you control the weather now as you control everything else?" she murmured, sleep catching her eyelids and dragging at her limbs.

"Not everything," he whispered, and touched his lips to her brow. "Not my duchess," she thought she heard. "Not my heart." But she knew she was already dreaming.

THE DAY BROKE splendidly clear and blue, as he had prophesied. Arabella awoke alone. She climbed from the cot, dressed, and made her way to the top deck. He was there and greeted her as he had since their journey began: pleasantly, lightly, impersonally.

He did not come to her at night again. When they set out on the road to Shropshire, he once more rode alongside the coach. It was a magnificent carriage, lined in the softest fabrics and leather, with gold tasseled curtains on the windows and the ducal crest on the door. Four gorgeous black horses drew it, their harnesses gleaming, and the coachman and postilion both in crisp blue livery. The innkeeper at the posting house at which they stopped along the road fell over himself backward to make the *comtesse* happy after the *comte* made it clear that was his only wish. Her husband immersed her in luxury and comfort and showed her no more intimacy than he did the servants.

She did not fight it. He had thwarted her plan to visit his brother in Paris. In some manner she would manage to discover the truth behind their rushed wedding, even if he remained distant from her.

By Jacqueline's account, Christos Westfall was an entertaining companion when he lived at the chateau during her time there. An artist, he kept mostly to himself in the studio he had in a cottage at the far end of the gardens tucked just inside the woods, and the princess had seen him little. She said he was mercurial of spirit and devoted to his brother, who adored him equally. He seemed unexceptionable.

But because of his unsuitability to inherit, Arabella had married his brother. She hoped the Duke of Lycombe's ancestral estate would offer her answers. The Duke of Lycombe's heir clearly would not.

ARABELLA HAD PASSED the residences of dukes in London many times, but she had never seen a duke's country house. The first glimpse of Combe dropped the bottom out of her stomach.

Presiding over emerald fields dotted with sheep and here and there a solitary grand old oak, it sprawled atop the crest of a hill in a majestic expanse of turreted limestone tempered with windows that caught the rays of the waning sun and set the house afire. Below in the valley, a curving river reflected the house's brilliance like a protective band.

She dragged her gaze away and to the man astride his horse nearby. He had halted and sat very still with his face to the house.

The drive wended its way around the north side of the hill until it came level with the house. Passing between rows of ancient firs, abruptly it burst into the open and Combe was right before them, towering and broad and indisputably ducal.

Two dozen servants stood in perfect lines from the colonnaded front door along either railing of the front stairs. On the bottom step stood Arabella's sisters and a huge black dog.

Ravenna ran to the coach, Beast loping in her wake. Eleanor followed. The moment the footman lowered the step, Arabella burst from the carriage door and fell into her younger sister's arms. Eleanor grasped her hand and they embraced without speaking. There was too much to say. It had been too long.

Arabella pulled back.

"Welcome home, *duchess*," Ravenna exclaimed, her dark eyes laughing.

"I told her that she must call you 'my lady,'" Eleanor said, squeezing Arabella's hand tightly, "but the servants are all insisting you will be a duchess soon anyway, and in any case our sister will do whatever she wishes no matter what I say." She smiled sweetly.

Arabella kissed her on the cheek. "How I have missed you both." Her voice broke.

"But you have been busy, it seems," Eleanor said with another smile, and glanced over her shoulder.

Luc was dismounting. He gave the reins to a servant and came forward.

"Good Lord, Bella," Ravenna whispered, "he is smashingly handsome. I thought you were determined to marry some scabby old hoary-headed prince, but this is— *Ouch*."

Eleanor's hand slipped away from Ravenna's elbow. She dipped her golden head and curtsied deeply as Luc came to them. "My lord," she said.

"Miss Caulfield." With great elegance he bowed.

Ravenna offered a quick dip of her knees. "Hello, Duke. It's lovely to have you in the family. Who had the mending of that wound across your eye? Whoever he was, he made a wretched hash of it."

Luc's beautiful mouth slipped into a one-sided grin. He bent to give her old dog's furry brow a rub. "I thought the same thing, Miss Ravenna, so I had him dispatched. Easy to do aboard ship, you know. One just pushes a fellow over then sails away very quickly."

Ravenna's mouth split into a sparkling smile. "I approve, Bella. You may keep him."

Eleanor smothered her chuckle.

"Now, ladies," he said, "if you will allow me to make your sister acquainted with the household, I will then give her fully into your keeping."

He did not look at Arabella as he took her hand upon his arm and introduced her to the butler and the housekeeper.

The housekeeper looked fondly at Luc. "May I say, we are all happy you've come home to stay . . . your grace."

"Thank you, Mrs. Pickett. I am happy to be home." He looked it. He looked like a man at perfect ease. "But you mustn't put the cart before the horse. 'My lord' will do."

"Mr. Parsons is eager to speak with you, your grace," the butler said with perfect sobriety. "He awaits you in the study."

None of the other servants arrayed on the drive batted a lash.

"See? I told you," Ravenna whispered to Eleanor.

Luc shook his head, then led Arabella up the steps and through the front door. Inside the majestic limestone mountain all was color and elegance and glittering light, from carved wooden stair rails and gilded furniture, to portraits of gaily gowned ladies and richly robbed gentlemen, to harlequin tiled floors and beeswax candles burning in bronze sconces and crystal chandeliers.

"What do you think, little governess?" he said quietly. "Does this offer you sufficient material to command, or should I build an additional wing and hire a dozen more servants?"

She looked up at him. His eyes shone not with teasing or censure, but pride and guarded hope. Her heart ached—the heart that he owned despite her efforts.

"This should do," she managed.

He smiled slightly and withdrew from her. "Miss Caulfield, Miss Ravenna: she is all yours."

The housekeeper gave Arabella a tour of the house, her sisters and Beast in tow.

"And you thought you could only have a palace if you married a prince," Ravenna whispered as they passed through a library lined with books up to the ceiling.

"She never wanted a palace," Eleanor said. "Only the prince."

"This is not my house," Arabella said quietly. "We are only here to see to matters until the duchess's baby is born."

"This is Ellie's favorite room in the whole pile." Ravenna gestured around them at the bookshelves. "Of course."

"Dinner is served at five o'clock, your grace," Mrs. Pickett said when she finally brought them to the door of her bedchamber. "If that suits you?"

"It does. Thank you, Mrs. Pickett. But you mustn't call me your grace," she said gently. "It is disrespectful to my husband's aunt."

"Yes, your grace." The housekeeper curtsied and left. Arabella turned to Eleanor, seeing again her sister's thinning gown, which she herself had sewed for her five years ago. Ravenna's gown was newer; her employers paid her a decent wage. But it was serviceable for the work she did with animals and not at all elegant.

"You are biting the inside of your lip, Bella," Eleanor said with a dip of her brow. "What troubles you?"

"Do the servants behave well with you?"

"Of course they do. We are your sisters."

But she had worked in too many aristocrats' houses not to know the truth of it, and she did not speak her thoughts: that the people of Combe must have anticipated another sort of woman to be their new mistress. An actual lady.

"Clearly they do not have trouble imagining you as the duchess," Eleanor said. "Indeed, they seem eager to do so."

Arabella straightened her shoulders. She would fulfill their expectations. Dreaming of a prince, she had trained herself to this life for a decade. She would be a duchess, or least a *comtesse* living in a duchess's house. He would not have cause to be ashamed of her.

"Come now. Let us see your bedchamber." Eleanor took her hand and opened the door. "We haven't been allowed a peek since it was being redecor . . ."

Her words died. They all halted in the doorway. The bedchamber was spectacular, elegant and understated and utterly feminine with ivory and pale pink silk damasks, subtle gilding on the dressing table and chairs, sparkling mirrors, and draperies of the thinnest rose-colored gauze embroidered with gold on the four-poster bed and windows.

"It's . . ." Ravenna's mouth opened and closed.

"Fit for a princess," Eleanor said.

Arabella's stomach was tight. "You say it was recently redecorated?"

Ravenna moved into the chamber. "The duke sent instructions weeks ago, apparently."

Weeks ago, before she had known she was a *comtesse* or a duchess-in-waiting. When she had still believed herself to be the widow of a merchant shipmaster.

"Look, Bella." Ravenna opened a door and poked her head inside. "A dressing chamber bigger than Papa's entire cottage in Cornwall. The duke could house his carriage team in here. And it's bursting with gowns. You could wear a different one each day for a month, I daresay." She looked across to the opposite wall. "Presumably that is the door to his chambers."

Eleanor grasped her hand. "Now, Bella, I will ring for tea and you will tell us how this all came about."

LUC DID NOT join them for dinner. The butler informed Arabella that his grace had been called elsewhere on the estate by pressing matters and wouldn't her grace like to enjoy the 1809 Burgundy with her *cailles en sauce de la reine*?

Later, in a nightrail of the finest silk edged with soft lace, she curled up on her wide mattress and listened to the sighs of the fire and sounds of her husband in the next chamber. Finally his door closed and his footsteps receded down the corridor.

SHE BREAKFASTED IN her bedchamber alone until Ravenna scratched on the door. She wore a gingham skirt with large pockets, a shirt, and snug waistcoat. Her wild, silky hair was bound back in a ribbon.

"Can I share your chocolate?" Ravenna asked. "Cook hadn't made any by the time I went out to the stables. It seems that servants don't drink chocolate in ducal mansions." She wiggled her black brows and took up Arabella's cup to sip.

"Do servants drink chocolate where you live?"

"I certainly do. But the nannies spoil me because I spoil their dogs." She smiled.

"Do you like them?"

"I do. And they adore me. I am the only person in England, apparently, that knows how to keep twelve pugs, three wolfhounds, and two parrots all healthy and happy at once. It's quite a marvelous arrangement."

"But you are not entirely happy there."

Ravenna picked at the toast. "You have always seemed to know my thoughts, Bella," she said. "But I will make do. If you want to worry, worry about Ellie, shut away in Cornwall doing Papa's work for him."

"Is she unhappy?"

"She says she is content." She shook her head.

A maid came to the door. "Your grace, the duke wishes you to join him at the stable in three-quarters of an hour. He asks that you dress to ride. May I assist you?"

STANDING AT THE grand entrance to the long, low-roofed complex of stables, he watched her with leisurely and undisguised appreciation as she approached across the drive.

He bowed. "That habit suits you."

She smoothed her palms over the velvet skirt the

color of the autumn sky. "It is almost as though it had been made with me in mind."

"Isn't it?" He smiled.

"I should be wearing mourning for your uncle."

"Rather, you should be wearing diamonds for me."

"You—"

"If you tell me that I mustn't attempt to purchase your obedience with pretty gifts, I will probably say something to the effect that I fully intend the beautiful gowns for my pleasure without any regard as to whether they would bring you pleasure too, or indeed ensure me any sort of other advantage. Then you will glower at me—"

"I do not glower."

"—and we will quarrel and you will stalk away—"

"I do not stalk away, except perhaps twice."

"—and I shan't be afforded the pleasure of enjoying the beautiful gowns after all. So do spare me the chastisement, duchess." He bowed. "If you will."

"I do not wish to chastise you." She could not bear this teasing when her heart was so confused. "I only wish to thank you for the gowns. For my chambers. For all that you have given me. But especially for bringing my sisters here."

He studied her face for a moment, his expression unreadable. "It is my pleasure." He turned to the broad door of the stable from which a groom was leading two horses. She touched his arm to stay him, and he paused and looked down at her hand. She withdrew it.

"Luc, it is unseemly that the servants address us as they do, as though the matter of the inheritance were already settled."

"I have mentioned this to them several times, to no avail. They seem to have made up their minds on the matter." His gaze glimmered. "And I have been told that servitude does not always teach a person meekness."

Her cheeks warmed.

"Now," he said with a gesture to the horses, "I aim to show you about Combe." He did not invite her; he expected her compliance.

"I would like that."

He assisted her to mount, wrapping his hands around her waist and sending her heart into her toes. She longed for the closeness he had given her on the crossing and for his hungry gaze. But he gave her only the most cursory glance as she arranged her skirts about her legs and the horse's rear, and then he moved to his own mount.

The October day was fine, bright and crisp with only the barest wisps of clouds above the river, and the path was well trodden. It skirted a copse of ash and oaks and cut across a field speckled with sheep toward a farmhouse far in the distance nestled in a nook in the hill. Spread out from the house, regular, carefully furrowed plots sat fallow beside budding crops of winter wheat.

"Combe has been in my family for four centuries, though the present house was built in the time of Elizabeth," he said. "I thought you might like to pay a call on some of the tenants. The family that lives in the house there, the Goodes, is the most prosperous." Atop his great black horse, surveying his family's land, he was at perfect ease, just as he had been on the deck of his ship.

"You seem familiar with the estate. Did you visit here often before you went to sea?"

"Until I was ten years old I lived at Combe with my parents and my brother. My father had a house in the North, but my mother preferred to reside here, where news of France traveled more swiftly from London. It was rarely good news in those days. Not for her family."

He was silent then, and only the horses' hoofs in the

grass and the chatter of birds and an occasional sheep's bleat stirred the air.

"When you were ten, did your father move your family to that house in the North or to London?"

"When I was ten my father died in a carriage accident. In her grief, my mother fled to France to take comfort in retrieving her family's lands from the Jacobins that had come into power. My brother and I were sent to live near London in the house of our aunt's brother—our uncle the duke being something of an indolent pleasure-seeker and not wanting to be bothered with raising two young boys."

"It was that guardian you spoke of at Saint-Reveé-des-Beaux, wasn't it? The man from whom your brother later fled?"

"The very one." He gestured to a man coming from the farmhouse. "There is Goode now. I knew his father, Edward, when I was a boy. Thatcher has precisely the look of him."

Thatcher Goode greeted them with deference, then studied her with a shrewd eye. He was neatly dressed and well spoken, but his clothing was worn nearly to threads at the joints and his cheeks were lean. He took them into the house and made known to them his wife and three sons.

The house was bare, the walls stripped of decoration, and the floors cold wooden planks without benefit of rugs. Mrs. Goode offered Arabella tea. The brew was thrice boiled and the biscuits lacked sweetener. Mrs. Goode and the eldest boy watched her carefully and said little.

Riding away from the farmhouse, Luc seemed in a pensive humor and Arabella remained silent.

The next tenant family and their house were much the same.

"Luc . . ."

He lifted his head from a study as they rode toward the bridge that crossed the river. Away in the distance the enormous house on the hill gave no hint of the state of the estate's residents.

"Duchess?"

"Are they all Quakers?"

His brow drew down. "No," he said shortly.

"Forgive me. I thought perhaps it might explain the bareness of their homes, and their—"

"Poverty?" The reins were tight in his fist. "No. They are simply poor."

"But the fields have all been harvested and there must be at least four hundred head of sheep and lambs—"

"It is the first I have seen of it." He rubbed the scar beneath his hat brim. "But it is worse than I even imagined."

"You knew of it before?"

"My uncle's steward reviewed with me the estate's books last night." He looked at her. "I regret that I was unable to join you and your sisters for dinner."

"I should say that Combe's starving tenants are more important than quails in queen sauce," she said. "Is Mr. Parsons dishonest?"

"He is frightfully honest. He simply does not know where the tenants' income is going. He wrote to me monthly before my uncle died, pleading for me to intervene. I could not; I had no authority. And . . ." He paused. "Other matters kept me abroad longer than I intended."

Matters about which he would not speak with her.

"They are afraid," she said. "I can sense their fear. And suspicion. But . . . I do not believe it is directed at you."

He regarded her carefully as their horses clopped across the bridge.

"I—"

"You mustn't trouble yourself with it," he said, and turned his face to the road. "I will see to it."

"I haven't anything else with which to trouble myself. You have taken me from a life in which I worked every day to a life of thorough leisure. I am unaccustomed to inactivity."

"In time you will find sufficient diversion."

He spoke then only of light matters, complimented her on her seat, and later on the gown she wore at dinner and the arrangement of her hair, and she wanted to seize him and shake him back to the moments of candid honesty he had briefly shared with her. Then she wanted him to hold her in his arms and make love to her as he had before, as though he needed her.

But she did not demand his honesty and he did not do as she dreamed. Neither did he invite her to ride out again. The moment of intimacy was gone. She saw him only at dinner when he was all charm to her sisters and all masculine appreciation for her. He was the lord of the manor and she was merely the ornament who shared his house.

Chapter 14

Enticements

$\mathcal{A}$rabella did find many activities with which to busy herself during the days.

"The house has been without a mistress for more than a year," Mrs. Pickett explained while by the light of candles they sorted through piles of ancient laces and linens, separating the hopelessly threadbare pieces from those that could be salvaged. "I've tried to keep all in order, but I wouldn't presume to make decisions that the lady of the house should."

Arabella did not bother pointing out that she was not in fact the lady of the house, for she already knew it would have no effect, and instead stifled a yawn. But she was not yet exhausted enough to fall swiftly into sleep. Imagining even a moment lying in bed waiting in vain for him to come to her drove her hands again to the heap of musty table linens. Her sisters had gone to bed, but Mrs. Pickett seemed eager to pursue the project.

"I understand that my husband's uncle was ill for some months before his death," Arabella said conversationally.

"Yes, your grace. For fourteen months, in fact, though at the beginning he could still walk about the grounds, of course. It was only in the last months that he grew too ill to leave his chambers."

"Fourteen months?" Her hands halted. "Did the duchess not live here during all that time?"

"No, your grace." The housekeeper kept her eyes on the piles of linen, but her lips pursed. "Her ladyship chose to reside in the house in town."

It was hardly uncommon for aristocratic husbands and wives to live separately for part of the year. But the duchess had clearly abandoned her ailing husband.

"I suspect she visited regularly, then." Arabella knew Mrs. Pickett would think her a gossip. But she must know. "It isn't such a long journey, of course."

"No, your grace."

No?

She could not ignore the opening the housekeeper was clearly offering her. "After he fell ill, did she ever visit Combe?"

"She is not fond of travel." Mrs. Pickett's eyes connected with Arabella's for a brief, instructive moment.

Suddenly the servants' insistence that Luc was the duke did not seem like impertinence. And the suspicious eyes and sunken cheeks of the Goodes and the other tenant farmer families became clear now. They did not fear Luc. They feared Adina's unborn child, who they believed to be illegitimate.

Even so, why fear a helpless infant? Unless they actually feared the infant's guardian.

"Mrs. Pickett." She pressed a crease into a lace doily, set it on the pile, and turned to the housekeeper. "Do you know where I might find the comte now?" She was ashamed to admit that she knew nothing of her husband's activities in the evenings after dinner. But Mrs. Pickett's eyes gleamed with satisfaction.

"He is in the study, your grace."

It required all of Arabella's discipline not to run.

She knocked, then entered without waiting. Buoyed by her newfound knowledge, she refused to accept the distance that he had imposed on her.

Lit by a single lamp on the desk and a blaze in the hearth, and furnished with masculine elegance, the study was sunk in shadows along walls paneled in walnut and painted above in dark blue studded with silver stars. A pair of bookcases flanked the marble mantel, and he sat before one of them, books and journals at his feet and an open volume across his knee. On a table at his elbow rested a silver tray with a crystal bottle and glass of amber liquid. Another, empty glass sat on the tray.

He looked up and seemed to take a moment to focus.

"Duchess," he only said. His voice was quite low.

"What are you . . ." Her courage faltered. The firelight cut dramatically across his scar and he looked very large, male, and forbidding. When she did not see him frequently she forgot how his nearness made her weak-kneed. "What are you reading?"

He closed the book and set it beside him, then stood. "Nothing, now that you are here. I imagined you long since gone to bed."

"I was engaged in a project with Mrs. Pickett."

"Industrious of you so late at night."

"It is not particularly late." She glanced at the gold and crystal clock on the desk beneath the darkened panes of the window. She moved toward it. "It is barely eight o'clock." She drew the drapes closed. She knew he watched her, and it made her heart beat fast. She turned to him and he stood exactly as before, tall and broad and impossibly distant.

"Won't you offer me a drink?" she said. "Or is that empty glass intended for another?"

"For whom else would it be intended? The butler is a Puritan and my valet turns up his nose at French brandy."

She tried to smile. "Brandy?" Now her hands were shaking.

He lifted a brow. "Would you care for some?"

She nodded, and as he poured she moved to the other side of the hearth. She traced her fingers nervously along the gilded leather bindings of the books.

"It seems as though you are engaged in a research project." She turned, and he caught her hand in his. His touch was warm and complete. He tucked the glass into her palm, wrapped her fingers around it and released her. But he did not move away. She'd not been so close to him since the Channel crossing.

"I was reading about crop rotation and corn yields," he said close to her, the scents of brandy and leather about him. "Fascinating stuff. Shall I share what I have learned with you?"

She lifted the glass to her lips and sipped. "I would like that."

He leaned closer. "While I would like instead to admire this fetching confection you are wearing. Very nice . . ." He lifted his glass and with the back of his knuckles stroked across the bared skin of her bosom above the tiny fichu. She shivered. " . . . design," he finished, and held her gaze as he raised the glass to his mouth.

"Are you drunk?" she whispered.

"Only on you, duchess. Only ever on you."

She pressed a palm to her hot cheek.

"Too close to the fire?" he said. "You can step away if you wish."

"I do not wish." She wanted to plunge into it. "I want to help you."

"With what?" His voice now hesitated.

"I want to help you with whatever it is you are doing to solve the mystery of the tenant farmers' losses. Tonight I—"

"Tonight when you were sorting linens like a housemaid?"

"How do you know that was my project?"

"I make it my business to know what you are doing always, little governess." He passed his cheek across her hair. "Mm. *Eau de* dust. Positively enchanting."

"If you don't like my *parfum domestique* then do not stand so close to me," she said without any conviction whatsoever.

His breaths stirred the hair that had fallen out of its combs and over her brow.

"Why are you laboring like a servant, Arabella? Do you believe that in this manner you are fulfilling your role as the dutiful wife, as you promised?"

"You . . ." she began, then made herself speak the words. "You haven't given me the opportunity to be a dutiful wife in weeks."

He seemed to go quite still.

"If I offered you the opportunity," he said, "would you welcome it out of duty?"

"No. In fact I fear that if you made that offer I would prove a disappointing wife, for there would be nothing of duty about the welcome I would show you."

He set down his glass on the mantel. Then his hand came around her waist and slipped up beneath her arm. He held her firmly and his thumb stroked beneath her breast. His touch, even so slight and teasing, made her tremble.

"Arabella?" His voice was husky.

She closed her eyes and felt his hands on her and never wanted him to stop. "Luc?"

He seemed to breathe her in. "Will you marry me?"

A sob rose in her throat. She knew it was ridiculous, but a ray of pure happiness lit her.

"I understood, my lord," she said shakily, "that we were already married."

"Will you marry me?" His other hand encompassed her waist and he spoke against her cheek. His thumb caressed again, stroking up the side of her breast. "Yes or no?"

She wanted to see his face, but he held her tight. "Yes."

He cupped her breast and slipped his thumb across the nipple, and she felt her body open for him.

"You may have carte blanche in planning the wedding," he said. "Anything you wish. But it must be soon. Three weeks."

Only long enough for the banns to be read.

"Anywhere?" She could barely hear her voice or feel the books pressing into her back. His hands were on her, teasing her, and she ached for him.

"Where else but here?"

"London," she said. "The Thames. On the deck of the *Victory.*"

His hands stilled and she wished immediately that she had not spoken. He drew back and his expression was inscrutable.

"Can it be done?" she asked unsteadily.

"Yes." His smile was slow. "Yes, I believe that can be done."

"Uh, ehm." A man cleared his throat at the door she had left open. "My lord?"

Luc backed away from her, and Arabella thanked God for the darkness that hid her flaming cheeks.

"Arabella, this is Mr. Parsons, the land steward here at Combe," Luc said without any suggestion in his voice that a moment ago he had been fondling her breast and proposing marriage to her. But he was a lord, and a lord could make love to his wife on the high street if he so desired and the traffic would be obliged to go around him. "Parsons, this is—" He glanced at her and a slight crease appeared beside his mouth. "My *comtesse*."

Mr. Parsons bowed. "My lady." He said to Luc, "Information has arrived from Mr. Firth—"

"Excellent, excellent." Luc started toward the door. He gestured for her to follow. "My dear, this fellow's dedication to the estate is untiring, but in good conscience I cannot keep him up past his bedtime doing business. I will see to this swiftly. Would you excuse us?"

His hand was on the door. He was dismissing her.

"Of course," she only said, her palms cold but cheeks aflame with shame. Considering all, she had been astoundingly foolish. He wanted her in his bed; she had known since their first encounter that he wanted her like that. And their marriage must be validated by the Church of England. She was a foolish girl to dream for the first time in her life of a tender proposal and a fairy-tale marriage. She had been wrong to read what had just happened as anything but business. Nothing had changed. He would not give her his confidences.

"Good night, Mr. Parsons," she said, and left the chamber without revealing the tempest inside her.

THE CANDLES WERE guttering when Luc opened the door between their bedchambers. He came to her bed, pushed aside the gauze curtain, and shrugged out of his dressing gown. Then he took her hand and made her stand before him, her feet buried in the thick rug. First he removed the lace cap on her head, then the pins in her hair, then her delicate nightrail.

He touched her everywhere the glow from the embers of the fire touched her skin, and then everywhere it did not. He made her need him until she wished for nothing else but him, then he thrust inside her and made her need him more.

When it was over and she lay beside him, her body soft and damp with satisfaction, she watched the shadows flicker over his body glistening with sweat, and she touched him. With her touch she silently asked him for more.

He turned her onto her belly, pulled her hips off the bed and, with great skill and breathless force, gave her quite a lot more. She pressed her palms into the headboard and cried out his name again and again as she shattered.

He kissed her shoulders, her back, and the curve of her buttock as she sank into the mattress and into sleep. He left her without having spoken a word.

In the morning the maid brought breakfast. Arabella snuggled into the covers with her cup of chocolate and the glorious soreness of her body, and took up the note on the breakfast tray. The stationery bore the embossed crest of the Comte de Rallis. With a smile—then with sinking breaths—she read.

Duchess,

I am off to town. I will return to retrieve you in three weeks.

L.

Arabella had only cried when the man she did not yet realize she loved was dying, then again when she was grieving over him. Such a little thing as virtual estrangement and abandonment could not now rouse her tears, even after he had used her in a manner in which a man might use a harlot, and even if her heart felt as though it had been wrung out with the laundry. She had allowed him that use of her body, willingly and eagerly. And she had again unguardedly allowed her heart to hope. The emptiness inside her now was her own fault.

She rose from bed, dressed, and went to find her sisters. In the corridor outside her door a liveried footman sat in a chair. He was a large young man with sun-bright ringlets, tanned skin, and somber eyes. She recognized him, but not from the downstairs staff. He was from the *Retribution* and he had accompanied her and Mr. Miles to Saint-Reveé-des-Beaux.

He stood and bowed. "Yer grace."

In the breakfast parlor she found her sisters. When she left them sometime later, the curly-headed footman was waiting outside the parlor.

He followed her from place to place for the remainder of the day.

"Bella," Ravenna said as they walked in the garden, "did you know there are two footmen following us?"

"One is in fact ahead and one is following," Eleanor corrected.

"I think I would much rather be a poor animal doctor than a duchess after all, never mind your spectacular stables," Ravenna said with a glimmer in her dark eyes. "To be watched all the time would be positively unnerving."

"I don't think they are watching her, Venna," Eleanor said. "I think they are protecting her."

Arabella was not quite so certain. Luc wanted an

heir, and she had nearly run away once before. But long before that, aboard his ship, he had assigned the cabin boy to keep a watch on her, so that he would always know where she was, he had said.

She chewed on the inside of her lip. "Ellie, Venna?"

Her sisters shifted their attention from her liveried watchdogs to her.

"I am going to London."

SHE DID NOT travel to town immediately. A day visiting the tenants across the expanse of Combe became two, then three, then a sennight. The farmers' wives served her weak tea and sugarless biscuits and warily welcomed the baskets of fruit, bread, cheese, and nuts that she brought from the great house.

She delayed her journey again, and the following week visited the same houses, carrying sweets for the children, honey, and table linens. Mrs. Pickett looked on with disapproval, claiming that farmers did not need fine lace and embroidery. But the farmers' wives warmed to Arabella, and she no longer needed to guess at their emotions to know their thoughts; they began to tell her.

During the duchess's long absence from Combe, they said, her brother had come in her stead. On occasion he preached in the parish church.

"You've never seen a finer gentleman, milady, or heard such sermons as the bishop's," Mrs. Lambkin said, pouring tea into cracked cups. "He talked all about giving to the Lord the best of what He gives us." Her gaze slipped to her son sweeping the hearthstone. "In thanks, you see," she added, "so He'll know we're not hard-hearted and send us famine again." Her hands quivered on the pot. The boy's lean jaw was tight. "We can't hope to be given bounty when we won't first give to the Lord, can we now, mum?" Her eyes lifted to Arabella's briefly then slipped to the burly footman-guard standing just inside the door, then out the window to the other footman leaning against a fence. The woman's eyes were shadowed with fear.

Arabella tracked down Combe's land steward at the mill. She made conversation about the estate and he was proud to speak at length about it. But she found could not ask him outright the question she had foolishly never thought to ask her husband; she would not shame herself or Luc in that manner.

At the house, no one had much to say about Christos Westfall. The elder servants remembered him as a beautiful little boy overly fond of drawing and prone to periods of intense thoughtfulness. All assumed that, grown, he had left England for his mother's country, never to return.

RAVENNA ANNOUNCED THAT she must be off to check on the nannies and their pets before she joined her sisters again in London for the wedding.

"I will send an invitation to your employers," Arabella said.

"Then they will happily attend. They adore spectacles."

"I should be leaving as well, Bella," Eleanor said. "Papa writes that he anticipates my return daily. I will ask him if he will travel to London with me for the wedding."

"He will no doubt be obliged to remain with his parish. And I am certain he will be unhappy to see you go again."

"He will." Eleanor embraced her and kissed her on both cheeks. "But wherever you are, there too I shall be."

She stood on the drive and waved at the coach that bore her sisters away.

"Joseph," she said to her guard as she walked into the house. He was a giant of a young man, with arms the size of tree branches and legs like the trunks. "Tell your partner Claude that we will leave for London tomorrow."

He bowed. "Yes, yer grace."

CHEROOT SMOKE HUNG thick in the air and men grunted in various stages of inebriation, frustration, and satisfaction as cards passed through hands and bills, trinkets, and vowels passed across the tables. Luc swallowed the last of his whiskey and blinked to clear his vision.

It would not clear. How a man could win a game of anything in this cloud of vice he'd no idea. And how he could bear another night of such excruciatingly dull hedonism without gaining anything for his efforts he was equally at a loss to predict.

He wanted salt air, sea breeze, and a ship deck beneath his feet. Or alternately he wanted country air, wind off the Shropshire hills, and his wife's body beneath his own.

Actually, scratch the first. The second was all he needed.

But this must be done. Of all the clubs in London, Absalom Fletcher, the Bishop of Barris, exclusively frequented White's. The last time Luc saw his former guardian he'd said he would cut him into little pieces with a sword and feed the bits to sharks if he could but get him aboard ship, so he thought it prudent to approach him in this subtle manner. Paying a call on him at his house near Richmond probably wouldn't do. The old duke's man of business, Firth, had requested a meeting of Combe's trustees to which Fletcher had not yet responded.

The last had not come as a surprise to Luc. It seemed that the Bishop of Barris employed a one-thumbed coachman. The coincidence with the sailor Mundy's claim that a one-thumbed man had hired him in Plymouth was too great.

Thus Luc's current strategy. A skillfully prepared accidental meeting might accomplish what a direct assault never could.

After a fortnight, however, he was beginning to doubt.

"Probably too busy fleecing innocent churchgoers out of their bread money to come out for a game of cards," Tony muttered, his hand on his hip. The doorman had collected his sword.

Cam strolled into the chamber and wandered over. "Care for a visit to the opera tonight, gentlemen?" he said casually.

"Good God, Charles," Tony groaned. "All that screeching is enough to send a man back to war, no matter the temptations of the green room. If we must see a show, why not Drury Lane?"

"I have just heard that tonight's patrons of the opera might be even more interesting than the denizens of the stage or the green room." Cam lifted a speaking brow at Luc.

Luc threw in his hand and stood. "I am particularly fond of the production tonight. What show is it again, Bedwyr?"

"Hamlet."

Luc cast him a glance over his shoulder.

"They don't play *Hamlet* at the opera house." Tony followed, weaving a bit. He peered at the doorman who gave him his sword. "Do they?"

"Only the version in which Uncle Claudius employs a coachman who is missing a thumb to murder Hamlet," Cam said.

Tony screwed up his brow. He turned to Luc abruptly. "Hamlet murders Claudius."

Luc shot Cam a scowl. "And dies moments later."

Tony shook his head. "Charles, you rapscallion, there is no version of *Hamlet* that includes a coachman."

Luc's carriage pulled up before the club and they drove to Lycombe House, where he changed his clothes for the opera. Not black for his uncle Theodore, who had allowed the people under his protection to starve, but brilliant blue with a silver and yellow striped waistcoat. Cam's tailor had clapped in glee when Luc selected the fabrics. He would be the most fashionable man about town in the robin's egg blue and canary yellow.

Luc could barely look at the avian monstrosity. But if it roused the sober, severely disciplined, and righteous Fletcher's ire, he would wear a basket over his head and trot up Bond Street braying like an ass.

In point of fact he was an ass. He should not have left Arabella so abruptly. He should have invited her to come to London with him. But he could not protect her when all he wanted to do was ravish her.

Not true. He did want to ravish her. Often. But holding her in his arms during the Channel crossing had been nearly as satisfying. And watching her take tea with the tenant farmers' wives and listening to her speak with their children and hearing her laugh with her sisters made his chest hurt the way it did when her chin ticked upward with courage. And when she looked at him and her eyes asked questions that made his gut ache and stole his reason, he could not think straight.

Ravishing her was infinitely easier, especially when they didn't speak.

His hands were clumsy on the neck cloth. Miles *tsked* and gave him another. He botched that one too.

"If your grace would allow me—"

"I can tie my own damned cravat, Miles," he growled.

"All evidence to the contrary, your grace. Perhaps a glass of brandy would soothe your grace's nerves."

"My grace's nerves are just fine." He grappled with the linen. He didn't need more to drink. He needed a fiery-haired temptress with cornflower eyes hazy in passion, supple raspberry lips, and the softest—

He snapped himself out of fantasy. He'd had to leave her at Combe. With Absalom Fletcher and his one-thumbed coachman in town, she was safest where she could not get caught in the cross fire between him and his would-be assassins.

"This is futile," he grumbled to his cousin as they took their seats in the box Cam had arranged at the opera house. "I'm wasting my time. Even if I do speak with Fletcher, he is unlikely to confess to hiring men to murder me in France."

"Too true." Tony nodded and drew a flask from his uniform pocket. "And I'll say, these shenanigans are becoming tiresome, Luc. That hideous coat is an absolute travesty. And that little race we enacted in the park yesterday to shock the bystanders left me fifty guineas in the hole."

"Luc will pay it back to you," Cam said.

"I wouldn't have it! He won it fair and square, galloping down Rotten Row like hell was after him."

"All for show," Cam said, producing a folded journal page. "It was in the gossip columns today, as hoped. I quote: 'Are the sporty amusements and defiance of mourning for his uncle merely the fruit of Lord W's frustration over his continued distance from the ducal title? Or—'"

"Idiocy," Luc scowled.

Cam casually surveyed the theater's gathering patrons. "But what tack do you propose to take instead, cousin? Break into his house to search his private documents for proof that he tried to kill you?"

"Not a bad idea, though terribly illegal of course." Tony quaffed from the flask and carefully wiped his moustaches with a kerchief.

"Anthony, you are occasionally a perfect imbecile. It is a wonder the Royal Navy allows you a dinghy."

"Exceptional service to the king," Tony pointed to the ribbons and medals pinned across his chest. "Order of the Garter and whatnot."

"God help our empire," Cam murmured. "Any word from your brother, Lucien?"

"Nothing. But I have cause to believe he sailed from France a fortnight ago. My man in Calais—" His tongue failed.

From across the theater a slender man with a narrow face and a cloak of black velvet slung dramatically over his black coat, cravat, and knee breeches met Luc's gaze. He scanned Luc and his eyes narrowed.

Luc's palms were cold and slick. Streaks of silver swept across Absalom Fletcher's temples, enhancing the portrait of severe, sophisticated sobriety. But otherwise he looked like the same pious, sanctimonious bastard Luc had last seen a dozen years earlier.

On that occasion he had gone to him demanding to know where Christos had gone. Not yet a bishop but striving diligently by making connections in Parliament and at court, the priest denied having any knowledge of the boy's whereabouts. He recommended that if Luc found his brother he should return him to his house in Richmond, where Christos would be cared for in a manner suitable to one so prone to hysterical fits.

If Luc had had a sword on him at that moment he would have drawn. Fletcher never admitted to doing wrong, saying that he had cared for them as well as a humble man might, teaching them discipline and the inner strength that they must have to be men of character in the world. Weaponless, instead of murdering him Luc had spat on him.

Then he bought a commission in the navy.

It was the obvious choice. Christos had fled to France, beyond Luc's protection while the war raged. So Luc had gone to the only place where as a child he had been able to escape Fletcher.

Like Luc's wife, the Reverend Absalom Fletcher was terrified of open water. And he could not swim.

Now Luc saw nothing of the drama unfolding on the stage below, or the other patrons tittering over his defiance of mourning, or felt anything except the burning in his gut. But at the break in the show he leaned back in his chair as though merely enjoying the company of his companions, and waited.

Fletcher did not make him wait long. Within minutes he made his austere way around the theater to Luc's box.

"Lucien, what a delightful surprise." His voice was the same urbane purr that it had been twenty years earlier. A large elegant cross of gold rested on his chest, glittering with tiny diamonds. "Charles." He flicked a glance at Cam, then at Tony. "Captain." None of them bowed. Luc silently vowed that if Fletcher lifted his bishop's purple-gemmed ring to be kissed, he would break every bone in his hand.

He perused Luc's clothing again.

"You do not wear mourning out of respect for your uncle, I see, Lucien." His steel gray eyes were stern with censure.

"No doubt because I did not respect him," Luc could only say. His fists and throat were tight.

"News has come to me of your race in the park yesterday, and of your frequent gaming these past weeks."

"Has it?"

"Do you care nothing for your aunt's grief or the honor due your family's name?"

"I suppose I don't."

"It seems you have not changed since you were eighteen, Lucien. It is with great regret that I discover this. I had hoped you would grow to be a man of character, but alas the seeds I attempted to sow in your youth fell on infertile ground."

Luc couldn't breathe. "It would seem so."

"It is a pity. I shall have to counsel my sister to withdraw her support for your trusteeship of the estate during her son's minority. A duke cannot disport himself as you, and the child must have guardians that teach him well and minister to his lands wisely until he is of age."

"Since you purchased your way into the episcopate, Fletcher, have you now a direct conduit to God's ear," Luc ground out, "so that you already know that my unborn cousin is a boy?"

Not a muscle on the bishop's face twitched. "I understand that you have wed a woman of the serving class, Lucien." He shook his head dolefully. "You were never even as intelligent as your brother. As feeble-minded as he was, at least he knew when to behave according to his best interests."

Luc saw red.

With a glance at Cam, Fletcher left the box.

Tony gripped Luc's arm, holding him still.

"Gentlemen," Cam said, "shall we depart? I've had

enough of the show for this evening and I happen to know a bottle of brandy with our names on it."

"Two bottles, I hope," Tony said. "The soprano gave me the most dreadful megrim in the first half. If I'm obliged to suffer through the second half I may go deaf. Then you would have to go mute, Charles, and the three of us could set up a booth at the fair and sell tickets."

"I will go mute when you do away with that ridiculous sword, Tony."

"Sword's been in the family for—"

"Decades. Yes, we know. That doesn't make it any less vulgar than the day it was forged."

"Eye of the beholder and all that."

"Speaking of, aren't whiskers like yours disallowed in the navy?"

"Got a special privilege, don't you know."

"Special privilege?"

"Already told you, Charles: king, Garter, whatnot. You ought to have been there. Ceremony was excellent. Now *that* was a rollicking good show."

They were speaking nonsense to cover his silence. Luc was grateful.

HE DID NOT accept Cam's invitation to drink himself into temporary oblivion, but made his way home. Already in her confinement, Adina was ensconced in a suite of chambers in Lycombe House, surrounded by servants and attended by a companion, and Luc had seen little of her except in initial greeting. The ducal physician reported that the infant was growing as it should, and the duchess was well albeit weak. It was entirely possible, he told Luc in private, that this child might survive. The duchess required rest, however, and not to be bothered by anything other than the most inconsequential matters.

But Luc could not delay speaking to her any longer. As he had hoped, his charade of hedonism had sufficed to draw out Fletcher's threat: his intention to cut him out of the business of the estate and raising Adina's son—if it were a son—was clear. Legally the bishop could not remove him as a trustee of Combe; Theodore's will was inviolate. But Fletcher was the principal trustee and he must hope to gain through it, and he saw Luc as an impediment. Perhaps he imagined that if Luc were out of the way, Christos could be controlled—whether as heir to the child or as the duke himself if the child were a girl. Then Fletcher would control the dukedom.

According to Theodore's will, Adina now had no legal control over Combe or her child's future. Given his uncle's devotion to the beautiful young wife with which his old friend Fletcher had provided him nineteen years earlier, Luc wondered why.

It was time to have an interview with the expectant mother.

When Luc returned to the house, Miles fussed over him like a mother hen. He drew the coat from Luc's shoulders and held it pinched between forefinger and thumb.

"Burn it. The waistcoat too, and all the other carnival clothing I've worn this past fortnight."

"Thank heaven!" Miles deposited the coat in the corridor. "Then am I to understand, your grace, that you encountered the bishop tonight finally?"

"Yes, but how you know that—" He shook his head. "Bedwyr."

"His lordship saw fit to inform me of the reason for your atrocious decisions concerning fashion and amusements of late, your grace."

"I'm sure he did." He drew on his dressing gown and went to the door.

"The library tonight, your grace? Or will it be the parlor? I have given each a careful survey and I find that the chairs in the library are considerably more comforta—"

"Don't henpeck, Miles."

"Forgive me, your grace."

"I always do."

"Your grace, I must inform you of—"

"No more tonight, Miles." He pulled open the door, more exhausted than he'd been since he was lying on a cot recovering from a stab wound to his gut. "I am finished for tonight."

HE AWOKE IN a cold sweat from a dream of his six-year-old brother riding along the crest of Combe Hill and falling off a cliff that was not there in reality. A woman appeared on the hill, walking steadily upward, her fiery hair catching the sun. Luc called to her but she did not answer. She marched toward the crest.

Arabella's name was on his lips as his eyes flew open. Daylight peeked through the library curtains.

He reached for the half-finished glass of brandy on the table beside him and swallowed it. Warmth trickled into his chest, but not enough to offset the ache in his side and neck. Miles had clearly never slept in one of the library chairs.

He went to his chambers and dressed in a black coat, black breeches, and black cravat. His uncle, who had never believed the stories Luc told him about Fletcher, did not deserve it, but the Lycombe name and his *comtesse* did.

Miles minced around him, clearly bursting to speak.

But years ago Luc had warned his valet that if he ever uttered a word before breakfast he would discharge him from the *Victory*'s thirty-two-pound gun into the depths of the ocean.

In the breakfast parlor the servants seemed peculiarly alert. He didn't know them; they were all Adina's people and he'd had only a fortnight in the house. But every time he looked up from the paper or his beefsteak he caught them peering at him with bright eyes.

Their attention soured his appetite. He pushed away his plate and went up to Adina's suite.

Her sitting chamber was rich with gold and yellow to compliment her guinea curls, brimming with satin pillows and lacy fripperies and dainty porcelain gewgaws, and awash in flowery perfume. In the middle of this gluttonous mass of feminine excess—like a lissome ebony candle lit with the purest flame—was his wife.

Chapter 15

Secrets

*A*rabella arose, smoothed out her black skirts, and fought with the competing desires to throw herself into Luc's arms like a strumpet or remain coolly aloof like a *comtesse*. He looked tired, the scar pulling at his right cheek tighter than usual and his tan skin pale. Dissipated, if what she had been hearing from Adina's companion was true.

When she was not with the duchess, Mrs. Baxter spent her time flitting about from drawing room to drawing room gathering the juiciest *on dits*. According to that gossip, the new duke had spent a fortnight in town carousing and gaming and getting up to larks, and generally dishonoring the Lycombe name. It was so thoroughly unlike the man Arabella knew, she hadn't believed it.

He did not, however, appear happy to see her.

He bowed and said graciously, "What a bevy of angelic beauty I have stumbled upon. But perhaps this is not Earth. Perhaps last night I perished in my sleep and I am now in heaven." His gaze shifted to her and his brow creased.

"Lucien, how lovely of you to come see me," Adina bubbled, and laid out her hand to be kissed. Luc bowed over it then nodded to Mrs. Baxter. Her lashes fluttered at least twenty times as she drew out the word *commmte* as though she could not bear to give it too little emphasis.

Arabella was obliged to offer her hand as well. His was warm and strong, and she had missed him so powerfully that now she could feel the life waking up in her again. He brushed his lips to her knuckles and her toes curled.

"Comtesse," he said.

She curtsied. "My lord." Her voice did not quaver. *A tiny triumph.* She could manage this. There were more important things at stake than her foolish, girlish heart that wanted to beg him to love her, or her body that remembered quite tangibly what he had done to it when they had last touched.

He released her and she regained a trace of the composure she had practiced so diligently until meeting Luc Westfall caused her to throw it all to the wind. She knew she should still be angry and hurt and stalwart in defending the walls around her heart. But those walls had long since crumbled. She could only stand atop their ruins and hope the invader was merciful.

"How perfectly delightful," Adina cooed. "To witness the reunion of a love match." She sighed, then her sparkling eyes went wide. "Dear me, Arabella, I have not yet asked you how you and Lucien came to fall in love. Your beauty speaks for itself, of course, and we know how gentlemen value that above all other feminine traits, do we not?" She nodded in wisdom. Mrs. Baxter mimicked her.

"You are quite right," Luc said. "Men are profoundly stupid when it comes to beautiful women."

Arabella's heart thumped. He could not mean to be cruel. But his jaw was tight.

"Adina," he said. "I should like to speak with you at your leisure. After, that is, I enjoy a private moment of reunion with my wife."

Adina's smile glowed. "Of course, Lucien," she said, and waved him toward the door. "Do take this lovely girl away and kiss her soundly. It shan't be said by anyone that I would stand in the way of lovemaking." She laughed softly and gaily. Mrs. Baxter giggled.

Arabella felt embarrassed for them both, nearly forty yet behaving as foolishly as fifteen-year-olds. But she was likewise guilty, wishing for kisses from the man who had tied her in knots of infatuation for months, this despite her plan to wed a prince and his careless and dishonest treatment of her.

Luc gestured her before him. In the corridor, Joseph's straight back jerked even straighter as they passed.

"Cap'n!"

"At ease, Mr. Porter."

Luc opened another door and again ushered her in. It was a parlor, furnished with an eye for high style and little comfort. She went into the middle of the chamber and did not sit.

He closed the door and came to her until he stood quite close. "I told you I would return to Combe and bring you to London myself."

She clasped her hands together. "Ah. It seems you have learned the art of my disagreeable greetings."

He did not smile. "Why did you come?"

"To make plans for the wedding, for which you gave me carte blanche if you recall. And to share with you information that I have learned which could not safely be conveyed in writing."

His brow dipped. "Information?"

"Adina's child is not your uncle's."

His eye widened. "She told you that?"

"No. I learned it from Mrs. Pickett and had it confirmed by nearly everybody else on the estate."

"You *asked* them?"

"Of course I did. I first went to the house servants and inquired as to the true identity of the child in the duchess's womb. Then I made the rounds of the gardeners and stable hands. And finally I put the question to the tenant—"

His hand jerked forward as though he would take her arm, then it dropped to his side. "How did you learn it?"

"By some very complicated addition and subtraction. I was a governess once, you see, and my arithmetic is especially good. I realize it may seem remarkable to you, a man with some university education, but I can count above the number nine. It is so convenient to possess these little skills sometimes."

He lifted his hand again, this time to rub at the scar beneath the lock of dark hair that fell over his brow. But Arabella espied a crease in his cheek.

"After you left Combe abruptly without notice or explanation—"

"I wrote you a message."

"—I busied myself by going about to visit the tenant families—"

"Like the duchess you are well suited to be."

Butterflies alighted in her stomach. "Everybody was eager to make it clear to me that Adina had not visited the estate since before the famine, and that the old duke was too ill to leave Combe during that time. Luc, they wanted me to know the baby is not Theodore's."

"It isn't proof."

"What do you mean, it isn't proof? Hundreds of people are certain of it, the housekeeper inclu—"

"It is Adina's word against all those people, and Adina's word will carry the day." He shook his head. "I am afraid that is simply the way of it in the world of the licentious peerage, little governess."

She bit the inside of her lip. His gaze dipped to it.

She gathered her courage. "Speaking of licentious, Mrs. Baxter has heard the most astounding gossip concerning you, Lord Bedwyr and Captain Masinter lately."

"Has she? I wonder what sort."

"Gaming. Drinking. Carousing." She paused, her breaths short. "Loose women. You know, the usual."

"The usual, hm?"

"For some men." She was suddenly fidgety beneath his intense regard. "I feel like we are standing on the deck of your ship again," she whispered.

"Because you are experiencing the urgent need to clutch a railing?"

"Because you are looking at me now as you used to do then." She made an attempt to square her shoulders. "Why?"

"Perhaps because I feel like I did then," he said in a strange, low voice. "Like a beautiful little mystery wrapped in self-righteous modesty and recklessly brave determination has just landed before me and I don't know quite what to do with her."

Her heart blocked her throat. "You could—"

The door opened.

Kiss her.

"My lord? Oh. Pardon me, my lady." The butler

bowed. "Joseph said I would find you here, my lord. Captain Masinter's carriage has arrived. He awaits you on the street."

"Thank you, Simpson. I will be down directly."

The butler withdrew.

"Well, there you have it," he said easily, the intensity gone from his gaze. "There is apparently more carousing to be had, and at only eleven o'clock in the morning. Ah, the life of a hedonist on the town." He moved away from her.

"You cannot be serious," she uttered to his back.

"I am not," he said, his hand on the door handle, his head bent. "Of course. But I've nothing else to say, Arabella. So that shall have to suffice for you."

Her stomach hollowed out. "It does not. But I don't suppose I have any choice in the matter. Luc, why did you set guards on me at Combe? Do you not trust me, after all?"

"I trust you," he said.

"Eleanor thought that you assigned Joseph and Claude to protect me."

For a moment he was silent. "Did you believe her?"

"I don't know. From what do I need to be protected?"

Her foolish heart and his indifference to it.

"Tonight we will have dinner guests," he only said. "Nothing inappropriate during mourning. Only a few close friends to announce your arrival in town."

"I—"

"The housekeeper will see to all the arrangements. You needn't do anything to prepare for it except dress suitably." He looked over his shoulder. "Wear your hair down, please."

"I am in mourning. And a married woman. It would not be seemly—"

"Wear it down, Arabella." He left.

SHE SPENT SEVERAL hours that afternoon closeted with Adina and Mrs. Baxter, who took to wedding planning with gleeful enthusiasm. Adina's wan cheeks colored prettily with her excitement. When conversation turned to a debate about which florist would provide the freshest roses in November, and a disputation on how the river would not be especially odiferous in this season so they needn't arrange for nosegays, Arabella went to dress.

She had dismissed her maid and was sitting at the dressing table considering the expanse of bosom and arm that her ebony gown revealed when Luc entered.

"Ah. The lady at her toilette. A man's greatest fantasy and nightmare at once."

She tried to breathe evenly as he approached behind her and she looked at him in the mirror. He wore black well, the kerchief about his brow now a mere extension of his forbidding beauty.

"Nightmare?" she said.

"Feminine decisions, of course. For instance, which jewels to wear."

"I haven't any—"

He drew forth a box from his coat and opened it. In the mirror two strings of crimson gems glittered in tiny gold florets. "I thought perhaps since you were accustomed to wearing rubies and gold, this gift would not be rejected."

"They are beautiful, Luc."

"I imagined them glimmering from within your hair." He caressed a neatly confined lock from her brow back to the combs that pulled it away from her face. Then he captured it all in his hand and drew it away from her shoulders. "You do not wear the ring tonight," he said as though he had not before accused her of infidelity with that ring.

"I . . . No." Perhaps if she told him, he would not scorn her. But she was afraid. "Thank you. You are generous."

He set the box on the table, withdrew an earring, and dressed her with it. "A beautiful woman needs no embellishments. But a prideful man may give them to her nevertheless."

She allowed him to place the other earring on her and she turned her head to watch the gems sparkle in the candlelight. He lifted a hand and stroked her cheek softly, then her neck, then her shoulder. She drew in a steadying breath, her breasts pressing at the edge of her bodice full and round and tender with the echo of his touch. She wanted him to touch her and trust her, and to give her cause to trust him in return.

One of them must begin it.

"Many years ago my sisters and I were told that the rightful master of this ring knows our real parents. We were told that the man is a prince."

His caress halted.

"Reiner?"

She met his gaze in the mirror. "We do not know who he is, only that he would not recognize the ring unless one of us first wed him."

His hand fell away from her and moved to his neck cloth. He peered at himself in the mirror and made a minuscule adjustment to the linen. "That sounds like a Gypsy tale if ever I heard one."

"You think me foolish. And you are correct, for I was foolish to believe in the story. But I keenly wished to know my father. And I wished to know if my mother was the woman that Reverend Caulfield always said she must have been to have abandoned us. If she was a whore." She swiveled around to look directly up at him. "Do you believe me? About the ring?"

"What reason have I not to?" It was not a statement. It was a question for her.

At this moment she could beg him to believe in her fidelity. She could insist that she would never take another man to her bed like Adina had taken a lover, perhaps like her own mother had long ago, producing three so very different daughters that to believe they shared the same father was naïve. She could tell him that he needn't hide her in the country with guards to watch her every move because she would never be unfaithful to him.

But she had already told him this and he was still holding secrets from her.

She took up a lacy black shawl and went to the door. "Our guests will arrive shortly. I shouldn't like to be late." She turned and for an instant thought she saw a shadow of bleakness on his scarred face. Then it was gone. Possibly she had only imagined it.

She waited for him to come to the door and open it for her, and went down the stairs on his arm, the Comte and Comtesse of Rallis appearing to all the world like they were in perfect accord with each other.

AFTER DINNER, A sumptuous affair with a dozen removes, sparkling conversation, and much laughter, a game of cards was gotten up among the gentlemen. Alone with the ladies, Arabella negotiated the torturous trek between governess and *comtesse* with every sentence she uttered. Her guests were people of sophistication, though, and all of them affectionate toward Luc, and Captain Masinter and Lord Bedwyr's easy acceptance of her made it natural.

After midnight she climbed the stairs to her bedchamber thoroughly exhausted. Luc did not come to her bed. Lying awake, she heard him leave his bedchamber and descend the stairs, but he did not return.

After breakfast, leaning back into her cushions, the round lump of her baby protruding from her excessively slender body, Adina waved Arabella away when she offered to assist with the wedding arrangements. Mrs. Baxter busily opened invitation replies and wrote names carefully on the ever-growing list of guests. Arabella left the women to their enjoyment.

Joseph was again at her side, which she took to mean that Luc was not in the house. Accompanied by her burly footman, she made her way to the front of the house and began exploring rooms. When she came upon a modest-sized chamber furnished with a desk, two chairs, and a sideboard sporting an array of crystal carafes and glasses, she backed out of the doorway. Then she paused and went in again, shutting the door in the face of her guard, with a smile for him.

Her nerves were raw, her head aching and stomach queasy. A spot of brandy seemed just the thing to take the edge off of her agitation. Whenever it was that Luc allowed her to see him again, she would be calm and strong and not allow his teasing and secrets to hurt her.

She removed the stopper from a bottle, sniffed, her eyes sprang with tears and she coughed.

Brandy.

She took up a glass and dribbled a thimbleful into it, then made her way a chair and settled down. The pure luxury of doing nothing at ten o'clock in the morning but sitting in a comfortable leather chair and sipping spirits made her smile.

She was still smiling when she glanced at the papers piled in three neat stacks before her. She set down the glass and took up the folio on top of the stack in the center of the blotter.

*Pursuant to your intention to petition Parliament
for grant of a divorce: a complete and detailed
accounting of your wife's infidelities must be
compiled, including dates, places, names, and all
possible witnesses. In establishing her True and
Undeniable Infidelity in preparation for a hearing of this sort, you must be willing to expose her
thoroughly, including those factors in her family
and youth that could provide grounds for character assassination. There is no easy way about
this, and although I know that a man of your character will be loath to expose his family to public
censure, these are the steps that must be taken to
ensure your desired result.*

It was clearly the draft of a letter, with smudges where
the author had dipped his pen anew and words crossed
and corrected in the margins. Arabella's stomach
churned nevertheless.

It must be a mistake. Perhaps a prank? Luc would
not insist that she wed him in order to immediately
divorce her.

But he was hiding secrets from her.

She pulled the stack of papers toward her, and her
hands threw each page aside after her desperate eyes
scanned them. Her gaze arrested finally on a letter written in the same hand, another draft but signed this time.

*The lady in whom you have expressed interest is
Miss Caroline Gardiner, the eldest daughter of
Lord Harold Gardiner and Lady Frances Gardiner. A new title, the estate is fifty miles north-
west of Combe and prosperous. The portion to
be settled on Miss Gardiner is fifteen thousand
pounds, including rights to the operation of the*

mill at Gardiner Crossing. Potential investment in the mines on Lord Gardiner's lands is to be considered separately from any marriage settlement. But in my estimation the lady's portion is more than sufficient to reinvigorate the estate at this time, leaving ample surplus for future projects or to be spent on your properties in the North and in France, as you wish.

If I may, there is an added attraction: the girl is remarkably pretty and recently out of the schoolroom. As her parents are not longtime members of society, they are unaware of the exigencies that could serve as potential deterrents to the marriage. Indeed, I have it on good counsel that they will be more than eager to ally their family with Combe.

I will await your instructions before drawing up an official offer.

Sincerely,
Thomas Robert Jonas Firth, Esq.

An *heiress*?

Arabella felt astoundingly dizzy. She set the letter atop the pile and tried to draw even breaths. She suspected she would shortly succumb to panicked misery, but at present she felt only cold, metallic nausea and thorough confusion.

Luc had insisted she marry him. *Insisted.* Then he refused to give her an annulment. Then he asked her to marry him—*again*—not quietly to fulfill the requirements of the Church, but in a wedding entirely of her choice.

It made no sense. Except that Combe would benefit enormously from fifteen thousand pounds suddenly emptied into its coffers. With that money, the tenants would be round and merry in no time.

The tenants he had wanted her to know.

She pressed a shaking hand against her face. What sort of game was he playing?

Abruptly she could not be still a moment longer. She bolted out of the chair. Her head spun and stomach heaved. She grabbed the edge of the desk and swallowed back her gorge.

With a wash of pure, hot awareness, she understood. Her body was rebelling because she was no longer alone in it.

She sank onto the chair and her hands stole to her belly then to her breast. The nipple was tender, her flesh ever so slightly fuller. It was not her gown the previous night that had displayed her bosom to such great advantage. It was Luc's child growing inside her.

She smiled. Then she laughed. Then she cried.

Then she wiped the tears from her face and went to the door.

She would not release him. Despite his secretary's letters and his continued distance, she did not believe he wished to release her. She would deliver him an heir as he needed and it would have brilliant green eyes. And she would help him solve the problem of the tenants' poverty.

Armed with uncertain courage, her first order of business would be to send a footman to bring the modiste to the house. She was to be married—again—in ten days. She needed a wedding gown.

Chapter 16

The Wedding

Must be nice to be nearly a duke, Luc old friend." Captain Anthony Masinter of the HMS *Victory* stood at the helm of the hundred-twenty-two-gun man-of-war and surveyed his realm. "You can demand that the Royal Navy send its ship not only into port but up a river, for God's sake, and the Admiralty leaps to it."

Festooned with garlands of white flowers, paper lanterns, and servants rushing about, the vessel was nothing less than an elegant festival afloat on the Thames. Adina Westfall was a silly woman, but she knew the pomp that must attend such a wedding. All was celebratory.

Except his bride.

As the day drew near, she had been increasingly evasive. Claiming herculean tasks yet to accomplish, she took her dinners with Adina and Mrs. Baxter and spent much of every day in meetings with caterers, florists, and the like. Luc visited his club and met with Firth again, and tried not to crave a glimpse of her in passing. Pathetically, in the hopes of actually sitting in a room with her for several minutes, he visited Adina's chambers. Arabella was not present, but Adina was loquacious.

"Oh, Luc, you will be the most splendid guardian to my baby, whether it is a boy or a girl," she gushed. "I am delighted my darling Theodore arranged it thus."

She was not intelligent enough to be a good actor; he believed her. Fletcher had not yet spoken to her. His threats were either for show or he did not wish to distress her until the baby was safely born.

Word came from Parsons that several of the tenant farmers had requested the opportunity to meet with him when he returned to Combe. The land steward asked him how long he would be absent on his wedding trip. Luc could not give him an answer.

He sent a note to his *comtesse* . . . who lived in the same house. Nearly six years as captain of one of the navy's finest vessels, and he felt like an absolute imbecile that he could not even command the voluntary attention of his wife.

As Miles pulled his coat over his shoulders—a coat he would undoubtedly wear to dine alone—she poked her head into his dressing chamber. She wore a simple black gown that climbed all the way up her neck, and her glorious hair was braided in two thick plaits that fell over her shoulders. A Valkyrie's hair. Rather, she looked like a girl training to be a governess. Both, combined. She wore no jewels or ribbons, not on her hands or in her ears or about her neck, and the lump of the ruby ring was missing from beneath her bodice. Her cheeks were flushed with pink and her lips parted.

"You wished to see me?"

In every way through every hour of every day.

His mouth was dry.

He gestured for Miles to leave and he walked to her. "I did."

The tilt of her chin was high. But he could not resist touching her. He took the end of a braid between his fingers and stroked the satiny tress.

"I was reminded today that newly wedded couples often embark upon a wedding journey after the nuptials," he said, feeling ridiculously clumsy, his tongue stiff. He looked down at the fiery locks in his palm. "Would you like that?"

"We will not be newly wedded, however," she said. "And as we have already traveled quite a bit recently, I don't really see why we should now do so simply to suit convention."

He allowed the braid to slide from his fingers. He clasped his hands behind his back and met her gaze.

His heart jerked beneath his ribs. For a moment her eyes were soft, the light in them almost seeking, it seemed. Then they shuttered again.

It was this swift shuttering each time they spoke that restrained Luc from going to her bed at night. He could demand his rights as a husband and she would acquiesce; she was a woman of passion. But he could not use her like that. She deserved more than the treatment a man might serve his mistress. She deserved to be treated like the princess she had once hoped to be.

He didn't know how much longer he could stand it, though. A sennight had already seemed like a millennium. If life with her were to be this slow, tortuous death of wanting her and not having her, he would have preferred to die on that beach in Saint-Nazaire after all.

But as he looked down at her lovely face and saw in it both wary reticence and adorable determination, he could not wish that in truth. Even brief moments alone with her were better than a lifetime without her. His madness, it seemed, had become complete.

"Do you?" she said.

"Do I . . . ?" He grasped at the strands of his reason unraveling in her presence, as they always did.

"Do you think we should bow to convention?"

He reached up to rub the back of his neck as though he were considering the matter. He was stalling for time. This issue was about to be settled, the conversation concluded, and she would leave.

"I have never found convention particularly inspiring," he said. "But forgive me, little governess. I realize that teaching conventional manners must have been the ballast of your livelihood for some time."

"To the girls who possessed no natural spark of originality, yes. To those with unique spirit, however, I encouraged . . ."

"You encouraged?"

"I encouraged them to follow their dreams in whatever manner they thought would most benefit them."

His chest actually hurt. She had tried to follow her dream and he had trapped her just short of achieving it.

"I don't suppose you offered the same counsel to their mothers." He didn't know how he accomplished a grin.

"Not precisely." Her perfect raspberry lips curved into a small smile. "But one becomes proficient at speaking around the truth when one is in an unenviable posi—" Her throat constricted. "—position." She took a quick breath. "I should go now. I have a hundred and two tasks to accomplish this afternoon." Her entire demeanor had altered to agitation. "Is that everything you wished to discuss?"

"Yes," he lied.

She glided away, and he stood still long after she had gone, his heart beating hard and slow.

He had not seen her in the two days since. And now he was to take her as his bride a second time, this time with the sanction of the Church of England.

"After you have captained this ship for nearly six years during war," he said to Tony, "you will not have to be even a baronet to be given special privileges."

Tony snorted.

From the quarterdeck Luc watched the wedding guests arriving across the pontoon boats that had been arranged as a sturdy walkway from the riverbank to the ship.

His heart turned. Upon his cousin's arm, Arabella picked her way carefully across the fabricated bridge to the deck, her head high and shoulders back. She showed no hint of fear as she boarded. Her shimmering hair was swept up in cascading curls, and her gown of the palest pink left her neck and arms bare and offered a tantalizing hint of the feminine beauty beneath it.

With Cam, she passed beneath the white canopy erected above the gangway and came on deck.

Luc went forward.

"Ah, my dear," his cousin said. "Here is your groom."

She reached up and touched her hand to Cam's cheek and kissed him there. "Thank you, my lord."

Luc's collar felt hot.

Cam offered her an elegant leg. "It has been my greatest pleasure to facilitate your nuptials. Again."

Luc took her hand and drew her toward him. Her lashes lifted and the cornflowers were bright.

"Bugger off, Cam."

"Charming, Lucien. Have you the rings?"

"With the sacristan at the church." He did not shift his attention from her. "Now go away."

"Ah, the Eager Groom. It seems that elusive creature

does exist after all. Fascinating. My compliments to you, dear." He grinned at Arabella and wandered off.

"He was kind to assist me aboard," she said with a small smile.

"He will seize any opportunity to touch a beautiful woman."

"And you, my lord?" she said with that directness that had dazed him from the first.

"I wish to touch only one woman."

Disquiet flickered in the cornflowers. "I hope the woman to whom you refer is me."

"For some time now, in fact." He tried to speak lightly but he feared he sounded as much of a buffoon as he felt. "Are you well?"

She nodded, quick little jerks of her head that revealed she had not done away with her fear but with great effort hid it now.

"Why did you do this, Arabella? Why the ship when you are terrified of the water?"

"I have no wealth—"

"You have mine."

"Wealth of my own." Her chin remained high. "I wished to give you a wedding gift. I wished to please you in a manner— In a manner in which I had not pleased you before."

"Duchess, if you had not already done so, do you think I would be here now?"

She curtsied as gracefully as a swan dipping its neck. "I am honored, my lord."

"Arabella, I have—" Beyond her shoulder, a figure in black strolled onto deck. Fletcher looked left and right, and held the railing as though casually but with tight fingers.

Luc's breaths stalled. "Did you invite that man?"

She turned. "Which one?"

"The one with the gold cross about his neck."

She looked into his face. "Who is he, Luc?"

"The Bishop of Barris. Absalom Fletcher."

"I did not see the final guest list. Adina supervised it. It is not peculiar that she should invite her brother." She placed her hand on his. "I am sorry, Luc. Do you wish me to ask him to leave? Adina will not attend, of course, and I see no reason to have him here if it displeases you."

He looked into her wide, compassionate eyes and wanted her to know everything. She had taken another woman's children into her care until they were safe. She had begged for mercy for a thief because he was starving. She had sought to protect the Lycombe name from her family's uncertain past. Yet he could not utter a syllable to her now. He could not tell her the shameful secrets of his past or his fears of the present. *He must protect her.*

She clasped his hand in her slender fingers. "He will not disturb our celebration," she said firmly. "We will simply ignore him. I have been studying the art of the cut direct. According to Mrs. Baxter, it is a necessary weapon of a duchess. I don't see why I cannot wield it as a *comtesse*."

He wrapped his hand around hers.

"A siren with hair like white flame and eyes like summer cornflowers." The young man at Luc's shoulder spoke swiftly and with a soft flavor of the Continent. "My brother did you justice, *belle enfant*."

Arabella feared she stared.

He seemed to hover upon the toes of his shining boots, leaning into Luc, his green eyes vibrant and mobile. "Your beauty does his admiration justice in return." He smiled a gorgeous smile that lit up his face.

Luc's hand slid from hers and went to the young man's arm.

"You have come."

"I could not miss my brother's wedding." He stepped around Luc and lifted her hand to his lips. "Christos Westfall. *Enchanté.*"

"Arabella, this is my brother." Luc's stance had broadened and his voice sounded fuller.

She curtsied but Christos urged her up. He angled close and his bright eyes swept her face, assessing.

"Luc, *elle est exquise*," he said, drawing out the words. Then quickly: "Where did you find her?"

The corner of Luc's mouth turned up. "In a tavern."

"And yet her bones shout of royal blood." Christos's long fingers grasped her chin, tilting her head left then right. She allowed it, trying to smile, her belly a tangle of nerves. "You must dress her in purple and ermine and I will do a portrait of her. You will wear a crown, Belle. *J'insist!* No scepter, though. Scepters are for old whiskered kings, not princesses."

"As you wish," Luc said easily, but he watched his brother with the same intensity with which Christos studied her.

She drew gently from the cage of his fingertips. "I am so pleased you have come." She held her voice level with effort. "The two of you must have much to speak of, and I have guests to greet. Please excuse me."

She went blindly forward.

A small, strong hand grabbed hers.

"He looks just like the duke!" Ravenna whispered.

"In a manner, though slenderer and less substantial." Eleanor came to Arabella's other side. "Is that his brother, Bella?"

She nodded and gripped her sisters' hands. "Stay with me. Please. I know so few of the people here and at this moment I think I may not be entirely prepared to be a *comtesse*."

Eleanor returned the pressure. "Of course. But you are much stronger than even you realize, Bella. If you weren't, you would not be a *comtesse* now."

But that was not true. She was a *comtesse* because she had been indescribably weak, not strong. Now the man whose supposed unfitness had propelled her into marriage stood yards away, as perfectly fit a person as any other on the ship.

She greeted people she did not know with practiced poise, gracefully accepted their congratulations, and ignored their curious stares. There were elegantly garbed earls and impressive ministers and old dukes and fashionable countesses and barons and admirals and their lady wives in number, and she spoke to them all without trouble. The only man she could not speak easily with now was somewhere in the crowd with his black-sheep brother, his stance confident and a smile across his dashingly scarred face.

Eleanor and Ravenna had fallen into conversations with others. Her breaths increasingly quick and shallow, not from the gray water of the river all around but because of the panic rising in her, Arabella fled belowdeck.

Christos and Ravenna found her there.

"Belle! At last we have discovered you!" He moved with lightness and great grace. He was a beautiful man with all the character and intensity in his face of Luc's yet none of the confident command. He sat down beside her and took her hand. "Your guests, they seek you out. Why do you hide?"

"*Are* you hiding, Bella?" Ravenna stood before her, hands on her hips, brow worried.

"No. Yes." She faced Christos directly. "You and he have not seen each other in a great long time."

"A half dozen months only. But"—he waved his hand dismissively—"months and years matter nothing when there is affinity of spirit and great affection, *non*?"

Ravenna nodded.

Arabella's hand twisted in Christos's and broke free. Desperate words that had been caged inside her rushed to her tongue. "Would your brother make plans to divorce his wife without telling her of that plan?"

"Not the brother that has been writing me letters in praise of her for the past many weeks," he said without hesitation.

"I found letters to him, written by his man of business. They spoke of preparing a petition for divorce, and of an heiress whose portion could restore the fortunes of Combe."

"Oh, Bella." Ravenna's dark eyes went wide. "Did you ask him about them?"

"She did not," Christos said, nodding thoughtfully. "There is great fear where there is uncertain love, I think."

Ravenna's brows rose. Arabella could not meet her sister's gaze.

"This heiress," Christos said, tilting his head. "Was she named?"

"Miss Gardiner."

His face relaxed into a smile. "Ah, then the mystery is solved, *ma belle*. It was my uncle who wished to make her my wife."

Air flooded Arabella's lungs. "Your uncle?" She tried to picture the letters. They had lacked dates and Luc's name. "When did your uncle tell you this?"

"A twelvemonth ago."

"But what about the divorce?"

"To excise Combe from the grip of his wife's brother," Christos said immediately.

Arabella sat forward. "What do you know of this?"

"What my aunt told me a year ago when I paid a call upon her, that her brother required her to remain in London while my uncle died alone in Shropshire. She is a weak soul, though benevolent. Her innocence is to my brother's disservice, I fear."

"But what does either have to do with the other?" Ravenna demanded.

"Ah, *mon chou*," he said with a shake of his head. "You know little of the greed of men, I think."

"Happily." She squinted. "What's a *chou*?"

"A cabbage."

Arabella's thoughts sped. "Why didn't he divorce Adina if he intended to? Her child is not his."

Christos offered an elegant shrug. "Perhaps he did not know she was with child."

"He must have. Why didn't you wed Miss Gardiner?"

"Ah." He lowered his chin. "Though I would like it very much, I think—the affection and companionship of a woman with whom to share dreams—it is not for me. I am not fit for such a gift, *ma belle*."

Not fit.

"Christos?" She took up his long, beautiful artist's hand. "How exactly are you unfit?"

With a crease of his lips that shaped them into a wave, he turned their hands over together. "I have peaks, and I have valleys." He drew back the lacy cuff of his shirt. His wrist was crisscrossed with thick, straight-edged scars, overlapping one upon the next. "The valleys, they are oftentimes quite low. No gentle lady deserves to be bound to that."

There was a silence between them in which the shuffling of feet on the deck above, the muffled conversations of four hundred people, and the muted delights of violin and flute could be heard.

Ravenna lowered herself to a chair and placed her palms on her knees. "What can we do, Bella, so that with a mind free of burdens you can marry your duke again?"

"*Oui, ma belle.* Your sister—though she speaks of the mind where I would speak of the heart—we shall help. For I believe as surely as I am a man that my brother has no ill intent toward you. Rather, the contrary."

"The tenant farmers of Combe are being extorted, I believe," Arabella said, "but they offer me only fearful hints. No proof. I believe that the Bishop of Barris, Adina's brother, is behind this. But I have little upon which to base this."

"Except his hatred of my brother and his manipulation of my sweet aunt. And, unless my brother becomes the duke, he is the principal trustee of Combe."

"That isn't enough to prove a crime," Ravenna said.

"Then she must find the proof," Christos replied.

"Where?"

"In his private chambers."

"Do you truly believe that a man who commits crimes involving thousands of pounds would hide proof of those crimes in a drawer in his study?"

"I do." He blinked his intense green eyes. "For I have seen it done. The fools. *Pft!*"

"Where is Barris?" Ravenna said, abruptly eager. "We will go there and—"

"Barris is a speck of an island in a far off northern sea, *mon chou*."

"Does he usually live in London, then?"

"When I was a child, he had a house near Richmond. We lived there, my brother and I, for some years."

"He still has this house," Arabella said. "Adina mentioned it."

"You could pay a call on him," Ravenna said, "and when he is in the other room you can search his desk. I read a lending library novel in which the hero did that."

"Ah, *oui*. And the art, it always reflects the reality, *non*, *mon chou*?" he said with a lift of a brow.

"I think you should stop calling me your cabbage, or our siblinghood will swiftly become uncomfortable for you."

"But it is too far to go to Richmond," Arabella said, "and then to sit and wait to enter his house after he has gone out."

Ravenna's lips screwed up. "With all his servants, presumably."

"Then she must go while he disports himself in London."

"How would she know when he'd be doing that?"

"Is he not doing that at this very moment, above our heads, *mon—*"

Ravenna glared. He laughed.

"Perhaps . . ." Arabella's heart raced. She wanted to help Luc. She needed to help him. This was the trouble that he was hiding from her. She did not have all the pieces: why he would not share it all with her, nor why Christos's arrival today had transformed his distress into ease.

Her fists bunched. "He refuses to allow me to help him protect the people of Combe."

"Ah, *ma belle*," Christos said. "My brother seeks always to protect. To share that burden is a foreign thing to him."

She stood up. "I could go to the bishop's house now, while he is here. I might not have this opportunity again. My footman Joseph could go with me. You two would remain here and make excuses for my absence."

"From your own wedding?" Ravenna hopped out of her seat.

"Immediately after it. I must go, Venna. When I arrive, the servants will ask me to await his return, then they will forget about me, and I can look around at my leisure." She bit the inside of her lip. "I hope."

"This seems far-fetched."

"*Non*. It is not. The house, it is plain and empty. The places to search are few. The servants are aged, their interest in guests poor."

"In a bishop's household?"

"In his household." Christos rose to his feet like a cat, slender and graceful. "I know this, you see. For it takes a madman to recognize a madman."

CHAMPAGNE HAD FLOWED freely during Arabella's sojourn below, and conversation was lively atop. *Just like her imagination*. It was pure foolishness to consider running off to Richmond to search a bishop's house for documents that probably didn't even exist. The same sort of foolishness that had taken her to a dark alley in a port town she did not know and began the series of events that led her here.

There remained but half an hour until a small party of guests and family were to leave the ship with her and Luc to go to the church nearby for the ceremony. They would return to the *Victory* afterward for supper, dancing, and fireworks. Adina had spared nothing in her plans.

Arabella could not wait half an hour. She needed to see Luc. She searched between clusters of guests. Her nerves were twisted to rawness, and as much as she feared his distance, she wanted only to be alone with him now.

At first she thought those strained nerves were the cause of the peculiar glances some of the guests were throwing her way—ladies, especially, ducking behind parasols to avoid her gaze while the gentlemen turned their heads away when she passed. She was imagining it, of course. No one would cut a bride at her wedding.

Wending her way between people under the main canopy spread across the front of the ship, she found Eleanor.

"Bella?" Her sister's brow creased. "I have something to say to you that I think will be difficult for you to hear. But you should know it."

Luc?

"What is it, Ellie?"

"I have just heard an unsavory rumor—for rumor I know it to be—told to me by a woman because I think she did not know that I am your sister."

"Tell me, please, quickly."

"It seems that it is being said that you have been unfaithful to the *comte,* that you have taken a lover or perhaps several already, and are eager to make him the father of a bastard."

The air flattened out of Arabella's lungs and heat flushed through her body and into her cheeks.

"It is a rumor."

"Of course it is. It is perfectly obvious to me that you adore him, and even if you did not, you have too much integrity to do such a thing." Eleanor looked about. "But someone is telling this tale here today. Just look at that pair of women over there, staring at us like we are a curiosity at an exhibition."

She must not allow gossip to hurt her. She had held strong against unkindnesses and cruelties her entire life. That this unkindness hurt Luc was the only source of her misery.

"The woman who told me said the news was to be believed because its source was within the family," Eleanor said. "But not the duchess; her brother, the bishop. Isn't it the most astounding thing you've heard?"

"No." Her heart racketed. "He hates Luc. I think he would do this to hurt him." As he would extort money from Luc's tenants. But only to hurt him, or to ruin him entirely? Or for some other purpose?

It was all too much. Desperation snatched at her reason again, the plan that Christos and Ravenna had laid out seeming less like foolishness and more like her only hope.

As she lifted her head to search the crowd again for Luc, a hush descended over them. Oh, good heavens. Were they to go in solemn procession to the church now? With her head awhirl and nerves frayed, she doubted she could bear it.

But no one was looking at her. They had all turned to another. At the head of the gangway in a ray of sunlight cut with shadow lines from the rigging above, the Bishop of Barris stood with his hands folded over his enormous gold pectoral cross. His amethyst ring glittered.

"It is with great solemnity that I share news now that affects my family deeply," he said with the measured confidence of a man accustomed to the pulpit. The guests went silent, all mouths closed. Even the ladies' tiny parasols stilled. Sick heat crept from Arabella's womb into her throat and to the tips of her fingers. He would declare her to be a Jezebel before everyone. He would shame Luc irreparably.

"My sister, the Duchess of Lycombe, has just now given birth." He paused and Arabella's eyes closed. "To a healthy boy."

Chapter 17

The Strength of a Man

$\mathcal{M}$y only regret is that Theodore," Fletcher continued, "whom we all admired, and whom his wife loved deeply"—he offered a rare, rueful grin—"though it was of course shockingly unfashionable for her to do so"—titters of amusement from the crowd—"I regret that my dear friend Theodore cannot see with his living eyes his son and heir. But I have faith that his spirit rests happy knowing his wife and child are well. If you will, raise a toast with me to the new Duke of Lycombe. And to Lucien, whose wedding we honor today, who will so ably remain heir until we all attend another wedding two decades or so from now." More laughter. The clinking of crystal.

Luc didn't care. Arabella was nowhere to be seen. The malicious gossip circulating throughout the party must have reached her.

He lifted his glass, accepted the sympathetic nods of his actual friends, and bowed. Then everyone began talking. He set down the champagne and wove his way through the guests, searching, his limited field of vision never more frustrating.

She might be devastated. *No.* Not his sharp-tongued little governess. She would be more likely to throw the incivility back in a gossip's face than accept an outright lie spoken about her.

He knew it was a lie. Rational thought fled when he was with her, but he knew her all the same.

"Looking for your stunning bride, Westfall?" A ship-master he'd known during the war stepped into his path. "P'raps she's flown the coop now that she's heard she's not to be a duchess after all, hm? Poor sod, losing your title and wife on the same day." He laughed and clapped Luc on the back. He was drunk. Luc saw it in his red-dened eyes. He was roasting him. All in fun. Tasteless and callous, but innocently so.

But accurate?

Aloof. Evasive. Unavailable. She had been all of these since coming to town. And before that . . . In France she had tried to escape him.

He could not believe it. She must know that wherever she ran, despite his blindness he would find her.

GIVEN HER RAW nerves, it was with considerable energy that Arabella descended from the carriage before the Bishop of Barris's modest house on the edge of Richmond. It sat alone at the back of an extensive park far from the main road and another quarter mile from the next house, which seemed to be a school of some sort. The river came close behind the house, offering a natural border at the property's rear.

Buoyed by determination, she went toward the door. "I should not be too long, Joseph. An hour, I suspect."

"I'd like to come in there with you, milady."

"No. This is an errand of extraordinary delicacy. If you come in with all your imposing size and glower, it will alarm the bishop's staff."

His brow descended over his serious eyes.

"Wait here in the carriage for me. The *comte* would be perfectly happy with you if he knew of it." The *comte* would turn Joseph off if he knew of it, then throttle her soundly. Verbally, of course. He had never touched her violently, not even roughly when she had not begged for it.

With heat high in her cheeks, she went toward the door, tugging her cloak about her shoulders. She had not paused to change from her wedding gown; she wasn't quite ready to discard it yet. She wanted Luc to remove it, slowly, on their wedding night. Rather, tonight. The church ceremony was supposed to have taken place an hour earlier, and she had not been present. So tonight would not be his wedding night either.

But they could pretend it was . . . if he ever spoke to her again after being abandoned at the altar just when he learned he would not be the duke.

What had she done?

But the tenant families must not continue to suffer. The bishop was now trustee to the little duke and in control of Combe. She wouldn't have this chance again.

She banged the plain brass knocker. Despite the bishop's elegant dress, his house lacked ostentation. An elderly thin woman in gray muslin opened the door.

"Inform his excellency that Mrs. Bradford is calling."

"His excellency's not in. You'll have to come back later." The woman made to shut the door. Arabella stopped it with her hand.

"I shan't mind waiting." She slipped through into the whitewashed foyer.

The housekeeper gave Arabella's fine gown and cloak and the ruby and gold earrings peeking out from her hair a perusal. Then she gestured her toward a door. "You can wait in here, mum," she said, opening it to a parlor. "I've no idea when he'll return. His nephew's getting married today in town."

"Yes." Arabella ran a fingertip along an unadorned table in the center of the room. "I think I had heard that. I shall read while I wait. What a marvelous collection of books."

"I don't know, mum. Not a reader myself. Will you have some tea?"

"Oh, you're very kind. No thank you."

The housekeeper nodded and closed the door behind her.

Arabella sprang up and went to the door. But there was no key in the lock. She searched about the room for a drawer that might hold a key, but the only furniture were the bookcase, table, and three straight-backed chairs upholstered in faded red velvet. If the bishop was siphoning money off Combe's tenant farmers, he certainly wasn't using it on his house.

She peered between books. It seemed the most obvious place to hide precious papers. She found nothing except dozens of tomes on religious matters marked with endless margin notes taken in an exceedingly neat hand.

She looked behind the two pictures hanging on the walls.

Nothing. But she had never imagined the parlor would offer up treasures anyway.

She opened the door as though she wished to recall the housekeeper then stood very still, listening. No footsteps sounded anywhere. The house was quiet.

Removing her shoes, she shut the door behind her.

At least the hinges were well oiled. On silent feet she padded to the next door and went completely motionless again. No sound came from within. There was nothing like creeping around someone's house in one's stocking feet to rouse suspicion; in the event that the room was in fact occupied, she donned her shoes again.

It was a dining chamber, immaculately clean like the foyer and parlor, but likewise small and plain, without even a closed sideboard in which to hide a chamber pot. *Useless.* And her nerves were a quivering shambles. Skulking around had never been her forte. She preferred to meet matters head on.

Except lately. Since reading Luc's secretary's letters she had been in hiding, running away from what he might tell her if she allowed him opportunity.

No more. When this unwise adventure was over and she returned to London, she would beg his forgiveness and finally tell him everything.

Slipping off her shoes again, she backed out of the dining chamber and shut the door, this time with a creak in the hinge, quiet as a mouse's squeak but it may as well be a gong banging in the silent house. She flinched and listened.

Thirty seconds became a minute. Nothing stirred. The housekeeper must have fallen asleep somewhere.

She crept toward the stair, praying they were as uncompromising as the rest of the bishop's home. Her prayers were answered: the steps did not squeak. She mounted the landing and pressed her ear against the first door. No sound. She put her shoes on yet again and opened the panel.

Success.

She slipped into the bishop's study and left her shoes at the door. The floors were plain wooden boards covered with an equally plain red carpet that masked the sound of her steps. A massive desk occupied at least half of the chamber. The only objects atop it were an inkwell, pen and blotter, and a single sheet of blank paper. The was another bookcase like those in the parlor, a small table, and two straight-backed chairs. The only object to disturb the drabness was a picture on the wall of an impressively austere building set on a broad park. The caption read:

WHITECHAPEL SCHOOL
READING, BRITAIN
EST. 1814

The curtains were partially drawn, the afternoon sun slanting directly into the chamber. Anyone outside would see only reflection from the pane.

She went around the desk and tried the center drawer. It opened smoothly. Within, she saw a stack of plain stationery, a letter opener shaped like a long, slender cross, a knife to sharpen pens, and a small pistol. Without pause, she grabbed up the knife and pistol and dropped them into her cloak pocket.

The drawers to either side of the chair were locked fast. *Of course they were.* Without locks on the doors the bishop must have some way of keeping his private matters private from prying servants. She reached up under the center drawer, her fingers searching for a hidden key but without hope of finding one. She pushed her arm deeper into the back of the drawer and her fingertips brushed metal. She drew forth a key.

The bishop was an odd man indeed. Or he had the dullest, least curious servants in England. Or servants with very short arms.

The key opened the drawers to either side easily. Her fingers sped through files as her frustration mounted.

Nothing looked especially odd; it was all correspondence to church officials and records of the Whitechapel School. She had no idea what she was looking for. She had been phenomenally foolish to do this. She'd left Luc standing at the altar and would have nothing to show for it but a furious husband who had just lost his dukedom to a bastard child.

She slid the drawers shut and replaced the key in its hiding spot. Then she took a deep breath. It would be the worst sort of weakness to admit defeat so easily.

Nothing stirred in the corridor so she repeated her earlier stealth and went to the next door. It was a bedchamber, this time with a lock on the door, and sparsely furnished but not currently occupied; the surfaces were bare of personal belongings, and the small bed was not made up. The next was another bedchamber, also with a lock and likewise empty.

The third bedchamber included a shaving stand, clothes press, and dressing mannequin garbed in a complete set of richly brocaded, embroidered clerical robes. Their opulence was at thorough odds with the rest of the house. Arabella had been imagining the Bishop of Barris and Reverend Caulfield like two peas in a pod. This dashed that notion from her head. The Reverend could sermonize for a month of Sundays on the sinful excess of these robes alone.

She stood in the middle of the bishop's bedchamber, arms folded, and thought about all the lectures on vanity that her adoptive father had given her over the years. A man who exalted personal appearance but who seemed to care nothing for domestic luxury . . . What had the Reverend always said about her vanity and pride? That she could hide her hair and pretty face, but beneath them would be the same sinful girl?

She dropped to her knees on the polished floor and looked under the bed.

It seemed too simple; like the key in the desk drawer, beneath the bed was a cedar chest. She pulled it forth, cringing at the scraping sound across the floor, and opened it.

Her shoulders dropped. More papers on Whitechapel School. Exhaling tightly, she flipped through them.

Her fingers stalled.

Last names of Combe's tenant farmers with pound figures beside them covered one sheet, including first names, all male, certainly the heads of the households from which he was extorting their income.

She frowned. Mr. Goode's name was Thatcher. But the name beside Goode on this list was Edward. She closed her eyes, picturing Mrs. Goode's kitchen on her second visit to the farm, the chipped teapot, the plate of tasteless biscuits, and the smiles of the Goodes' three sons when Arabella gave them the sweets. John, Michael, and the youngest Teddy, named after his grandfather, Edward.

"Well, well. A lady in the bishop's bedchamber. Never thought I'd see the day."

Arabella's head snapped up.

The man standing in the doorway was large, thick in the chest, and somewhat heavy in the belly where the fabric of his waistcoat strained, with squinting eyes and slick, well-combed hair. With the two first fingers of his left hand he wiggled a toothpick between his lips; the thumb on that hand was missing.

Arabella released the papers, stood and brushed imaginary dust off her skirt. Her shoes dangled from her other hand. "This is not as you imagine it, sir."

His lips pinched around the toothpick and he nodded

thoughtfully. "Actually, I 'spect it's exactly as I imagine it," he said with an unhurried grin, "*comtesse*."

THE ARCHBISHOP OF Canterbury gestured Luc to collect his lady and hasten to the church for the ceremony. Luc could not, however, tell him that his lady was nowhere to be found; it would expose her to yet more gossip.

Fletcher stood beneath the wedding canopy like a bridegroom, serenely accepting congratulations as though he were head of the family, and in no apparent hurry to shorten this moment of glory. Far to portside, Arabella's sisters huddled close together, removed from the other guests. Ravenna cast Luc a quick glance then turned away abruptly.

Heart in his throat, he started toward her.

Christos stepped in his way. "*La jolie brune* had nothing to do with it. *Eh bien*, very little."

"Nothing to do with what? Where is my wife, Christos?"

Christos turned about and headed toward the companionway. Servants rushed up the steps bearing trays laden with delicacies. He made way for them then hurried down. Luc followed along the low deck lined with cannons.

"Why the devil can't I find my wife?" he demanded when his brother finally led him into the captain's quarters. "And what the devil do you have to do with it?"

His brother peered at him intently. "Do you not know, then? Of the birth of the boy of our aunt?"

"Of course I know."

"And you have no unhappiness with it?"

"Of course I have unhappi— Of course I'm unhappy about it. And disappointed. But I am rather more concerned with how Arabella has taken the news."

His brother's eyes lit with the smile Luc remembered

from their childhood, before their father died and the world fell out from beneath them.

Then Christos's face sobered and he lifted his palm. "Fear not. She has not abandoned you. Rather, she has gone to help you."

"Help me? What, is she a witch that knows some sort of spell that will change a boy child to a girl?"

A fresh grin split across his brother's face. "Ah, that you are able to jest at such a time . . ." He shook his head. "I am in great awe of you, *mon frère*."

"I am immensely gratified. Now *give over*, Chris."

He dipped his head and folded his hands. "She fears for the safety of the child and his patrimony."

"What?"

"The infant's guardian—that man—will ruin Combe. She believes he already has, and she seeks proof of it."

"Damn it, Christos. Fletcher is not the child's only guardian. I am as well. He will not have complete control over the boy or Combe."

"But he will control our aunt, as he always has."

"Then I will take Adina and her son out of his realm of influence. The house in Durham will do for distance. If that does not suffice, Rallis will. Fletcher will never cross the Channel."

"And what if you die, *mon frère*?" Christos said matter-of-factly. "Who will protect the young duke from him then?"

Luc stared at his brother, his chest tight. "You do remember. Don't you?"

"Remember what?" Christos waved it away. "Brother, *la belle* made me vow to withhold information from you that however you must now be told."

"Why now?"

"Before, I knew you admired her beauty and courage. Now I know you cherish her heart."

More than his life. "What information, Christos?"

"She has gone."

Luc's stomach twisted. "Where?"

"I cannot say. I made a vow. A man that breaks a promise to a lady is no man at all. But she has taken the stalwart footman with her."

"Damn you, Christos, tell me."

"Where would you go now if you were she?"

"As far away from Absalom Fletcher's poison as I could."

"Ah." Christos lifted his forefinger. "But I said if you were *she*. Not you."

No.

"Damn it. How could you allow it?"

"I have no authority over anyone, *mon frère*, least of all myself. And she wished to do it."

"Why, in God's name—"

"*Pour toi*, of course."

For him.

If he had told her about Fletcher . . . If he had told her the truth . . .

Luc replaced the decorative épée in his belt with a rapier from Tony's weapons trunk, grabbed up a pistol, and slipped a dirk in the top of his boot, where he'd had a slot sewn for a knife.

"Fletcher won't be there." He laid out her plan aloud as he imagined it. "He is here now. Then he will call on his sister and the infant, perhaps for the remainder of the day. It's a clever plan."

"*Merci.*"

"But it will gain her nothing. Fletcher isn't such a fool to leave proof of his misdeeds lying about. He will have hidden it well. Have you a horse here?"

"A very good one."

"Take me to it."

Christos followed him across the gun deck. Arabella's younger sister came clattering down the companionway. Her gaze darted between him and his brother.

"Did you tell him where she's gone?" she demanded of Christos.

He slapped a hand over his heart. "I made a vow, mademoiselle."

"Well, I didn't, you *chou*." She turned to Luc. "She went to the bishop's house near Richmond."

He was already mounting the stairs three at a time.

"Hurry!" she called after him.

He needed no encouragement. But he paused and looked back down at his brother.

"Christos, how might Fletcher have acquired a portrait that you drew since December?"

His brow creased. "In March I found myself without funds. I sold all my work on the street in Paris to a Sicilian and his English companion. After, I drew a picture of the Englishman. That man, he was a beast, but he was an interesting study: he had only one thumb."

The Sicilian assassins from Saint-Nazaire had been with Fletcher's coachman in Paris.

"Did the work they purchased include a portrait of me?"

"*Mais oui.* I liked that picture. You looked fierce. *Comme un pirate.*" He shrugged. "But I can draw another."

"First you will do that portrait of my wife." Luc went swiftly up the steps. "As a princess." As she deserved.

"YOU ARE MISTAKING me for somebody else," Arabella said. "My name is Mrs. Bradford. I have called on his excellency to—"

"Your name is Westfall. And you called to poke into his excellency's private matters." The man slid the toothpick from between his lips and tucked it into his waistcoat pocket. "Can't be having that."

"I don't know what you mean. I was simply very tired after waiting at such length for his return and the housekeeper told me I could rest here." She dropped her pretty pink and ridiculously impractical wedding slippers to the floor, slipped her feet into them and started toward him. "Now that I know this is the bishop's personal chamber, however, I don't think that is a good idea after all." She halted before him. "I should like to return to the parlor now."

"I don't think you'll be doing that." He stood before her like a great big rock of malice. Joseph was at least as tall and less round. But Joseph was in the carriage.

She had failed. She had now effectively shamed Luc twice, heaping scandal upon scandal, this one by her own volition. Even if he had not been planning to throw her off, it was entirely possible he would now. But what a feast for the gossips! *Governess-turned-comtesse is accused by bishop of infidelity to her comte then found in said bishop's bedchamber with her shoes off.* Ravenna's lending library novels could not invent better.

The squinting rock clamped his fleshy hand about her arm and dragged her across the corridor to another bedchamber and locked her in, and her amused musings fled.

She banged on the door. "Let me out of here this instant," she demanded in her grandest voice. "This instant!"

"We'll wait for his excellency to decide that," he said through the door.

"But the housekeeper said he would not be home for some time. You cannot leave me locked in this chamber until then. It is outrageous." And terrifying in a manner she had never before considered. The room was small, and now she saw the bars across the window, quite like the sort one saw on houses in certain neighborhoods of London. But the bishop's house sat on a private park. Thieves could not be plentiful here.

Unless the bars were intended not to keep thieves out but to keep guests in.

She backed away from the door.

"This is kidnapping." she called. "You will be jailed for it. Or hung."

"Only if you live to tell about it." Heavy footsteps receded along the bare boards of the corridor and down the stairs.

Arabella sank down onto the bed and began trembling.

A QUARTER HOUR later, after having lifted the window sash and tested the width of her body against the bars, and found them far too narrow, she started banging on the door and shouting. The housekeeper might hear, or even Joseph.

Her jailer returned quickly, so she guessed he had not gone far.

"Be quiet or I'll tie your hands and mouth," he grunted through the closed door.

"All right. But first I would like to ask you something."

No sound came from the other side of the panel.

"Does the bishop pay you well?" she said. "That is to say, are your wages from him commensurate to the income he illegally culls from my husband's family's estate?"

"My wages are my own business," he said like a surly cur. But he didn't walk away. Arabella did a silent little leap of victory.

"I wondered," she said, "because those papers under

his bed, the ones that I was poking through, they make it quite clear that your master is now a wealthy man. Much wealthier than this house suggests. Why, with his annual income now," she fabricated, "he could have a house four times this size if he wished. Go see for yourself. It's all in the papers he hides."

Silence.

Then the man said: "Must use it on that school he's got over there in Reading."

"Yes. The Whitechapel School," she gambled.

"Poor brats' families can't pay, and they've got to eat, I suppose."

Poor children?

"Mm. I daresay." She worried the inside of her lip between her teeth, her nerves frayed. "But one would suppose he could share at least a little of the surplus with you and his other servants, wouldn't one?"

"There's nobody but me and Mrs. Biggs," he said. "And I ain't no servant. I drive the coach, is all, when there's a job."

"If you drive a coach for him, I am afraid you are his servant," she said, tiptoeing the fine line between instigating rebellion against his master and inspiring antagonism toward her.

"He says I'm his partner."

He sounded angry. *Not ideal.*

"He is not your partner if he is not paying you a fair wage according to the work you do." She paused for a moment. "But I can."

There was another silent interval, this time lengthy.

"What're you offering?"

She took a deep, fast breath and closed her eyes tight. "A ring of ruby and gold." Her heart thudded. "A ring of inestimable value. The ruby is very large. You could remove it, melt down the gold, and sell it, and no one would be able to trace you," she said quickly. "And if you agree to the trade, I won't tell a soul. It isn't in my interests for anyone to know I have been here, and I could never explain how you had gotten it otherwise, could I? Imagine: you could buy a new waistcoat to replace the one you wear now that does not fit. You could buy ten new waistcoats and a house of your own too. You would never have to work for another man again. That is how valuable this ring is."

By the time she completed this speech her hands were damp and shaky. One of them slipped to her pocket and the only thing of value she had ever owned . . . until she became a *comtesse* and the lord who had stolen her heart tried to give her a tiara fit for a duchess. She'd taken the ring from the house before her hasty departure for Richmond. She didn't know why at the time she had done it.

She knew now. *Destiny.*

She waited for his response with a sick stomach.

"What d'you want to trade it for?"

"My freedom and the documents. Let me go, and let me take those papers with me, and I will give you that ring."

"How do I know you'd pay your side of the bargain?"

"You would have to trust me."

From very far off she heard knocking on the front door.

Her captor grumbled and clomped down the steps. Arabella pressed her ear to the door, but the panel was thick and she could catch no sounds. Perhaps Joseph had gotten impatient. Good Lord, let him not be injured because of her naïveté. But she had not been prepared. Her mistrust of men had never extended to this sort of villainy.

Finally, footsteps sounded on the stairs, not the heavy

tread of her captor, but another man's booted steps, confident and clean. Behind those came the thunderous clomp of her captor.

She backed away from the door, her hands tight about her cloak.

The door opened. Her heart stopped.

Hands bound at his back, Luc entered. Behind him was both her captor and the old housekeeper.

"Unbind me now," he said as calmly as though he were instructing his butler to serve dinner.

Her captor nudged him forward. A pistol glimmered in his fist. "She can do it."

Luc walked to her and turned his back. "If you please, duchess."

Her hands shook as she freed him. He drew his arms forward and rubbed his wrists.

"Toss the rope here," her captor said.

She looked at Luc. He nodded. She tossed the bindings to the threshold.

"Now I'll take that ring, milady," he said to her with a squint.

"I—" She shook her head. "I don't have it."

He cocked the pistol with an ominous click. "The ring now. Or do you think his lordship would prefer if I tied him up again while I looked for that ring on you at my leisure?" He grinned. "Fine wedding present that would be, now wouldn't it?"

Luc's face was white.

She reached into her pocket, pulled out the ring, and crouched to roll it across the floor. It made a soft clattering sound as it rolled, coming to a stop by his feet. The housekeeper picked it up and dropped it into her pocket.

Her captor stepped back, closed the door, and the key clicked in the lock.

Beside her Luc was shaking, his jaw hard.

"I cannot begin— I don't know how—" she stuttered. "I am so sorry. I never imagined a bishop would do *this* sort of thing. Why are you here? Why did you allow him to—"

He gripped her wrist. His palm was icy. *"No,"* he said in a peculiar rasp. He released her and went to the door. Slowly, his hand moved to the handle. He turned it and the door remained fast.

"He locked it," she said stupidly. "I would have shouted to warn you off, but I heard nothing until you were at the top of the stairs. It is a very thick door—"

"I know," he said in that scratchy voice. "I allowed it." He heaved in breaths and leaned his brow against the door, his hands flattening against the panel.

She stepped forward. "What—"

He turned his head. His eye was closed, his face taut from brow to jaw. A hard shiver shook his entire frame.

"Luc?"

"I fear, little governess," he said on another convulsive shake, "that I may shortly disgrace myself in a manner in which your former charges—the especially tiny ones—probably did quite often."

"Luc?"

"I may be sick."

She went around him and touched his face. His skin was cold and damp.

"You were not ill this morning. Have they— Oh, God! Have they poisoned you?"

"No," he said tightly. "Though that might have been preferable."

"Then what—"

"When I was ten—" He breathed hard through his nostrils, his entire body rigid.

She had never seen him ill, never anything but strong and vital. Except when he was dying.

She stroked his face, curving her hands around his cheeks. "When you were ten, after your father's death?"

Sweat beaded on his brow.

"Fletcher brought you and your brother here to live, did he not?"

"This was my bedchamber."

She looked behind her. It was nothing more than a cube furnished with only a small bed, a side table, and a single wooden chair. It was Spartan, and the furnishings were old, no different from the dormitory at the foundling home.

"What did he do, Luc?" she said, seeing so clearly the brick wall of the dormitory that she had been told to face each time the directress of the foundling home took a cane to her back, as if every crack, crevice, and discoloration of that brick were before her now. "Did he beat you in this chamber?"

"Nothing so pedestrian," he said with a harsh laugh.

She grabbed his hand. His fingers clamped around hers.

"He starved us," he said. "For days, sometimes weeks, he withheld food. He told us it was a discipline to be able to withstand extreme hunger. That men like us, who would eventually be wealthy and powerful, must learn great discipline while we were still young. He locked me into this room each night with the promise of breakfast in the morning, but only if I did not complain to his manservant or housekeeper. He promised the same to my brother—"

"Oh, *Luc*."

"—but he locked himself in my brother's room too."

Her stomach turned and she went cold all over. "Oh, dear God."

"He said that God would punish us if we told anyone. But I never believed him. God had made my father, after all. He had shown me what a good man could be." A tear slid down his cheek.

She wrapped her arm around him and held him. He bent to her, sank his face against her shoulder and trembled fiercely in her embrace.

When he pulled away, his cheek was damp. She reached up to wipe the tears, but he did not allow her. He removed her hand, and his own hand shook only slightly as he swiped away the moisture.

"Did you know you would find me in danger?" she said.

He did not respond.

"What have you done?" she whispered.

"What I had to do to ensure that you would not find yourself alone with them. Admittedly, I did not quite count on being greeted at the door with a pistol, nor on becoming a quivering mess."

She snapped her gaze up. "You should not have done this."

"I could not have done otherwise."

"But you—"

"Arabella, enough."

"But after all I have done—today, and before—and what you must believe . . . Why would you do this for me?"

"I would die for you." With a hard breath, he moved around her and across the room. "But not tonight. I am no longer a boy and this is just a house like any other." He pushed the windowpane open, braced a foot on the sill, and stretched his arm upward through the iron bars. "That oaf made me give over my sword and pistol. Even the knife in my boot. But he could not take every weapon at my disposal." He closed his eye and pushed on the bar against his shoulder.

"Luc." She went toward him. "Luc, you mustn't. You will harm—"

The bar snapped out with a scrape and a clang and fell away.

He cut her a quick, satisfied grin. "What I might have done then with the strength of a man." He heaved his shoulder into the next bar. "But then I might have simply killed him," he said, the veins on his neck straining as he pushed, "and ended up shipped off to Australia." The bar broke loose and jutted out for a moment before it disappeared. "That would have been inconvenient."

He climbed off the sill and rubbed his hands together.

"What did you do?"

"You needn't look so flabbergasted. A man learns a few tricks after a decade spent on the sea."

"But—"

"Poorly designed hardware." He gestured to the iron grill, his hand trembling slightly. "I knew it then, but I was not tall enough to reach the pins or strong enough to force them loose." He swept his gaze over her, still brittle, but he was trying to mask his fear—for her or for his pride, or perhaps both. "The drawback, of course, is that now I am rather too big to depend on the stability of the drain pipe that runs along the wall just outside."

"I'm not." She leaned out the window. The park was quiet and wooded, with plenty of places to hide as she ran if she managed the descent successfully. The pipe looked sturdy. She turned to him. "I will not go without you."

"You will have to."

"I cannot leave you here with those people."

"Arabella, this is not a discussion. Climb out of that window and onto that drainpipe and run for help. The fence around the park has a gate on its northern end. You will find it by following the river downstream to a tight copse of trees. On the other side of that copse are the fence and the gate. Go now."

"But what about Joseph and my coachman? My carriage—"

"Before I arrived, the oaf paid a visit to your carriage. I found the coachman hiding in the shrubbery and terrified, and Joseph injured."

Her hand flew to her mouth. "How injured?"

"Shot. I sent them home."

"They *shot* him? But—"

"Arabella, the Bishop of Barris has tried to kill me twice, with poison stolen from my ship and with a knife wound administered to me on the beach in Saint-Nazaire."

"But those men—"

"Were hired assassins. Fletcher wishes me out of the way so that he can control Combe's wealth through my aunt's child. While I imagine he would have preferred disposing of me in France, I will not put it past him to attempt to do so here." He moved toward her. "Now, you—"

The key rattled in the lock.

Luc swept his arm to the draperies and pulled them over the missing bars. He went to the middle of the room as the door opened.

Their captor, the housekeeper behind him, jerked the pistol toward Arabella. "I don't want her. She'll have to go."

Arabella froze. "Go?"

"Go home," he said as though she were an imbecile.

Luc circled his arm around her waist loosely. "She goes nowhere without me."

"No more of your talking, milord. She *goes*."

Luc dipped his hand into her cloak pocket and swept the pistol forward and her body behind him in one quick movement.

"Now," he said, "calculate if you will the likelihood

of your pistol firing and you managing to hit me anywhere vital, and the speed with which I can fire at you,
which I assure you I can do quite swiftly and quite ac-
curately. Are you calculating? Good. Now set down
your weapon."

Astoundingly, the man did as Luc commanded. The
housekeeper's face was stark.

"Back away from the door," Luc said.

They obeyed.

"Duchess," he said, and went toward the doorway and
through. "Take up that pistol and pass it to me."

She did. He dropped the bishop's pistol in his pocket
and stepped forward, motioning her to go past behind
him. She hurried toward the stairs.

It happened in an instant: the housekeeper flung her
fist forward, a gray cloud burst over them, and she and
the oaf threw their hands over their eyes. Luc staggered
back, coughing, his palm covering his face.

"Arabella," he gasped. *"Run."*

She ran. But she was not quick enough. Her captor
grabbed her shoulder, spun her around and knocked her
head with the side of his fist.

Pain. Her stomach lurched. She scrabbled for a hold
but her hands only found his thick body. She struck
him. He grabbed her wrists and pinned them together,
then hauled her back up the steps. Luc lunged toward
them. The man released her and slammed his fist into
Luc's jaw. She jumped forward then jerked back; the
housekeeper's fingers clamped around her hair. She saw
Luc reel and the oaf pointed the pistol at him.

"No!" she shouted. "I will do whatever you want.
Lock me up. Do whatever you wish to me. Just don't
harm him. I beg of you!"

The man shoved her back into the bedchamber. The
door slammed shut and the lock clicked.

She wasted no time in further begging. Throwing off her cloak, she went to the window, pushed the curtain aside, and climbed onto the sill.

The ground was remarkably far below. She grabbed hold of the pipe, found a nail for a foothold, and prayed.

She fell more than climbed. Her feet hit the ground hard and she tumbled over, then pushed to her knees and, torn and bleeding from her descent, set off at a run around the side of the house.

Figures moved in the distance near the river, and she flattened her back against the house.

From afar she saw the bishop's man shove Luc with the pistol. Luc struggled, but with his arms tied behind his back again he seemed unbalanced. His captor lifted an arm, hit him in the head with the butt of the pistol, and Luc staggered. He kept his footing, but the man pushed him to the edge of the riverbank where a small rowboat was tied up. As Luc's head came up slowly, painfully it seemed, the man just stood there, no longer even pointing the pistol at his captive.

Luc looked off to the side. The man threw back his head and laughed, the sound lost to her against the rumbling of the river and her own roaring heartbeats and labored breaths. His captor stepped forward and struck him again and Luc stumbled back. Then, with a mighty shove, the man pushed him into the river.

She clamped her lips over her cry and gripped the wall behind her. If he saw her, all was lost.

Her heart was screaming. Luc's hands were tied. She had only minutes.

The man watched the water for a moment, then turned and lumbered toward the house. As soon as he was around the corner of the building, she broke into a run.

Chapter 18

The Bull and the Boar

Wet and stiff, the knots would not respond to his fingers, and he was sinking fast. And running out of air.

He shook his arm thickly through the water. The penknife from Arabella's cloak pocket slipped from inside his cuff into his palm.

He cut his wrists and fingers then finally rope, and his hands burst free. He swept his arms around. His shoulder slammed into a rock. He was moving with the current. He knew this river. But he could see no light, no sun from above directing him. His lungs screamed for air. Her voice shouting his name came to him through the blackness and noise. *A dream.* An illusion. Desperate men heard mermaids in the sea's depths. Arabella was his siren. She had always been, calling to him over the gurgle and rush of the river, the confusion in his head.

He broke free to the surface. He gulped in air. Midnight enveloped him. Complete darkness.

Her voice called him again. His dream. But closer now. *Real*.

He marked the sweet, strident sound. He turned his body toward it, against the current, and swam.

SHE SAW HIM struggle, go under, and disappear.

The oar was slippery in her hands, her head dizzy, the water all around seething, silver sunlight slanting off its surface. She could not see him.

"Luc! Oh, God, Luc, where are you?" she shouted. "Luc!"

She leaned forward, pushing the oar into the water, but she was flying past the place where he had gone under, speeding forward. The boat smacked against a rock and jerked to the side. She grabbed at air. The oar hit another rock and flew out of her hands. She lunged for it. The boat tipped.

She fell in. With flailing arms and flying skirts and an enormous splash she sank into the river. Water poured into her mouth. She choked, struggling to hold her head above, coughing and paddling, her legs caught in her skirts. She sank. She would drown. Her nightmare coming true. Before she told him. Taking his child. The river sucked at her, dragging her beneath.

Strong arms came around her, lifting, scooping, pushing away the water. She gasped in air, coughed and sputtered and breathed.

His arms were around her, holding her above water, pulling her toward the riverbank.

He hauled her onto the bank.

His hands came around her face, wiping the streaming hair from her eyes. She coughed and then she was in his lap and he was holding her and hot tears covered her cheeks.

"Duchess," he said harshly, then "Duchess" again, over and over, his lips upon her brow and cheeks. She sought his mouth with hers. He kissed her, fusing them, his hands cradling her head, holding her to him.

Her fingers tangled in his shirt. He was warm, solid, strong, and whole. She had gone without him for too long. Now she wanted to pour herself into him.

He pulled away abruptly and grabbed her shoulders. "On which bank of the river are we now? The house side?"

She shook her head.

His hands tightened on her. "*Which bank?* Speak!"

"The opposite bank." She lifted her hand to his face. His eye was closed and swollen red, his brow tight. An angry welt crossed his temple. "Downriver a hundred yards at least. Beyond the copse."

He pulled her up as he rose. His hands were cut in a dozen places. His head was bent. "Do you see the fence?"

She nodded. "What—"

"Do you see the fence?"

"Yes! But I don't under—"

"I cannot see, Arabella. You must lead us to the gate. Quickly now. They will discover your absence."

He couldn't see?

"Yes. Yes." She wrapped her arms around his and drew him quickly away from the river and toward the copse, her skirts dragging and his steps faltering. He stumbled many times, but she held onto him tightly and gave him what little strength she had and her sight.

HIS KNOCK ECHOED for at least a minute before Arabella heard the bolts being thrown, and then the great door slowly opened. She shivered, frozen, her gown clinging.

The young woman before them stared open-mouthed.

"I am the Count of Rallis and this is my wife," Luc said between teeth clenched against chattering. "We should like an audience with the headmistress at once."

The woman ushered them in.

Within minutes Arabella was seated before a fire in a comfortable sitting room of amber hues. She clutched a blanket around her.

"I had not thought I could be c-colder than that night on your ship," she stuttered. "Do you suppose they will give us b-brandy?"

He said nothing. He stood beside her, his hand clenched on the back of her chair.

The door opened and a woman came in and directly to them, the hem of her plain dark gown nearly to the floor.

"Good day, my lord. My lady." She curtsied. She was not young; her brown hair was streaked with silver and her voice was mature.

Luc bowed, his hand never leaving the chair back. He did not open his eye. "My wife and I have come upon a spot of trouble and wonder if you might assist us in returning to London."

"We should be honored to assist you, my lord. My lady, if you will"—she gestured to the door where another woman stood now—"Miss Magee will show you to my personal chambers where she can assist you in changing into dry clothing." She turned to Luc. "My lord, I fear that the only men in residence in our school at present are the drawing master, who is a considerably smaller man than you, and our coachman, who is rather more your size."

"I shan't mind changing my wedding finery for another sort of groom's garments," he said.

The headmistress's brows rose.

"Today we were to be wed," Arabella explained. "A second time."

But the woman seemed to be studying his face. He had not yet opened his swollen eye, and the scar showed livid against his cold skin.

"My lord, despite your civility you are clearly unwell," she said. "I shouldn't mind helping you both today, but I don't fancy finding myself burdened with a lord in a burning fever while trying to hold the curiosity of seventy-six innocent girls at bay. Let us get you both dry with haste, and then you can tell me all about your thwarted wedding."

Arabella laughed.

Luc did not quite grin, but his shoulders seemed to relax. "Madam, at the risk of broaching the delicate subject of a lady's age, I don't suppose you were the headmistress at this school twenty years ago?"

"I was, in fact. Newly headmistress. The challenges of the position weighed upon me greatly in those days, and I used to take walks about the park to settle my thoughts. Once, in fact, I invited another refugee into this chamber, a boy who wandered onto our property several times," she said, watching him carefully. "In the twenty years since, I have sometimes wondered how that boy fared."

Arabella did not understand, but she wanted desperately to touch him and tell him she was near.

He turned his face toward the fire, or perhaps toward her. "He fared as well as any boy could hope."

SHE CHANGED INTO dry clothing and was told the drawing master was assisting Luc to dress. She waited at the door, and when he came out she took his arm, and whispered directions to him as they walked. His steps were careful; she allowed him to set the pace. But even in her exhaustion she felt the bunching frustration in his muscles and saw the anger in his tight jaw.

He declined tea. Night was falling and he thought it best to return to London without delay.

When they were inside the school's carriage, she reached for his hand.

"Luc—"

He drew his hand away. Arabella swallowed back her grief and allowed him his silence and his distance.

"YE SAY IT burned till ye went in the strict, then the pain went aff?"

"Yes, the river water seemed to wash away the initial hellacious agony. But you have asked me this before. Two dozen times in the past three days."

"I'm a man o' science. I must be thorough."

"You are a quack and I am astounded I have been allowing you to see to my physical welfare for twenty years."

Gavin's callused fingertips pressed against Luc's brow, pulling his eyelid wide.

Luc knocked away his hand. "I can do that myself. I've still got hands."

"Aye, all cut up but ye winna allou me to bandage them."

"I look enough like a fool with this bandage across my eye."

A splash of warm liquid hit Luc's eye. Drops. He blinked. All the sensations were still there—cold, heat, pain—though considerably less pain than at first. Only the pictures were gone. The light.

"Yer a trying patient, lad."

"I don't care to be fussed over."

"Ye dinna care to need anybody. Makes ye as mad as a bull no' to be the one protecting everybody else." He replaced the bandage. "'Tis a guid thing all my patients aren't like ye, lad."

Luc settled the kerchief over his scar again. "You haven't got any other patients. Not paying patients, anyway."

"As sore as a boar, ye are." He slapped Luc on the shoulder.

Luc sat forward and rubbed his temples. His eye still wanted to see and it made his head ache like the devil. It hadn't been nearly as bad with the first, but this eye was still whole. Only useless. "Well, make up your mind. Am I a bull or a boar?" he grumbled.

"Both. But I'd be worse if it were me." The clasp of Gavin's case clicked shut. "I've no' got a bonnie lass to read to me an' to caress ma scars when they ache, nou do I?"

There'd been no caressing of scars—or of anything—in the three days since he'd been blinded by the housekeeper's dust. Gavin thought it must have been pepper. Luc only knew it'd felt like fire.

And now his whole world had changed. It had become black, and confined to the chambers in Lycombe House that he had already come to know well enough that he could mostly avoid bumping into furniture. He feared to fall. He feared her seeing him fall. Even more so he hated that if she fell he would not know it, and that he would not be able to help her rise because he could not go to her.

He feared that if she disappeared he would not be able to search for her.

She had thanked him for dragging her from the river. *Thanked him.* And he had barely spoken a word to her since, because he simply could not. He could not bear the shame of weakness. He could not bear to be, after so many years, helpless again.

"Tell me again, Gavin," he said. "Tell me this could be temporary."

The Scot grasped his shoulder. "Ye already know it, lad. Nou ye've got to wait."

MILES SHAVED AND dressed him, fussing like Gavin but much the same as before.

In other matters—matters that Luc managed himself—he was clumsy. He spilled food from his plate and had to bear the footman cleaning it without a word. After that he began to take meals in his private chambers. He walked with his hand on the wall, slowly, carefully, like an old man with the gout. He had navigated oceans and now his landscape narrowed to the route between his bedchamber and the library.

He should leave his infant cousin's house and take a house elsewhere. Lycombe House was not his; he did not have the right to live in it. But he could not go to his club and query friends for suitable residences to let. Even if he asked his man of business to hire a house for him, he would be obliged to learn it inch by inch. He could take Arabella to his house in the North where he had never lived, but there would be many more chambers to learn, and she would be isolated with him only.

He could not ride, read, play cards, or write correspondence. He could not drive a carriage. He could not sail even a yawl. He could not see his wife's eyes.

Tony and Cam called. They talked and drank and tried to make him laugh until he wearied of idleness and sent them away like the surly boar Gavin had called him. He could drink himself into oblivion every day if he wished; the footmen were wonderfully prompt about refilling his glass before he asked. He supposed they preferred him insensible to surly. But after the first night of drunkenness to dull his remaining senses, when she announced that she was leaving the door open between their bedchambers so she could hear him if he needed help, he ordered all the brandy in the house locked up.

He needed her more than she understood. He needed her with a desperation that ate at him and made him sick now. He had nothing to give her. She had never wanted the title; she wanted a prince so she could find her parents. He had wealth, but she never coveted that either, not his little governess who had made a good name for herself on the edge of society entirely by her own merits.

But with his money, he might be able to find the one thing she did want. He could find her real family.

"My lord?" The butler's voice came from the left—the library doorway. Luc sat by the window. He welcomed the pale warmth of the winter sun he could not see.

"Yes, Simpson?"

"Mr. Parsons has come from Combe. He has brought several persons with him. I have told him that you are not at home to callers. But he insists that you see—that is, that you allow these persons an audience."

"Send them in." As a trustee of the estate, he could hardly turn away the land steward. And soon enough the Surly Lord would acquire a reputation in town as a boar and a recluse. He might as well enjoy the company of callers now while they still came, and Parsons's attention while Fletcher allowed it. Luc had no doubt the bishop would use his blindness as an excuse to rob him of what small power he had over the estate and his cousin's future. Trapped, helpless, he wouldn't be able to do a damn thing about it.

"My lord," the steward said. "Good day."

"What brings you to town, Parsons?"

"I have information to share with you, my lord." The man sounded downright meek. It was the blindness. Everybody was tiptoeing around him now, using lowered voices and gentle words as if he were an invalid. Which he was.

"First, my lord, may I tell you of the profound horror and grief of everyone at Combe over the consequences of your unfortunate acci—"

"Yes, that's fine, Parsons. Thank you." *Accident.* Christos and Ravenna had come to him apologizing for their parts in Arabella's visit to Fletcher's house. He assured them she would have done it without their encouragement. No one else knew the truth. Christos had tried to tell him about the story they invented to explain both their disappearances from the wedding and his loss of sight, but he didn't want to hear. It was done. He was blind. Society could believe what it wished. That was an end to it.

Fletcher knew, of course. He had not come to Lycombe House since. Probably busy burning all those files Arabella had seen.

"My lord, three of the tenant farmers from Combe are with me: Goode, Lambkin, and Post."

Luc nodded and hoped he was looking in their direction. "What news from the land, gentlemen?"

"Milord, we've come to you with a petition."

Subtly, he adjusted the angle of his head to face the voice. "A petition? That sounds downright revolutionary of you, Goode." He guessed it was Goode who spoke. Arabella would know. He wished she were here with him to read these men, as he could no longer read anything. He should have called her. He needed her.

"Not at all, milord. It's only that, you see . . . we're afraid."

"Afraid?"

"With the new little duke, God bless him, we're— Well, we hoped with you as duke matters would be settled. But our wives and our boys are afraid now and we've got to do something for it."

"Of what precisely are your families afraid, Goode?"

"Of *who*, milord."

Luc drew a slow breath and nodded.

"We need your help, milord." This came from another of the men. Lambkin? "We're that desperate."

"I do know a thing or two of desperation, Lambkin."

They responded with silence to that.

"Tell me."

"The bishop—that is, her ladyship's brother—he came around last year telling us we had to give him our quarterlies. He told us to tell Mr. Parsons that the duke wanted it all to go to charity. Well, when we told him them rents weren't anybody's but ours and the duke's and we'd only give them over to Mr. Parsons, he got all friendly and said he'd like to take our boys for a school he'd made for country folk. It's a charity place, so the boys can learn their letters and arithmetic and be clerks in town someday. He said he needed some good farm boys to get the place going and he'd like ours as much as anybody's."

"He told you that, did he?" Luc said. "What did you think of it?"

"We didn't trust him, milord. Never mind that he's supposed to be a man of God."

"Why not? Did you, perhaps, see the bishop's generous offer a threat in response to your refusal to give him your rents?"

"Yes, milord."

Silence. One of the men shifted his feet.

"You see, milord," Lambkin finally said, "my young-

est son—my Toby—he stayed after church one day
when the bishop was preaching at the parish, to help
with cleaning up as he does. He's a good lad." His voice
crackled. "That day Toby came running home with a
tale that made my missus weep for a fortnight."

"I see."

"Milord." It was Goode again. "We're asking you to
help our boys. It's them or Combe."

AFTER THEY DEPARTED, Luc made his way—slowly,
awkwardly—back to his bedchamber and penned a
brief letter. He had no idea if it was legible, but he could
not dictate it to another. He would be obliged to ask
Miles to read the response. That was enough.

On the front he printed Fletcher's name, and he gave
it to the footman whom Arabella had assigned to sit outside his door—Claude, the same footman Luc had ordered to follow her about Combe. He told him to deliver
it by hand and wait for a response.

The footman did not move away.

"What is the trouble, Claude?"

"Well, Cap'n . . . maybe you could tell me where you
want it to go?"

"You cannot read the name and direction."

"Nope, Cap'n."

"Hm. I never realized quite how poor my penman-
ship was before."

The footman smothered a guffaw.

He made Claude memorize the message and then
threw the letter into the fire. The sailor had been mid-
shipman for seven years on the *Victory*. He was quick-
witted and loyal, the very reason he had brought him to
Combe with Joseph to look after Arabella. He simply
had to trust him now. He had no other choice.

THAT NIGHT, LUC did not retire to the library. With steps he had counted a hundred times that afternoon in practice, he went to the door between his chamber and Arabella's and opened it.

He heard her quick intake of breath. Surprise, or alarm? "Mary, you may go now," she said, her voice composed. She was on the right side of the chamber, perhaps at the dressing table. He tried to imagine the space but felt disoriented. He had come into this chamber only once, the evening she told him about the ring and the prince and her dream—the dream that she had given up for the families of Combe.

The bed was straight ahead, three yards away perhaps. He remembered that much. He'd thought about it quite a lot.

The maid's quick footsteps passed between them. The door clicked shut.

"Are you unwell?" Skirts rustled softly, swiftly. Then she was before him, her scent of summer roses and wild lavender inside his head and all around him. "May I help you?"

"I haven't come for help," he said awkwardly. He had prepared a speech, and a rather good speech at that. She liked his teasing—when it didn't infuriate her—and he wanted to charm her now. But nothing came to his tongue. "I had a speech prepared," he mumbled. "I—"

The brush of her fingertips across his jaw was the caress of heaven. He steadied himself against his need. She curved her hand around his neck and drew his mouth down to hers.

She kissed him tentatively at first, then more surely, then with hunger and urgency quite like he was feeling. He ran his hands down her sides and tugged her close, wanting her against him, such a slight little thing, but strong. And eager. She tried to burrow closer, her hands sliding beneath his waistcoat.

He swept her up in his arms and stepped forward. She broke her mouth free.

"Left! Go left!"

He halted.

She laughed, sweetly, lightly, and the knot of anger around his heart unwound.

After a brief misdirection to her ear that started her giggling again, he found her mouth and kissed her hard. She drew away.

"Left, one step. Then forward two. Then left one," she whispered a little breathlessly, and nuzzled his jaw. She wound her arms about his neck, her fingers slipping into his hair. "You will learn the route if you do it often enough, you know," she added almost shyly.

"Often, hm?"

"Or . . . perhaps you wish to make this excursion just this once." Her voice was smaller.

He stepped to the left, then forward twice, then to the left, and laid her gently down on the mattress. Slowly, he bent to her, finding her with his hands then his lips—her brow, her cheek, her mouth. "Just this once in this half hour, at least," he said, and kissed her again. She wound her arms around his neck and gave him her sweet mouth and tongue and her soft breasts pressed to his chest.

"But, little governess," he said, tasting her, drinking in her eager beauty in the supple dampness of her mouth. His fingers sank into her satin hair. "I suspect I will need more lessons before the night is through."

Her hand stole beneath his shirt, and her breaths deepened upon a sigh. He had never known such a beautiful sound. It filled him with longing and profound satisfaction at once. She stroked him, her palms smoothing across his skin. She wound her leg around his back, digging her heel into his buttock. Her scent was everywhere, her body perfect beneath his. He pressed her into the mattress and she arched to him with a soft moan.

"Many more lessons," he said huskily.

"Then, my lord," she whispered in his ear and nibbled on it, "I am the right teacher for the job."

IT TURNED OUT that her husband did indeed require many more lessons. There were textures that he demanded to be allowed to spend time memorizing, and then memorizing again to be certain he knew them by heart. Then there were hands and legs and other parts of her that had to be traced with fingers and often his tongue; so he could create a mental map of the landscape, he insisted. At times, especially the occasions involving his tongue, Arabella felt that she became the student rather than the instructor.

She gave herself up completely to education.

He repeated lessons. She protested, saying it was not necessary for him to do so if he did not wish, that really he had already been an exemplary student from the start, that he had not actually needed any instruction. But her protests were remarkably weak, and he would not hear of it. He applied himself diligently.

She slept in his arms.

When he climbed from her bed shortly before dawn, he kissed her lips and her brow, and she invited him to visit her schoolroom again that evening. With a handsome smile and a gallant bow, he said he would be happy to return for further instruction.

Then he grasped the bedpost, tilted his brow to it, and

quietly requested her assistance to navigate the treacherous strait between their bedchambers.

As she fell into sleep she wept, though she did not know if her tears were of grief or joy.

LUC STEPPED ONTO the bridge in the freezing drizzle and knew he was the greatest fool alive.

If so, he was a happy fool. A happy fool whose wife deserved much better than a blind lover and a defunct duke.

Clutching the rail, he went slowly forward. Chill mist whisked beneath the brim of his hat. But Fletcher had demanded this location and time.

Luc wondered if his old guardian was an imbecile or if he truly believed that he was one. A man did not bring a blind man to a bridge over the Thames before dawn unless he intended to deposit him in said Thames.

Clearly the bishop did not want another near miss. This time he would see to the deed himself.

Behind the muffling patter of rain, Luc could hear a heavy cart and draft horse clopping down an alley close by, the slurps of the river against the hulls of fishing boats moored on the bank, and the complaints of hungry gulls awaiting the daylight. The rain was icy, the footing slick, but he knew the sounds and scents and texture of river and sea like he knew his name and that he loved Arabella. He made his way carefully, by feel, upright, struggling to recall the lay and breadth of this bridge. He'd only seen it once or twice before.

"Are you unarmed?" Fletcher's hushed voice came out of the darkness ahead.

Luc halted. "As required. But I'd have no use of a

weapon now. Not even a blade, unfortunately. Unless of course you stood quite close and I could slide it across your throat."

"*Tsk tsk,* Lucien. Murder is a sin."

"Then I am damned already. What's another soul gone to his maker at my hands for me to fear the consequences, hm?"

"Send your servant away with the horses."

"You and I both know he is not going away until that ring is in his hand."

There was a long silence while the rain turned to mist and Luc waited, his muscles tensed.

A whiff of stale tobacco smoke and the tang of hair oil approached before he heard the heavy breaths before him.

"You're a good swimmer, milord," Fletcher's coachman said closer than he'd expected. "But I don't think you'll be swimming away this time."

Luc extended his hand, palm up. The man pressed the ring into it, then grabbed Luc's hand and with a burst of tobacco-scented breath whispered at his shoulder, "I'd kill you myself for making a fool of me, but his excellency wants to do it."

"I am honored by the both of you." Luc pulled free. "Now back up fifteen paces."

"What—"

"Do it," Fletcher said.

"Have you come as I required, Fletcher?" Luc said.

"A hood conceals my face and my servant's. Your servant will not know us unless you have told him who we are."

"Among the two of us here, only one man is without honor, and it isn't me."

"How noble of you, Lucien." Fletcher spoke with no

sarcasm, as though he were only the bishop, only the priest, mildly commenting on a truth. Even in the midst of his villainy he did not know he was a villain.

Luc lifted his hand with the ring above his head. Footsteps splashed on the bridge behind him, approaching at a jog.

"Cap'n," Claude said as he came beside him.

Luc passed the ring to him. "Is it as I described it to you?"

"Yessir."

"The markings and color?"

"Exactly, Cap'n. It don't look like a fake, sir."

There was no way to know for certain except when Arabella saw it. He could only hope that Fletcher hadn't had sufficient time to commission a paste copy in the few hours since he'd contacted him.

"Can you see these men's faces?"

"No, sir."

"Where are they?"

"Three yards and another three yards farther." Claude's voice grinned. "Would you like me to take care of them, Cap'n?"

"No, thank you." God bless the loyalty of sailors to their captains. "I want you to walk to the horses so that you do not lose sight of these men, but watch about you as well."

"So they can't jump me and take the ring while you're standing here."

"That's the idea."

"Cap'n," he said. "I don't like to—"

"Then I want you to mount and with the other horse in tow call to me as you leave. Ride directly to the house and give that ring to Mr. Miles, but do not tell him how you acquired it. Do you understand?"

"Yessir." The sailor's voice was no longer amused, instead grim.

"Go now."

"Aye aye, sir."

His footsteps smacked along the bridge, receding. A moment passed, then another. Hooves clacked on the cobbles.

"I'm off, Cap'n!"

The rain had become a fine mist, cold on Luc's cheeks.

"You have your trinket again, Lucien. I trust you are satisfied."

"Adina's child is not Theodore's."

"Come now," Fletcher chuckled. "You cannot hope to play these games now, when you are beaten. Look at you, blind, ruined. What sort of duke would you be?"

"I seek only the good of my family. That child is not my family, and neither are you."

"My sister is a virtuous woman."

"Your sister is easily led by you. If you tell her to make a public confession, if you insist that it is for the good of her soul, she will do it."

"I have no such interest." Fletcher's voice was flat. To Luc it sounded like the Devil's.

"There are dozens of people who will testify that the old Duke and Duchess of Lycombe did not once meet during the fourteen months prior to his death."

"Half the titled nobles in English history have been bastards. Your claim will be laughed out of Lords." A hint of bravado marked the bishop's tone. *Unusual.* He never wavered from serene confidence.

Discomfort built behind Luc's eyes, deep. The scar ached, but the left eye sizzled with pain. He wanted to close it. He could not. Fletcher would see it as weakness, even with his blindness.

"I don't make the claim for myself," he said.

"Then for whom? For your poor, feeble-minded brother?"

"For the people whom you have hurt and seek to hurt more gravely through this child who is not the rightful lord of Combe. I will—" The pain spiked. A pinpoint of golden light darted across the blackness. His throat constricted.

It was his imagination. It had to be. His hand tightened on the rail. The palest smudge of gray floated before him.

"What will you do? Claim the duchy? Come now, Lucien—"

"I will petition Parliament." The golden dart came again, like a hummingbird, there for an instant then gone. "I will make my claim to the title, and if you fight me I will tell them everything. About the extortion. About the innocents. About my brother if I must." The gray smudge widened, deepened. The gold star sparkled. *Dizziness*. He gulped in breaths and closed his eye. The gold star vanished with the gray.

"You are as mad as him," he heard as though from a distance.

The rain had stopped and the air off the river was frigid. Luc opened his eye and the star flickered before him again in the smudge of gray. His heart pounded.

He stepped forward.

"Remain where you are."

"I am blind, Fletcher." *Not forever.* Dear God. "What do you imagine I can do to you at such a distance without a weapon?"

Fletcher laughed, but it was not an easy sound. Luc blinked. The smudge of gray was a patch the color of early dawn marked by a dot of pale cream. *Fletcher's face?* Below it, the flickering star. *The pectoral cross.*

"You are angry, nephew. Anger discolors judgment.

It is a sin for a rational man to succumb to anger, and inconvenient. If you do something rash now, you will harm yourself."

"You are afraid," he said. "Even of a blind man. You are so afraid you will burn in eternity for your many sins that you fear death beyond reason. Even now you fear me because of what I would do to you if I could see." With each moment he spoke, his world expanded, shadows, shapes in the dimness, the bridge's railing, the silhouette of the man.

"You have never sought to harm me before," Fletcher said. "You ran from me. You should run now."

"I'm finished running."

"Not yet." His voice had changed again, like silk cut through with slashes made by a knife. "I will make certain Christos is given the credit for your murder."

Luc jerked forward.

"Stand back," Fletcher barked. "Or this will be more painful than necessary."

Now Luc saw a glimmer of silver beneath the pale oval face and the sparkle of gold. He dropped his eyelid halfway and fought to focus on the bishop's henchman farther away. A darker shadow in the dark dawn, he stood three yards away. *Far enough.*

"You cannot hurt me again," he said, and it was the truth.

"I have the confession letter ready," Fletcher said. "He will kill you and the infant and be so remorseful that he will lose his mind entirely."

"He is stronger than you know." *Continue talking.* Talk until the shadows were clearer, the glinting rail of the bridge and shimmering puddles and golden cross no longer distractions from the pistol's dully shining muzzle. "He will not oblige you by going mad. He is a good man and he will be a good lord."

"Let's see about that, shall we?" The pistol cock clicked. Luc threw himself forward. A crack sounded then a burst of smoke.

No pain.

Luc slammed his fist into Fletcher's face. The bishop fell against the rail. He grappled in his cloak. Luc hit him again. The henchman would be upon him in moments. He could not win this fight with only shadows and sparkles to guide him. But he'd take Fletcher with him if he could.

Footfalls pounded behind him. He pivoted, swinging his arm, catching the man's chin. With a grunt the henchman jerked back. Silver flashed in his hand. Luc grabbed for his wrist and kicked him in the groin. With a groan the brute doubled over. The knife clinked to the bridge.

Pain sliced through the back of Luc's arm. He roared and spun.

Fletcher leaped back, the knife glittering in his hand stretched toward Luc.

"Now, Lucien." He took another retreating step. "You mustn't fight m—" He stumbled. His arms windmilled. He fell back, tumbling into shadow. Luc lunged forward. His foot dropped into nothing. He jerked away from the hole.

A dull splash sounded below.

He advanced with his hands first, finding the railing, grabbing it, bending his head over to peer down. He saw nothing, only the blackness of the river until he thought he was blind again.

Footsteps thumped on the bridge. Luc swung around. The bishop's coachman was running away. He disappeared in the fog of Luc's imperfect sight.

Luc sank to his knees and breathed deeply. Then again. A glimmer on the ground caught his eye: the golden cross, its chain broken, lying on the rain-washed stone.

He pushed to his feet, the chill dawn settling around him in stripes of pearl. Below him the river rested, quiet, no fishermen about yet, nothing to disturb the tranquility but the cries of a few impatient gulls.

He found the pistol in a puddle and tossed it into the Thames. Then he walked away.

Chapter 19

The Lovers

As early as she dared, Arabella knocked on Adina's door. The new mother slept at all hours now, enamored of her tiny son, insisting on nursing him despite the advisements of Mrs. Baxter, the housekeeper, and a dozen of her friends.

After returning from Richmond, Arabella had delayed speaking privately with Adina. The birth had been quick but Adina had not recovered from it immediately. But Arabella could delay no longer. Luc would never claim what he deserved. Not now. His pride was too strong. So she must claim it for him.

She stifled a yawn as she waited for the door to open. She had slept very little.

A smile crept over her lips. She closed her eyes and bounced a bit on the balls of her toes.

A sleepy maid finally opened the door. Adina greeted her sleepily as well, though with a happy countenance. She was thin and pale, but a breakfast tray beside the bed bore the remnants of chocolate, toast, and a lemon custard. The sight of it made Arabella's stomach turn. Nothing tasted good to her now. But she ate anyway. Her baby needed it.

She could not hide the news from Luc any longer. The fear that had kept her from telling him before—the fear that, assured his goal of an heir, he would never seek her out again—was now gone. And with his new attention to the details of her body, he would discover the changes in her soon enough. Perhaps she would tell him and show him tonight at the same time.

A delicious little shiver scampered through her.

"Darling Arabella, how happy I am to see you with smudges beneath your eyes. It is lovely not to be the only woman in the house that looks so wretched." Adina said it so sweetly that Arabella had to chuckle. "But your sleeplessness, I suspect, is caused by another sort of activity than mine." She cast a besotted glance at the cradle in which her infant slept.

"Adina." Arabella sat on the end of the bed. "I need to tell you a story. I hope you will listen to it carefully before you make a decision."

Her pretty gold lashes spread wide. "A decision about what?"

"About whether you will confess publicly that your son is not your husband's and allow Luc to take his rightful place as the Duke of Lycombe."

Adina's face crumpled.

But she listened.

When Arabella finished speaking, Adina dipped her head.

"My brother said he would never do it again." Her voice was thin. "After I found him that time with my page boy—" She closed her eyes. "He promised."

"He lied."

"Not only about that." She met Arabella's gaze. "He told my dear Theodore that I was unfaithful to him. After that, my husband would not allow me at Combe. Then Christos came to visit me here. He had been to see Theodore. He brought a friend with him." She plucked Arabella's hand from her lap and squeezed it. "I did not intend it, Arabella darling! You must know: I adored my Theodore. But I was so lonely and he was so far away, and Michel comforted me." She made a sad little shrug.

"Adina, will you write this and sign the document before witnesses? Will you stand before Parliament and the king if you must and declare the truth?"

Her pretty brow creased. But she nodded. "My baby . . ."

"Luc will care for him. He will be a member of this family even if he does not bear the Westfall name. We will never abandon him."

Adina's lashes flickered with uncertainty. "Michel wishes to wed me. Even if it means our son will not be a duke, he wants to claim him as his own. Men are sometimes very contrary, aren't they?"

ARABELLA DESCENDED THE stairs, heart and step light, and went to the library. Luc had spent the past several days there. She would tell him her news in private and watch his face. Then she would tell him everything.

He was not in the library.

She looked in the parlor, the drawing room, and the dining chamber. The garden was gray and damp and empty.

She climbed the stairs to his bedchamber and knocked. Her stomach fluttered with impatience. *Silly.* But imagining seeing him was always so much easier than actually seeing him. He was large and a little bit dangerous and still gorgeously confident despite all, and he made her so wretchedly weak with pure longing she was furious with him for it. Then he would kiss her and wrap her in his arms and she felt as powerful as a goddess.

She was utterly hopeless.

Miles opened the door. He stared at her, his face pale and eyes wide. He said nothing.

A tickle of cold nerves stirred in her. "Is his lordship within?"

"No, my lady."

"Do you know where I can find him?"

The valet's face seemed to turn paler. "Not precisely, my lady."

"When does he intend to return?"

His mouth opened then closed.

"Mr. Miles, where is my husband?"

He widened the door. Heart speeding now, she walked inside the chamber. Luc was not within. She pivoted to his valet.

Mr. Miles stood with his palm extended, her family's ring upon it.

She couldn't breathe.

"Where is he?"

"Claude and he rode to the East End this morning, my lady." His voice was clipped. "His lordship met with the bishop."

"No." Her lungs were folding in upon themselves. "No." Her head snapped up. "When? And where exactly?"

WAITING FOR THE carriage was a torture Arabella had never imagined. When it came around, she flung herself inside and called to the driver.

The avenues of Mayfair disappeared swiftly, but as they neared the City, the streets grew crowded with carts, carriages, and horsemen. She gripped the seat with frozen hands. He would not be there now, still. But she could not believe that. She would scour the dockside taverns and sailor's haunts to find him as she had in Plymouth. She would find someone who had seen him, a fisherman or river warden, *anybody*. Someone must have noticed him. Blind lords did not go wandering about the banks of the Thames alone on foot every dawn, after all.

The carriage was not moving. She snapped open the window and poked her head out to call up to the coachman. They were jammed in a row of traffic. The street was filled with people, on foot and horseback, all watching a parade—a circus parade, it seemed, with stilt walkers and boys in shining waistcoats and women riding beribboned ponies and gay music from flute and cymbals and brightly painted carts. A pair of performers passed by, juggling sticks of fire like the performers in Saint-Nazaire the night she had first given herself to an arrogant ship captain, despite her dream of wedding a prince, because even then she loved him.

"No." Her heart twisted. *"No."* She pressed her palms to her eyes and tears soaked them.

The parade passed and the crowd began to move from the street into shops and down alleyways. Her driver shrugged the carriage along. She pulled in breaths, willing away the despair, and peered out the window.

From out of the thinning crowd, Luc appeared, walking.

Choking on a sob she threw open the door and tumbled out of the carriage into a run.

He walked straight toward her. It seemed he smiled at her.

She flew at him. She threw her arms around him and he tucked her into his embrace. He was cold all over, his clothing and hair, and shaking lightly. She reached up and pulled his face to her and kissed him, then kissed him again. "You can see," she uttered. "You can *see*." She kissed his cheeks and his jaw and his brow and pushed the black kerchief aside and kissed his scar.

"Duchess, you will unman me," he said quietly, roughly, but smiling, his hands tight on her waist. Stragglers in the crowd watched curiously.

She tugged the kerchief into place and kissed it, then his whole eye and his cheeks and mouth again. "You could never be less than a great man."

His hand came around her chin and he looked down at her soberly. "Arabella, he is dead."

"Did you kill him?"

"No. I would have. But it was an accident."

"You did the right thing."

"Yes, I did." He stroked her cheek with his thumb. "But with you, Arabella Anne Westfall, I have done everything wrong, from the moment we met, at nearly every turn. I have been arrogant and overly confident and short-tempered and deeply, insatiably lustful"—a bystander gasped—"and afraid of this between us. I was everything that must have been abhorrent to you when all you wished was to find your prince charming. Instead you ended up with a blind, surly, autocratic fool. If I could turn back time, if I could do what I should have done—"

"Before I fell in love with you?"

"—b-before I stole your virtue." His brow cut down. "By God, woman, you will always say what I least expect, won't you?"

"I tried again and again not to love you." She tucked her hands inside his coat. "I failed."

"You failed." He smiled.

"But I did not fail in all matters. Adina has written a confession of her affair with a Frenchman who is eager to claim their son as his own. You are now the duke, your grace."

He laughed and shook his head. Then his gaze took on that intensity that made her knees weak.

"I am lost without you, duchess."

"Then you are found. Because you will not be without me ever again." She dipped her brow to his chest. "I will never leave you."

"This declaration is because I am no longer entirely blind, isn't it?" he said a bit unsteadily. "You feared having to instruct me every night, but now you needn't worry about that."

She arched her brows. "Of course not. The reason I will not leave you is because you are a duke."

"I see."

"I always wanted to marry high."

"Did you?"

"And I want my baby to be a duke. Or perhaps the sister of a duke."

He blinked. "Your baby?"

She offered him a small smile. "Your baby."

"My . . ." His throat jerked. His hands tightened on her waist. "We need to go home." His voice was hoarse. "Now."

"Now? All right. But—"

"I want you."

"You—"

"I want you now. Always. Everywhere and as my everything—my lover, my friend, my sharp-tongued beauty, my drinking companion, my children's mother, my courage in the face of certain defeat. My sanctuary." He captured her lips. "My duchess."

He kissed her. She returned his kiss with great enthusiasm.

"But at this specific moment," he said between kisses, "I just really want you in my bed."

With eager compliance, she accepted his kisses on her throat. "I can oblige you in that, your grace."

"Or your bed. Whichever we come to first."

"You are all that is wise and efficient."

"Or the carriage."

She grabbed his hand. "Let's be off then, shall we?" Laughter bubbling from her, she dragged him toward the carriage.

He snatched her back to him and with his hands around her face said, "Arabella, I love you."

"Luc?"

"Yes?"

"Will you marry me?"

Epilogue

The Fairy Tale

Frothy skirts of snow white silk glittering with tiny diamonds and cascading down the long train spilled over the arms of the chair upon which the Duchess of Lycombe perched in her dressing chamber. A diamond tiara sparkled in her hair falling like spun copper about her shoulders and the puffed cap sleeves of her wedding gown.

Her sisters sat across from her. On the table between them a lone object glimmered gold and crimson.

"I do not expect it of either of you." Arabella's gaze darted back and forth between them, radiant joy in her eyes. "I have all I wish—your well-being and Luc's." She placed her palm on her belly. "And I will do what I can now to search for our parents."

"But you don't really believe guineas will suffice to make that search successful," Eleanor said. "One of us must wed a prince."

"Now you believe in the Gypsy fortune too?" Laughter lit Ravenna's dark eyes.

"I have never not believed in it," Eleanor said. "I am merely skeptical that any one man can be the answer to anything."

"Faith is not like scholarship, Ellie. You either believe or you don't."

"Like you don't."

Ravenna stroked her dog's brow. "I believe in friendship. And I am perfectly content to leave happily-ever-afters to princesses like Bella."

"You needn't adopt my quest." Arabella took up the ring and carried it to her dressing table, to a box of gold and enamel. She nestled the ring in the velvet within. "But if either of you do, you can find it here."

A knock came on the dressing room door. The Duke of Lycombe entered, resplendent in wedding finery, the black kerchief across his brow dashing and a bit dangerous. Arabella's heart danced. He was wonderful and he was hers.

She tried not to smile too foolishly. But he already knew she was weak for him. Always. Forever. His gaze upon her shone with confidence.

"Wife," he said, conveying in the single word his pleasure and affection.

"Husband," she said, as deeply happy as he.

"Our guests expect us downstairs." He bowed to Ravenna and Eleanor. "You too, ladies."

Eleanor offered him a soft smile and left the room. Ravenna went onto her tiptoes, pecked him on the cheek, and skipped out after Beast.

He extended his hand to Arabella. "Duchess?"

She reached for him and he drew her into his arms. He bent to nuzzle behind her ear as she slipped her palms over his shoulders.

"Luc?"

"Mm?"

"Now that I am truly your duchess, what will you call me?"

He brought his lips to hers. "My love."

Author's Note

Serious debate rages today over the terminology used for the people often known as Gypsies, more properly referred to as Romani. And for good reason: words have power. Derogatory names for any group or individual can divide and destroy if used intentionally or in ignorance. For this book I have chosen to use the terms common to the places and period in which my story is set. The English of the early nineteenth century typically referred to Romani as Gypsies.

For their generosity in sharing their expertise, I thank Dr. Marie-Claude Dubois, Professor Leslie Moch, Dr. Christine E. Lee, Professor Molly A. Warsh (for her timely intervention concerning pearls, which provides you, gentle reader, with an example of how an insane author can write one descriptive line—"lips satiny as [fill in blank] pearls"—and subsequently spend days researching the appropriate descriptor), and Samantha Kane. Thanks also to Carol Strickland and the ladies of the Heart of Carolina Romance Writers BiaW group for inspiration and fun, and to The Chambermaids: Anne Alexander, Nita Eyster, Carrie Gwaltney, and Christy Krupa.

Fulsome thanks go to Marcia Abercrombie, Georgie Brophy, Mary Brophy Marcus, and Marquita Valentine for their thoughtful reading and recommendations. Big thanks and hugs also to Kieran Kramer, Caroline Linden, Sarah MacLean, Miranda Neville, and Maya Rodale, without whose affection and wisdom I would have been bereft while writing this book. Myron Lawrence and Georgann Brophy came to my aid more times than I can count, and for their infinite patience and understanding I am deeply grateful.

Special double thanks to Georgie Brophy, Nita Eyster, and Miranda Neville who rescued me at the last minute, and to Laurie LaBean for saving me and this book.

Many say I am blessed by the cover gods, but I know who should really get the credit. I offer a hearty *Huzzah!* to the art department at Avon for yet another beautiful cover.

My agent, Kimberly Whalen, deserves thanks for every book I publish not to mention for my continued sanity. To my editor, Lucia Macro, whose direction on this story was both spot-on and offered with compassion and unflagging confidence in this humble author, I send up a mighty thanks.

For my husband for his loving support, and for my wonderful son and my sweet Idaho, who every day help me feel the joy and adventure of love that makes it possible for me to write stories, I thank heaven.

Don't miss the next two books in

The Prince Catchers

by KATHARINE ASHE

Available from

AVON BOOKS

Summer 2014 and Winter 2015!

At Avon Books, we know your passion for romance—once you finish one of our novels, you find yourself wanting more.

May we tempt you with . . .

- **Excerpts** from our upcoming releases.

- Entertaining **extras**, including authors' personal photo albums and book lists.

- Behind-the-scenes **scoop** on your favorite characters and series.

- **Sweepstakes** for the chance to win free books, romantic getaways, and other fun prizes.

- Writing **tips** from our authors and editors.

- **Blog** with our authors and find out why they love to write romance.

- **Exclusive content** that's not contained within the pages of our novels.

Join us at
www.avonbooks.com

AVON

An Imprint of HarperCollinsPublishers
www.avonromance.com